SOUL WOUND

The Beginning

GLORIA KNIGHT

HIGH BRIDGE BOOKS
HOUSTON

Soul Wound: The Beginning
by Gloria Knight

Copyright © 2021 by Gloria Knight
All rights reserved.

Printed in the United States of America
ISBN: 978-1-954943-19-3

All rights reserved. Except in the case of brief quotations embodied in critical articles and reviews, no portion of this book may be reproduced, stored in a retrieval system, or transmitted in any form or by any means—electronic, mechanical, photocopy, recording, scanning, or other—without prior written permission from the author.

Unless otherwise indicated, all Scripture is taken from the New King James Version®. Copyright © 1982 by Thomas Nelson. Used by permission. All rights reserved.

Scripture quotations marked NIV are taken from THE HOLY BIBLE, NEW INTERNATIONAL VERSION®, NIV® Copyright © 1973, 1978, 1984, 2011 by Biblica, Inc.® Used by permission. All rights reserved worldwide.

High Bridge Books titles may be purchased in bulk for educational, business, fundraising, or sales promotional use. For information, please contact High Bridge Books via www.HighBridgeBooks.com/contact.

Published in Houston, Texas by High Bridge Books

Contents

Acknowledgments v

Characters vii

Chapter 1 1

Chapter 2 13

Chapter 3 49

Chapter 4 89

Chapter 5 99

Chapter 6 127

Chapter 7 143

Chapter 8 161

Chapter 9 175

Chapter 10 191

Chapter 11 205

Chapter 12 225

Acknowledgments and Events that Inspire the Book 289

Acknowledgments

I want to thank my extremely talented writing source and assistant Maverick Wrights for contributing to exciting ideas. He helped to create much of the suspense in the book. He also made the Diesel and Alfred characters, supplied many ideas for most of the other male characters, and helped create Angel's near-death experience. He and I worked together continuously. Maverick took my thoughts and direction for the book and created more suspenseful and exciting ideas. In addition, when I started provocative concepts, he made them even more thrilling. I call him my action and adventure man.

I loved C. S. Lewis and his books about Narnia. They were an inspiration for my near-death experience for Summer. Also, Karen Kingsbury's books, like *Coming Home*, had a considerable impact. I was so impressed with the crossover experience of the family members who died in a fatal car accident were then reunited in heaven. I wanted to create a crossover experience of my own with Summer meeting Mike and Ruby in Heaven. In Summer's heaven experience with Mike, I wanted him to be the first to give Summer away to Larry. I also wanted Mike's deceased sister, Ruby, to be included in the book. This work is the first book of a trilogy I have planned. The eventual ministry in which Larry and Summer will engage is called *Soul Wound*. I want to stress that Larry and Summer's becoming a couple is God's purpose for the *Soul Wound Ministry.* Since it is crucial for Larry and Summer to be together, Mike gives them that extra push.

Maverick had the idea for Angel's near-death experience—a more dimensional and personal presence of God; it also detailed Angel being under God's conviction and then later receiving His forgiveness and grace.

Both near-death experiences involve the protagonists being in critical condition. After reading the book, one may wonder if God has a miracle in mind.

Characters

Summer Logan Hanley
Larry Calhoun
Mike Hanley
R.D. Hanley
Kevin Logan
Lindy Logan
Autumn Logan
Lynn Rothberg
Andrew Marks
Diesel Hamilton
Earl "the beast" Mason
Angelitto Garcia (Angel)
Alfred Dominguez
Traye Washington
Marcus Washington
Charles Henker
Monica Lewis Garcia
Dr. Craig Williamson

Chapter 1

Beginning Late January 2003

Summer was waiting for Mike to return home. For some reason, she was on her guard. Many perverts stayed at the Metro Hotel, but she was most concerned about Earl, also known as Earl "the beast" Mason. Earl was of average weight and height. He had pale, brown eyes, reddish-brown hair, and had average features—neither striking nor plain. Summer knew about the conflict Earl had with Angel and thought Earl would know better than to cross Angel. Angel had promised her protection against any offender who wanted to harm her. She knew he had even put the word out. What she didn't realize was that Earl was unaware of this.

Whenever Earl approached Summer, there would be interference. Mostly it would be the hotel's manager, Bill Blake. He wondered if the guy had ESP. Bill wasn't like the hotel's other managers. Managers in the past dressed in hippy-like attire and lacked cleanliness; however, Bill dressed professionally. He was in his early fifties, medium weight, height, and a little haggard—but with attractive features. Bill had a distinct fondness for Mike and Summer and tried to protect them as much as possible. He let the residents know from the beginning that there would be an automatic eviction for any resident who committed any crime against another resident. The padlocks on the residents' doors were proof that Bill meant what was said. He then spoke to Summer.

"Hi Summer, How's Mike doing?" He could tell Summer was apprehensive about something but didn't ask in case it was personal. Summer responded, "He's ok Mr. Bill; how are you?"

"I'm good, and you Summer, are you ok?"

"Yes, I'm doing ok." He noticed her features were pale, and she was extremely nervous. However, he had to take her word. He changed the subject "I love my job, but I hate this region. I have applied to many other Hotels in Nob Hill and other safer locations. It's been over a year, and I put in at least thirty applications. I only wish most of the other residents were as neat and respectful as you and Mike. Then working here would be more satisfactory."

"Mr. Bill, if you left here, I would have to insist that Mike make us move. However, I can't blame you, and I hope a job opening is available for you soon,"

Earl was eavesdropping and rolling his eyes. Saying to himself, "Enough already."

Summer understood why Bill wanted to leave because there were no rules about how many residents could reside in a single room. There would be as many as 20 or more drug addicts to a room to free up money for drugs. This order came from the top official. Bill had never agreed with it. Each resident had a separate rent charge, and it was quite a bit less than it would be for one or two to a room. Since Mike and Summer had a single room to themselves, the other residents considered them wealthy.

In an hour, Mike, along with many other residents, would arrive home. Earl was becoming desperate now, even angry. He wanted his opportunity, and by now, he was tired of waiting.

It wasn't much of an opportunity, but Bill went into his office. Earl looked to see if anyone else was around. There she was by herself at last. Summer was a swift runner with agility and athletic speed. However, she wasn't as easy prey as he had thought. She seemed to know she was being accosted and ran to the closed window to the fire escape. She thought she would never open it in time. Fortunately, she opened it. They were outside. Earl wasn't as swift—he was even awkward—but his desperation to execute his evil plan gave him the swiftness he needed.

He called out to her
"Beautiful girl, you'll be mine."

Lynn had her usual Friday date with Summer; it was usually a luncheon. Summer had mentioned that she would be running late, so they agreed to have beverages instead. However, Lynn was concerned because Summer was exceptionally late. She decided to get in her car and see if Summer was still at the Metro. She was desperately hoping she was because she didn't want to search for her in other places and end up calling the police. Lynn got into her vehicle headed to the Metro.

Summer was gaining speed and ground; she was aware that Earl was directly behind her. She grunted to herself, "Move legs, move faster" She moved swiftly. But so did Earl. He was close enough now to reach out and grab her, but something had frightened and deterred him. He screamed. "AHHHHHHHHHH" and then started running in the other direction. Summer was confused, so she turned around. The man looked to be about seven feet tall, with a muscular build. His face shone so brightly his features were hard to make out. She told him, "Thank you! You saved my life." Then something behind her caught her attention. She turned around and didn't see anything. When she turned around again, he was gone. She knew he was a heavenly being. She also knew he had been there for her before and always would be. Summer knew it was God. She couldn't understand why, as she had rebelliously turned her heart away from him. Then she had a sudden revelation—God's love was unconditional.

Lynn had finally arrived at the Metro. She was frightened and suspected the worse. She found Summer on the sidewalk crying uncontrollably. Everything had hit Summer at once—being chased by Earl and being rescued by the unknown stranger. Lynn dashed to embrace her. She thought perhaps Summer had been raped, not knowing it would have happened if it hadn't been for the sudden appearance of the mysterious stranger.

She held Summer, and Summer desperately clung to her. Finally, Lynn broke the silence. "Summer, honey, has someone hurt you?"

"No, yes, they tried to," Summer stuttered, her words coming out jumbled.

Lynn stopped her, telling her, "Calm down, sweetie, then speak." Summer held Lynn close and cried for a few minutes more. When she calmed down, she spoke more clearly. She told Lynn, "I know you won't believe me."

"You've never lied to me; you know I'll believe you."

"That horrible beast was chasing me. He was very close to catching me. Then in a hurry, he ran the other direction. A radiant man, very tall and muscular, frightened him away. I couldn't see his face; I know he was God's angel. I had undergone this presence before."

Lynn wasn't a person of faith, but she had heard of these encounters before. Summer then told Lynn, "I've made my decision to rededicate my life to back Christ. I was a Christian before

I met and married Mike. I rebelled and backslid because I just didn't understand his ways. I'll tell you about it sometime."

Lynn could tell a transformation had taken place in Summer.

She asked Summer, "Why don't you stay with me until Mike comes home each day. You know I'll provide your transportation expense."

Summer replied to her," that isn't necessary, Lynn. My guardian angel has been protecting me, and I believe he'll continue to do so."

For reasons Lynn couldn't explain, she believed Summer.

They went inside to find Mike beside himself because he couldn't find Summer. He saw her and cried, "Summer, where have you been? I've been looking for you everywhere!" Lynn thought to herself, *He wasn't looking hard enough; how could he not spot her?* He embraced her and then complained, "Summer, I'm starving. I've noticed you never prepared supper."

But then Lynn intervened. "Someone attempted an assault on Summer; that's the reason dinner wasn't prepared; besides, you must have forgotten this is Fish and Chips Day at *The Yellow Submarine*. I'll take us all out to eat. My treat." She then took them both out to eat anything to calm everyone down.

As Earl approached the hotel, the word was out that he had tried to assault Summer. Bill, the manager, replied angrily, "You have been evicted, Earl, for trying to attack Summer. But that's not your worst problem—Angel has a contract out on you because you tried to harm her." Earl went to his room and quickly gathered his few belongings and put them in his backpack. He then went to catch the next bus bound for Tijuana, Mexico. He was also hoping Angel wouldn't find him before he could leave.

Lynn, Mike, and Summer finished their dinner of fish, chips, and coleslaw. They then rested and finished their coffee. Summer had tea. Mike asked Summer, "About the assault, are you sure it was Earl?" Lynn and Summer both questionably looked at him, as he didn't seem that concerned about what had taken place.

He then explained himself, "No, you don't understand. Angel put a contract out on Earl and anyone else who would harm you, Summer."

Summer was appalled. She didn't want blood spilled in her name. Then she said, "Lynn, I have to go see Angel. I have to talk him out of this. He is going to ruin his life."

"Summer, you know Angel already has a lot of blood on his hands. He has already ruined his life."

"I know, but I can't let him do this. It will also make me equally responsible."

Lynn had a lot of doubt about Angel, but she also knew he wouldn't harm Summer. So, she immediately took Summer to Angel's apartment.

Angel's apartment was a luxury two-bedroom, two-bathroom apartment. In the master bedroom, he had a master bath, a water bed, and modern bedroom furniture. The apartment's location was in the Twin Peaks area, where he could view the city lights from his balcony. Angel lived alone and rarely had company (except for his and Monica's romantic escapades), but he wanted a spare bedroom and bathroom just in case a friend or family member came for a visit.

Angel knew Earl was at the bus depot about to head to Tijuana, and he was about to execute his plan to waste him. Angel had the party on the line discussing the matter about Earl when Summer rang the doorbell. He saw her and Mike standing there, and he was so emotional that he embraced her, concern written on his face. Mike was jealous, but he wouldn't dare cross Angel; so, he was silent. Mike also knew Angel had only sisterly affection for Summer. Monica was the only woman in which he possessed intimate feelings.

After Angel released his embrace, he said, "That monster will pay—I promise you, Summer."

Summer had counted on Angel to protect her, but she realized he couldn't always be there to deliver. But God was. She said, "Why would you do this now, Angel? Out of vengeance? You know I'm okay. You don't know me well if you think this is what I want you to do. Please, Angel, I need you to relent on this. I don't want Earl's or anyone else's blood on my hands."

Angel stood there, amazed by this young girl. He could also see the transformation in her. She had an aura now. In many cases, women loved Angel to fight for them, but here she was begging him to take his contract off her potential assailant.

He said, "Summer, baby girl, you know how fond of you I am. I normally wouldn't deny any wish you had, but you know that animal could come back and make another attempt. Baby, I can't ever take that chance!"

"He wouldn't dare. He is too afraid of you. Angel, you must know I have another protector sent by God. So, if you continue to pursue Earl, it will only be for revenge. Please, I beg you, don't do this in my name. I don't want the responsibility for this."

Angel couldn't believe what he was hearing. He could no longer protest. He had to give in to her plea. "Summer, you know Earl doesn't deserve mercy. I can't believe what I am saying, but okay, I will call off the hit for you. However, you better pray Earl never comes near you again. I am so glad you are safe, and I will leave you in the hands of your protecting Angel. After all, he was there when I couldn't be."

Bill Blake was glad to see Summer and Mike. He told them, "I evicted Earl because of how he tried to assault you. Earl went to his room and packed, probably leaving town. I hope he made it. He's a scumbag, but I still don't want his death on my conscience.

Yet, Angel is cleverer, and I'm sure he had him hunted him down." Then Mike told him, "No, Bill Angel changed his mind."

"You mean Summer changed his mind," Bill said, giving him a curious look.

Neither Mike nor Summer replied. In Summer's mind, the less said, the better. Bill didn't need an answer, as he had already figured it out. He was proud of Summer for her integrity. He also noticed a difference in her.

The encounter with Summer had broken Angel, and this was new for him. He was apathetic about most things. His weak areas were his parents; other family members; and Monica, Mike, and Summer. The gang had taught him that these attachments were liabilities. Yet, of course, the gang never knew he had them. What happened to him? Did God take down his wall? He hated what this vulnerability had created—the return of pain.

Angel had been inevitable pain would never again enter his life. He had hardened his heart to most things, especially to violence. Why did Angel have to go back down the road before all his involvement with gang activity? When he was 12, he remembered his pain and how his parents had attempted to be there for him. When he was nine, his father had a job with good pay and benefits, which they hoped would allow them to leave this crime-infested neighborhood. Sadly, that never happened. His parents explored other areas; however, the rent and expenses were out of their range.

So, Angel was left to be influenced by hostile forces. When he was 12, he joined a gang called the Terrors. He considered Jack Norris, this gang's leader, to be his best friend, and Jack taught Angel the gang world of crime and violence. He had told Angel, "Man, if you want to be successful in drug delivery, never get hooked on our merchandise, let the street people stay hooked, remember, that's how you rack in a lot of money."

Angel embraced career crime and became a Gypsy Joker when he turned 16. When he was 18, the leader, Frederico, died in a rumble. Angel was next in line for leadership and had been the leader of this biker gang for 12 years.

Gypsy Jokers were a Hispanic gang. Bikers, like other gangs, were in a race war. Hispanics mainly battled Caucasian gangs, which were called the Hell's Angels.

Yet, before all of this, young Angelito Garcia had a tender heart. He was sickened at his first rumble, though he hid it well. Then slowly, his heart hardened. Leaving dead bodies in the street didn't make sense. The loss of some of the Terrors saddened him. Jack seemed to notice Angel's reaction. He said, "You know the best way to avoid pain is not to become attached to anyone."

Angel said nothing but wondered whether he should stop loving his parents and others close to him. Yet, Jack's influence had won out because, except for his parents, Monica, uncles, aunts, and cousins, Angel became detached from everyone.

Angel's parents were Juan and Carman Garcia. Juan was slightly older than Carmen, in his middle 50's. He was of small weight and height with distinct but attractive Hispanic features. Angel looked like him. Carmen was in her early 50's. She was petite yet heavyset, and she also had attractive Hispanic features. They were Catholic and named their Angelito after all the heavenly angels, hoping Angel would fulfill his Christian destiny. Angel's choices broke their heart, yet, they still prayed for him constantly. They knew there was hope for Angel as long as he drew a breath. Still, they were concerned and wondered how long it would take for Angel to come around.

Juan was a highly valued worker at the beverage bottling plant where he worked. He was promoted to head foreman and had a huge pay raise. However, this was never satisfactory to Angel; he was more interested in the revenue brought in by his gang activity. Although they never could move into a better neighborhood, they moved into a better house in their community.

Angel was constantly involved in life-threatening situations. His parents would remember all the hospital visits, the knife, and bullet wounds. Angel had two bullet wounds; both times, he was in critical condition. After he survived his second bullet wound, the doctors and nurses had told them he would not survive the third one. Their utmost prayer was that Angel would not get re-shot.

The Garcias had finally left the high-crime hoods. They only regretted that they couldn't do so when Angel lived with them. Angel had chosen his life of crime. When he turned 18, his parents had asked him to leave because they never wanted to be in the position to turn him over to the law. It was a heart-wrenching decision. However, it seemed Angel was relieved about their decision. His parents never knew he was a drug dealer (though they had their suspicions). They asked him to leave.

They became prayer warriors because prayer was all they had. There was no time for worrying—only time to hit their knees and pray. They prayed with extreme passion, but they didn't realize their prayers were about to pay off.

Angel, still reflecting on his past, realizing his anger was toward God. It seemed to him God could have allowed them to move away from the hood and away from gang life. He blamed God for everything, from his injuries to his lost relationship with Monica. Then there was Summer. Her transformation and the way she had asked for mercy for Earl influenced him. Earl didn't deserve mercy. Others Angel had ordered a hit on deserved more mercy than he did. It was like this small, adorable young girl was ordering him around. She reminded him of Monica, which is why he had become so fond of her. Of course, she wasn't Monica.

Monica captured his heart the moment he saw her about two years ago. This woman was a little younger—24 to his 28—very petite and curvy. Monica was lovely, with ha. She zel eyes and brown hair with auburn highlights. Angel was mesmerized by her beauty, and Monica was also deeply in love with him. However, life as a biker's wife was more than she had bargained. It was an insane life to her, yet she so loved Angel.

It tormented Angel when he recalled how a rival gang member had held her at gunpoint, calling out to Angel. "First, it's her Garcia and then you. Don't worry; I'll give you plenty of time to mourn her before I kill you." Fortunately, Angel had the drop on him; then, she had to deal with the fact that a man was dead on her behalf. Angel would never forget the tortured look in her eyes and how she had abruptly ended things. "Angel, I'm a nurse; how can I live with this man's death on my conscience?" She was shaken and sickened to her stomach.

"Baby, if I hadn't have wasted him, that would be you and me dead on the ground."

"Angel, I realized that you saved my life, and I appreciate it. However, I shouldn't be where these events take place. Angel, I love you, and I never want to pine for you. I just never realized the high risks you take. I just need to be out of the picture. I have to have a more stable life."

"I understand baby, being my wife puts you at risk with my enemies. I think we need to be discreet when we meet." Nonetheless, he won because he was still as irresistible to her as she was to him. So sometimes, they met secretly for stolen moments of passion. He prayed no one would find out: because he didn't ever want her life to be in jeopardy again. Neither his gang nor any rival gang must ever know she was his weakest link.

Angel had to decide whether he would follow Christ. He was like the rich man who refused when Jesus asked him to give up all he had for the poor. Angel knew he would have to give up his blood money, and he wasn't ready for that. Just as the rich man felt sorrow for his wrong decision, so did Angel. He then dismissed his thoughts about redemption. If only he could get

Summer's transformation out of his mind. Why? Why was he softening? He hated being weak and vulnerable.

Angel's parents reared him to worship God as a Christian Catholic. Yet, it had all changed. In his mind, it was a weakness. Now he didn't consider it a weakness. He just didn't want to give up his financial independence.

Chapter 2

On August 15, in the mid-summer of 1985, 22-year-old Lindy Logan was great with child. It was a pleasant summer afternoon, and she and her 25-year-old husband Kevin were having a picnic at the local park in Minion, Texas. Lindy had prepared fried chicken, potato salad, fresh fruit, and dinner rolls. They had eaten and were playfully frolicking when Lindy's labor pains began. Kevin took her immediately to Saint Mary's hospital in Lubbock. Within about five hours, Lindy Logan had given birth to a beautiful and tiny baby girl. She was named Summer for the pleasant summer day of her birth. They were the happiest couple. Lindy wanted a little girl. Kevin had hoped for a son, but this tiny, loud, crying creature had captured his heart.

There was no happier toddler than three-year-old Summer Logan. She had the adoration of her mother and father for the last three years. Then on November 28, 1988, her sister Autumn was born. She was named Autumn for the unforgettable autumn day of her birth. That's when all Summer's attention from her mother came to a sudden standstill. She took care of Summer's physical needs of food, hygiene, and safety and granted her desires for material possessions; however, Lindy doted only on Autumn. At first, Kevin felt Lindy was giving all her attention to Autumn because a newborn was very demanding; on the other hand, he soon noticed that Lindy favored Autumn more than Summer.

At first, he never really paid a lot of attention because his first concern was how he would support this growing family. He was an insurance agent and had landed a great job with the Mills

Insurance Agency. He tried to spend as much time with his daughters as he could. Kevin sometimes allowed Summer to spend time with Autumn, and Summer was delighted, stating, "She's like my baby doll." However, Lindy disagreed, but Kevin stood his ground and told Lindy, "Summer can spend time with her sister as long as I'm supervising her. Lindy, you are unreasonable." Lindy couldn't argue but told Kevin, "I hope you don't regret this, Kevin."

Sadly, Kevin rarely followed up on this routine with Summer. He was working late hours and was extremely tired when he came home. Summer was jealous of Autumn, but she also longed to be with her. She counted on Kevin to support her. She would try to get his attention and let him know, "Daddy, please can I spend time with Baby Autumn?" he would say "Ok" a few times, giving in even when he didn't feel he could. Eventually, he just thought he couldn't, which left little Summer feeling heartsick and lonely.

Early one spring morning, Summer wandered out of the house. When Lindy noticed that she was gone, she immediately alerted Kevin. They went out to the backyard and saw Summer playing with a tiny Beagle puppy. Kevin and Lindy were both enchanted, watching the two at play. Kevin hadn't heard Summer laugh so much in a while. He really couldn't recall her having this much amusement since Autumn was born. Kevin then joined in and started playing with the pup, but Summer held the dog tight, saying, "No. Mine, mine" repeatedly, barring Kevin from the tiny creature. Finally, Lindy scolded her in a harsh tone screaming, "Summer!" Kevin stopped her. He then reasoned with Summer by asking, "How would you like to keep this little fellow as a pet?" "Yay, Yaaaaay," Summer exclaimed gleefully, clapping her hands. Then I'll talk to the dog's owner. But you have to promise not to be selfish with him," Summer laughed joyfully and then let Kevin also play with him. The dog had a commanding bark, appearing to order him and Summer around. Considering how authoritative the dog was, he thought that

"General" would be the perfect name for him. So he asked Summer, "How about we name him General?" Summer repeated the name, calling him "Genwal." Kevin immediately called the neighbor who had the puppies, explaining what had happened. "Sam, this is your next-door neighbor, Kevin; your little one wandered over to my yard. Summer fell in love with him, and I was wondering if you would sell him to me.?" He knew the puppy was expensive, but seeing the joy he gave Summer was priceless to him. Sam then replied, "Certainly, however, it'll be two more weeks before he's weaned; after that, he's all yours and Summer's. By the way, since he's in a loving home, I'll give him to you, papers and all."

"That's more than generous, but I'd like to give you something for him."

"Your loving care is all that's required."

"Wow, thank you so much." Then he hung up, "Summer, he's all ours but not for a couple of weeks."

"Two weeks!" Summer repeated shouting

Summer cheered and laughed gleefully. She just didn't how long the two weeks were going to drag by.

While Kevin took the dog back to the owner, Lindy coaxed Summer into the house. "Come in, and you can play with Autumn for a little while. Now daddy lets you hold her, but I won't do that. Do you understand?" Summer nodded; Kevin would hold Autumn with Summer making Summer think she was doing it independently. This action made Lindy cringe because she thought Summer would attempt to hold her by herself. Summer was too small for this and couldn't support Autumn. "Ok, then just go to the crib and speak to her"

"Autumn." Summer began, "This is big Sissie; I love you, Baby Autumn." Autumn cooed and laughed. It was apparent that she also enjoyed her time with Summer. However, that came to a sudden cessation in less than fifteen minutes. Lindy had chores and errands to take care of, and she didn't want Summer to be alone with Autumn.

Summer felt that she had lost General too. He had two more weeks before being weaned from his mother. Kevin tried to explain to Summer, "He still needs his mother, Honey." but he could see the lonely expression on her face. He knew that until the dog could be with her, he would be spending time with her, and he was anxiously waiting for the day that General took over. Lindy, however, didn't want General at first. She knew she would have all the responsibility for his care because Kevin's schedule wouldn't allow for it, and Summer was much too young for the obligation. Moreover, she was resentful because now not only would her attention for Autumn be divided with Summer, but also with a dog.

In time, Lindy was grateful for General because he was becoming a suitable babysitter for Summer. By the time General was six months old, he was very protective of Summer. Autumn was also fascinated with General, but Lindy had to supervise them, as Autumn was abusive to General. Finally, General understood that Autumn was just a baby and allowed her to hit him and pull on his fur, even though it was painful and he would yelp. Lindy, however, wouldn't allow it, but she quickly learned that she couldn't swat at either child in General's presence—he was protective and would snarl at her.

When Summer noticed that the canine was shielding her, she tried to stay with him until her father came home. She also brought him into the house whenever Kevin came home. Lindy had stated her objections, "Kevin, that dog is going to smell up the house. I was taught that animals belong outside!"

"I'm not going to be deprived of a greeting like this. I want my dog here every night when I come home."

Lindy noticed Summer's smile of triumph, and she gave her a threatening glance. Summer then knew that she had to be aware of her mother's harshness, and she was grateful for General. He was her hero and her bodyguard. The affectionate canine delighted the Logan family for many years, and he became part of the family. Lindy never resented General for snarling at her;

she understood his protecting instinct because she possessed it herself. When Autumn was older, she tried to possess General, "I want General for my dog," She exclaimed. Summer wasn't worried. She stated. "General is my dog." She whistled and called him, and he came to her immediately. Autumn then witnessed his loyalty to Summer. He loved all the family, but Summer and Kevin were his masters. Lindy taught both girls how to care for him, but Summer assumed most of the responsibility because of her love and devotion for him.

General was in the Logan household until Summer was 11 years old. Then, when General was only eight, he gave his life for Summer, who had unconsciously stepped off the sidewalk as a car was speeding by. Summer caught herself and stepped back up onto the curve, but not before General had rushed to her rescue and was hit by the speeding car. "General!" Summer screamed, heaving heavy sobs, as though her life was over. Her best friend, confidant, and bodyguard were now gone. Lindy worried about Summer; she called out to her, "Summer, Summer!"

Then she found her on the sidewalk holding General and crying uncontrollably. Their neighbor, Mr. Marshall, picked up General from the street and allowed Summer to mourn him. Lindy also held on to General, crying. Finally, autumn joined in, and all the Logan women were tearing up over General. Lindy then called Kevin, and he said, "Lindy, please take General to the house until I arrive home so that I can say goodbye to him. I'm going to try my best to be home early."

They buried General in the backyard—the first place they encountered him when he became part of the family. Kevin had bought a marker for him with his name, birth, and death dates. General Logan, April 3, 1989, to June 20, 1997. Summer had much comfort from the marker, as she had a place to speak to General and share her troubles. In life and death, General was Summer's sole comfort.

The Logans lived in a high-middle-income neighborhood. They had a four-bedroom house with two-and-a-half baths. Kevin and Lindy had the master bedroom with a master bathroom. It had a king-size bed and beautiful antique bedroom furniture—a chest of drawers, a dresser, and bedside tables. There was also a wingback recliner in the room for nights when one of them didn't want to go to bed immediately and wanted to sit up and watch TV. Summer and Autumn each had their bedroom with a full-size bed, a chair, a chest of drawers, a TV, and an entertainment system. The other bathroom was between the girl's bedrooms. The other room was Kevin's home office with a desk, computer, loveseat, and chair. The half bath was next to it.

When the girls were older, Kevin thought they could share a bedroom for a while, which would allow them to become closer. Only Lindy disagreed. She was very overprotective of Autumn and feared Summer might severely hurt her. So, for the sake of harmony, the girls remained in separate bedrooms.

The house also had a large living area, kitchen area, and a den, with beautiful kitchen and living room furniture. The family mostly stayed together in the den. On the other hand, during weeknights after dinner, the girls went to do their homework in the living room under Lindy's supervision.

Summer was thinking about the house that she grew up in, reflecting on her family and the recent loss of General. The same neighbor who gave them General had offered Summer another Beagle puppy, but Kevin refused. The loss of General was hard for him. It was the second beloved pet he had lost. The first was a female pit bull that he had when he was a child. The Pit's name was Tony, named after his cousin, who he thought was tough. He thought the dog was tough because she was a pit bull, but Tony had proven to be a gentle dog. Tony was five years old when Kevin's father, Frank, noticed her abdomen was enormously distended. She also lacked an appetite, and her breathing was shallow. The vet discovered that she had heartworms. Her condition was too far along for treatment, so the vet lethally injected her, and she was gone. Kevin's father felt Tony was finally at peace, but Kevin's whole world was shattered. At this time, Kevin was only 12 years old. As he remembered Tony's death and suffering, he made sure General had extraordinary care. He had heartworm prevention and prevention from other diseases. There was no doubt General would have lived for many years; however, Kevin never anticipated that an accident could end his life. So once again, he suffered the unbearable pain of losing another pet. This time it was worse because his family, especially Summer, were also experiencing the same loss and sorrow.

Summer also remembered her school and recalled receiving salvation in 1997 when she was 12 years old. Her middle school counselor was Sally Ames. Sally had led Summer to Christ. Summer had issues then because her mother, Lindy, had shown favoritism to her sister, Autumn, since the day of her birth. Their mother, Lindy, was small, with dark brown hair and brown eyes. The women had attractive features. Autumn manipulated their mother, and whenever she was disrespectful to Summer, their mother never corrected her.

On the other hand, she was harsh to Summer anytime she tried to defend herself or her belongings. When Summer, corrected Autumn she was rude and often brutal when she dealt with her. She hated and resented her. She also hated and resented Lindy for allowing Autumn to get away with so much and resented their father for not being t

here for her.

Summer was petite with light brown hair, piercing blue eyes, and striking features. She resembled her father. Autumn was tall, almost as tall as Summer. At that time, she was nine years old. She had dark brown hair and brown eyes and the striking features of her mother, except her mother was petite. Every day, a fight would break out between Summer and Autumn. "Mama," Autumn cried, "Summer's trying to hit me," and Lindy automatically came to Autumn's defense. Autumn demanded control. She didn't respect Summer's possessions and would hide them or destroy them. And Lindy allowed it. Autumn loved tormenting Summer, but she hated the consequences, "Autumn, you brat!" Summer screamed as she wrestled her to the ground, demanding her belongings back—striking her sister a time or two. "Ma-Ma," Autumn would scream in pain. Lindy was out of earshot until Autumn had to give an alarming and ear ringing screech. When Lindy returned, Summer sped out of the house and went to her secret hiding place. Neither parent knew where it was, and it caused Lindy much strife.

Kevin, Summer's father, was a handsome man with striking features. He was tall, about 6'0 muscular build, with light brown hair. The man had blue eyes that could pierce the soul. He had started a new insurance agency with his partner, Leo Harper. Leo was of average height and a little heavyset, but he was handsome with dark brown hair and hazel-colored eyes. He recently married Trudy Miles. She was of medium size and built. She had long, blonde, curly hair and blue eyes and looked like Reese Witherspoon. Trudy helped out in the business on hectic days. She had experience because she had a partnership in another business, which she had sold to her former partner. Kevin would tease Leo, "Leo, how did you get so blessed with a beauty like Trudy with brains to match."

Leo agreed; "I've adored Trudy from the first day we met. I just try to love her like Christ loved the church."

"That's how you won her heart" He was referring to the time when Trudy had to break up with her boyfriend because she fell in love with Leo.

"I never thought of it as conquest; I'm just glad that Eric was a good sport and became my good friend."

"You can't get no better break than that."

"True," Leo answered, and then their break ended, and they went back to work.

The Logans and the Harpers attended the same church and worshiped there together.

Leo had recently inherited money from his grandfather, Jacob Harper. He loved his grandfather and mourned for him.

One day when he visited his grandfather's grave, "Grandpa, I miss you so much. I rather have you back than to have all this money. I promise I'll use it to make you proud." That's how the idea of Harper and Logan Insurance Agency began. Before this, Leo and Kevin had worked together at the Mills Agency. Leo left his grandfather, then approached Kevin with the idea.

" What do you say, Kevin, partners?"

"Only if I can contribute my half in some way,"

"You can just contribute out of your proceeds taking the equal salary you already have."

"Accept a small down payment from me, and you have a deal." So, they shook hands and agreed. They also had legal papers drawn up, though neither one ever thought it necessary. Kevin's share would come out of his proceeds. He would accept a salary equal to that of the Mills Agency, and the remainder would go toward his balance in the partnership. The agency was a success, and their clients from their former agency followed them to this agency. There were also many new clients.

Summer's secret hiding place was a church a few blocks from her house. She escaped by singing and playing the church piano, singing her heart out as if playing a concert for millions. One day she was daydreaming as she sang and played, unaware there was an audience of one. When she looked up, she saw Pastor Brim taking in her beautiful music. She shied away from him, afraid she was in trouble. But the warm look on his face told a different story.

"I won't say a word about your being here without consent," he said, "but why are you hiding such a beautiful talent?"

Summer gave him a heartwarming smile. "I'm sorry, I just got lost in my dreams."

"Dreams always begin with action. I would love for you to play and sing for my congregation."

Summer hesitated. "Could I have time to think about it, please?"

"Of course, you can, but the sooner you begin, the sooner your dreams will come true."

Summer was afraid that Autumn and her mother would find her hiding place if she performed at this church. She had been in performances, musicals, and plays in grammar school, and her parents were rarely present to lend their support. So, it didn't matter to her anymore. However, Pastor Brim's attention had impressed her. Finally, someone cared enough to recognize her talent.

Lindy was beside herself about Summer's absence. She was angry and worried, but, primarily, she was concerned. She and Kevin constantly argued because Kevin kept accusing her of partiality regarding the girls. Autumn was undisciplined, and Summer was rebellious because of Lindy's harsh treatment.

Summer was still gone, and Kevin would soon be home. She hoped Summer would come home first, so she didn't have to hear him say, "Someday, she won't come home. I wouldn't if I were, she." Then the battle between them would begin. "Why was it my fault?" she would say" You are rarely there for her either, or for any of us for that matter."

"Is that why you take your resentment out on her because you resent me?" Before she could answer, Autumn arrived home from visiting her friend, Nancy Allen. Then Summer came into the house. She was home shortly before Kevin. Summer waited for her father to go into the house first. Lindy was so glad to see

Summer that she hugged her. She didn't notice that Summer never hugged her back. Lindy had a supper of meatloaf, mashed potatoes, green beans, and dinner rolls on the table, along with southern sweet tea. They were all seated and asked God's blessing; then, they ate in total silence.

Summer then recalled the time when she met her school counselor, Sally Ames. Sally was younger than her mother, but she was Summer's role model. This woman genuinely cared about Summer. Sally was a born-again believer and always reminded Summer of God's love for her. Summer remembered the first time Ms. Ames had mentioned this to her. Only she wondered if He loved her so much, why did she always have to struggle? Why did she have an uncaring mother, a neglectful father, and a nasty brat for a sister? Why did she have to hide to get away from home when she wanted to be home in peace? It was almost as if she was a girl without a home, as the man without a country. She wanted to live somewhere else, but where?

Autumn had been to her friend Nancy Allen's house. She was different around Nancy. Autumn's parents loved Nancy, and Kevin appreciated her positive influence on Autumn. Even Summer could tolerate Autumn when she was around Nancy. Nancy was nine years old; like Autumn, this child was blonde-haired and fair-skinned. She had plain features, but her disposition made up for it. She had the favor of God, and most people flocked to her. Lindy always invited her to eat with them, but Nancy always declined. Autumn and Nancy had been friends since kindergarten. They were inseparable.

Sally Ames was the new counselor at South Granby Middle School. Her heart went out to Summer Logan. She could see that this adorable, sweet young girl was troubled. She prayed for her constantly because the Lord kept Summer in her heart. Sally was a graduate of Texas Tech University and had a master's degree in counseling. She was a Word of God Church member, where the Logans and many others attended. She had also noticed Summer in church, which is when she befriended her.

Sally had noticed Summer becoming impressed with the mean girl trio, Taylor Miller, a striking blond with blue-green eyes, fair-skinned and petite. Lilly German, an African American beauty, light-skinned, dark permed hair, dark eyes, and medium height and build. And Mary Franklin, who had brunette colored hair, brown eyes, tall, slim, and striking. They were two years older than Summer and were about to graduate from the eighth grade. (Summer was an overachiever and skipped a grade in school. She was in the seventh grade) The clique was from different backgrounds and of different financial statuses. Taylor was close to the upper-middle class, Lilly came from extreme wealth, and Mary was from a lower income bracket. Taylor and Lilly's most positive thing was to protect Mary from her stepfather, who physically and sexually abused her. It wasn't a positive move, but Lilly used her wealth to rent Mary an apartment. Mary could pass for 18, so no one asked questions.

When Lilly picked out the apartment, they decided it would also be their party pad. It had a large living area with a large kitchen and dining room. It was completely furnished and had one bedroom. The couch also pulled out into a bed because Lilly and Taylor spent the night there on most weekends. "Free at last," Mary cried out when they first walked in.

"Amen," Lilly replied,

To ensure that Mary could stay at the apartment, Lilly threatened Hugh, Mary's stepfather, "I'll have you arrested, and Mary will never stay here again." Lilly's threat got his attention because he had attempted to molest her. Mary's mother seemed relieved for Mary to be away from Hugh because she also feared him. Mary's mother requested to stay in touch with Mary, and of course, Lilly had no objections. Mary was closer to her mother.

Lilly also had "Mom," as Lilly referred to her too, sign Mary's report card and other school documents to keep suspicion down. Sally was concerned because she knew these girls lived fast lives and had wild, unchaperoned parties at Mary's place. Only Sally was unaware that Mary had an apartment.

Ella Nix had been Summer's best friend since kindergarten. Ella was petite, pretty, with blond hair and blue eyes. Then the mean girl clique befriended Summer. They were bullies, but they had prestige. Lilly asked, "Summer, we want you to be a part of our group."

Summer was elated and asked, "Can Ella belong too?"

"Are you kidding? Can't you see we are rescuing you from her!" Summer was speechless. She was in indecision, yet the prestige of the clique had won her over, though she never forgot the look of betrayal on Ella's face.

Sally Ames was observant. She knew Summer had abandoned her lifelong friend to become a part of the mean girls. She also feared for Summer, as she knew she wasn't as used to fast living as the trio was. These girls had made themselves up to look older, which impressed Summer. She wanted to look older, too. She was unhappy at home and envied Mary for having her apartment. She wanted to live with Mary but was too shy to ask. She remembered her vow of secrecy to Lilly "Remember, Summer, you can't ever mention the apartment to anyone else. I need you to promise me you never will," Then Summer promised. Lilly must have known that Summer was faithful in her promises because she seemed very confidant.

Summer was helping to plan a party at Mary's apartment. Taylor's adult brother, Norman, who was medium height, thin, and handsome with dark hair and eyes, would provide the alcohol. He spoke, "Lilly, I will provide the alcohol, but I need your money to cover it, and all I want is to be able to drink some at the party." "Sounds like a plan to me." Lilly agreed. These young girls were naïve and were unaware of Norman having a suspended license and DUI arrests. They couldn't know the consequences if, for example, Norman ever committed vehicular homicide while intoxicated. Summer was excited to be planning this party. She wanted to be a grown-up like the trio tried to be. But, of course, they weren't grown up.

Ella felt betrayed and hurt when Summer joined the clique and excluded her from her life. But, she also knew the potential danger for Summer. The mean girls had wild parties with boys in high school. They made themselves up to look older to attract these boys, and now Summer wanted to do the same thing.

Lilly had a chauffeur named Alex, who transported her and her friends to all events and activities. One evening, he took them to an out-of-town movie theater because the local theater didn't show the movie they wanted to see. It was at this movie theater in another town that the trio had met these boys. The girls had made themselves up to look older than they were. Lilly took the lead and had her eye on Jimmy Smith, who also seemed to be in the Lead. Lilly looked at Jimmy, then began, "I guess you attend high school in this town."

"Well, of course!" Jimmy replied, but I don't recall seeing any of you at school."

"We don't go to school here. Taylor and I are seniors at South Granby high. Our friend Mary has already graduated with her apartment."

The apartment idea instantly caught the boy's attention. Jimmy was the oldest, and the others were juniors. The boys were impressed because they thought older girls approached them instead of the other way around.

The boys believed their story because the girls looked like they could be even older than they stated.

It was Wednesday, and the party was on Friday night. Summer anticipated the party because it made her feel grown-up. She was highly organized and resourceful as she helped with the planning, which impressed the mean girls. They were also looking for someone to carry on their legacy, preferably a seventh-grader, but the seventh graders they had observed were less mature than Summer. The girls admired Summer's maturity, but not her innocence. It was a threat to them. They didn't know why, but it was.

It was Friday afternoon, and Summer had impressed the trio with her decorations and table design. She had hung the decorations over the table and placed balloons and bunny rabbits along the wall. They loved the bunny rabbits stating, "How adorable, but I'm sure the boys won't be impressed." The boys never noticed much except the girls anyway. The trio was excited about the boys coming. Summer was only excited about the party. She didn't know it would involve alcohol and sex. The trio then gave Summer a makeover, using eye makeup that brought out her eyes and gave her an adult-like appearance. The trio was envious and even jealous because they knew the older boys would notice her.

Summer had been lying to her parents about her whereabouts these days. They thought she was still hanging out with Ella. She kept them in the dark about her newfound friends, but they never kept tabs on her. However, Ms. Ames had given Summer her private number in case she ever needed her. Summer felt it unnecessary and that she had everything under control. She was excited about the new direction her life was taking. Tonight would be a dream come true.

That night, Summer and the trio were waiting for the older boys to arrive. Norman came with the beer and other alcoholic beverages with mixers and chasers. Summer was never exposed to alcohol in her house, so this would be a new experience.

Other boys began to show up. There was Jimmy Smith, the football captain. He was handsome with dark features and a stocky build. Lilly had her eye on Jimmy and was coming apart at the seams when she noticed he never took his eyes off Summer. Jake Taylor was another handsome football player. He also had a stocky build, with dark hair and brown eyes. Arnold South was not so striking but had enough charisma to attract the girls. When they came in, one would have thought Summer was the only girl there because of the way they all kept gazing at her. The last one to come in was the one the other boys had chosen for Summer. His name was Paul Bale, and he was more devastatingly handsome than the others. He was also taller, not so stocky, and had almost black hair and sea blue eyes. Lilly and Mary couldn't take their eyes off of him. But Summer wasn't as impressed with him as they were.

All the boys, including Paul, couldn't take their eyes off Summer. They wanted to toss a coin for her, but they knew that would be too insensitive. Besides, they learned with the trio; it was a sure thing. But, they couldn't be confident with Summer. So, they introduced Paul to her. Summer thought he was cute, but she didn't understand the arrangement. Yet all the attention flattered her, so she didn't question much.

Summer tried to make it look as though she and Ella remained friendly to her parents; so, the party would go off without a hitch. They wanted them to believe she was with Ella on the party night. At church, she walked up to Ella as though they were never on the outs. "Hey Ella, how are things?"

Ella was significantly hurt and wasn't playing along. "Ok, I guess." She spoke. She wasn't warm, but she was also trying not to be rude. It still seemed funny to Summer that her parents never asked questions when she and Ella had been estranged at church. They spoke politely to each other, but anyone could tell they weren't the best buds they had been. So, many people had questioned her as to why they went their separate ways, but her parents never did. Summer wondered if they even cared.

Paul was the blind date she never expected. He seemed polite enough until his hands were all over her. Summer was uncomfortable with this. Finally, he appeared to give up; he said, "Let's call a truce. I have delicious refreshment for you." He offered her something to drink. But Summer could tell something was in her drink which was supposed to be ginger ale. She was lightheaded, "Something's in this drink!" she cried out, then Summer ran, but she didn't get far. Paul caught her and led her to the couch. "Come on; it's going to be fun." Summer knew his intentions. She pulled away and began fighting. "Leave me alone!" In the struggle, she bit Paul and then lost her balance and hit her head on the sharp edge of the coffee table. A pool of blood was seeping out around her head. Paul and everyone else panicked and fled the scene. "Let's get out of here!" Paul said to others following behind. They thought that she might be dead.

In a few moments, Summer regained consciousness. She then remembered Ms. Ames and reached into her handbag to look for her number. She became anxious, thinking she had lost it, but she looked again and found it. There was no one in the apartment. She thought maybe the group ran because they thought she was dead. But she was glad they were all gone. She dialed Ms. Ames' number.

Lindy awoke around 1:00 a.m., screaming from a nightmare about Summer; she was drowning in her sweat. Lindy's restlessness woke Kevin up. When he saw Lindy's sweat, he thought she was ill.

"Are you okay, Lindy?" he cried out.

"It's Summer. I need to know she's okay."

"Lindy, Summer is probably sound asleep at Ella's. Is it necessary to wake her up?"

"Kevin, she's not over there. I know she's not there. She and Ella haven't been together for a while."

So, Kevin reached for the phone and called Ella's house. Tom, Ella's father, sleepily answered the phone. "Hello"

"Tom, this is Kevin. I am so sorry to disturb you, but I need to speak to Summer."

"Summer? She's not here."

Panic shot through Kevin, and he dreaded telling Lindy. How on earth did she know? "Thank you, Tom. Would Ella know where she is?"

"Ella hasn't been in touch with Summer for a while. I hope she's okay. Can we help in any way?"

"Thank you so much. I will let you know if that becomes necessary." They said their goodbyes and hung up

"Lindy, where's Summer?"

"I knew she wasn't at Ella's. I am praying. She's in danger, or she was. I just want her home!"

Kevin's voice was now shrill with panic. "Lindy, she's not at Ella's! We don't know where she is!" He put his clothes on, and then the doorbell rang. Kevin just knew it was a police officer with the tragic news about Summer. First, he heard Lindy answer the door. Then Kevin heard Summer's voice and another voice. When he went to the door, they introduced him to Sally Ames. Lindy warmly said, "Thank you so much. We were so worried; she wasn't where we thought she was." Summer cringed at Lindy's remark. But hugged Ms. Ames and said, "Thank you, Miss Ames, for caring so much."

Lindy and Kevin then asked, "Won't you please come in?" but Sally said, "Maybe another time."

They remembered her from church and would plan to invite her to dinner after church one Sunday or take her out to dine.

Summer knew she was in trouble. But it had been a long time since she had been so lovingly embraced by both her parents. Could it be they cared after all?

When Kevin released her, he said, "You are grounded for a month!"

Even that was an embrace to Summer.

"Make that two months," Lindy added

Summer also remembered the childhood crush she had on Larry Calhoun. It was odd how her mind embraced this from time to time. After all, a desire isn't supposed to be forever. And she was now married to Mike. Larry was recovering from a drug issue. He turned to drugs after losing his best friend to a fatal car accident. This abuse almost cost him his job as a business administrator. His company's insurance provided for him to be in drug rehab. It had a statute of limitations and was almost up when he made his decision.

Pastor Joel Richmond, the senior pastor of the Word of God, introduced him to the congregation. He then gave his testimony, and Summer was infatuated with him. She had daydreamed about him from the first moment she saw him. Afterward, every time she went to church, she found herself gazing at him, and she would try to stop herself. Larry was muscular, tall, and devastatingly handsome, with dark hair and blue-green eyes and a smile that would melt ice. Summer's feelings for Larry were real. She knew the age gap meant he could find someone else, but she prayed for God to reserve him for her. *"Dear Lord, I know I love Larry. I know I'm only a child, but I won't be forever. Please let him be mine!"* She didn't think of it as a selfish prayer—she only knew her feelings for him were genuine. Summer considered sharing this confidential matter with her best friend, Ella, but she knew Ella would only express disapproval. She wouldn't understand a 12-year-old girl dreaming about a future relationship with a 22-year-old man. Summer decided this would be a matter between

God and herself only. The only problem was that Summer hadn't given her heart to Jesus yet.

Twelve was a crisis year for her. Eventually, she said the sinner's prayer and gave her heart to Jesus. Sally Ames had led her to the Lord, and her conversion was profound. Sally asked Summer, "Have you ever invited Jesus into your heart."

"Not really!" Summer expressed

"Would you like to?"

"I guess so." Summer stated unsure

"It's effortless, and you will discover Jesus is your best friend."

"I could use that."

"Then what are you waiting for?"

Then she said the sinner's prayer with Sally Ames.

She was also impressed with Larry's testimony. She was on fire and had passed Bibles out at school. Unfortunately, she was also under fire, and she faced severe criticism from the parents of students she had led to Christ. Finally, the principal called her into the office and said, "Summer, I'm proud of what you do. But unfortunately, school is not the place for passing out Bibles and holding Bible Studies." She knew this violated her first amendment rights, but she decided not to make waves. "Ok, sir, I'll do my studies somewhere else, and I'll pass the Bibles out there too." The Bibles had comic book excerpts.

Summer's favorite scripture was Psalm 23:4-6. "Yea, though I walk through the valley of the shadow of death, I will fear no evil; For You are with me; Your rod and Your staff, they comfort me. You prepare a table before me in the presence of my enemies; You anoint my head with oil; My cup runs over. Surely goodness and mercy shall follow me All the days of my life; And I will dwell in the house of the LORD Forever." The shadow of death represents depression and thoughts of suicide for preteens and teens, among other issues. In Summer's Bible studies, they prayed consistently about these concerns.

The Bible studies were held once or twice weekly. The other days were spent creating music at God's Temple Church, making beautiful music, and Ella joined her. They had Pastor Brim's consent, and Pastor Brim was even more impressed with Summer and Ella's duet.

Summer hadn't heard the last from the trio. They seemed to have amnesia about how they had left her unconscious and didn't seek medical attention when they thought she was severely injured or dead. They wanted revenge Lilly began, "There she is, the homewrecker." That's how Lilly referred to her because their boyfriends wanted nothing more to do with them. "She's lying about Paul," she continued, "he's not that hung up her to be so desperate.". The night that Sally Ames brought Summer home, Summer mentioned her drink was spiked. Her parents took her to the emergency room for a drug test. They found a minute amount of powerful alcohol, which could have caused her to be date raped if she had consumed the entire amount. Kevin and Lindy knew they had to press charges. At first, Summer fiercely objected, "Mom, Dad, if I do this, everyone at school will hate me." But the staff at the hospital told her, "Summer, if you don't come forward, another young girl can become a victim. Do you want that?" Summer shook her head. "And Summer, this young man is a minor. He will probably have a chance to be in the *Scared Straight* program to remind him of the consequences of his behavior continues, and we pray he won't become an adult offender."

"Jimmy let me have it because he didn't know our real ages, and they still wouldn't know if it weren't for Summer." Lilly continued.

"I guess it's a big deal that Summer's only twelve," Taylor remarked.

"What about your brother Tayler? Isn't he in jail because of her?" Norman was arrested for contributing to the delinquency of minors

"He's in and out of jail a lot anyway."

"And how about Mary? She's in a foster home, and they don't allow her to do anything."

"I know you're right." Taylor didn't want to argue with Lilly anymore.

"And we have to sneak around to be together anymore."

"True."

They blamed everything on Summer. When Sally Ames rescued Summer that night, she was appalled when she saw Mary's apartment, a party place for the trio. She had to inform Child Protection. Lilly's parents were humiliated and ordered Alex to keep a more watchful eye on Lilly's activities. Child protection had advised Lilly and Taylor's parents that the girls needed to dissolve their association with each other and with Mary. So, outside of the school grounds and phone contact, the trio never communicated. Lilly and Taylor's parents told the school staff not to permit Lilly or Taylor to associate with each other or Mary. At first, the staff tried to enforce this request, but the school couldn't babysit just three when there were hundreds more. Lilly then stated, "I have an interesting idea. How about we convince Summer we're her friends again. Then think of something that would expel her from school, make her lose her good standing with her church, and show her Bible study students the real hypocrite she is."

Lilly was giving her a devious look and then proceeded with a sinister plan. "Maybe we can take pictures of her when she undressed in gym class and make it appear that she sold the pictures to a nude magazine for money."

But Taylor was not comfortable with this idea. This line is hard for her to cross because it crosses a line with God. She's not a believer but fears God enough not to push him to the limit.

Things weren't going any better in Summer's home life. Lindy still declared Autumn to be the reigning queen. Kevin was still more devoted to his job than to his family. Larry left to attend Seminary, so Summer had a greater interest in God's Temple Church. She wanted to attend there, but she kept silent since it was her secret hiding place. Summer had great support from Ms. Ames and Pastor Brim, and with this, Summer could soar through it all. They had reminded her she was an eagle. She was faithful and needed this support from her counselor and her pastor. She had experienced severe persecution for her Bible studies, but the most severe persecution was just ahead. Her eagle-soaring days were about to be tested.

The trio was putting their plan into action. The girls had a friend set up a hidden camera between her gym locker and the nearest shower. Summer always showered after gym class, so they knew she would be visible on camera. But they had to win Summer's trust to make sure the trick was effective. This sickened Taylor. She thought of how she would feel to have such a vulgar trick played on her. She empathized with Summer. Yes, she hated that her brother was facing prison time, but he had sealed his fate. She couldn't blame it all on Summer.

Taylor thought the matter over realistically. "Lilly, can't we do something else to Summer. I'm not comfortable with this plan."

"Well, Taylor, how comfortable are you with how Summer destroyed our lives. Doesn't she deserve the same thing?"

"I'm not saying to do nothing, just change the plan."

"To a honey-coated plan, I don't think so. This plan is perfect. I hope you're not getting cold feet because you know this plan has to be confidential."

"Of course, it's confidential. I've never betrayed you."

"Then let's keep it that way."

Taylor hated that Lilly was so headstrong, and she had the most influence over Mary. So, getting either of them to change their mind was futile. Now she was torn about whether to help execute the evil plan or do the right thing. As she didn't want God for an enemy, she opted for doing the right thing. It would be hard, as she knew the venom of the other two could prove tragic for her. However, it was more important for her to win God's favor and protection. Summer knew a lot about God, so Taylor thought maybe it was time to ask Summer some questions.

When Lilly and Mary saw Taylor being friendly to Summer, they thought she was setting Summer up. Summer also saw it as a setup until Taylor came right out and said, "I'm a mean person, and I can do some despicable things, but this is going too far. I can't come against a worker of God." She wanted to tell her the plot, but she wasn't yet ready to betray her friends. However, she would keep her eye on the situation and come to Summer's rescue.

Summer didn't know what to make of Taylor's offer of friendship. She knew she and the other two girls had to be furious. Taylor's brother could be facing a lengthy prison term. It was hard to trust her, but she decided she would pray about it. She told Taylor this and then added, "Know this, Taylor Miller, if I decide to trust you, believe me when I say you don't want to cross God."

She soon felt God had beckoned her to trust Taylor. So, she answered Taylor's handful of questions about God. Finally, Taylor shot the central question, "Will God protect me for doing the right thing rather than to do what is wrong for the sake of friendship."

"That's deceit, Taylor and God will never honor deceit."

"Summer, how do I have God in my life?"

"Come to our Bible study tomorrow. I would like you to meet many who asked the question you just did."

Taylor had tears of repentance in her eyes. She, Summer, and Ella had just recited the sinner's prayer. She apologized to Ella for how cruel she had been to her. And, of course, Ella forgave her, hugged her, and expressed, "This is a very courageous move, Taylor taking a stand for your faith." Taylor knew she was going to feel Lilly's and Mary's wrath. She also knew she wasn't backing down.

Lilly and Mary were noticing how chummy Taylor was becoming with Summer and Ella. Lilly scowled at Mary. "Taylor has probably told Summer all about our plan, and now we can't go ahead with it. But little Taylor is going to pay the price for this!"

"Really? What do you mean?" Mary asked, puzzled.

"Do you remember the little secret our Taylor told us a few years ago? Well, I think it's time to talk to her about it again."

Mary didn't want to betray Taylor, but she knew she couldn't express this to Lilly. So she only felt she had no choice but to go along with Lilly.

Kevin and Leo were in their agency doing paperwork. Their assistant June Hart was a reasonably attractive middle-aged widow of medium height and weight. She wore her greying hair pulled back. She was a widow and displaced homemaker, and this was her first job outside of her home. Trudy had trained her, and she learned rapidly. She was very resourceful. For Kevin and Leo, she was the best assistant. Word of God Pastor Joel Richmond had recommended her. Kevin and Leo talked it over and gave her this opportunity. Trudy instructed her because she wanted more time for homemaking. Lindy was her role model, and Trudy discovered her passion for making a proficient home and cooking healthy meals for Leo. She was addicted to his praise. Neither Leo nor Kevin had ever hesitated about hiring June. She was finished and about to retire for the day, "I'm leaving now." She announced and then left. The office bell rang, and Joshua Brim entered. He came to pay his semiannual insurance premium.

Kevin greeted him. "How's everything going, Joshua? you know you had a grace period."

"I know, but I'm here to kill two birds with one stone. I love hearing Summer performing, and I wish you would persuade her to be a part of our Christmas concert." Kevin asked Joshua some questions.

"Joshua, when did you hear Summer practicing her performance?"

"Quite some time now. Didn't you know?" He explained how Summer used his piano in his sanctuary to practice piano.

"Oh yes, of course, I knew. I hope my daughter had your approval." Kevin lied

"That's no problem." Pastor Brim stated, not wanting Summer to be in trouble. However, the only thing that mattered to Kevin was knowing her whereabouts.

Kevin now knew where Summer's secret hiding place was, and he was relieved. He then answered Joshua, "I'll speak to Summer and try to encourage her to be a part of your play. It would be perfect for her." Summer was different these days. He reminisced about the many times Summer sang his favorite songs. Suddenly, he missed his family. He thanked Joshua but didn't want him to know how his discovery about Summer gave him mental peace.

Lilly and Mary recalled the time Taylor told them a family secret—her brother, Norman, had killed a man named Arturo. It was the only name anyone knew. He was an illegal alien from somewhere in El Salvador. He was of medium height, heavy set, had dark-colored Hispanic skin, dark brown eyes, and a rugged and worn appearance. No one knew anything about him. Arturo approached Norman as he left work. There had been bad blood between Norman and him for a while about some drug issue.

The argument escalated to violence; Arturo punched Norman in the face and knocked him down. He was turning to leave when Norman broke a beer bottle, took the broken edge of the bottle, and pierced it deep into Arturo's chest. He died instantly.

Norman panicked and called his Uncle Rick, "Uncle Rick, I just killed a man, and I swear I didn't mean to."

"Is anyone around?"

"I don't think so."

"Then hide the body and tell me where you are. We'll take care of the rest when I get there."

"I don't know; maybe I would feel better if I just called the cops. But, I can't live with this."

"Are you crazy? You'll be in prison for the rest of your life. Hide that man, and then I'll get him into my truck."

From what he could tell, no one was around. He pulled Arturo's body out of direct sight. His uncle arrived shortly, but it seemed like an eternity to Norman. They placed Arturo's body in the back of Uncle Rick's truck and took it to the city dump, where tons of trash and garbage would soon cover it up.

His neighbors didn't miss Arturo because he would disappear for weeks on end. They just figured he had decided not to return. They knew he was an illegal alien, so they thought that was why.

Lilly watched as Taylor came to their meeting place. Taylor had thought she could trust Lilly and Mary with this information, and they made an oath never to tell anyone. But today, because Taylor decided she would rather pal around with Summer and Ella, that oath became null and void.

Kevin and Summer arrived home at the same time. Kevin told Summer he wanted to speak to her after dinner. Summer gave him an "Am I in trouble" look.

"No, sweetheart, you haven't done anything. That I know of?" He stated, giving a mock suspicious look.

"Daddy, quit that!" Kevin laughed; he loved teasing her.

"Let's get washed up for dinner."

They were both famished.

Lindy had prepared chicken and dumplings, squash, dinner rolls, and southern sweet tea. The family ate, enjoying the spread.

Autumn began, "I made two as in school today Mama."

"Why didn't you bring you them home."

"I will tomorrow."

It had always annoyed Kevin to see Lindy and Autumn talking as though no one else was in the room. He looked at Summer, but she didn't seem to notice. Summer seemed so at peace these days. When they had their talk, he would have her sing his favorite song by George Strait, "Carrying Your Love with Me." It was about how love is with him even when he's not with his family. How did he become so removed from the situation? Maybe it wasn't right, but since Lindy insisted on giving Autumn all of her attention, he would make this a special time for Summer and him.

Summer ended up singing several songs to Kevin. Once Summer shared her lovely singing voice, Kevin was hooked. He then made his announcement.

"I talked with Pastor Brim this evening. He also loves your performance."

"Dad, I have to have my privacy from Mother and Autumn, and if I perform, it's going give away my hide away."

"Summer, you make your mom worry when you take off each day. It's not right to put her through that. But I'll tell you what, you arrange your performance, and I promise you that neither your mother nor Autumn will disturb you."

"You know Autumn does what she wants."

"You leave that to me."

He told Summer to begin her homework. Then he called Lindy into his office.

"I know where Summer's hideaway is."

"Really, where? "

"I will tell you, but Summer doesn't want you to know because it appears she's afraid you and Autumn will pester her. And if I tell, you have to promise to give her privacy. Lindy promised anxiously. "Now I need to talk to Autumn."

Lindy was apprehensive about getting Autumn when she saw the serious look on Kevin's face. However, she found her and took her into Kevin.

"Autumn, I need for you to give your sister her privacy. It seems you bother her stuff."

"It's just a joke." Autumn tried to interrupt.

"No more interruptions, Autumn. Also, you will not bother Summer at the church where she's going to perform. Thus, if you do interrupt her, you will feel my strap. Is that understood!"

"Just one thing, can Nancy and I perform at the church too. I promise to be good." The mention of the play intrigued Autumn so much that she wasn't even fearful of Kevin's discipline.

"That'll be up to your sister."

"Slim chance then."

"I'll talk to her"

Kevin's true dream was to see Summer and Autumn be close as sisters. So, Kevin thought maybe the church musical could be the answer.

Summer met with the Christmas concert cast and auditioned for Mary, Jesus's mother; however, she got the part of Elizabeth, the mother of John the Baptist. Ella also auditioned and got the role of Mary. Summer was disappointed, but God taught Summer humility, and she was happy that Ella got the part.

Lilly and Mary cornered Taylor. "Are you having fun with these total Jesus Freaks? Have they converted you now?" Lilly asked.

Their attitudes alarmed Taylor, but she knew she had to get this over. "Yes, Lilly, I am a Christian now. But you don't have to worry. I'm not and have never been a snitch."

"That's good, but I don't trust you. Just in case you do think about snitching, remember the info we have on your murdering brother."

"You know you took an oath not to tell."

"That was an oath of the sisterhood. You no longer belong, and neither does the oath."

"I promise I won't tell. This knowledge will kill my mother."

"Remember, your brother's fate is in the palm of my hand. But that will change if I find out you told Summer or Ella about our plot."

Taylor's family wasn't aware she knew about Norman. She overheard her father and her Uncle Rick talking about how Norman had killed the man in a drunken rage and how they disposed of his body. They wanted it to be a secret between the three men, which meant even her mother didn't know. What should she do now? She had to trust God, but her baby Christian faith now staggered. She didn't want to confide in Summer, but Summer's walk with God was closer than hers. Norman was in jail, and now his term could be even longer. She loved him and hated how she had made such a mess of things for him.

Summer could tell by Taylor's expression that she had troubling news. She wasn't going to press her about it. She only hoped Taylor understood that God helps us through our troubles.

Taylor had to speak to someone, and she trusted Summer. She was just afraid of losing her friendship once Summer knew a member of her family was a killer. However, she couldn't keep it to herself. Summer asked Taylor, "Are you ok?" Then, Taylor began uncontrollably sobbing as Summer embraced her. When she regained control, she poured her heart out. "When I was eight years old, I woke up one morning and overheard a conversation between my father and uncle about how my brother, who was seventeen years old at the time, had killed a man. He was in a drunken rage, and afterward, he was afraid and called my uncle. They disposed of his body. I don't know where. I felt close to Lilly and Mary, and I shared this with them. Now they are using it to blackmail me."

Summer was concerned, but now she knew Norman had committed a critical crime. She felt inclined to pray to receive an answer from God fervently. Taylor became alarmed by Summer's lengthy silence. In compassion, Summer embraced her again and assured her, "God has the answers, Taylor, and we are going to give this to Him and wait for His answer." But how should she approach this matter? She didn't feel inclined to notify the police. Norman should do that, he at least had to have that chance, and she just told Taylor to wait on God. So, she knew she had to, also.

She looked at Taylor as God compelled her to say. "You have to go to Norman. First, he needs salvation, and then he will do the right thing."

There it was again, Taylor reflected. The right thing, Yet the right thing was always tricky. But God beckoned her to obey and gave her peace that everything would be okay.

Norman was still in jail because no one in his family would provide for his bail. He knew he would be there until his court appearance a month away. Then it would probably be on to prison. The chaplain at the correctional facility had told him he might have his time reduced if he went to rehab. He didn't know if he could overcome this addiction, and the man couldn't pretend he could. Yet, he wanted his freedom badly. He had to at least think about rehab.

He had stayed drunk and high over the last six years so that he couldn't reflect on his life back then. But even drugs and alcohol only relieved a part of his guilt and pain. Of course, staying silent had made it worse. He knew he should've gone to the police and told them he never realized what he had done. It happened so fast, and if Norman hadn't been high and drunk, he wouldn't have done it. He was about to go to his cell when the guard told him, "Norman, you have a visitor." Norman left to go to the visiting room.

Taylor was sitting opposite the inmate booth, waiting to visit with her brother. She hated the thought that he would feel she betrayed him, but she needed the truth to set her free. Taylor also hoped the truth would set Norman free. She was lost in her thoughts when he arrived.

Norman adored his baby sister. Their mother was close by because an adult had to accompany her. But she requested to speak to Norman alone and had obtained the Chaplain's consent. Norman observed Taylor's long face, but he was adamant about cheering her up. He didn't know that before he finished, he would need the cheering up.

"Norman, I have something to confess to you, something's that's festered in me for too long," Norman observed her and knew what she was going to say. But how could she know? Taylor then began, "Early one morning, I overheard Daddy and Uncle Rick talking about how you had killed a man, and you and Uncle Rick buried him. I was in shock and couldn't believe it. I wanted to feel better; so, I confessed this incident to Lilly and Mary."

Norman felt betrayed and said, "Taylor, how could you?"

Taylor broke down in heavy sobs. "I didn't know what to do. I was hurting, and I just couldn't keep it inside. I'm sorry, Norman, but Lilly and Mary are blackmailing me because I gave my heart to Jesus. They are threatening to tell the police."

Norman tortured, seeing his baby sister in pain. How could he accuse a then eight-year-old child of betrayal when she was only seeking comfort? It was time to come clean. "Honey, it's not your worry anymore," he said. "I'm coming clean about it; I need it off my conscience, anyway."

Taylor pleaded with him, "Please, Norman, let Jesus into your heart, and He will take care of everything."

"I want to believe this, Taylor, but I don't know."

"Please, Norman, give him a try. He won't fail you. You have to give Him a chance." Norman then remembered when he was eight years old and had a childlike faith in Jesus. What happened? He couldn't remember when it left. However, maybe it was time to get it back. "How do I do it, Taylor?"

"Repeat the sinner's prayer after me." Taylor spoke, and Norman repeated, "Lord Jesus, I need you. Please come into my heart. I am a sinner, and I've greatly sinned against you. Please cleanse these sins. Take away my old life and give me a new one. I believe you are the only way to salvation. Please give me salvation. In Your Holy Name, I ask this. Amen!"

Taylor then saw the light and aura in Norman. She knew he was saved, and they were both ready for whatever plan God had. Norman thought *If I go to prison, God will use me there. If I'm set free, God will use me there. I will go wherever God wants to use me. I will no longer think about myself. Just God and then others.* He then remembered Ephesians 1:3, Paul's prayer, *"Blessed be the God and Father of our Lord Jesus Christ, who has blessed us with every spiritual blessing in the heavenly places...."* All of a sudden, he wasn't in a jail cell anymore. It had become a heavenly place.

Summer and Taylor then went to Pastor Brim. Summer went with her family to Word of God Church, but Pastor Brim was her pastor. Taylor's parents didn't attend church, so she attended God's Temple Church. On many Sundays, Summer attended with her. Today, they wanted Pastor Brim to speak to Norman. He agreed and made the arrangements.

At the inmate booth, Norman received him enthusiastically. He asked, "Pastor Brim will you baptize Me?". He didn't know Pastor Brim, but Taylor spoke highly of him. Then Pastor Brim stated, "something tells me Norman; you won't have to be baptized here. Let's wait."

Norman made his confession. The correctional officers were sad because they liked Norman. When he had his court date, they would ask the judge to take his excellent behavior into account. Everyone prayed he would have favor with the Judge. They knew he had to serve time, but everyone prayed at least for leniency.

Judge Tom Jenkins, seated in his black robe, had balding, light hair and wore glasses. After all the testimony and Norman's confession, he just asked Pastor Brim, "Pastor Brim will you give a recommendation."

"How about the recommendation of 500 community service hours and probation time."

The judge stated, "500 community service hours and probation for five years. Even though I don't condone the taking of the life, young man, I do believe you when you said you had remorse and were under the influence. That was several years ago, and you've never had a violent offense since. Your victim was also violent. I'm taking that into account also. If the D.A. agrees, we'll just let this recommendation stand." The D.A. nodded his head. The judge continued to proceed, "I also recommend Rehab at Minion's Mission Shelter" Norman had a big smile of relief.

His probation officer was a member of God's Temple Church. The following Sunday, Norman was baptized. George Fields, his probation officer, told him, "Congratulations, and together, Norman, we will defeat this enemy. You will have a new life because you are a new person."

Taylor and Summer were ecstatic at how well the court decision went. It cleared any doubts that either Taylor or Norman had about God. They knew only God could arrange this kind of mercy. More over the best part for Taylor was that it foiled Lilly and Mary's plans. Taylor knew it was facetious, but she had to tell Lilly and Mary. "Not only is confession good for the soul, but it also cancels out blackmail." Lilly and Mary gave her a murderous look. After Norman's rehab, he did his community service hours serving the homeless addicts who later found a temporary home at the local Mission Shelter. Norman participated in the shelter's drug and alcohol rehab program. Norman worked to help them get jobs and eventually permanent places to live. He felt this was his calling, and he was dedicated. Doing these service hours helped him decide to become a social worker. He registered as a student of Sociology at Texas Tech University for the upcoming semester.

December 15 was opening night for the Christmas musical, *The Nativity*. Ella had the part of Mary. She crushed on Jeremy Scott, who played Joseph. Summer had the role of Elizabeth, mother of John the Baptist. Everyone loved the way she held her stomach as she said, "My child has leaped inside of me because of the child in your womb."

The music was magnificent, and all the children's voices were in perfect melody and harmony.

Taylor played the Angel of God who came to Elizabeth and Mary. God had convicted Summer to include Autumn and Nancy. They played two of the wise men. The performance received a standing ovation.

Summer was in the dressing area when she received flowers and a note from a devoted fan. It was Larry Calhoun. Summer's heart was on a cloud. She knew she was still too young, and Larry just loved her talent. Yet, she believed this was a sign that Larry would one day be reserved for her.

Chapter 3

At sixteen Summer's appearance was the same, only more mature looking. She had remained faithful to God. Although, events that occurred when she was sixteen had shaken her faith. She heavily relied on both Ms. Ames and Pastor Brim for support. Then before school began in the fall of 2001, Ms. Ames had been fired. She had been warned repeatedly by the school board not to witness to the students whose parents were atheists. Nonetheless, she listened to the Lord rather than the school board. She continued to witness, and, as the school board promised, Miss Ames was fired. Summer didn't understand. She had received salvation through Ms. Ames's ministry. She had a million questions, but the biggest one was why? Why did this happen? What was Ms. Ames going to do without a job? Why does the devil seem always to win?

Her home life was also diving. Nothing had changed with her parents, and Autumn (now 13 and looking the same, but more awkward and taller than Summer) became a nastier brat. Summer tried to be at either Taylor's or Ella's house as much as possible. She had to escape from home. It would be more bearable if her father were home more. However, even when he was home, he worked from the home computer. To her, he may as well not have been there. He wasn't there for her. He wasn't there for anyone.

Now, though, she was looking for different friends. She was discouraged about being a Christian. If God was a provider, why would someone as faithful as Ms. Ames lose her job? If he loved her, why did she have to endure abuse from Lindy and Autumn?

Summer hadn't had a physical altercation with Autumn for a while. It never solved problems. Moreover, since Kevin stopped Autumn stealing and destroying her possessions, there wasn't much reason to. Instead, she rebelled and verbally attacked her mother. She would continually remark, "I hate you, and you hate me. Just admit it. You only care about your little Autumn angel. She never does anything wrong. I wish you weren't my mother. I just wish I had another family" Lindy would look at Summer and was in a state of shock and anger. It was pointless to try and run after her. She knew she would never catch her. Then Lindy told Kevin about it "Kevin; Summer is getting uncontrollable. She disrespects me, and she doesn't care what she says to me. Please help me with her. You never discipline her." Lindy stood as Kevin admonished her, "Like the way you always discipline Autumn. You don't notice how mean she is to Summer. You say Summer doesn't care how she talks to you; well, Autumn doesn't care how she speaks to Summer. Lindy! You made this trouble. Bail yourself out!"

Summer was also tired of hearing her parents argue about Autumn and her. Her father's attitude and how he always blamed Lindy and never saw how neglectful he was. She wanted just to run away. But to where?

Summer stopped hanging out with Taylor and Ella. She wasn't into praising the Lord anymore and didn't want to be around it. Taylor and Ella were disappointed with Summer's new attitude, but they left her alone and committed her to prayer. Then, one of Summer's new friends, Linda Jenkins, asked, "How would you like to join our group for a picnic at Buffalo Springs Lake? We don't do drugs or have orgies or anything like that."

"That should make my folks happy." She thought to herself. She remembered how they cared about her traumatic experience in middle school. Only, did they still care? They approved of her new friends, yet it didn't seem to matter to them that she wasn't seeking Christian fellowship anymore.

The friends had fun and water skiing. Some tanned California boys were there, and all the girls were impressed. That's where Summer met Mike. He was 19 years old. The boy was a blond-haired, blue-eyed surfer type who looked like Brad Pitt. Many of the girls swarmed around him, but he couldn't take his eyes off Summer. He walked up to her and spoke, "Hi, I noticed you standing here by yourself. I thought you could use some company." He didn't use the usual lines with her. She intrigued him more than any girl he had ever met.

"Thank you. So, you're from California. I've lived here all my life; how is life in California?"

"Probably no different than here."

"I hope it is because I would like to leave here." Summer said this before she realized it. She never knew she had thought it.

"Wow, are you serious? Are things that bad with your folks?" He was shocked yet also intrigued. Summer couldn't believe she had shared something so personal with a total stranger---even if he was a gorgeous stranger. And maybe that was why.

Mike was from San Mateo and attended San Francisco State University. He traveled here with his best friend Ernie Maddison and other friends. When he saw Summer, he had a strong desire to stay where she was. There were sparks between the two of them from the start.

Mike was respectful in the beginning. He didn't want to discourage her, but he had to determine how many liberties he could take with her. Summer had never been with a guy. She was taught in church to wait for the mate God had for her. But Summer had become discouraged about church matters and stopped believing its teachings. However, she wanted him to respect her; so, she refused his advances. He approached. "Summer, you are so beautiful. I want you." He was tempting, but she was having reactions to her experience of the attempted date rape. This incident made her cautious of any male company. Still, she had to admit that Mike was more tempting than any other boy she had met. She stated back, "Please stop hitting on me. It makes me uncomfortable, and I don't want to stop seeing you."

"I don't want that. I apologize. But please understand I was just complimenting you, not hitting on you. So I'm sorry if it appeared that way." Mike then knew he was forbidden to take liberties with her. He was glad she addressed this before he made a move on her.

They met most nights at Buffalo Springs. One night, on Labor Day weekend, they found a secluded spot. Summer was daydreaming and having romantic thoughts about Mike. That and the cool breeze gave Summer goosebumps, and Mike hadn't even touched her yet. Her daydreams about him and being alone with him were too overwhelming. She wanted him to touch l her. She wanted her dreams to become a reality, but her shyness prevented her from letting him know.

Mike sensed Summer's aspiration for him. He just didn't want to make a mistake and be wrong. Suddenly, Mike saw sparks of electricity in Summer's eyes, and her longing for him evident. He knew then he was not mistaken. He approached her and told her everything she ever wanted to hear "Summer, you are the most beautiful, thrilling, and desirable girl I have ever met. I can't help this electrifying desire I have for you. But, sweet baby, it's all up to you. I'm your puppet, and I'm letting you pull the strings."

"Consider the strings pulled," Summer stated in stirring and sincere passion. Now all her thoughts about wanting respect were gone because all she wanted was Mike. He had fulfilled her beyond all her expectations and released her of all her inhibitions. Then it was all over, and reality set in. She was taught that a boy loses respect for a girl who gives in.

She had to ask him. "Do you still respect me? I was taught that boys lose respect for girls who give in." He stated quietly, "Of course, I respect you. You just gave me a gift. I've never been the first with any girl; I have never been with a virgin. That's extremely special to me. Though, I am concerned that you could be pregnant. After you take a pregnancy test, we'll have to take precautions from now on. I don't think we're ready to be parents."

"I never thought about that." Summer then pictured how she could face her parents if she were pregnant. Then she heard Mike talking.

"Summer to Earth, Earth to Summer. I just asked you that since you want to leave home anyway, you can come back to California with us."

"Do you mean it?"

"I wouldn't have asked if I didn't mean it." It was the perfect answer; at last, Summer felt the freedom she hadn't had in a long time.

Kevin and Lindy were concerned because Summer was so late coming home. They found out her friend Linda had already returned home. It was hard for them to sleep that night, and they called the police.

Kevin asked the officer on the phone, "Our daughter never came home from her outing. She's only sixteen years. Can you please try to find her?"

"Where did she go?"

"Buffalo Springs Lake."

"Ok, we'll try to find her, but there's a curfew, so there's a good chance she won't be there."

"Just please try to find her."

Lindy felt Summer was ok but sensed she had run away. In the morning, they found a goodbye note from Summer in the mailbox. It didn't give a hint of her whereabouts. It was a "don't try to find me because I'm okay" note. Kevin turned pale, and Lindy sobbed mournfully.

At first, Summer wanted to tell her parents about her decision face to face. However, Mike immediately persuaded her not to.

He said, "Don't you know they'll lock you up and throw away the key. And send me packing. Maybe they'll even call the cops on me."

She said, "Well, I at least need to leave them a note. They are my parents, and they will worry."

"Ok, leave a note then." Summer borrowed a pen and paper from a friend and then wrote:

> *Dear Dad and Mom, by the time you get this note, I will be gone. I can't tell you where I am going because I don't want you coming after me. Just know I am safe and with someone capable of looking out for me.*
>
> *I haven't been happy at home for a while. Autumn seems to be Mom's only child. And Daddy, you just don't seem to care because you are never there. And I am fed up with Autumn's nasty attitude toward me. I haven't been able to bear being at home for a while. Since I was 12, I always had to find somewhere to get away. So now I feel I just need to get away for good.*
>
> *You are my parents, and I will always care about you. I even care about Autumn. I just don't feel it's returned. I feel at total peace with this decision. Therefore, once again, please don't try to find me.*
>
> *Summer*

Kevin was pale as a ghost. Lindy sobbed mournfully. Kevin held her, but he could tell he wasn't comforting her. A million questions and thoughts ran through Kevin's mind. *How did this happen? Where was Summer, and who was with her? He had no idea she was this unhappy. How on earth are we going to find her?* First, they went to Linda's house. She said, "I'm sorry, but Summer never confided in me about anything she was doing. I wish I could help you."

Kevin remembered his teenage years and how teenagers didn't snitch on each other. He knew getting her to break pointless, but he had to try.

"Linda, what if she's in danger? If you know something, you have to talk."

"I don't know where Summer might be, but I'm sure she's not in danger."

"Then you do know something?"

"I'm sorry, but I know nothing that will help you find her."

Lindy and Kevin had to give up. Linda's parents also tried to encourage Linda to speak. But it was pointless. They knew their next stop had to be the police station to file a missing teen report.

Autumn had spent the long weekend with Nancy. Nancy's father, Henry, had been out of town. Lindy and Kevin agreed she could go to the airport to meet Henry, and then her mother Nan would take them both to school. It was exciting for Autumn to spend a long weekend away from home. As they walked through the airport, Autumn noticed a girl who looked like Summer sitting at the San Francisco gate. She was with the most handsome guy Autumn had ever seen. Autumn took a closer look and realized it was Summer. She was confused; she had no idea Summer was seeing anyone. The child wanted to run and speak to her, but the boy summer's charisma prevented her. She was star-struck. She thought Summer was seeing him off. It never dawned on her she was leaving with him.

Summer never saw Autumn. She was highly anxious about the flight, as she had only a little experience with flying. But that was the least of it. Most of her anxiety was guilt over leaving her parents without even personally telling them goodbye. She knew if she didn't make this move now, she never would. Then the announcement rang out

"Flight 6098 was leaving out of gate 24A to San Francisco." Summer knew once she was on the flight, there was no turning back.

Kevin and Lindy were at the police station speaking to Officer Jones, who asked the usual questions

"How was her home life? Did a relative abuse her? Did she suffer any abuse?" Kevin and Lindy were annoyed by these questions, but they had no choice but to comply with them. It was the only way to get Summer back. Unfortunately, after the questioning, the officer didn't offer any hope. He said, "Many runaways are never found because they don't want to be found. An Amber Alert is only sent out for abductions, and your daughter's note rules that out. However, we will do a routine investigation and talk to her friends who had seen her last. That's the best we can do."

Kevin and Lindy left the police station with no more hope for finding Summer than before entering. So they went home to be there for Autumn and break the news to her.

Lindy offered to make lunch. It was past lunchtime, but they hadn't eaten all day. Lindy couldn't eat. Kevin didn't have an appetite but felt he needed to keep up the strength he would need for the hunt for Summer. The police weren't going to do much, so he discussed with Lindy, "Why don't we hire a private investigator?" That got Lindy's attention. "How about I use the proceeds from the agency? Then we can better afford it."

Lindy had a gift for interior home design. She only worked on occasion

"And I'll go to work with an agency in Lubbock for my home design. I was offered a position a few months ago. I hope it's still available. However, we have to think about Autumn. I can't leave her alone."

"She's always at Nancy's house anyway. Maybe we can pay Nan to let her stay with her until one of us comes home."

"Wonderful idea!"

She then got Nan on the phone. "Nan, this is Lindy. We have a major crisis. Summer has run away."

"Oh, I'm so sorry!" Nan stated shockingly

"Yes, and we have to take measures to bring her back home. I have to go to work so we can afford it. Is there any way we can hire you to keep Autumn each day until one of us comes home?"

"Of course, and you don't have to pay me Autumn's over here most of the time anyway."

"That's very generous, but Kevin and I insist that you be paid."

Autumn returned home after school, wondering what to do with her discovery about Summer. She had planned to tell her parents until she saw they were upset about Summer. Instead, Lindy greeted Autumn and then shared the news, "Autumn, honey, Summer has run away from home." Autumn was jealous of the concern Lindy was showing. However, she convinced herself loyalty to Summer was her reason to be silent. She couldn't blame Summer for wanting to leave with her handsome boyfriend.

So, she chose to stay silent, at least for now. Her parents thought they were breaking the news to her. Little did they know that she knew more than they did. She justified it by declaring Summer to be the lucky one with the hunk. So, Autumn, trying not to expose herself, acted shocked. "Are you kidding me? Summer ran away?" She also honestly didn't know; she had witnessed Summer's running away.

The plane landed at San Francisco International, and Mike and Summer were greeted by Mike's parents, Gerald and Susan Hanley. Gerald was tall like Mike. Mike had his features, except Summer noticed grey blended with his dark blond hair. Susan had greying dark auburn hair, green eyes, and striking features. They were an attractive couple, and they complemented each other. Gerald and Mike carried the luggage to the car.

Gerald was a biochemical engineer. He had worked for a firm for fifteen years and then started his firm. His dream was for Mike to become a part of the firm. Mike went to San Francisco University, the same school where he graduated. Gerald is now semi-retired and has a staff to run the firm.

Susan introduced herself to Summer. "It's wonderful to meet you, Summer, Mike; you never told us how beautiful this girl is."

Mike replied, "There's only so much to say on a phone conversation to people you were going to be with soon anyway. And she is beautiful."

"That she is!" Gerald added

Summer just blushed.

Summer was little, and without makeup, she looked younger than sixteen. Mike said, "She's eighteen." Susan had compassion for Summer's parents and wondered if they were beside themselves with worry. She had doubts that Summer was eighteen, but she had to dismiss these thoughts since she didn't have proof. They all got into the Hanley's Lincoln and headed for their luxury San Mateo home. The home was a large six-bedroom, four-bath Victorian. It was 23 years old. The couple had it built using their floor plans, and it took Summer's breath away. "Wow," she said, "I've never seen a mansion before!"

"You just gave it an upgrade!" Gerald said amusingly.

The living area was almost the total size of the house where she grew up. The dining room was separate. There was also a dinette set in the kitchen area— the most spacious kitchen area she had ever seen. There was also a huge den. She wasn't surprised when Gerald and Susan gave her a bedroom separate from Mike's. She knew this was also how her parents would have handled the situation.

Summer stated, "I have never slept in such an enormous bed. Look at all this beautiful antique furniture." That's when Susan noticed that Summer didn't have much to put in the chest of drawers. All she had were the jeans and t-shirt she had worn to the airport, the swimsuit she had worn at Buffalo Springs, and her few underclothes. Susan gave Summer a gown and a robe. Since Summer only had the clothes on her back, she said compassionately, "Tomorrow, young lady, we are shopping for you some clothes." Summer was embarrassed, but going home after clothes were out of the question. She was taught not to take advantage, but she couldn't argue since she needed at least a small wardrobe.

Lindy and Kevin hired a private investigator named Andrew Marks. Marks was tall, medium build, and muscular. He had light brown hair and dark hazel eyes. He had handsome features and was in about his mid-50s. Kevin and Lindy chose him because he was a Christian and had fair prices. He always prayed with his clients. He lived in New York City, and he was the best. Kevin and Lindy went to see him in New York. Kevin commented, "I'm told that you are the best and were also one of New York's finest."

"Those are rumors," Andrew said modestly. "Tell me more about your case."

"Our daughter ran away, and we don't know to where," Lindy said sadly.

"If you hire me, we will find her," Andrew stated confidently. Thus, his confidence gave Kevin and Lindy great comfort.

"Consider yourself hired," Kevin responded abruptly. Lindy looked harshly at Kevin. She agreed to hire Marks but would have liked Kevin to speak to her about it first. Andrew was very wise and asked, "Is this ok with you too, Mrs. Logan."

"Certainly," Lindy responded, grateful that he was more sensitive than Kevin was. "Who wouldn't want to hire the best?" She complimented, letting him know he had her approval.

"Ok, then," Andrew continued, "I will probably have to come to Minion a few times. I don't think it would be necessary for you to come back here, but you might a time or two. I will try to save you some travel expenses. I think we can conduct most of our business over the phone." He gave them his card. Then he added, "I have an upfront fee. I also need money for expenses for any travel I need to make. You'll find I gave you a break in my prices. I don't believe that you are wealthy, and I'm not going take advantage of you." The Logan's were relieved and knew for sure they made the right choice.

Kevin then said, "When do you start?"

"Immediately, I will come to Minion tomorrow if you want me to so that I can investigate the group of teens who saw her last." Kevin and Lindy were praying that he would find out more than he or the police did.

Mark's cases were always kidnappings and runaways. He had a critical reason to undertake this endeavor. Approximately 20 years ago, the body of his daughter, Mandy, who was 14 years old, was found in Central Park close to the body of a renowned businessman. The cause of death was a bullet wound to her frontal lobe, the exact cause of death as the businessman. Andrew was a Homicide Criminologist and the best in New York City. It didn't take long for him to figure out Mandy was in the wrong place at the wrong time and had witnessed the hit on the businessman.

He also knew who the killer was. He had been tracking Diesel Hamilton for a long time, and now the scumbag had made it personal. He thought of his wife, Vivian. She had been gone now for ten years. She had never gotten over Mandy's loss. Her's was another death he had tagged on Diesel. After Mandy's death, he decided to resign his position from the NYPD to conduct private investigations into only kidnapping and runaway cases.

"Vivian," he said, "I'm thinking of retiring from the NYPD. I'm thinking of going into a private investigation of kidnappings and runaways. I think this would be a wonderful memorial to Mandy." Vivian had then expressed her approval. "I think this would be most appropriate; Andrew and I know our sweet Mandy would be so proud."

He was going to make sure that what had happened to his daughter would never happen to another child. Hamilton was elusive because he worked locally, nationally, and internationally. However, Andrew was not going to rest until he put Diesel Hamilton behind bars.

Mike and Summer moved swiftly from San Mateo to the Metro Hotel in San Francisco. Mike and his father fought. "Mike, why would you drop out of college? You always follow the leader; why can't you be a leader?" He said, "Dad, I need a job now. I have to take care of Summer."

"If you two would get married, I could allow you to share a room. I'm not in any hurry for you to get married. However, you can't live in sin in my house. The two of you could live here and not worry about expenses."

"That's wonderful of you to offer Dad, but I don't want Summer to see me as a freeloader."

"Son, this is just a temporary situation. Surely Summer would understand that you have better opportunities with higher education."

"Ernie has already found me a job. I'll begin in two weeks. I can't let him down."

"I don't understand why you and Ernie quit school for fewer prospects. Education is everything. Please don't throw this chance away."

"It's my life, Dad; let me live it."

Gerald became angry now and said words he wanted to take back. "Son, every generation in the families of your mother and myself have been professionals. Why do you want to shame us?"

"That's enough, dad, you've gone too far. I'm calling Ernie tonight, and Summer and I are going to San Francisco tomorrow instead of in two weeks unless you want us to leave tonight."

"That's up to you, son, but you don't have to leave. Just don't' tell anyone I threw the two of you out."

"Why not? There's more than one way of being thrown out. And in this way, you are making it unbearable for Summer and me to stay."

"Have your way. You have always been tenacious." He retorted.

Mike immediately went to the phone and dialed Ernie's number.

Mike's friend, Ernie Maddison, couldn't have picked a better time to get Mike on at Barc Brothers Construction. The work site was approximately two blocks from the Metro. Mike had noticed that other Metro residents worked there. Ernie even loaned Mike enough money to cover his rent, groceries, and personal expenses. Mike never told Summer he smoked weed, but there wouldn't be enough money on his paychecks to cover it all for a while anyway. Fortunately for Mike, Barc Brothers needed overtime workers because it was the only way Mike could catch up.

Summer was appalled by the condition of the hotel. She never recalled seeing such rundown conditions in her young life. This place was a total wreck. The carpet was completely worn. The walls were dirty—with cracks, holes, and ugly graffiti. An aspiring artist had designed a beautiful mural of street people, but it looked out of place in this filthy place. Once Mike and Summer settled in the rented room, all Summer could see was the work and attention required. She spent her days on it like spring cleaning; their room stood out above the others. It was the most out-of-place but immaculate room in the entire hotel. The room was large, with a small double bed, a large walk-in closet with a chest of drawers, and another chest of drawers across from the bed. It had a tiny bathroom with a tiny shower and sink. It also had a small stove and refrigerator and a tiny kitchen sink. Plus, it had a cabinet above the stove for dishes and groceries.

While Mike was filling out his paperwork at work, his friend Ernie mentioned, "You know Mike, if you and Summer married, you would be given the best tax break for a couple, and if the two of you had children, it would be even better."

"I'm not ready for that, Maddison. However, I wouldn't mind being married to Summer. I love her like no one else in my life,"

So, he and Summer applied and received a marriage license and were married by a judge. The judge said the traditional vows. "Mike, do you take Summer to be your lawfully wedded wife, for better and for worse, and remain faithful to each other from this day forward." Mike said, "I do." He repeated the same vows to Summer, and she said, "I do." This small, informal ceremony was not how she pictured her wedding day. She felt a degree of sadness. She suddenly wished Kevin was giving her away. However, Mike was the man in her life now. So, she quickly got over it. In a short time, she went from Summer Logan to Summer Hanley. Their honeymoon would be brief because overtime was going to steal Mike's attention from Summer temporarily.

Diesel Hamilton was tall and tan-skinned, with dark curly hair, blue-green eyes, and desirable features. He was in his early 50s. He had been on the run from Andrew Marks since he killed his daughter 20 years ago. It was as if Andrew could smell when Diesel was in New York. He would always find him and tell him, "Your days are numbered, Hamilton. I'm going to snake you out because you are a snake. And all snakes get their heads ripped off. You'll make a mistake, and that will be the end of you." He knew Andrew was baiting him, and it was working. His confidence was shaken. If he didn't get away, he was going to get caught. How on earth was he to know he had killed the daughter of a renowned criminologist? A real Pitbull? So, he got in touch with his contractors. "Hey man, I need to get out of New York. It's too risky here. I'll go anywhere in the world. But I want money from you. You owe me for the risks I've taken."

"Ok, but let me get with some of your other contractors, and we'll be better to afford your hush money with our combined resources." This man would have hired someone to kill Diesel for bleeding him. However, it wouldn't have been worth it because Diesel was the best.

Diesel didn't need hush money because his career of fulfilling death contracts made him extremely wealthy. Nevertheless, he was going to take advantage of having more monetary increases.

Summer was lonely with Mike gone all the time. She was also bored and frequently walked or took public transportation to see the city's sights. Little did she know a dangerous admirer was watching her. Diesel loved beautiful women, but none affected him as this beauty was walking and catching streetcars and cable cars. He was close enough to her to listen to her speak and say "Hi" to other sightseers, and her Texas drawl transfixed him. He wanted her to keep speaking. To him, it was like hearing a beautiful song.

Summer was unaware of Diesel as he boarded the streetcars and cable cars with her. He watched as she entered the souvenir shops in China Town and North Beach. He stared at her from the window of a shop in North Beach she had entered. She was looking at an elegant Chinese lamp. She was used to a room with exquisite novelties and figurines. He saw this as an opportunity to make his appearance and was there at her side before she knew it. For some reason, Summer felt uncomfortable in his presence. He was older, much too old to have an interest in her. He was considerably older than her father. Even still, he had striking features; only there was an eeriness about him that told her she didn't want to be around him. Using all his charm, he said, "Young lady, I noticed you admiring this lamp. I would be happy to purchase it for you."

"Sir, I do appreciate your kindness, but I will have to say no." Her Texas drawl again made him powerless—her voice, beauty, and charm had enchanted him. He knew he had to have her. Yet, she had just refused his gift, which he knew was not a good sign. Most women noticed his charm and good looks—why not her? He wanted her, and he was going to have her.

"You have the most interesting voice," he said, "and I am overwhelmed by your charming southern accent."

"It's a Texas drawl. Sir, before you go any further, you should know I am happily married. So please respect!"

Yes, she was a challenge to Diesel, so he made up his mind to eavesdrop on this couple to see how happy they were. He had never seen them together.

Mike was working more extended weekdays and weekends. He was in bed sleeping when he wasn't working. This man was up long enough to eat, then back to bed and up for work. He didn't mind—he had always been a hard worker. He had to work overtime to cover all of their expenses, which now included birth control pills. Mike was going to make sure Summer took them. He was relieved that she wasn't pregnant after their first episode. He would make sure she wouldn't become pregnant at any time.

The extra work also affected his love life. He was active but not as passionate and spontaneous as Summer was accustomed to. They had bitter fights. Summer felt neglected and let him know it. "Mike, I miss you. I know you're tired from working, but I need you as my husband."

"Since I work and make all the money, Summer, I would think you would be more grateful."

"And I don't work and make an exceptional home for us? Especially in this dive with nothing to work with."

"Enough, Summer. I have to go back to sleep so I can be rested enough for work."

Summer left home because of fights with her family. She thought she had gotten away from home to avoid disputes. And things are no different. She had hideaways at home, and now her hideaway is San Francisco public transportation.

Autumn missed Summer. So out of curiosity, she checked the internet for news of San Francisco. Details the child observed caused her much concern. Every week she saw statistics about teen killings. She saw a picture of a young girl who looked similar to Summer. This image immediately set off an alarm in her. She had thought she was doing the right thing keeping this knowledge from her parents, but now she knew Summer could be in danger. She knew there would be dire consequences; however, she didn't want harm to come to Summer. Her first thought was to call Andrew Marks and tell him Summer's possible whereabouts. Only, she knew he had integrity and would tell her parents-or insist she tells them. So, she went to the living room and delivered the news to them. "Mom, Dad, I have something to tell you."

"Ok, Autumn shoot!" replied Kevin

"You aren't going to like it." She stalled

"Let's get it over with," Lindy added

"Do you remember the sleepover I had on Labor Day weekend with Nancy?" Kevin and Lindy looked intensely at each other.

"Yes, the weekend Summer ran away, but why do you mention this?" Said Kevin observing her suspiciously. "What do you know?"

"I saw Summer at the airport the morning after Labor Day. She was with the most interesting-looking boy." Kevin was in a tirade, and so was Lindy. They chorused together, "Autumn, why hadn't you mentioned this to us before?"

"I told you she was with an interesting-looking boy. He was "drop dead" gorgeous. And if this were me, I wouldn't want you to interfere either."

"Don't give me that." This time it was Lindy. "I don't think you care that much about your sister's well-being."

Autumn, unconsciously, confessed. "That's not true. I care about what happens to Summer. I guess I love her more than I thought because she's in San Francisco, and it's a dangerous place."

Kevin and Lindy both were relieved of Autumn's concern. However, they were still angry because if Autumn had come forward sooner, they would have found her by now.

"I'll take care of this." Lindy commented, "Autumn, I'm sorry for this, but you will be grounded from all school activities for a month. You are to go straight to Nancy's house after school. I'm glad you love your sister, but she's in danger now."

"It's ok, Mom, and I deserve it." Autumn's heart hurt for Summer, and she didn't care that they punished her. She even started talking to God.

Autumn was their daughter, too; therefore, Kevin and Lindy couldn't stay angry at her. She was a child, after all. They couldn't expect her to make reasonable decisions.

They immediately called Andrew Marks to give him the latest development.

Diesel was in the Metro outside of Mike and Summer's door, eavesdropping on a fight they were having. He knew now he was going to have to portray the compassionate friend to her. He heard the door handle turn, so he disappeared quickly. Mike came out and left for work. Diesel was excited about her being in there alone. Of course, it was too premature for him to make his move. It was going to take a lot of thought and planning.

Andrew had just gotten off the phone with Kevin, who had given him the latest update. "Thanks, Kevin, and I'm glad you're not staying angry with Autumn. She's not at fault, and I know you know this. I promise you; I will find your daughter."

He had his plans to head to San Francisco. He was in the house, the beautiful three-bedroom, two-bath home Vivian had created for them. He was in their bedroom, reflecting on their intimate moments. The man stared at Mandy's room that stayed virtually the same as it was before she died. Then he passed the kitchen and dining room where they cooked, ate, and talked as a family. In the living room that held the most memories of Vivian and Mandy, he stared at their pictures. He couldn't help but think of the life Diesel had robbed him of—seeing Mandy graduate from high school and college, giving her hand in marriage, and having grandchildren, and having Vivian for his twilight years. The only thing he hated about his cases was that they took time and energy away from finding Diesel. He was well off financially, so he could give full time and attention to this case. However, his heart was for the parents of kidnapped children and runaways, so Summer Logan was his top priority.

He made his flight and hotel reservations. He would be leaving on an early morning flight. He packed his suitcase and caught a flight before dawn out to the city of the Golden Gate.

Diesel's attraction for Summer was increasing. He had to plan how he could win her heart. Winning hearts was never any problem for Diesel—he was the love 'em and leave 'em kind. He had even thought he might be in love, though love was never part of Diesel's life. However, with the challenge Summer had presented him, he was confused about everything, even love.

Summer was in the room, hurting from the fight she had with Mike. She knew Mike had to work overtime, but did he have to be so mean about it? She never had a problem living in San Mateo, but Mike had fought with his father and left abruptly, without a red cent and deep in debt. Summer felt she was patient with Mike. She tried never to complain that he wasn't giving her adequate time and attention. It did hurt, and anytime she wanted to discuss it with him, he snarled at her. And, of course, she got angry and fought back. Summer's life had prepared her for altercations. Autumn had given her many experiences with this. But she never liked to fight. It was a big part of why this girl had run away. She loved Mike and knew they had to work things out.

Wearing a short-sleeved, plaid shirt and blue jeans, she headed out the door to sight-see. Then she saw Diesel Hamilton. He had flirted with her but never told her his name. She didn't care; she couldn't let him get in the way. She didn't need Mike to be jealous on top of all their other problems. Diesel kept speaking, "Southern Belle," he yelled out at her as this was his nickname for her, but Summer ignored him. Finally, she was in a foul mood and vented, "Stop following me, leave me alone." He looked hurt. "Look, I'm sorry," Summer apologized, "but I'm just not interested." Finally, they both boarded the cable car to North Beach.

Diesel rarely experienced rejection. It was a feeling he despised. Yet, he also knew he would only be patient for so long.

Little Miss Summer better watch her step with him; however, he wasn't giving up on winning her over for now.

Andrew's plane had landed. He was in his rental car heading to the San Francisco Hilton. The hotel staff remembered him. He had solved many runaway cases here. Some runaways were reunited with family—other families were given sad news. The hotel owner remembered Andrew from when he had found his niece. She had been kidnapped but managed to escape her offenders. Andrew found and arrested them, but the girl was gone. He checked the closest police precinct, and she was there. So, whenever he came to San Francisco, he reserved a suite at a considerable discount. This deal, of course, was a blessing to Kevin and Lindy, as they paid all of his expenses.

Andrew settled in and ate a late lunch of a chef's salad with crackers and drank lemon water. He was looking for Mike from the description Autumn had given him. He had questioned Linda Jenkins. She admitted, "I knew about Summer and Mike, but Summer had asked me not to say anything to her parents. I just never thought it was that big of a deal. I had no idea a P.I. would be involved." He thought to himself, *yes, sweetheart, but you knew the police were involved*. The reality is Marks was just a skilled investigator. He had a gift for dredging out the truth.

In no time, he found Mike's parents in San Mateo. He introduced himself. "I'm Andrew Marks, and I'm a private investigator for Summer Logan's Parents." Then Susan recalled how concerned she was when she first saw Summer and how young she looked. He gave her his card.

"Wow, I knew she looked young. My son said she was eighteen."

"He lied about her age. Understandable!"

"She does look eighteen wearing makeup."

Now, the truth was coming out. Susan figured out either Summer had a fake ID or forged her parents' consent when they married. "Mr. Marks, I hope you understand that I can't just give you my son's address. But I will get in touch with him and have him reach you. Now that I know that Summer's parents are concerned for her, could you give me their phone number, and we'll keep them posted about her? "

"I will let them know that you want to reach them if you give your phone number for them to call you."

"Of course," Susan commented and jotted their phone number down, and handed it to him.

He was sure Mike and Summer wouldn't get in touch with him, so he was on his own to find out where they lived. The Hanleys did hint that they lived in the most impoverished community. He knew that to be the Tenderloin. It didn't take long for Andrew to find them. He knew the street people, and when he gave them a few dollars, they immediately gave him the address of the Metro.

He saw Summer from a distance. She looked like the picture he was given; only he could tell she was wearing makeup to look older. He also noticed a man following her. The man looked familiar, and he adjusted his binoculars for a closer view. It was his enemy, Diesel Hamilton. Suddenly, he feared greatly for Summer. The cable car was approaching, and he ran to catch it while Summer and Diesel did. He put on a hat and sunglasses so Diesel wouldn't recognize him as all three of them boarded. Diesel let Summer get a head start and was about to follow her when a strong hand grabbed him from behind and took him to an alleyway. In extreme anger, Andrew said, "Hamilton, if you know what's good for you, you better leave that girl alone. You will make me forget my integrity."

Diesel wasn't worried. If not for Andrew's integrity, he would have been long dead. Diesel knew he would have wasted anyone who killed his daughter if he had one. Yes, Andrew did harass him, but he never crossed the line of violence, and he wouldn't now. He responded, "As long as I keep my hands to myself, Marks, you have nothing to say. Maybe I'll tell the police you are harassing me."

"I'm watching you. You may not see me, but I'm watching you!"

Diesel hopped back on the cable car and headed back to his disrupted. Now Marks had disru[t his opportunity with Summer had been whereabouts. He would now have to find ways to keep Andrew busy and eavesdrop to keep up with his apartment. The problem was Andrew was as clever as he was.

Andrew was worried now. The Hilton wasn't close enough to the Metro for him to protect Summer from Diesel. So, he was going to move into the Metro. His line of business has had him living in dives before. He always detested it, but he never had a choice. He wanted Diesel with a vengeance, but protecting Summer came first. Summer reminded him a lot of Mandy. Under all the lipstick, blush, and eye makeup, he still saw a little girl not much older than Mandy, and he would make sure that that rodent didn't come near her. Though all he ever wanted was to catch Diesel and lock him up, at the moment, he wanted him to go away and leave Summer alone, even if it meant he would never capture him.

Diesel was desperate now. Andrew now lived at the Metro. How would he make his move now? Andrew had a life, and this man would have to leave to take care of personal matters. He could tell Summer wasn't playing hard to get; however, he believed he would have won her in time. Diesel didn't have time now. He gave her admiration he had never given to any other woman. He thought to himself, and *I'll have my opportunity, and Summer will be mine, whether she likes it or not. And if she put up a fight, I'll have to kill her.* He usually used the term *waste*, but not for this rare beauty. Yes, he did have feelings for her, but they weren't mutual, and she would have to pay for rejecting him.

Andrew was settled at the Metro and noticed he forgot his phone and address book. He would be gone for a short while. But he knew he had to make it back as soon as possible. He was unaware Summer was at an amusement park across the city attending a party. Diesel knew she was there. As soon as Andrew left, Diesel waited at a streetcar stop.

Andrew noticed Diesel waiting for the streetcar. He had to forget his book for now. He heard a couple of people talking, "They are having a costume party at the amusement park." The persons were out of range, but he kept hearing their mumbles. Quickly he had enough information to find the park. He missed the streetcar Diesel was on, but within a few minutes, he caught another one. He had a hunch Summer was at the Masquerade Party, and Diesel was following her. He prayed he would get there in time. There were masqueraders in the car, and he was going to follow them.

Summer was having the time of her life at the Masquerade party. She wasn't in costume, but an older, heavyset lady named Lottie, blond and resembled a middle-aged Joan Blondell, had an outfit for her to wear. She was Marie Antoinette. She was modeling the costume and play-acting. Lottie and others laughed and were charmed by her "Ms. Antoinette!" Lottie exclaimed, curtsying and playing along. It was apparent she was fond of Summer. Diesel was at a distance, watching and waiting for her to be alone. Summer was still into her play-acting as everyone was leaving to gather somewhere else.

"Where are all of you going?" She pleaded, missing the attention.

When they were completely out of sight, she attempted to follow after them when Diesel made his move. He moved in front of her. She tried to get away from him, but he had her cornered. Summer feared the evil expression on his face, which told her he meant her harm. He ushered her into a vacant room with a lock on the door. He dared her to scream. "It would be best if you didn't scream, sweetheart. You just don't know how much I desire you." She hadn't prayed for a long time, but at this moment, praying was all she could do. "Precious, Holy, Heavenly Father, I need your presence in this room. Please drive out this evil." Then she began to pray in unknown tongues. She was overwhelmed as God's Spirit, and Holy Presence entered the room. This encounter freaked Diesel out because it was unfamiliar and strange to him. The presence in the room paralyzed him, and the only offense he could commit against Summer was to rant, rave, and threaten. He couldn't even lift his weapon to shoot her.

At that exact moment, Andrew entered the room by kicking the door down. Andrew was familiar with this presence and guessed what had taken place. Nevertheless, he couldn't help but give Diesel a gloating look of satisfaction.

"I told you, Hamilton, this day would come!"

He took Diesel's gun, and then placed him in handcuffs, and was hauling him off to jail. He asked Summer, "Are you ok?" She nodded. But as he observed hers and Diesel's appearances, he could tell she was in better condition than Diesel was. Diesel had a look of fright. He escorted her and Diesel both to his car. Summer in the front seat and Diesel in the back. He dropped her off at the Metro first.

Andrew had friends in jail who detested child killers, so they made sure Diesel was in with these hardened criminals who hated offenders who attack children and women. They knew who and what Diesel was all about. Diesel knew it and wondered then if the same God who had so passionately protected Summer would also now protect him. He knew, however, that he didn't deserve it. He asked the guard. "I wonder if I could speak to the prison chaplain."

Chaplain Neal Andrews had been chaplain at the San Francisco County Jail for 17 years. He always became attached to the inmates who were on death row. They arrived hardened and vicious but softened when they knew death was inevitable. Most received salvation because they didn't want an uncertain eternity. He had witnessed compelling transformations. He was now about to meet Diesel Hamilton, who had requested his visit.

SOUL WOUND

Diesel had hard questions for Chaplain Andrews, but he knew the answers to give him.

Diesel began, "Chaplain Andrews, I just had the weirdest encounter. I'm ashamed to admit how it emerged. It's about committing the crime for which I was arrested. I've always successfully escaped my crimes, but this presence allowed me to see myself. I hated the picture I saw. I just don't understand any of this. I know that there are occurrences in the Bible about these kinds of events. Could you please explain it to me?"

Many chaplains don't know about the supernatural or the presence of God. Diesel didn't know how fortunate he was to have Chaplain Andrews answering his questions. "Yes, I will first read from Exodus and How Moses encountered God through a burning bush. Then there's Joshua's battle with the walls of Jericho, from 2 Kings and Elijah and the raising the Shunammite's son from the dead, and from 2 Chronicles when God's spirit in the Ark of the Covenant had enormous power that took place when the Ark entered the Temple."

As Diesel listened, he knew this same presence had protected Summer from him. He requested to the Chaplain, "I know it's a strange request, but could I please have Summer visit me. She invited the presence in, and I want to know about this God." He had questions for her about her God. Chaplain Andrews went to see the prison warden, knowing what Diesel had asked for was impossible.

Warden Sam Jackson was of African American descent, in his late 40s, tall, physically fit, and with rugged features. The warden had been a Christian since childhood. He was a tough but fair warden, now about to be presented with an unusual request. He was waiting for his appointment with Chaplain Andrews. He was happy the chaplain was spirit-filled. He was able to answer complex questions. He always prayed first and relied on God for his decisions. Now would one of those times.

The chaplain knocked on his door, and the warden immediately opened it and greeted him. "How are you, Neal."

"I'm ok, Sam. How are you?"

"I'm okay, considering the tough job I have. I keep trying to give it to God, but I keep taking it back."

"We're all guilty of that."

"So, Neal, what brings you here?"

"An unusual request from an inmate."

"Which one?"

"Diesel Hamilton?"

"And the request?"

"A visit from his victim." Neal thought he would shoot it straight: Because Sam Jackson didn't like surprises.

"Explain, Neal."

"I think Diesel has a transformation. He keeps asking about God. When he attempted his attack on Summer, she ushered in God's spirit, and obviously, Diesel can't get it off his mind."

"Wow, that's powerful. I'm going to pray about this, but I'll probably get back with you in a day or two."

"You're not afraid for Summer?"

"Not with the power she has. Not when Diesel was afraid of her. I just need time to pray for Diesel's soul. I want this transformation to have staying power."

Neal Andrews left the warden and was amazed at his attitude. Christians are a peculiar people. Neal understood where Sam was coming from, but non-believers would say he needed to see a psychiatrist.

Two days later, the chaplain finally returned with an answer from the warden. Chaplain Andrews had a pleased look on his face, so Diesel was optimistic, except that the chaplain looked happy most of the time. Neal immediately told him, "Warden Jackson will agree with your request if Summer is comfortable with it." Diesel could only hope she would agree. Diesel was never one to want to wait, but he had never been in a position like this one. He had to have answers. The chaplain couldn't stay with Diesel long; he just presented with the news and left.

Summer thought a lot about what had happened and how she had prayed, and God rescued her. She was still confused about many things. She didn't know if she wanted any more changes, for she remembered her disappointments as well. She was grateful. And she was well aware of the outcome if God had not been there on her behalf. She knew she would have to go back to her roots, but she wasn't ready yet. Then the girl heard a knock on her door. She opened the door and saw a handsome man, young with sandy hair, wearing a minister's collar. He introduced himself, "I'm Chaplain Neal Andrews from San Francisco County Jail." Summer was confused yet curious. "How may I help you?" she asked suspiciously. Neal didn't know how to begin, so he just explained the strange encounter with Diesel in jail. Summer remained quiet. Summer had many mixed feelings, then Neal continued.

"You left a lasting impression on Diesel when you invited the presence of God in. It's all he talks about."

"I hope this isn't a trick he's pulling to have my attention."

"I don't think so. I am usually sensitive to deceiving spirits. I think this man is sincere." Curiosity had gotten the better of Summer, and she agreed to the visit.

At the jail, feelings of eeriness came over Summer. She remembered Diesel's evil presence when she first met him. At least there was a solid piece of glass between them. When he arrived in his orange prison attire, she saw a different expression on his face. They spoke and greeted each other.

"Summer," he said, speaking her name as though he had always known her, "I want to tell you many things about myself, but I have so many questions about your God. I never in my life believed in any God. I am a killer for hire and have always been successful. I got paid for it. I also sometimes killed just to survive. I attempted to kill you to mollify my lusts. But never in my long career, as a hit man has, I encountered the presence of a God who let me know I would meet my doom if I touched you. Why you? You must have pleased him at one time."

Summer looked amazed. She had thought he wanted to meet with her to satisfy his lusts further and had used the chaplain to trick her. He was only curious about God. "Yes, Diesel," she said, "I was once on fire for God in middle school. I passed Bibles out to all the students who wanted them—special Bibles with comic book excerpts. I distributed them like hotcakes and held Bible studies. That was a long time ago."

"Well, apparently, your God remembered because he would have taken me out had I touched you."

Summer was overwhelmed. Why was she so special to God and not Andrew's daughter? In a way, it didn't make sense, except maybe God still wanted to use her. She prayed, and though she felt like she was a flawed testimony, she asked him, "Diesel, do you want to accept Jesus your heart.?" He hung his head as he nodded and then asked, "Will He still accept me knowing the suffering I have caused? "

"He's no respecter of persons. He loves you as much as he loves me."

"I have to admit He took me away from the danger of the hardened inmates who intended to kill me and arranged solitary for me. I never thought I would be so relieved to be in solitary. Yes, let's pray, but first, Summer, I need to ask your forgiveness for the harm I intended."

"Of course, you're forgiven. Now repeat after me. 'Heavenly Father, I come before you a sinner repenting of my sin. Please forgive me. Please cleanse me. I accept your Son Jesus, who died for my sins. He has risen, and he is the only way to salvation. Make my life new. Free me from my old life's wrong desires, and help me live my life for you. Take away my chains of sin and set me free. I ask this in Jesus' Holy Name. Amen.'"

Diesel repeated everything she said. He then had the aura all Christians have. Summer had no doubt he was a changed man, and she was glad God used her for this conversion. As she said goodbye, she saw a warm expression on Diesel's face where there was once an evil one.

SOUL WOUND

Diesel wanted baptism. Warden Jackson's church had a movable baptismal, members used on warm days, to be baptized outside. On many occasions, he requested permission to use it to baptize the inmates. When he asked for it to baptize Diesel, his pastor granted permission as he always had, and arrangements were made for Diesel to be baptized. Chaplain Andrews performed the baptism, Warden Jackson and many born-again inmates on death row were there, congratulating Diesel. When Diesel was baptized, he experienced peace in his heart like he never had before. His past fears had disappeared. He sensed he would be receiving the death penalty, and he was totally at peace about it. He felt this was how the Holy Spirit came upon him in the form of a dove. (From Matthew 3:16.)

Many months had passed. There were other states where Diesel had committed murders. These states didn't want the expense of extradition, so they requested DNA evidence to be sent to one state. The only offense he committed in San Francisco was the attempted murder of Summer. The local DA wanted to have the trial here. He stated, "I want the trial here, and I want the death penalty." Diesel's attorney objected, "Counsel wants to fight the death penalty." but Diesel told him, "I'm guilty, and I want to accept the death penalty. I can't take back the lives I've taken, but I can give mine."

Diesel's confession and decision solved the extradition matter. His attorney pleaded with him, "Please, Diesel change your mind. I'm a pro-lifer, and I want to fight for you to keep your life." "No," Diesel said. "I'm not losing my life. I have eternal life. It won't be over for me; it will be the beginning. Do you have eternal life?" His lawyer didn't answer, and he didn't argue any further. Diesel pleaded guilty, and the judge then said," I accept all the DNA evidence against Diesel Hamilton and declare the death penalty sentence, death by legal injection to be set in the county jail exactly on two months from today, August 2; of this year." He wasn't transferred to prison since the court would carry out the sentence in such a short time. He remained in jail and Solitary. Warden Jackson had also requested that Diesel remain there.

Andrew Marks planned on attending the court date, but he heard about the guilty verdict and changed his mind. He had initially hoped that the courts would try Diesel in New York, not for just Mandy's murder, but the businessman and others. Only when Diesel confessed was the man satisfied with Diesel's decision. He also decided to decline to be present when Diesel was lethally injected. He had a full workload and had to remain in NYC. God had also convicted him for deliberately putting Diesel's life in jeopardy. He wrote this letter of apology.

July 5, 2002

Diesel,

I know you have to be in shock to hear from me. I am too. I never thought I would allow God ever to bring me to this place of forgiveness. But His Word clearly states we all have to forgive others to receive forgiveness from Him. So, I apologize for everything from the first moment I ever harassed you. I was wrong. I wasn't trusting in God for Mandy's vengeance. I guess I always thought the vengeance of God as taken out His wrath on our enemies. And some cases, that is true. But, not in your case. In your case, you've received your salvation, and I couldn't be any happier for you. I've had my salvation for over thirty years. Since before Mandy was born. Please forgive my actions. I have been at total peace since absolving you. I never knew the burden I was carrying. Anyway, please forgive me. I know I will see you in heaven. I'm just sad that you're going there first. I have no delight about your death. I know you are a new person. I'm just jealous that you will see Vivian and Mandy before I will. Please give them my love.

There's nothing more to say. God bless and keep you always.

Andrew

The letter was the first time that Andrew had used Diesel's first name. He was suddenly saddened and overwhelmed. Yes, he was happy about his eternal life, but he thought of how his life could've been different. Maybe a life where he and Andrew could've been close friends. A life where instead of murdering Mandy, he could've been her Godfather. Yes, Diesel had redemption, but he never mourned the lives that he took. He's mourning them now and for Mandy the most. Tears were streaming down Diesel's face. He thought about calling for Neal or Sam. He became on a first-name basis with them. They loved Diesel like a brother. But he wasn't going to call them because he wanted t time alone with God. He knew Jesus was the only comfort for his hurting heart. Diesel answered Andrew's letter.

July 11, 2002

Andrew,

I can't ever tell you how much your letter means to me. I am so sorry for causing you and your wife so much pain. I'm also sorry you no longer have your wife. It's hard not to envy you. I never thought about marriage or family before, but I think about it all the time now. It's too late now, and I hate the mess I made of my life. I had the hardest heart. A heart that couldn't desire or want love. But it all changed on that day when Summer invited God into that room. The day I thought would be her last. She is so special to me. She will always be my spiritual sister. She saved my life and brought in Jesus to save my soul.

I will be so honored to meet Vivian and Mandy in heaven. Mandy's become so special to my heart. And if God would permit it, I would like to be a substitute father to her until you get there yourself. I say substitute because I know I could never take your place.

I'm signing off. And once again, thank you for your grace.

Diesel

Andrew cherished Diesel's letter and was happy he now treasured his Mandy. He also enjoyed hearing about his salvation experience and his new spiritual relationship with Summer. He wrote to him once more, expressing the joy his letter gave him.

July 20, 2002

Diesel,

Thank you so much for your expression of redemption for Vivian and Mandy. It means more to me than gold. We all wished we had made different choices. I wished I had spent more time with Vivian and Mandy when they were here. We can't go back, but we can move on and become stronger and better-quality people. I have to commend you because your transformation is the most amazing I have ever encountered.

I would love to see you one more time on the earth, but my cases have me too bogged down. I do this work in Vivian and Mandy's memory. I hope to know this gives you some degree of comfort. All things are used for God's glory. If not for my losses, I would probably still be with the NYPD. Being there would not be as satisfactory or have as much purpose.

I love you, Diesel; I want you to know this. My heart is very saddened by your departure. I do look forward to seeing you in Heaven. Please take care, and God bless you always.

Andrew

This last letter had Diesel in tears. He was amazed that a father who adored his little girl the way Andrew did could show so much mercy and love. He verbally expressed love to him. How can I even answer him? But Diesel had to write to Andrew once more.

July 27, 2003

Andrew,

Thank you so much for your last letter. I had to wait a day or two to answer. I don't have much time left. You'll never know the gratitude I have for the mercy you have shown me. I love you too. And please don't be sad. I will live a better life in eternity than I ever did here. I look forward to it, my chance to start over and get things right. I've kept a short journal while I was here and memoirs of the past. It's not an excuse for how I've lived, but maybe you can understand more about my life as a child. It will be here for you if you choose to come to San Francisco, or I'll have it mailed to you. Just call Sam and let him know. God bless you always.

Diesel

God taught Andrew a true lesson of forgiveness. Once he forgave Diesel, he then lived in peace in his home without being further tormented by the ghosts of Vivian and Mandy.

Andrew then recalled how angry Kevin Logan was. He didn't take the news of Summer's marriage well. He said, "I'll have that marriage annulled." Mark asked, "Kevin, would you rather have your daughter living in sin or be legally married? Because she and Mike were going to stay together regardless. Also, in California, it's easy for minors age 16 to be emancipated. In the eyes of the State, Summer had proven she could live on her own. It's also possible that your plea for an annulment would be denied."

"Oh, why California. I have lost my little girl." He said with dripping tears.

And Kevin said nothing more. He knew then his hands were tied. He had college dreams for Summer, and she hadn't even finished high school. His heart was broken because Summer was making life hard for herself. He also cringed when Andrew described the horrific neighborhood she lived in and her close brush with death. It caused him to have frequent nightmares about her. If only she would stay in touch. But he did have a way to know how she was because he, Lindy, and the Hanleys stayed in communication. He was grateful, but it wasn't the same as hearing her voice.

Diesel called in Chaplain Andrews to make a special request; he had no family to see him leave the earth. The person he wanted to be there was Summer. She was his sister in Christ now. "Chaplain Andrews, I would like to make a special request. I want Summer to be there to say goodbye to me if it's possible?"

"I can only try Diesel, but I can't promise. Together we can pray that she will. I would like that for you. But it's up to Sam too."

"Thank you so much. I can't ask for anything more than that."

Chaplain Andrews spoke to the warden "Diesel is requesting for Summer to be present with him when he enters the chamber."

"Sure, I'll let Summer visit Diesel if she agrees to it, and I have a funny feeling that she will."

Sam had congratulated Diesel on his decision for salvation. He, Chaplain Andrews, and Diesel read the Bible daily. The warden loved Diesel and was sad about his pending death. Granting Diesel his last request gave him peace. Now Chaplain Andrews was praying for Summer to honor Diesel's request.

Summer was now getting used to Mike's overtime, but she couldn't get used to his insensitivity. He had been concerned about her incident with Diesel, but Mike was only jealous when she visited him in jail. He never showed that he cared about her safety. She was also tired of being the one to bite the bullet no matter how often Mike was insensitive. She did want to stay in contact with Diesel to make sure he remained faithful to God, but she was apprehensive because of Mike's jealousy.

She was about to head out to sight-see when she ran into Chaplain Andrews. She couldn't imagine why he was there. She'd had no further contact with Diesel. She hoped he was okay. She invited the Chaplain in with her humble offer. "It's nice to see you, Chaplain Andrews. I have few refreshments, but you are welcome to them."

"That's ok, Summer. I am full. But thanks for the offer."

"How is Diesel doing?"

He took the opportunity and said, "Summer, Diesel is going to be lethally injected, and he has no family to see him to the end. He has requested for you to be there for him."

Summer had seen a lot of death in the city. Now she was being asked to witness another. Chaplain Andrews noticed the severe look on Summer's face and decided not to pressure her.

"Summer, you don't have to make any decision that makes you feel uncomfortable. I know Diesel will understand."

Summer replied, "Give me a day or so, and I would like to tell Diesel my decision. I was already going request to see him."

Chaplain Andrews hoped Summer would have good news for Diesel. He had to be true to his word. Neal stayed and talked to Summer for a few more minutes. Then he had to return to jail. Summer went to the jail two days later.

Summer was once again at the inmate window, waiting to speak to Diesel. When he arrived, he looked like a different person. He *was* a different person, though some people will never believe that. Summer had made her decision.

Diesel picked up the phone mic and began. "Summer, I hope I haven't made you feel pressured. I would rather you not attend if you would feel uncomfortable to see me go home to Jesus."

"No, Diesel, I'll be there for you."

Tears flooded Diesel's eyes. His voice cracked as he said, "Summer, you have no idea what this means to me. I know God will be there for me. Chaplain Andrews and Warden Jackson will also be there. But, Summer, you led me to the Lord. You are my spiritual sister."

Summer was amazed at the change that had taken place in Diesel—a hard heart softened. A dead soul brought to life like Ezekiel's dry bones. A broken spirit.

"Diesel, I can't stay long, but I had to let you know. I hate death, I see too much of it, but I won't let you down."

"Thank you." Diesel said one more time. He wanted to blow her a kiss (as he still secretly had a crush on her), but he didn't want to give her the wrong idea. He and Summer had a rewarding yet short visit. She was then glad about her decision.

Their short time passed, and, in two more days, on August 1, 2002, Summer would be there for him to say goodbye. Diesel had received a call from Andrew the night before. He requested to share the conversation with Summer. So, one more time, he and Summer had a visit. However, this time she was allowed to be with him in person. They met in a room close to the chamber. She was so happy to see him and had to hug him. Diesel hugged her so hard but was respectful. He began, "I got a call from Andrew last night, and I wanted to tell you."

"That's so wonderful that the two of you have become so close. But Diesel, you aren't that same person."

"I know. I wish things could've been different. Andrew is an amazing friend."

"Diesel, I am so proud of you. And I'm going to miss you. My heart is so heavy right now. Life is unfair. Now you do deserve to live. God tore out your hard heart and gave you one with abundant compassion."

"Summer, my time is up. I have to go now and be with the Lord."

"Ok, just one more hug."

They hugged one more time, and then Diesel took his place.

Deeply saddened, Summer took her seat outside of the chamber. Family members of some victims Diesel had killed were also present. They all viewed him through the window. Diesel was strapped down and looking out at Summer. There wasn't a look of fear on Diesel's face, but one of total peace. Summer could sense resentment in the room. These family members didn't understand Diesel's change, and they didn't want to understand. They were only there to make sure Diesel got what he deserved. Summer decided they were the ones who needed prayer most.

They were about to inject Diesel. Summer could barely contain herself. Yet God was there with her. and she saw that Diesel was at total peace. He wore an angelic smile as his life left him, and it remained on his corpse. Summer also left in complete peace, knowing she was going to see Diesel again.

Two weeks later, on August 15, Summer turned 17. She had hated learning that Mike smoked weed. "Weed? Mike, are you serious?"

"Baby, it's ok. I just never could afford it before. Now with all this overtime, we are finally caught up on the bills, and I've paid Ernie back every cent."

"Mike, I smell weed in the hotel all the time, and the smell turns my stomach."

"Baby, you have to give it a chance. You can't knock something until you've tried it."

"Well, maybe you're right."

Mike had such influence over her that she agreed to try it for her 17th birthday.

Mike mentioned. "Since we're all caught up on bills, I won't have to work so much over time. That means I'm all yours. I will work at least an extra weekend a month to pay the premium for your life insurance."

Then he brought in her gifts. "Summer, I have something for you." Summer loved her flowers, and she fell in love with her jewelry box. It was the jewelry box Summer had admired at the curio shop in North Beach. How could Mike have known?

Her friends at the Metro threw Summer a party and made her a chocolate cake and ice cream. There was plenty of food, as they would all have the munchies after this weed party. They were all seated and passed the joint around. This experience was Summer's first time, and she was frightened and sick. Nonetheless, Mike knew how to console her. Before much longer, she began to enjoy the high.

Chapter 4

Early Spring of 2003

Summer remembered when she first arrived at the Metro and the streets of San Francisco. She had to adjust to many conditions. There were horrible and horrific sights she never dreamed she would encounter. The Tenderloin district was the most drug-infested and crime-filled in the city. Crimes committed daily were in broad daylight and plain view. Summer saw people being mugged, shot, and knifed, sometimes to death. She was overwhelmed with fear and paranoia, believing these criminals were after her as well. She was terrified at a knock on her door, thinking she was next. She often didn't leave her room.

Some residents at the hotel helped Summer adjust. "It's ok, Summer. We have to teach you to be street smart. Just act as though it doesn't matter, and no one will bother you." Stated a young girl following her direction. This attitude wasn't like Summer's, but she did soon build a wall of apathy. The residents consoled her, and she was less apprehensive and paranoid. She even enjoyed rides on public transportation and went with them to different areas of the city. Their favorite areas were North Beach and China Town. Summer loved these areas as well. She needed this getaway.

Mike was always working. He wouldn't refuse overtime because it helped cover the extra expense of the weed parties. He had to bring his weed and contribute somewhat to the food expenses. Weed increased one's appetite, so food was a significant expense, and the weed was also expensive. To Summer, it seemed Mike never had any time for her. He was always irritable and moody. He was not the same young man she had met at Buffalo Springs Lake. She almost dreaded his coming home in the evening. He also complained about her sightseeing trips. It seemed there was no way to please him. She thought maybe it was the overtime, and she was ready for it to subside.

After seeing beautiful and unique sights from the streetcar, she arrived home to see lifeless-looking winos on the street. If they weren't passed out, they were panhandling money for their habit. Just a few cents got them a cheap bottle of wine.

She also recalled gay individuals. She had never been around them much, and they once gave Summer sick feelings in the pit of her stomach. However, she found most of them to be kind and caring and not as violent as other street people were. She also became accepting of their lifestyle. She just had to avoid lesbians, as they would try to recruit her into their lifestyle. However, things changed when she rededicated her life back to Christ. God revealed the truth to her from His Word. She loved her gay friends unconditionally and remained friendly with them; still, she had to stand firm and hold to the Word. The girl prayed for them and for God to reveal the truth to them. She tried to minister to them and not preach at them. She never failed to tell them God loved them unconditionally. But she couldn't consider herself a friend if she didn't educate them of what God's Word said.

She recalled witnessing Diesel going home to Jesus, and she seen a lot of death and was used to it. She often thought about eternity. She wanted to believe the other people she had known who had died from drug overdoses or foolishness had also gone to be with the Lord. But, of course, she was uncertain. She recalled seeing ambulances hauling off corpses on stretchers and covering up their faces with a sheet. It was more than she wanted to see. She remembered a sweet girl named Dana doing laundry with Summer one day, then carted off on the death stretcher the next. It was a drug overdose. She was the same age as Summer.

Summer knew then that she wanted nothing more to do with drugs, not even marijuana. However, from time to time, Mike convinced her to smoke it. She did it only to get along with him, and she controlled her intake.

About two months after her 17th birthday, some Metro residents encouraged Summer to visit the Sunset district. "Summer, we want to show you a place we think you would love. The people there are more like you. They dress in beautiful clothing as you have. We will go with you on this first trip; however, we won't stay because we don't feel like we belong there." They took a streetcar there, and she visited a restaurant called the Yellow Submarine. Her friends had left. She had the money for lunch, but these prices were out of her range. She felt she'd be rude to go, so she purchased a coke.

An attractive, older stranger, not much older than her mother, sat at a table across from her. She was sitting at the table Summer was unaware she was observing her. She walked over to Summer and introduced herself. "I'm Lynn Rothberg." Summer was amazed at how they complemented each other. She then noticed her shiny salt and pepper. She remarked again, "I'm Lynn Rothberg."

"Summer Hanley."

Lynn said, "You know, I am starving. Let's get a menu and order something, and, honey, it's on me."

"I don't know. I hate to take advantage."

"Please, child, it's not taking advantage. I'm delighted to do this."

"Well, I guess it's ok."

"Fish and Chips is their specialty."

They had ordered the fish and chips; Summer was famished.

It was a huge order, and there was enough left for her and Mike to have for dinner. Lynn motioned to the food server;

"Please give us a box, please."

"Certainly, ma'am."

"Thank you."

They both left the restaurant, jumped into her vehicle (A pink Cadillac she received when she had sold Mary Kay products), and left for the Metro. When Lynn saw Summer's living conditions, she was appalled, though, of course, she tried not to let it show. She just hated to leave this lovely, sweet young girl in this dive. She offered, "I can drive you to the Yellow Submarine every week, my treat."

"Thank you I do look forward to your company, and I'll let you drive me home; I prefer to arrive on the street car." She looked forward to her friends' send-off. So that was their arrangement every Friday at lunchtime.

The weekly weed party was held every Friday night at the Metro. Most residents attended, and each resident had to bring their weed. Mike looked forward to it—it was his relaxation and unwinding time, only after her friend Lynn told her weed was addictive, Summer decided to be drug-free. Mike complained. "What's got into you, Summer? You aren't fun anymore. Besides, I want us to do everything together. Please don't bail on me for this."

"Mike, I never wanted to start smoking weed. I only tried it to please you. I'm not going to get hooked on drugs. Lynn has told that weed is addictive."

"Well, maybe it's time that you stop seeing this uppity friend. She's breaking up our marriage."

"Mike, you are so ridiculous."

"I need you to stop seeing her." He smirked. But Summer didn't answer because Summer felt her visits to the Sunset district and having lunch with Lynn kept her sane. So, she ignored Mike's selfish advice. She seemed to look forward more to seeing Lynn than she did to Mike coming home. Mike was never in a good mood. Making love appeared to be the only positive thing he could offer. For a while, it was enough. However, it soon wasn't worth it that she had to suffer with him.

Lynn Rothberg was happy to have her new friend. She could tell Summer was troubled. She had been married to her husband,

Harold, for twenty years, and he had been gone for five. They had yearned dearly for children, but that never happened. The saddest part of Harold's death was not to have a child as a part of his memory. Today she had found a true purpose by befriending this sweet young girl at the Yellow Submarine. Being in her company reminded her of how lonely she was. Also, the void of a child was finally happening. She couldn't help but think about that horrifying hotel that looked like it needed to be condemned.

Summer looked so young. She never talked about any family other than her husband. Lynn wondered if Summer had parents or siblings. Moreover, if she did, they had to be crazy with worry about her living conditions. This woman knew if Summer were her child, she would try to persuade her husband to find a safer place to live. She wanted to do that, but it didn't seem appropriate, so she remained silent.

Summer had noticed for a while a group of bikers in North Beach. They always appeared hostile, and she witnessed them harassing people. North Beach was a tourist attraction, so the police frequently patrolled it. The bikers would leave when police appeared, but it seemed they would find an unprotected area. The leader of this gang wouldn't permit his gang members to harass innocent citizens. However, the gang would harass them when he wasn't around. The gang was only allowed in a particular location of North Beach and never where tourists were. Sometimes tourists accidentally gravitated to the area where the bikers were. Even when bikers weren't harassing them, they would be in the crossfire of a gang war. This group was called the Gypsy Jokers.

It was another new experience for Summer. One day they surrounded her and barred her from escaping.

"Look, what we have here!" A biker came at her. He was heavyset. Had long greasy hair, tattoos, and a distinct gold front tooth, he motioned his gang to come as they kept closing their circle. Summer was terrified. Before long, a young, tall, slender gang member arrived.

"What are you idiots doing? You know this is not our style. Leave this girl alone, and from now on, I'm going to be watching you. If this continues, you will be barred from the gang in style." He meant they would be severely beaten and barred from the gang; only Summer didn't know this.

"Thank you so much. I don't know what would have happened if you hadn't shown up!" She said, not aware that she was embracing him and trembling with fear. She let go of him quickly and blushed with embarrassment.

"What's your name?"

"Summer"

"Well, Summer, I think you better be careful of the areas you visit. Where do you live?"

"The Metro Hotel."

"That's a worse area than here. I hope you've learned street smarts."

"Yes, I had to. It's the only way to survive."

"Well, you have learned something. But my gang isn't the only ones who attack young chicks like you. So please be careful. I'll let you know the safe areas and the bad ones. Please stay away from the bad ones. And never be alone in the Tenderloin!"

"I'm usually not."

"I go to the Metro sometimes for business; maybe I'll see you there. By the way, my name is Angel."

"Nice to meet you, Angel, and I do hope I'll see you at the Metro." That was the last of their conversation, and Summer left immediately.

Angel had one of his most trusted gang members escort her home. Angel was slender and had dark, attractive Hispanic features, and appeared to be kind. He thought Summer was beautiful and reminded him of Monica, the love of his life. Summer, however, was a lot younger. He decided to adopt her as his little sister. This man would guard and protect her. He reprimanded his gang members for terrorizing her. "From now on, when you see Summer, you will protect her. Is that understood?" They agreed because they were intimidated by him.

Earl, "the Beast" Mason, was a member of the Gypsy Jokers. His mother was of Hispanic descent, but his father was Caucasian. Earl was also a drug addict; Angel had told all the new gang members, "There will be no drug users in this gang. It's an easy way to get caught. We don't do drugs; we sell them."

Earl tried to hide his addiction for several months, but Angel had guessed his problem. Angel had been more patient with Earl than he had with any of his gang members. Using always made the members ruthless and dangerous, which was a risk to Angel and the gang. Even in the world of gangs and crime, Angel wanted his members to be straight and alert. Drug-free decreases the risk of making the mistakes that cause incarceration. Earl was just too much of a chance, so he was about to be expelled from the gang.

Alfred Dominguez had admired Angel when he was ten years old, and Angel was 16. That was 14 years ago. Alfred is now 24, and Angel, 30. Back then, Alfred looked up to Angel as a role model. He was like a little brother to Angel. Alfred always referred to him as "Big Bro," and to Angel, he was "Little Bro." He followed Angel around, begging him for a role in his gang. "Hey, Big Bro, let me join your gang. I can do anything you want me to do. Please give me a shot."

"You are too young. The gangs are dangerous. I wouldn't want anything to happen to you, Little Bro."

"But I rarely see you outside of the gang. And I want to be with you. Please just give me one chance. I promise I won't let you down."

"Ok, I'll let you be a runner. You'll go after our food and supplies. And, if this works out, I'll promote you."

Surprisingly, Alfred was highly proficient. Angel promoted him quickly as a standby on drug deals. He was young and had an innocent appearance that worked well, as the police initially were never suspicious of Alfred. Later, Pedro and Maria Dominguez became concerned for him, as his grades had suffered. He went from being a straight-A honor roll student to a barely average student. His parents were Catholic. They were extremely poor, and because bills needed to be met, they didn't question him much. He lied and said he ran errands, did lawn care, and many other odd jobs. He was careful not to show too much of his actual income. He continued to lie to his parents about his revenue as he became older. He was bright and clever, but his parents had always suspected his earnings weren't legal. They just remained silent about it.

Pedro Dominguez was a janitor at a private Catholic school. It didn't pay well, and he would try to find odd jobs in the summer and on the holidays. Maria would find housekeeping work on occasions. Even in the hood, expenses were devastating; they struggled to get by. Alfred joined the gang to help out with finances. He just couldn't tell them the source of the money. Pedro and Maria also never questioned him. Desperation to manage their finances prevented them from ever asking.

Angel learned he could rely on Alfred to be a confidant. Angel was also a confidant to Alfred. Other gang members were jealous and often suspicious of how close Angel and Alfred had become

"Hey, what's up with you two? Are you gay or something?" A gang member scowled.

"Flesh and blood can't be gay." Angel joked. "This is my little bro who works rings around any of you. I wonder how I managed before he came, with you procrastinating losers." He heard a lot of sarcastic whispers among the gang members, but none spoke out loud. They also noticed Alfred could keep Angel calm when he flew into a rage. Alfred didn't know Angel put contracts out on people. Alfred being in the dark was how Angel wanted it. He didn't want Alfred to follow his example. His gang members did know but remained silent. As Alfred grew to maturity, the members loved and respected him as much as they loved Angel.

Angel was tired of Earl's drug dependency and finally had to oust him from the gang.

"I can't afford for you to remain in the gang Earl. I know you use." In most gangs, unwanted members would never make it out alive, but Angel wasn't worried about Earl. Earl avoided the police at all costs; However, he wouldn't leave without a confrontation. Earl approached Angel. "I can't leave. I have nowhere else to go, man; please give me another chance."

"You've used all your chances, countless chances. I can't afford you." Earl surprised Angel by pulling out his blade. But just as quickly, Angel threw out his chains. Chain fighting was a common practice among gangs, and Angel was highly skilled. Angel was referred to as the "Bruce Lee" of chain fighting. His flair had the similarity of Bruce's fast pace as he flung out his nun chucks, hurling them at top speed. Angel had this same high speed in flinging out his chains, and, at the moment, Earl was in serious trouble. Earl lashed his blade at Angel, clearly missing. Angel hit Earl several times before hitting the hand he held the knife in. His knife fell to the ground. Earl attempted many times to retrieve his knife but was unsuccessful. Finally, Angel's chains hit him in the head, knocking him out. He was knocked out, and the gang members placed him in an alley. Earl thought now he had no other place to live; Earl was forced to live in a few other skank residential hotels before residing at the Metro. He was also forced to deal with drugs. His payment was obtaining drugs for his habit and rooming at the cheap hotel. He was also provided with food when he felt like eating.

Summer reminisced about the big hole in her relationship with her parents. God had convicted her to reconcile with them.

She knew she had only thought about herself and never once thought not communicating with them caused them unnecessary concern. The girl deeply meditated on this. Summer had a conflict with her pride, the same pride that terminated contact with her family in the first place. She had to pray for God to remove it from her. After all this time, she didn't want to face her shame. She now needed the courage to confront her family.

She was now determined to be obedient to God, so she went to the phone, with heart in hand, and dialed her parents' phone number.

Kevin, Lindy, and Autumn had just finished dinner. Kevin reminded Autumn to do the dishes. Much had changed since Summer's absence. Kevin exerted his authority over Autumn and dared Lindy to defy him. He also suffered a hurt ego and pride. When Andrew Marks mentioned the horrific conditions Summer was living in and the close call with a serial killer, her father began having frequent nightmares. He was also angry with Summer for not staying in touch.

The phone rang, Lindy picked up, and he heard her scream in delight. He thought, *no, it couldn't be, but is it Summer?*

Chapter 5

Summer had the phone in her hand. "It's so good to talk to you, Mom. Could I please speak to Dad?" Lindy knew Kevin probably wouldn't talk to her, so she answered swiftly. "He's very busy with work right now; I'll have him talk to you later."

"Thanks' Mom; how about Autumn?"

"Autumn isn't handy now, but I'll let her know you want to talk to her." Summer knew her father and Autumn didn't want to talk to her, and she tried not to be angry. *Lord, let this not be about me. I want to reach my family. Take this bad attitude out of my heart. Please defeat the enemy. Be with me and give me guidance and direction. I need more of You and less of me. I ask all of this in Your Holy Name, Amen.*

Summer meditated on scripture. God reminded her of Luke 15:11–32, The Parable of the Prodigal Son. Yes, she asked God for a servant's heart to serve her parents' house. Summer recalled all the consternation this girl had experienced and realized none of it would have happened if she had stayed home. She had jumped right out of the frying pan and straight into the fire. Her stubborn pride wouldn't let her relent.

It was simply rebellion. The rebellion of never admitting to being wrong and paying a heavy price for it. The rebellion of not staying in touch with her parents and pretending the many long nights of homesickness didn't exist., However, it was all over because Summer had placed rebellion at the foot of the cross of Jesus. She joined a church support group called *Rebel Freedom*. Alas, freedom from the rebellion that had enslaved her for these past two years. She recalled her first meeting. She had felt total shame because many of the group members had faced aggressive abuse. Such severe physical, sexual, emotional, mental, and verbal abuse made her issues appear mild. But Bob Hines, the leader of the group, had told her the opposite. He said, "Summer abuse is abuse, and no one deserves mistreatment, no matter how great or small. Our purpose is forgiveness. That's the freedom from rebellion." Summer had to agree. She learned so much in this class. God had set her free, and she was able to forgive.

Summer and Mike had been at odds since she had made her new vow of faith. They had fought before, but Mike was adamant he was not going to deal with Christianity. Mike had gone to church most of his life, but when the young man left home for college and decided not to attend church anymore. He wanted no part of it. If Summer didn't abate, Mike would take drastic measures to ensure she did. He was going to force her to choose between him and her faith. He did fear she wouldn't choose him. However, he refused to hear about the church and Jesus continually.

Summer recalled a passionate episode she recently had with Mike. It was about the weed parties. "Mike, I can't attend the weed parties anymore. I'm sorry. I have my faith now, and I won't let God down. I'm just glad I never became hooked."

"No one gets hooked on weed. Get real!"

"I can't get my friend Dana out of my mind. She never missed a weed party."

"She was also into the hard stuff. She would have been ok if she only did weed."

"I'm not going to argue, Mike. It's just wrong!" He knew he was getting nowhere. "You know you are becoming an uppity bitch just like your friend in the Avenues." This comment hurt and infuriated Summer. Mike saw the crushed look on her face and regretted his words immediately, although his pride wouldn't let him apologize. She said nothing to him. Summer dug into one of the chests of drawers and came out with two blankets, and then the girl grabbed her pillow from her spot on the bed. She made a pallet on the floor as far away from the bed as she could. This action sent Mike into shock. "What's gotten into you, Summer? What are you doing?" But she was hurt and angry and pushed him away. She told him, "I want you to stay away from me. You are a total jerk."

For Mike, passion was always a deterrent to a fight. He grabbed and passionately kissed her, saying, "I love you, Summer, baby, you know how I love you." She noticed he never said." *I'm sorry, Summer."*

"I said leave me alone. I mean it." She fought him off at first but slowly gave in—because Mike was always irresistible to her. Then it was over, and they were back to being the lovebirds they were most of the time. Then she recalled that she'd forgotten to take her birth control pill. She had relied on Mike to remind her, but that night, he failed. He did remember to remind her every night since, but she feared that if she were already pregnant, the pills might harm the baby. So, she lied to him and said she took them.

Now Summer was waiting for Mike to come home, which she dreaded most of the time. But tonight, she was shaken up. She knew something was about to take place. She couldn't put her finger on it, but she knew her feelings weren't a good sign.

Mike entered the room. Summer had cooked grilled chicken, mashed potatoes, and green beans. He didn't want to eat. He only wanted to get down to business. "Summer, I never see you anymore. You are always at all these church events."

"Rebel Freedom is the only event I have in the evening. I'm always here to cook your meals and take care of all of your needs. We need a life outside of each other. You spend time with your friends away from me."

"I wouldn't object to just plain events, but not these church events."

"Why not Mike. It's what makes me happy. Since I've given my life to Jesus, I think I love you better. I pray for you all the time." Yes, she tried hard to love him, and she prayed for him. She even reserved her anger when he was unreasonable. *Why doesn't he notice I am trying harder? Lord, please help us. Help me reach Mike so he can have a relationship with you.* There was silence, but she felt God's presence.

Mike said, "Summer, I used to go to church. My parents made me when I was l at home. But when I left home, I stopped going. They don't have anything to offer me. Now here you are, trying to be Mother Teresa. Summer, I won't live under these conditions anymore. You either stop this nonsense, or we go our separate ways."

Summer was devastated. Jesus was always there for her when no one else was. So, she wasn't going to knuckle under to Mike's demands. She thought she would try to minister to Mike again. "Mike, God loves you."

"Shut up, Summer. Please stop it."

"I don't understand. Jesus gave it all."

"I am warning you, Summer. You have to stop this."

Summer adamantly spoke out, "I am not ashamed of my faith, and I will never stop declaring Jesus."

Suddenly, Summer heard crashes all over their room as Mike trashed their belongings. This frightened Summer. Mike was like a madman. She fled from the hotel as if fleeing for her life, with her adrenaline spinning.

Mike regained control, but when he turned to speak to Summer, she was gone. He looked out the window just as she was boarding the streetcar, and he knew it was too late to go after her. Mike was in shock. He thought, *"what on earth have I done?"* Then he looked at all the broken and torn objects on the floor and understood Summer's fright, only he thought, *I wouldn't have hurt her.* He went to the drawer where Summer kept her address book, found Lynn's phone number, and placed the call.

Lynn's house was a beautiful three-bedroom, two-bath, remodeled Victorian with a master bedroom and bathroom. The house had a quaint living room and dining area, with Early

American furniture, a loveseat couch, and a wingback chair and recliner. The kitchen area was extra-large, with a large walnut table and six chairs. Lynn heard the phone ring. It was Mike. She answered, thinking something was wrong with Summer. "Hello, Mike, is everything ok?"

"No, Summer and I just fought, and she left me. I'm sure she's coming to your house. Can you please have her call me?"

"Of course, but Mike, you don't sound very well. Are you ok?"

"Of course, I'm not ok. My baby's gone. I need her to call me." Lynn could tell Mike was in tears; his voice was broken up, and she felt deep compassion for him.

"Ok, if Summer comes here, I promise I will ask her to call you. But please, Mike, take it easy. We can't lose you." Lynn said this because Mike seemed despondent.

"Thank you so much, Lynn. I do appreciate your concern." Mike said this sincerely because he was overcome with Lynn's compassion.

Several minutes after Lynn's conversation with Mike, Summer knocked on the door. She saw the frightened look on Summer's face and embraced her. Summer was crying uncontrollably. Lynn kept embracing and comforting her, then she said, "Summer, Mike called me a while ago. He asked that you please call him."

"I just saw a dark side to Mike," Summer said, "and I have to stay away from him."

"I just experienced another side to Mike too, the broken side. Mike was crying on the phone, saying over and over again I have to talk to Summer."

She then tried to change the subject and cheer Summer up. She took her to the bedrooms.

"Summer, I'm showing you my two spare bedrooms, and you can have whichever one you want to sleep in." Lynn then had Summer choose which of the other two bedrooms she wanted to reside in. Summer thought they were both equally beautiful, so she closed her eyes and chose the one closest to Lynn's bedroom.

Mike was still in a state of shock. Summer was afraid of him, and now he was scared of himself. The man couldn't figure out his fit of rage. He knew now he knew he was paying a heavy price for it. He thought about how he had given Summer an ultimatum, but now here without her for less than two hours, he felt so lost and alone. Just knowing how terrified Summer was of him tore him apart. He wanted so badly to be with her, and he tried to make things right. Only, Summer hadn't returned his call.

Lynn was still comforting and consoling Summer. Summer loved Mike, but now she was also terrified of him. She had so many mixed emotions. Lynn thought Summer should have at least called Mike to hear him out. However, seeing the trauma Summer was suffering, she wasn't going to push it. Lynn was never a believer, but at this moment, this woman was honestly praying for Mike and Summer. There was a lot she didn't like about Mike. However, Lynn believed marriage was a lifetime commitment as long as there wasn't abuse. Since Mike had never been violent before, she felt there had to be a reason for his rage.

The following day Summer and Lynn went to the Metro for Summer's belongings. The broken debris on the floor was still there, though they could see Mike had attempted to clean it up. The food Summer prepared was in the refrigerator. Lynn could tell by the shattered mess that Mike had gone off the deep end. She didn't believe he would hurt Summer, but it was apparent Mike needed help. She wanted to encourage Summer, "Honey, maybe you should see a counselor who can help you with this decision. Maybe your church pastor can help you make sense of all this?"

"Maybe I do. But I'm not coming back here."

Then Lynn thought that maybe a separation from Summer would encourage Mike to get the help he needed.

Mike never told anyone about his and Summer's problems. Since some of his co-workers attended the weekly weed party, the word got out about Summer's leaving him and his fit of rage. He was taking heat at work from his co-workers making remarks about Summer. His so-called friend Ernie said, "Wow, man, you mean that gorgeous hunk of woman flesh is available now? Are you ever stupid!" Mike was about to fight him. "Watch your mouth, Maddison. That's my woman you're referring to."

"Hey, man, I didn't mean anything by that."

"Then you should've kept your mouth shut." Mike balled up his fists when the foreman pulled the two of them aside. "I want to remind the two of you that fighting on the job is automatic termination. The two of you are excellent workers, and I'm trying to save your jobs." Mike was enraged, but he also had his survival instinct and knew he couldn't settle matters with Ernie here. Then Mike told Ernie emphatically, "Meet me after work. We are going to settle this."

Ernie saw the rage in Mike's eyes and knew he would not be meeting Mike after work. Mike knew Ernie would chicken out, and he was disappointed because he wanted someone or something to connect with his fists. There it was again, the person inside him he despised—the person who had frightened away the love of his life. Mike noticed that all of her clothes and personal items were gone home, so he knew she had come to pick them up. He felt he had lost her and now had to deal with the vultures who couldn't wait to hit on her. He was now facing acute episodes of jealousy and lovesickness.

After a few days, Summer was no longer in shock but was still fearful and heartbroken. She was beginning to think about a future without Mike. She loved living with Lynn and enjoyed their walks through the Sunset district. However, she didn't want to be an imposition to Lynn. She arranged to talk to Pastor Thomas. She wasn't going to talk about the episode she had with Mike. Even though she felt she could no longer trust Mike, she was still loyal to him. Summer asked Pastor Thomas for prayer. "Pastor Thomas, please pray for a job for me."

"Talk to our church secretary; we have an opening for a receptionist."

"That would be wonderful." Laurie was the church secretary, and she interviewed summer and demonstrated her computer and phone skills.

"Mrs. Hanley, you are hired. I'm very impressed with your skills. It's just part-time, three days a week. We do have small apartments here at the church, and we can offer that to you, but then you would have to come five days a week."

"Thank you so much before I decide on the apartment. I need to talk to someone."

"That's fine; just let us know tomorrow, and then you can begin work on Monday. That's Mondays, Wednesdays, and Fridays if you choose three days. I will Look forward to hearing from you."

The church had studio apartments. These dwellings were located in the Haight Ashbury district, which was not the worst district of the city but also not the best. An apartment would be part of her pay to work five days a week. Summer talked it over with Lynn. "I have a job now, Lynn, and they are offering me an apartment with a small salary. Now I won't be an imposition to you."

"Honey, you would never be an imposition to me. You are like my family. I really would like you to live here if you want to."

"Oh yes, I want to, and I was hoping I could."

"Then it's settled we're roommates."

Summer wanted to remain with Lynn. She loved Lynn's house and also the beautiful district, so she decided to commute to her job, traveling by bus.

Lynn knew the salary from Summer's job didn't cover Summer's expenses, so she felt she should talk to Mike about supporting her. She hated to burden him because she knew the severe emotional pain he had. Still, he had an obligation to take care of her.

Mike was leaving for his break when the foreman told him, "Hanley, you have a visitor on the site." He looked out and saw it was Summer's friend Lynn. He and she had their differences, but he was relieved to have this connection to Summer. He slowly walked toward her, not knowing if she would be angry after hearing Summer's side of the story. He had his head hung down. He could tell by her expression she wasn't angry but compassionate. "How is she?" he asked.

"Not well, Mike. She's frightened and heartbroken."

"I'm heartbroken, too."

Lynn replied, "I know you are, Mike." She didn't know what to do or say because her first loyalty was to Summer, and Summer didn't want to see Mike now. She continued with the business at hand. She told him, "Summer has a part-time job, but it's not much money. She needs more to cover her expenses." Heartsick as Mike was, he was willing to relinquish his whole check to her. But he asked, "How much do you think she needs."

"Maybe a quarter of your paycheck. She does live with me, and I won't charge her anything."

"Will Summer be picking it up?" he asked, hoping to have this access to Summer.

"That will be up to Summer." Mike knew it was wishful thinking, and it would be a while before he saw Summer again. He would have to give her some recovery time. He didn't want it to be too much time, as he feared someone else would take her away from him.

Lynn returned home. She asked Summer, "How was your session with Dr. Thomas? Are you requesting counseling for you and Mike?"

Summer never considered counseling. She said, "We are beyond counseling!" She said, rolling her eyes.

Lynn wanted to say *so you are giving up on your husband*. However, she knew she couldn't push Summer, so she let it go.

Summer mentioned, "I am loyal to Mike though because I never mentioned our fight to Dr. Thomas."

Lynn had to butt in then. "That was a fit of rage, and Summer, you are not helping Mike by keeping this issue a secret. Mike needs help, and Pastor Thomas is just the person who can help." Pastor Thomas was also a clinical psychologist. Lynn had heard of him because of his successful reputation. Summer hadn't thought about Pastor Thomas's help, but she had to agree. But for now, it was hard to get past her fear. She would have to pray about it.

Summer had to admit that she longed for Mike. She was thinking of talking to Dr. Thomas. His schedule was hectic, so there was hardly an opportunity. When she finally got him, she asked, "Dr. Thomas is there any way I could schedule an appointment with you?" He said, "Summer, let me check my schedule, and I'll get back to you." However, the workday ended, and he had left for a meeting before getting back to her.

When Summer returned home, Lynn said, "Your mother called Summer, and she said it was imperative that you call back." Summer wasted no time and made the call. Lindy immediately answered. She said, "Honey, your father has had chest pains, and he's about to undergo a heart cauterization. I need you to please catch the next flight to Lubbock. I will book the flight for you and meet you there." Lindy was still in interior design and now had her own company. She wanted to wire money to her, but she feared there wouldn't be any time, and she didn't want to risk anything going wrong. Summer told Lynn, "It's my father, and I have to go to Lubbock right away."

"I'm so sorry," Lynn said compassionately. Lynn gave her the cash she would need and said, "Honey, this for you, you're going to be needing it." This time Summer didn't argue.

Then Summer called Dr. Thomas at home and told him, "Dr. Thomas, I hate to bother you at home, but I have an emergency. My father will be undergoing a heart procedure, and I have to be there, so I can't come to work."

"Please don't worry, Summer, I use a temporary agency for these kinds of emergencies. Your job will be waiting for you when you return. Please be in no hurry. I know you need this time to connect with your family," Summer agreed. She did need this time to be with her family. At least two weeks or more if her father's condition was severe.

Mike had made his mind up that when he got paid on Fridays, he would take Summer's portion to her. He knew she wouldn't see him. Yet, he needed to be where she was, whether he saw her or not. He just wanted a little glimpse of her. Friday was two days away. He already had butterflies, but he was going to plow on. He had to see Summer, even if she wouldn't talk to him.

Summer was about to take the red-eye to Lubbock. The flight left at 11:53 p.m., arriving in Lubbock at 5:55 a.m. Lynn accompanied her to the inspection gate. "I don't pray much, honey, but I will be praying for your father."

"Thank you so much, Lynn, and I will miss you. Please explain this to Mike."

"I will, honey." But, truthfully, Lynn had hoped that Summer had called to let him know.

They hugged and then left Summer to go onto the boarding gate. Summer hadn't boarded a flight since that day almost two years ago in Minion when she and Mike had left for San Francisco. They were such love birds then, and they had clung to each other since Buffalo Springs Lake. She missed Mike. They had been together for almost two years, and she had never seen this violent side. She recalled he did have nightmares on occasions, which left him screaming. Though she didn't understand the nightmares, she was glad to be there for him. She held him until he felt safe again. She thought, "Do *these nightmares have anything to do with his anger towards God?*" She had nightmares often after her attempted date rape episode. *Maybe Mike had an episode in his life that caused his nightmares. Perhaps I need to be more supportive. If only I can get past this fear.* She just didn't understand what was taking place, and she wouldn't talk about it. Lynn, however, did understand it, and she prayed maybe Summer's mother or someone could get her to open up. Lynn could see how sad Summer was, as well as how sad Mike was.

Summer's plane landed in Lubbock. She hadn't seen her family for almost two years. As she headed for baggage claim, Lindy was there waiting for her. Summer felt strange seeing her mother. Satan had tried to keep them estranged. Lindy held out her arms for Summer's embrace. Summer prayed against her apathetic attitude and hugged her mother. Lindy held Summer for a long time, telling her, "You feel so good in my arms. I have waited much too long for this." Her mother's affection warmed and overwhelmed Summer's heart. After the embrace, she held Summer out so she could take a good look. "Summer, you have become so beautiful." Summer was too overwhelmed to speak. They had a pleasant car ride to Minion. However, Summer felt a little apprehension about seeing her father. She wanted to make things right and convince him she wouldn't disappoint him again. She asked her mother, "Do you think Daddy will be glad to see me?" Lindy told Summer, "I know he will. He loves you. He's had frequent nightmares about you since he found out about the dangerous neighborhood you live in and the attempt on your life by that Diesel character." Summer wanted to tell her about how she visited Diesel in jail, and he had found salvation, but she didn't feel this was the time. "I don't live there anymore. I live in a wonderful area now."

"You'll have to give me your and Mike's new address."

Lindy was relieved. Then Lindy asked, "How is Mike doing? Does he like your new location?" Summer never anticipated these questions, and the mention of Mike's name was painful. She quickly told Lindy." Mike's ok." and hoped Lindy would ask no more questions about him. Then Lindy said, "Your father and I are looking forward to meeting Mike and were hoping to meet him on this trip." When she looked at Summer and saw the pain in her eyes, she knew something was wrong. She quickly changed the subject. "Anyway, it's so good you're here, Summer." She thought Lord *help to be her mother again,* she prayed. *We are like strangers, and it hurts because I know Summer needs me*

At last, they arrived at the hospital. Summer walked into Kevin's room. He was civil but not warm. This attitude hurt Summer, and she knew she had to win his trust back. Lindy and Kevin talked about his heart cauterization. "So, when do you have your test?" This health scare worried the family.

"In a couple of days. The doctor says it was a simple and fairly quick procedure, and if stents are needed, they'll be placed right away." Lindy and Kevin continued talking, but Summer drowned it out as she walked to the hospital window, looking out at a hood where a homeless family lived. She wondered if they were still there. It was a father, a mother, and two children. The oldest was a boy, and he'd be about thirteen. His sister would be 11. Summer turned away from the window when Lindy announced, "It's time to go, honey.". Kevin was still distant, but Summer tried to break the ice by kissing him on his cheek and telling him, "I love you, Daddy." Then she and Lindy left for Summer's former home.

Summer was in her old room and noticed everything was still the same. There were still posters on the wall of her favorite Contemporary Christian artists. Her favorites were Mercy Me and Avalon, among others. She observed all the memorabilia and took a trip back in time as she played their music on her old CD player. Finally, she was exhausted and went sound to sleep listening to their music.

The following day, Summer met with Pastor Brim. Her old pastor was glad to see her. He said, "Wow, Summer, what a beauty you've become. You have always been beautiful but not like now."

"Thank you, Pastor Brim; how are Taylor and Norman?"

"They are both well and talk about you often. Taylor works here, but she's off today."

SOUL WOUND

"I'll have to call her later. I know I disappointed her and Norman, but I have God back in my life now. Have you seen Ella lately? "

"Summer, I'm so happy you have God back. Yes, Ella's out of town with her parents. She's considering doing Missionary work." Summer wasn't surprised. Mission work was always Ella's dream.

She changed the subject. "Pastor Brim, have you heard anything about the Bertrands? I've thought a lot about them recently."

"Yes, I've known people who have run into them. The father had found a vacant lot. He made a roof for them out of the debris on the streets, tarp, and particle board parts. Surprisingly, it was well made. He sings and plays guitar and brings in enough money each day for their meals. Mostly, it would be sandwiches, chips, and whatever readymade finger food he could find. He purchases tomatoes and fresh fruit daily. He allows the children to visit a Friendship House for their education. The occupants of the house had told them the children coming there weren't met with truant officers."

"So, you have kept in touch with them?"

"As much as possible. The father is very proud and won't accept help from anyone."

But Summer thought of the handmade shelter and knew it wouldn't be enough. So the pastor began again, "On the coldest days, the mother takes the children to the local shelter. The father rarely goes with them, except when severe storms approach, and then he has no choice. So much more can be done for them. The church and the community have offered to help them get back on their feet. Except for the father won't permit it."

Summer was determined to persuade the father to do what was best for his family. She knew she had to be armed with scripture. Proverbs was full of scripture on pride. Summer thought about the most familiar scripture—Proverbs 16:18, "Pride goes before destruction, and a haughty spirit before a fall." But then she read James 4:10, "Humble yourselves before the Lord, and he will lift you up" (NIV). Yes, that was the right one. She showed it to Pastor Brim, who approved it, and then met with the family.

Friday was payday, and Mike hadn't been as excited for one in a long time. He had stopped attending the weed parties. Without Summer, there was no celebration. He also didn't care to be around his co-workers who had disrespected Summer. He went to the office and picked up his check. Then he went to the bank to make his deposit and get a money order for Summer's portion. He went home and put on his best blue jeans attire. He was hoping to see Summer, or at least be in her presence. For now, that would be satisfactory.

He left the Metro and arrived on Lynn's doorstep. Lynn came to the door and saw Mike all dressed up. She knew he was hoping to see Summer, and she would have to deliver some disappointing news.

"I have Summer's support check," Mike said.

"She went to Minion a couple of days ago. Her father's ill. Her mother paid her plane fare. I'm so sorry, Mike. Summer asked me to please tell you, and I forgot."

Mike's heart went to his throat. Have I just lost all my rights as a husband? He thought. Why Couldn't Summer have told me herself?

Lynn's heart went out to Mike. She could see the pain in his eyes. She also saw tears and was moved to embrace him. Mike hugged Lynn hard and poured out his heart, and released all the pain he felt. "Lynn, does she even love me anymore?"

"I know she does, Mike; she's just afraid."

"I'm so afraid of losing her. I never hear from her. She never told me she was going to Minion. I never even knew she was talking to her folks again." He was trying hard not to break down.

Lynn stayed silent and was praying something would happen and the pain for both of them would end. When Mike had composed himself, he left Summer's check with Lynn and went back to the Metro.

Summer won the favor of the homeless parents, and the children loved her. She talked to them and read James 4:10. She told them about the ministries. "Mr. Bertrand, I have been thinking about your family since I moved to San Francisco. I feel as though I had bailed on you, and I'm sorry. If you let me, I can tell you about some programs that get you off the streets and into a home. There's Habitat for Humanity, which builds homes for the poor and the homeless, and the churches in town would be more than willing to help you to get a new start."

Immediately, Sharon, the mother, chimed in and said to her husband, "Please, John, let's give these programs a chance. It would be so wonderful if we could all live in a house."

John wasn't sure. Summer then replied, "I know you have carpentry skills, and you can help to build your own home. You can probably supervise the other workers."

"Now that sounds very interesting. I wouldn't mind that at all. I miss working."

Summer continued, "There's also a program called Dress for Success. They provide clothes for job interviews and a wardrobe to go to work." Every program Summer mentioned held their interest. Finally, John gave his consent, and Summer met with Pastor Brim and everyone involved in this project. A new life for the Bertrands was underway.

Mike refused to let go of the score he wanted to settle with Ernie at the worksite. "I told you I wasn't finished with you, Maddison. I won't let you chicken out again. You disrespected Summer, and now you're going to pay the price." Mike constantly got in his face. Ernie even apologized. "Man, I told you I was sorry. I won't do it again; what else can I say." Mike stayed in his face and wouldn't relent. Ernie had quit attending the weed parties at the Metro because he was so afraid of Mike.

Dr. Thomas was a close friend of Bob Smith, the site foreman. He was there inviting him to a church banquet and noticed Mike bullying Ernie. Bob once again warned, "Mike leave Ernie alone on and off the work site. Is that understood!" Mike walked away in a huff. Bob was about to fire him when Dr. Thomas called him to the side. "I hope you weren't going to fire that boy because it wouldn't be a good idea."

"Why?" Bob asked, fed up with Mike's attitude.

"My guess is he has a post-traumatic episode. I would like him to be hospitalized—he's a walking time bomb."

Bob had to agree. He didn't want to fire someone who had an illness. So, he told Mike, "Mike, I think you have a problem, and I know you need help with it. I have to insist you be examined at a behavioral hospital, and I want you to meet Dr. Thomas, a clinical Psychologist. Mike, you have to do this. I can't have you continually harassing Ernie."

Mike then looked at Doctor Thomas and spoke.

"I guess I have no choice."

Dr. Thomas gave Mike a warm fatherly smile. Mike liked Pastor Thomas instantly, and he trusted him. So, he agreed to be under his care.

Lynn missed Summer. She started attending Glad Tidings and became good friends with Dr. and Mrs. Thomas. The lady found out from some church members that Mike was harassing a coworker. She demanded to know. "Why! I know Mike, and I know he wouldn't do this for no reason." One church member told her, "Someone told me that one of Mike's coworkers had made inappropriate remarks about Summer." Lynn knew Mike was jealous. She said to Dr. Thomas, "Can you please take me to see Mike." Dr. Thomas then reprimanded the group for gossiping about Mike. "It seems that you ladies never listen to my sermons about gossip." He then escorted Lynn to the Metro.

Mike told Lynn, "My job has commanded me to admit myself into the hospital for a psychiatric examination. I am so scared, and Summer needs to know I'm admitting myself. I won't go in until I see her." Dr. Thomas agreed, "Mike, I'll permit you to visit Summer to let her know of your commitment to the hospital. However, you told me the reason she left you. Someone can go with you, but you can't be alone with her."

"I swear to you, Dr. Thomas, I would never hurt her. I couldn't; she's part of my soul."

"After the visit, I'll let you know about being alone with her again, but not before then." Mike wouldn't argue further. He's was going to see Summer, and he didn't want to mess that up.

Lynn volunteered, "I'll go with him to Minion."

"I'll have to think and pray about that. I'll let you know soon."

Mike had been extremely compliant with orders, and Dr. Thomas could tell that Lynn's presence was therapeutic for Mike. He granted his consent for her to accompany Mike to Minion.

Kevin would have his heart cauterization tomorrow. He was standing by his hospital window looking out at the hood. He saw Summer and a friend unloading boxes from a car and giving them to the poor family. Everyone in town knew the family. Kevin was amazed his daughter had turned out to be so giving. He felt all the traumatic experiences she'd had would have damaged her or caused her to use drugs.

When Kevin underwent his heart cauterization, two stents needed were placed during the procedure. If everything went well, he would be discharged the next day. Everyone was relieved. Autumn rarely paid attention to Summer, but Summer knew she had to be patient. At the moment, all the family members were concerned for Kevin.

Lindy now regretted that she never encouraged her daughters to be close. She could see Summer was trying, but Autumn was full of resentment. This mother blamed herself. She knew things would've been different if she could've seen this day. They visited, and then Lindy decided Kevin and Summer needed some alone time together. So, she and Autumn went shopping.

Summer felt awkward with her father.

Kevin said, "I saw you the other day helping out that poor family."

Summer told Kevin. "Much is being done for them. The father has an interview for a carpentry job. The mother is considered to be hired in the children's new school cafeteria. I persuaded the father to move the family into the shelter while their home is being built. The couple has their privacy in a large room with two petition curtains, and the children also have privacy."

Kevin was amazed and reversed his opinion of Summer. He repented and realized he wasn't as gracious as the father of the prodigal son. He discovered his love for Summer was conditional. They cried together, hugging and forgiving each other. It ended with Summer singing his favorite praise song, "How great is our God." Lindy had dropped Autumn off at home and picked up Summer, and they went directly home. They didn't want to tire Kevin out.

The next day, Lindy was at the hospital awaiting word on Kevin. It looked favorable for him to go home. She was there by herself. Autumn wanted to stay in her room and keep to herself, and Summer claimed she was feeling sick. The doctor came in and said, "This young man has passed all of his tests with great results, and he can go home."

Lindy said, "Wonderful if I can now get him to behave himself." Kevin just smiled. He was grateful to be alive.

On the way home, Kevin told Lindy, "Things are great between Summer and me again. Thanks for being patient with me. Did you know she was helping a homeless family?"

"Yes, I did. I helped box up the clothing and other things. Summer has become so selfless you know she gave her boom box and all her CDs to the children."

"I am so proud of her. And I have missed her. I stayed so angry that I'm afraid I tried to refuse to miss her. But that didn't work."

"It never does. You were right all along; I did favor, Autumn. But that changed when I thought I lost Summer for good."

"I noticed."

"And you have been so patient and wonderful. I never want to lose you."

Summer had missed a menses, and now it was almost time for another. She was trying to hide her nausea; fortunately, she managed to be alone during her emesis episodes. Anytime her mother or Autumn was present during one, she went outside to heave. She had taken a home pregnancy test, and she was about to check it for results. In just a few seconds, Summer would know if she was pregnant with Mike's child.

Kevin was doing considerably well as they arrived home. Summer was up and appeared to be feeling better. However, Lindy could tell something was heavy on her mind. Autumn came into the room and hugged Kevin, "I'm so glad you are okay, Daddy. I love you." She then rolled her eyes at Summer. She seemed sure Summer would lose her temper the way she used to, but Summer saw through Autumn's attempt to anger her. It was a wasted effort. The Lord wasn't pleased with Summer's attitude either, and she prayed for God to reveal what kindness she could show Autumn. Lindy asked Summer, "Are you feeling any better, honey?". She had an idea of what the problem was but wanted to get the news from Summer.

The phone rang, and it was Lynn. Lindy handed the phone to Summer. Summer held the phone close, and Lindy saw the concern on her face.

Summer hung up the phone and calmly announced, "It looks like you will meet Mike after all." Lindy was too unsettled to be thrilled. She asked Summer, "Is everything was ok with you and Mike? Honey, I know you don't want to worry us, but the truth is the best."

Summer had never confided in her mother, and it felt strange. She honestly wished it was Lynn she was confiding in. But she just had to unload. Everything was overwhelming. The incident with Mike, taking care of herself, and now the pregnancy. She didn't know where to begin, but when she was through, Lindy knew it all. Of course, now she would meet her son-in-law, who had broken her daughter's heart, although she was thrilled about being a grandma. Now she had to pray for God to help her be pleasant to Mike. Summer told her that Lynn would be coming with him. She was happy about meeting her too. At first, when Summer talked about Lynn, Lindy would be a little jealous. Then she realized that Lynn was her answer to prayer. Lynn was the person Lindy asked God to send to Summer, but Lynn wasn't a tangible person at her prayer time. She knew she would have to treat Lynn special when she met her tomorrow.

The next day, Lindy and Summer met Mike and Lynn at the airport. Summer was apprehensive about Mike but happy to see Lynn. Lindy saw that Mike was tall, blond, and extremely handsome. She saw the attraction Summer had for him. Mike was shy when she introduced herself. "Hello, Mike, so nice to meet you."

"You too."

"And Lynn, I am so honored to meet you. Thank you so much for taking care of Summer."

"My pleasure, she and Mike are wonderful." Praising Lynn convicted Lindy because she had left Mike out.

Mike wasn't offended. He was more concerned about what Summer's parents knew about the cause of their separation, and he was ashamed. He wished he could be back in San Francisco; except he was happy to be here with Summer

He spoke his heart. "You look so beautiful, Summer." Summer's heart skipped a beat until she thought about Mike's episode, and now there was a child to protect

She graciously told him, "Thank you." Summer then noticed that Lindy and Lynn were speaking to each other as if they had always been old friends. Observing this had puzzled her yet also amazed her.

They all got into Lindy's car and headed to Minion. Kevin had wanted to come to meet Mike, but Lindy insisted that he rest. Lindy welcomed Mike warmly and asked him some questions about California. "Mike, I can't tell you how relieved I am about Summer's living in a safer district. She tells me how astounding and picturesque it is. Since you are a native there, I'm sure you can tell me more about it." Mike remained silent because he couldn't describe the Sunset District, and he didn't know if Summer's family knew why they were separated. Lindy's questions seem to indicate they didn't know, and he didn't want to be the one to report the news. Lindy understood why Mike was silent. He didn't want to talk about the separation. In addition, Lindy could see the painful expression on his face. It was the same expression that Summer had. Lindy could then tell this couple was in love. She didn't want to bring up the fact that she knew they were separated. Summer had asked Lindy to keep her pregnancy a secret until Mike left. Lindy understood why and agreed.

They arrived home, and Kevin gave Mike a warm greeting and a vigorous handshake. "Mike, I thought I was never going to meet you. Now I can see why you were able to steal my little girl away!"

"Daddy!" Summer exclaimed, blushing with awkwardness.

"Don't be embarrassed. Summer, this is your husband of two years after all." Summer appeared to go along with him because she didn't want her father to know about the separation. Summer insisted her mother not tell him. Her father needed recovery time and not shocking news. She was also glad that her father made Mike feel loved and welcomed.

Autumn, however, was once again entranced by Mike. Summer couldn't help but notice Autumn gaping at him, and she was jealous. Autumn was almost 15 but could pass for 18. Looking at Mike, she knew she didn't have to worry. He had eyes only for her since the day they met at Buffalo Springs Lake. If only she could trust him again. Lynn had explained on the phone that Mike wanted to visit her before entering the hospital. She asked herself why would he be hospitalized?

Mike wanted to be alone with Summer, but a condition for his visit was that they not be alone together. His heart was torn apart. It hurt him severely that anyone would think he could ever hurt Summer. It hurt more that Summer thought that way. But he hoped the hospital commitment would set him free to be with her. All he thought about and wanted was Summer. The separation was killing him. How could he tell Summer these things if they couldn't be alone? It looked as though everyone would know what he would say to her, and he was also going to plead with her to give him another chance.

Lynn announced, "We can only be here until tomorrow. We are only here because Mike has something to say to Summer." She then looked toward Mike. Mike had longed for this chance and also dreaded it. He wasn't a lover of country music, but these words from Alan Jackson's song "Wanted" stayed stuck in his head. "Wanted, a good-hearted woman to forgive imperfection in the man she loves. Wanted, just one chance to tell her how much he still loves her; he can't be sorry enough."

Yes, God had humbled him. He wasn't sure he was a believer yet, but, for certain, he was hollering "Uncle." He said, "Summer, life without you has been a living hell. I want you back so bad. I love you so much. I don't understand what happened the last time we were together any more than you do. That's why I have decided to get help. Honey, I need you by my side. I am going to get better, and I am going to be the man you deserve. I have been in such torment. From the first day I laid eyes on you, I thought you were the most beautiful girl ever. I don't want to be without you anymore. I realize you could just have any man you wanted, but please let that man be me."

Summer was overwhelmed, and she was in Mike's arms in a heartbeat. They shed tears together, held each other, kissed, and caressed each other as though no one was looking, and this couple romanced everyone who watched. Autumn was moved to tears. She had envied Summer from the beginning, but now she saw that this dashingly handsome man loving on Summer also had heart and soul. And surprisingly, she was also happy for Summer.

Summer called Pastor Brim. "Pastor Brim, It's Summer. Look, something's come up, and I have to go back home. Taylor knows all of our plans for the Bertrand's, so maybe she can take over. I will be back when Taylor needs me. I'll wait for her to call me. Thank you for everything." Pastor, out of concern, stated to Summer, "Is everything ok. Why is your trip cut so abruptly? I hope you're alright!"

"More than alright." Summer never mentioned being separated and wasn't going to now. My husband has come here, and I need to go back with him."

"Certainly, Summer, and take all the time you need. I hope your husband is ok."

"He's more than ok. He's wonderful."

"Then I say again, and please take your time." Pastor Brim didn't fully understand, but he could tell there was "celebration" in Summer's voice, and he was rejoicing too.

Summer was leaving to go back with Mike but planned to return to see the couple into their new home. Mike needed her, and she needed him. She had to be at the hospital for him; the staff said her presence would help Mike recover faster. She then called Taylor, "Taylor, I'm so sorry, but could you please take over the Bertrand project? I'm going back home with my husband. It's wonderful news, and when I come back, I'll tell you all about it." Taylor was baffled. Summer never mentioned her husband when she was here. However, Taylor could hear Summer's expression of delight, and that was all that mattered. She said, "Ok, Summer, and please don't worry; I can handle this. John and his family adore you, and they would want you to celebrate their new beginning."

Summer, Mike, and Lynn were back in San Francisco. Summer had spoken to Dr. Thomas on the phone. "Dr. Thomas, this is Summer; Mike and I have reconciled. I'm a little embarrassed to mention this, but it seems you have a medical order on my husband not to be alone with me. It's not going to be possible for us to have a honeymoon abiding by this order. Could you please lift it?"

"Of course, I will, and I'm so happy for you and Mike. I know when he recovers, life for the two of you will be more joyful. Congratulations."

Mike and Summer were honeymooning in Summer's room in Lynn's house. Lynn offered, "You can stay here now with Summer and me. All you have to pay me is what you paid at the Metro." Mike accepted graciously, "Just add grocery expense to that, Lynn, and you have a deal."

Summer and Lynn took turns cooking and cleaning the kitchen. Mike would move in when he was out of the hospital. Summer and Lynn retrieved all his belongings from the hotel. They would live there for a while and then save to buy a house. Summer was hesitant, but she told Mike about the baby. "Mike, you're not going to like this, but there's soon going to be three of us" Summer expected to get a lecture on not taking her birth control. Suddenly Mike surprised her. "I won't deny that I'd hoped to have you to myself for a while longer; however, I do look forward to number three." He made Summer so happy, and they embraced continually. Lynn always caught them kissing and holding hands.

Mike was in the hospital under strict psychiatric care. His parents visited him. They told the Doctor, "We tried to get therapy for Mike years ago. He fought it. We believe he persecuted himself because of his sister's death. Ruby was Mike's sister, and they were close." They continued to tell the doctor, "One day Summer Mike and Ruby had visited their grandpa's farm. It was when Mike was fourteen and Ruby was nine. One tragic day Ruby was in the path of a tractor with a harvester. It ran her over, and she was severely mutilated. Parts of her body were never found. We believe that Mike had witnessed this tragedy. He would suffer countless nightmares, and he couldn't eat or sleep. We worried that he wouldn't survive. We don't know what happened, but he recovered, except for the nightmares." His parents knew he needed help after the tragedy. However, since he had his appetite back, he seemed ok. Except for his arrogance toward God remained."

The doctors believe that Summer's speaking about her faith had triggered his episode. Then Dr. Thomas explained to Mike, Summer, and his parents. "It appears that Mike did witness his sister's tragedy. We think Mike was angry that God didn't prevent this tragedy or rescue Ruby. Then Summer left him; Mike experienced the same pain of loss as with Ruby. However, it was worse because Summer was his soul mate." The doctor continued. "Please try to understand, Mike, that God doesn't cause tragedy and death. He loved Ruby more than any of you. Remember he told Cain, 'Your brother's blood cries out to me from the ground' (Genesis 4:10 NIV). He's grief-stricken over tragedies." Mike admitted, "I did seek God and prayed for my marriage." Mike knew there were no atheists at the bargaining table. Then Dr. Thomas became Pastor Thomas. "Mike, none of us knows our fate or what day will be our last, and sometimes salvation never comes. Mike, have you ever accepted Jesus into your heart?"

"No, sir," Mike admitted, his voice choked with tears.

"Will you accept him into your heart now?"

"Yes, sir."

"Then let's say the sinner's prayer." Pastor Thomas spoke, and Mike repeated. "Lord, I am a sinner. I come to you in my sin, asking you to forgive me. Please give me a new life. Take away my old sinful life. Let me live only for You and be a testimony to others. Thank You, Lord, for Your mercy and grace, and accept me as Your child. I accept that Your Son Jesus is the only way to salvation. In Jesus Name. Amen." Mike wept uncontrollably.

Summer was overjoyed and embraced him. It was almost like she was married to another man, a changed man.

Summer wondered why she had never heard about Ruby before now. She had lived at the Hanley's house for over a week before Mike decided to move to San Francisco, and they had also visited them a few times. The visits were shortened because Mr. Hanley and Mike would have arguments. Yet, there was never any mention of Ruby. Summer recalled seeing a picture of a child who had dark, auburn hair and green eyes. She asked Susan. "Is the picture of the child in the living room, Ruby?" Susan replied in tears, "Yes, it's her."

"Why haven't I heard about her before?"

"Because it too painful for Mike, and us too. I'm sorry, you do have a right to know. The truth is we haven't been around each other a lot." Summer knew this was true. And she was going to try to change this. Mike needs to spend time with his parents. So, she would pray he and his father would end their fighting.

Mike and Dr. Thomas became close, and every Saturday, they went fishing off the pier of Fisherman's Wharf. On Saturday nights, Summer and Mrs. Thomas had a fish fry. Often Lynn joined them.

One night after a fish fry, Mike held Summer's hand and poured his heart out. "Summer, honey, I'm so sorry that I ever hurt you. I have been too proud. However, there have been times I never meant to hurt you. I still should've apologized. And I don't ever want to hurt you anymore, baby; I love seeing your smile. I never want it to leave your face again." Summer's heart lightened, she answered. "I'm not innocent, Mike, because I know I hurt you too. I should never have abandoned you. I know we won't hurt each other anymore, and we have a new beginning. We have God to guide us now. We'll have obstacles and challenges, but I don't believe it will ever affect our marriage. Hey, don't forget, we now have our number three to look forward to."

"Yes, indeed, number three, we can't forget him."

"You're so sure it's him?" He looked and saw a stern look come over Summer's face, and he then remarked. "Remember you said obstacles and challenges wouldn't affect our marriage." He looked so adorable and so like a little boy that Summer had to kiss him passionately.

Then Mike told Summer, "This is how it will always be. You will have all my heart's passion. I'll never again withhold anything from you.". Then, still holding hands, they went to their room.

Chapter 6

Mike and Summer had a brief but long-awaited honeymoon after they reconciled. He even took a few extra days off from work when he was out of the hospital. They wanted it to last forever. They continued honeymooning as they stayed affectionate toward each other and held hands all the time. Also, because he no longer participated in the weed parties, he didn't have to work overtime. However, he did work some overtime to save for a new house.

Now they were discussing their future. Before this couple separated, Mike had made all the decisions, but now he included Summer. God has taught them so much about respect for each other. An almost one-month separation from Summer had made Mike appreciate her more. However, summer felt remorse because Mike had a disorder and broken her vow in sickness and health. "Mike, I am so sorry I abandoned you. I only thought about myself and never tried to find out why! Please forgive me."

"Summer, you have to stop beating yourself up. I had to learn from this. If you hadn't left, I probably wouldn't have changed, nor had Jesus in my life."

"You're right, and I won't mention it again. But, Mike, you love me more powerfully than you ever had before. I know you love Jesus more, but it's hard to tell with all the attention you pay me now."

"Summer, I am so much happier letting go of my proud nature. I was never aware it was making me unhappy. And Lynn is incredible. I'm sorry I had such a bad attitude about her. I would apologize, but I can't let her know I had it."

"That is the best, Mike. I'm glad you see that Lynn is such a giving person."

"Yea, and payday, I'm going to treat us to fish and chips at the Yellow Submarine. I miss their fish and chips."

"Are you complaining about "home cooking?" Summer teased

"Heavens, no, you and Lynn are extraordinary cooks. I'm just tripping down memory lane."

"Ok, then you're forgiven," And then once again, they kissed with a powerful desire."

Lynn loved having the new honeymooners around. It made her feel young, and she reminisced about the days when she was with her Harold. "You two remind me and my husband and myself."

Mike and Summer asked Lynn many questions about her marriage. Mike began, "Lynn, how did you meet your husband?" Summer chimed in, "yea Lynn, I would like to know about him. I can tell his memories still make you happy."

"Okay, I was very young, only seventeen. Harold was twenty-three. We met at a movie theater in 1975. The movie was *Nashville*, with Keith Carradine and Lilly Tomlin. We went to the movie separately, but we left together, talking about the movie. I jokingly expressed to him, "I hope you're nothing like that Tom Franks."' Of course, he was the opposite. He was timid. I didn't think he would ever ask me out. He appeared interested, but it was hard to tell. At seventeen, I was very insecure."

"How did you get together?" Mike asked, engrossed in her story.

"Well, it was weeks before he would come around, and I thought I was going to have to ask him out. He followed me around everywhere. The movie theater and the Burger Shack turned out he was too tongue-tied to verbalize his feelings, and I was so attracted to him. It was hard to be around him without expressing how I felt, and wondering if he felt the same way, I gave him several hints, but he didn't seem to get my message.

We watched Nashville repeatedly. It was a romantic story for us. It was after we watched it for the last time he yelled out, "' Lynn would you do me the honor of going out with me?"' His voice was shaken. I blurted out back '"I thought you would never ask."' Mike and Summer then laughed. Lynn continued. "Yes, that's what we did. We had a hard-long laugh and ended up in each other's arms. It also took a few weeks for him to have the courage to kiss me. I thought I was going to have to kiss him; I patiently waited." Mike squeezed Summer's hand. Because just talking about kissing increased their desire for each other. It seemed odd to Summer that Lynn had these feelings too. Lynn then continued. "Our first kiss was electrifying. But Harold was a gentleman. He wouldn't allow our passion to plummet out of control, so he proposed marriage. He was so cute, all tongue-tied and unsure of himself. It's my favorite mental picture of him." Summer remarked, "That sure wasn't you, Mike. This guy was the role model for confidence."

"I just had you fooled," Mike replied, "you devasted me as much Lynn devastated Harold." Mike's response triggered another emotional reaction from Summer. Lynn continued. "After Harold proposed, we were married a year later. It was a private ceremony because both of us had no family to be present except for my mother. She and our best friends were our witnesses." Mike then asked, "What kind of work did Harold do?"

"He was a real estate agent. Throughout the years, we acquired several properties. We rented all these properties out, and this was our financial means of support. We lived like a retired couple except when Harold had repair work; he was very responsible and cared for his tenants' repair needs. I think it was because he was so responsible and took care of the tenants, was why God blessed us with a comfortable income." Summer replied. "I was wondering why you never had an actual job; I guess I think everyone punches a timeclock. It's wonderful that your husband is still providing for you." Lynn replied, "I never thought of it that way, but you're right." Mike added, "Lynn, I hate that I can't meet him he sounds like a wonderful man."

"The best." Then Lynn continued, "We did have our challenges. We both wanted to have children. The doctor examined us both. He never found anything that would prevent me from conceiving. Yet, I could never become pregnant. We just had to give up on that. So we decided to adopt pets instead. We adopted animals from the dog pound, a cat and a dog. They were like our babies. They greatly entertained us. Honey was our blond Labrador Retriever. Hollywood was our grey Tabby. They were beautiful and loyal pets. They were also devoted to each other. They played together and had us laughing most of the time. Honey was huge but was careful in his play with Hollywood.

One time, Honey was chasing Hollywood, but the chase ended with Hollywood chasing Honey. Honey lived to be 16. When he died, Hollywood mourned him, and he also died less than a year later. He was almost 17. We mourned them like they were our children. We had them buried in a pet cemetery. We refused to have any more pets because it was too painful." Summer then remembered General. She had told Lynn about General, but this was the first time she heard about Honey and Hollywood.

Lynn continued, "In June 1998, Harold had a massive heart attack. He died while in the ambulance. They tried to revive him in the ambulance and at the hospital, but it was pointless. I was devastated—Harold was my only family. My father had passed away just as I began high school, and I lost my mother ten years later. I had no living brothers or sisters. I had a brother who had died in Vietnam in 1968. I was devastated ." Mike offered comfort and a gentle hug. Summer hugged her too. Mike replied, "Lynn, I'm so sorry; it seems we're making you relive all of this."

"Not really. I had joined a grief support group for widows. The group helped, but I always knew there was a missing factor. I didn't know it then, but now I know it was Jesus. It's when I gave my life to Christ; I received true comfort. Harold had received Christ before he died. He ministered to me, but at that time, I didn't understand it. Summer, it was your influence and hindsight that helped me to take the step." Lynn and Mike were saved around the same time, so they decided to be baptized on the same day. It was a glorious day for Summer to watch her best friend and her husband take the plunge. Summer and Mike thanked Lynn for sharing her love story. It gave them a new perspective of her life.

Taylor Miller worked part-time at God's Temple Church; she was also a full-time nursing student. She and Pastor Brim had stayed in contact with the Bertrand family. In the next two weeks, the family would graduate from the Rescue Mission to move into their new home built by Habitat for Humanity and the many volunteers who helped build the structure.

The couple had a four-bedroom, two-and-a-half-bath home. It had a large living room area, a large kitchen dining area, and a huge master bedroom with a master bath. The children had the following largest rooms with a second bathroom between them. The spare room was a computer room. The half-bath was next to the computer room. A church member donated a PC. Lindy volunteered her services in home design. So, it was a beautifully furnished, decorated home when the community presented to the Bertrands.

John and Sharon Bertrand were business owners before their homelessness. John was tall and medium height and weight. He had brown hair, blue eyes, and handsome features. His wife Sharon was petite. She had blonde hair, hazel eyes and was extremely attractive. They had two children, Stephen, aged 13 — who was almost as tall as his father and his spitting image. Cissy, aged 11, was a tiny carbon copy of her mother. They were of German descent. They had lived in a modest but beautiful three-bedroom apartment. Stephen and Cissy each had a bedroom and shared a bathroom. Sharon and John had a master bedroom with a master bathroom. It also had a large living, dining, and kitchen area. They were the owners of a coffee shop. The business was excellent until an unfortunate incident happened. Somehow a customer became sick from the coffee they had served, and this customer sued them. Most of their money went for an attorney, and, eventually, they had to declare bankruptcy. This action ended the lawsuit. But they were broke and had no money for living expenses.

They had two children, Stephen, aged 13—who was almost as tall as his father and his spitting image. Cissy, aged 11, was a tiny carbon copy of her mother. It was over a year ago since they met Summer. Then she returned and told them about this opportunity. They missed her visiting them. However, during her absence, they acquired a strong faith in God. The father had a musical gift he used to collect money to keep them from starvation. "How great is our God." He would sing as a crowd gathered around. He took in enough money to feed them.

The homeless shelter kept the children in shoes and clothes. The shelter also had a place where the mother could wash the clothes. She kept all their clothes to a bare minimum. The shelter had a shower for the family to stay clean. There was also a shower at the local bus terminal, where John showered because it took coins. A couple running a friendship house educated the children. Now they will accept help from other organizations; that will provide them home, jobs, and clothes for interviews and work. Many businesses conducted the interviews, allowing the poor and homeless. Summer Logan Hanley had made this possible for the Bertrands, and she was their hero. Naturally, of course, Summer gave all the glory to God.

John Bertrand accepted a job as a carpenter. He had always loved this trade. He had even built additions onto the coffee shop they owned. His greatest satisfaction about the job was that it was the vocation Jesus chose. Sharon had accepted the job in the middle-school cafeteria where her children attended, which didn't interfere with time for her children. It was convenient, especially in case of any emergency.

Summer had Taylor arranged for two church congregations to collect the Bertrands' furniture and home decor once the house was ready for habitation. Taylor and Pastor Brim also took up a collection to fly Mike and Summer out for the housewarming, except Mike needed to stay in San Francisco to work. "I got my call from Taylor. We need to go to Minion to help with the Bertrand project. They want to book a flight for both of us." Mike replied, "Baby, I can't afford to go. I need to work to earn enough money for the down payment on our new house."

"Honey, I understand, and I know my family will too. Don't worry; I'm sure going to miss you."

"Oh, Summer, separation seems like an eternity. At least there's no uncertainty with this one. I feel at peace. Only, I'm anxious for us to have our own home." Mike and Summer were to buy a new house. Lynn had a place next door to her, and she offered for Mike to purchase it from her. Stating, "Mike, I really want for you and Summer to live close to me still. I would love to sell the property next door."

Mike then replied, "Lynn, we would love nothing better. We want you to be a big part of our child's life." Lynn felt like a new grandmother; only, she kept silent about this to Mike and Summer. Then Mike expressed himself, stating she would be the honorary grandma. She exclaimed," thank you, Mike I'm looking as forward to this number three as you and Summer are. I keep in touch with Lindy, who says she's a little jealous because I'm nearby for "her" and she can't be."

"Why are you and Summer so sure it's her It could be him!"

"A healthy child is what's important. But let's, please, continue our negotiations. I'll let you give me some of your savings as a down payment. I want you to put some of that aside for number three."

"That's way too generous, Lynn. I'll accept a ten percent discount as number three's baby gift, just let me earn a little more money. I want to give you a fair down payment."

"Ok, but I'll 'decrease' some more from my end, then you can 'increase' some more to yours. Then in a very few months, you and Summer will have your own home."

"Okay, deal, let's shake hands." So they shook hands on the bargain. However, this still meant Mike needed to work a little more overtime.

Then Taylor called about the flight arrangements. Mike told Summer, "Honey, it's so wonderful for Taylor's church to finance my trip to Minion, but if they insist on buying me a ticket, please tell them to use that money towards the purchase of the furniture for the Betrands'." Summer was delighted. She had never offered anything monetarily, and this was the perfect donation. She hugged Mike enthusiastically.

Summer was sad to leave for Minion without Mike. The night before she left, Mike planned a special night for them. He took her to a fine restaurant, and they had dinner by candlelight. A violinist played romantic music, and Mike and Summer slow-danced all night. Mike said, "Summer, my darling, may I have this dance?"

"Certainly, my tall, tan, and handsome prince." Mike then held Summer close, savoring every moment of the dance. And giving her the most romantic night of her life. The reconciliation had given them powerful feelings, romantic and spiritual. The romance was more engrossed when they included Jesus as a part of it. Other couples on the dance floor looked at them with jealousy but also favor. A couple, dancing so close that it could be one person. Mike and Summer held each other, and their mood filled the room. They would separate briefly in the morning, but tonight was all theirs. Since the couple's reconciliation, Summer wanted to recapture these moments. She tried to cling to Mike and never leave. Mike felt the same way, but life had to move on, and Summer needed to go to Minion and fulfill her promise to the Bertrands.

Mike and Lynn accompanied Summer to the check-in gate. Summer dreaded parting with Mike for some reason. She couldn't place a finger on the feeling, but she honestly didn't want to leave him.

"Mike, I have an eerie feeling, and my instinct is saying not to leave."

"It'll be okay; you have to keep your promise. I'll be just as lonely without you." But Summer knew it more than that.

Lynn added, "Honey, you and Mike have created a powerful bond. So it's natural that you wouldn't want to leave him now. No one wants to leave in the middle of a honeymoon." But that still didn't feel like the correct answer.

She held on to Mike as though he would disappear in front of her. Her affection only ignited Mike's feelings. He held her face, tenderly, in his hands and kissed her with emotions that were getting out of control. Then he stopped himself and said, "baby, we will continue this when you get back home. Oh, you have me not wanting you to go. But sweetheart, you have to." Summer's heart raced as her desire for him increased. Mike was right, and his words were a comfort to her. Finally, it was time to go to the boarding gate. "Bye, sweetheart," he told her with one last long passionate kiss. "I love you."

"I love you, Mike; I will miss you more than you'll ever know. But, Lynn, please keep him safe for me."

"Honey, you know I will. You take care of yourself and give your family my love."

"Thanks, Lynn; I love you. You are the best."

Summer kept looking out at Mike and Lynn as they faded out of sight. She was soon at her boarding gate. She waited, and finally, they announced her flight to Minion.

Taylor and Pastor Brim met Summer at Lubbock International. They hadn't told Kevin and Lindy, as they wanted to surprise them. Summer was happy to see them, but she had to ask God to help her let go of her gnawing feelings about Mike. She greeted her friends, "Taylor, Pastor Brim, thank you so much for coming to get me. However, I thought it would be my parents."

"We surprise them. Your folks don't know you're here."

"Wow," Summer said, overwhelmed.

The business she and the others were undertaking took her mind off her troubles. She decided to stay busy for the whole trip, and when she returned home, she would be elated to see Mike. This thought kept her at peace.

Taylor and Pastor Brim arrived at her parents' house. They stayed briefly. It was a wonderful surprise. Kevin and Lindy kept embracing Summer, and Autumn just stared. Suddenly Summer said, "Please, join in Autumn." Autumn did, but with reluctance. Summer was just glad to embrace her family. God had taught her about unconditional love—embracing and loving Autumn, whether she embraced or loved her back. She felt a peace about them she hadn't felt for a long time.

Kevin had just returned to work. The man was fit for work when he got out of the hospital, but Leo and Trudy persuaded him to take more time for his family. When Kevin did, he realized much he had missed out on when the girls were little. Before he went back to work, he, Lindy, and Autumn took a brief trip to Carlsbad, New Mexico, and visited the Caverns. Before, the only vacations taken were when Lindy took them with the girls and without Kevin. Lindy and the girls drove and t her parents, Tom and Liz Wyman, who moved from Minion to Arizona. Tom had severe asthma, and his doctor advised the climate in Arizona would extend his life. Lindy and the girls drove there at least once a year, and the girls loved staying in hotels before arriving. However, Lindy and the girls had always missed Kevin—even Lindy's parents desired him to visit. Now, Kevin had decided to take more time off for recreation with his family. He only regretted that it wasn't before Summer had left home. Kevin now understood why she left. He planned that the next vacation would include Summer and Mike. He would speak to Mike about taking time off for family and not making the same mistakes.

The time had come for the housewarming. The Bertrands strongly revered Summer; they were thrilled about her pregnancy and happy for her reconciled marriage. John offered to lay hands on her, and she accepted. John prayed, "Heavenly Father, thank you so much for placing Summer in our lives. She's our angel. Please take care of her and her child. And please take care of her husband, who had to stay behind. Thank you so much for all the abundance with you're a blessing to us. In Jesus Name Amen."

Summer remarked in gratitude. "Thank you so much for your prayers for my family, especially your prayers for Mike." She didn't explain why she was thankful for the prayer for Mike. But it didn't seem to matter. It gave her comfort.

The Bertrands were so grateful to Summer for the project that will bring them out of poverty. They were thankful to everyone involved, but Summer cared enough to have patience with John; while he was very determined. Her care and concern had led to the many blessings they had before them. So they just kept thanking her.

Taylor, Pastor Brim, and many of the church members had shown the Bertrands their new furniture and home decor. People from both congregations filled the home with dishes of fine China, as well as simple dishes—fine silverware, as well as daily flatware. They had fine pots and pans, many small electric appliances, along with linen, bedding, towels, washcloths, dish towels, and many other home necessities. Someone had bought them a Shark vacuum cleaner. Other congregation members took the children shopping for new school clothes, shoes, and school supplies. It was all overwhelming for the family. Never had they felt so loved and cared for; most of all, they knew it was God, and later they were going to take some private time to give him thanks.

Mike had reconciled with his co-workers, especially Ernie. He was ashamed of his treatment of Ernie. "Ernie, man, I'm so sorry for my anger towards you. I would have felt awful if I had beaten you up. But from now on, please be careful; men get testy when you show an interest in their women."

Ernie confessed, "I was wrong, man, but I was sincere. I wasn't just afraid of your beating, though I know you would have killed me."

"Man, Ernie, I hope I wouldn't." The two men hugged, reconciled, and were good friends again.

Mike was glad to be receiving counsel from Dr. Thomas. Dr. Thomas told him, "Mike, you could trigger episodes from time to time, please just stay close to Jesus. Please talk to Him; he's the one who changes things.". Mike stated to the pastor, "I've never felt a feeling of peace as much as now. I am the most blessed man in the world. The new desire I have for Summer is priceless. If I don't know anything else, I know I love her like Christ loved the church. She just can't return to me soon enough." He called her at least twice a day. He called before he went to work early in California, but it was later in the morning in Minion with the two-hour time difference. He also called around dinner time his time, which was early to the middle evening where Summer was. He would have loved to call her more often, but he didn't want Summer's parents to think he was a pest. Summer also relished his phone calls. She even timed them.

Summer and her parents were having breakfast together. Autumn had left for school. Kevin had asked Summer, "Do you remember Larry Calhoun? "Do I ever; I had a huge crush on him?" She remembered her schoolgirl crush and wondered why it never seemed to fade. Kevin mentioned Larry's name stirred her up. She continued, "Why do you ask?" Kevin told her, "He's the new senior pastor at Word of God, and he had recently broken up with Emily' Millet Honds." Summer, had been attending God's Temple with Taylor and Norman. She didn't know about Word of God and Larry. It seemed curiosity got the better of her. She told her father, "I guess this Sunday I'll attend Word of God."

"You better call Taylor and let her know." Summer then immediately reached Taylor and gave her the news. She didn't want Taylor to ask why she was attending another church; Summer just had to see Larry.

Summer hasn't been to Word of God in a while. She greeted many people at the door. She saw Mary Franklin, a former "mean girl." Mary greeted Summer warmly. "Wow, Summer, you look exquisite. It's wonderful to see you." Summer wanted to ask her about Lilly German, but she never did. Mary voluntarily voiced, "I know you remember Lilly. When we graduated from school, her parents sent her to live in Europe."

"She has the money, that's for sure. Have you heard anything about Ella?"

"Yes, in a missionary school and with dreams of living in South America."

"Things change too much. I miss seeing old, familiar faces. I was looking to see Sally Ames. Doesn't she live here anymore?"

"I understood that she went to Lubbock the same year you left for San Francisco. One of the church members kept up with her and her whereabouts." Mary explained.

"Sally planned to obtain her doctorate in counseling. There Sally had met and married her husband, Jordan Chandler, who was tall, handsome, with dark brown hair and blue eyes. Jordan is a devout Christian psychiatrist. When Sally met Jordan, he substituted to teach a psych class as a favor to a friend, and Sally was in his class. Sally and Jordan discovered they had strong chemistry together, but this posed a problem. Sally and Jordan knew for her first semester, and they could only be casual friends. However, their time was productive as Jordan helped Sally complete her thesis on *Promiscuity and Adolescent Behavior*. She had gotten the idea for the thesis from her years at South Granby. She got the idea from when she counseled me and the other two of the trio. Sally wanted to know the psychology that leads to this type of behavior in teens, especially teens as young as we were. She had counseled many teens—some of them would confide in her, and others wouldn't. I knew that child protection forced Lilly to see her after the apartment episode. Of course, she wasn't going to share her problems with her because Lilly probably figured out Sally reported our party life to child protection. However, the counseling sessions were still beneficial to her composition.

"When Jordan completed his teaching semester, he had to tell his friend he couldn't substitute for him anymore until Sally graduated. They then began a long-distance relationship for a while. Jordan lived in Corpus Christi. He had his practice and his staff covered for him most of the time, which was why he had the freedom to teach at other universities. Teaching psychology and behavioral medicine was his passion. Sally was beautiful and had countless suitors, but none ever captured her fascination the way Jordan had. He spent a lot of time in Lubbock to court Sally, staying with the professor he had substituted. A little more than a year had passed before anyone knew it, and with Jordan's help, Sally received her doctorate. Sally's family lived in Lubbock, so they married there. After their honeymoon, Sally moved with Jordan to Corpus Christi and joined his staff."

Sally's termination from South Granby was one of the reasons Summer rebelled. This reason, and her home issues. Sally had to leave Minion to find her soul mate and a new destiny. Now Summer sees that God puts all the pieces of a puzzle together.

Summer was lost in her thoughts when suddenly, without warning, he appeared with his hand extended to Summer. Summer's heart beat fast—it was as though time had stood still and awaited her reappearance. He was as devastatingly handsome as she had always remembered. She knew she was blushing and wanted to hide. She could tell by the man's expression he had his own experience. She shook his hand, and the handshake set off an explosion in them both.

Larry couldn't help but express how he thought she looked. "Little Summer Logan, what a beauty you've become. I am so glad you are here." She was wearing a loose-fitting yellow dress that hid her baby bump. However, it brought out the best in her skin tone and features. Larry Calhoun wore a navy three-piece suit, and every woman in the congregation noticed how devastatingly handsome he was. Autumn once again had her mouth hung open. She also noticed that, once again, another handsome man had his eyes on Summer.

Mike had heard from his friends at the Metro that the manager, Bill Blake, was taking another job at one of Nob Hill's finest hotels. Mike and Bill were good friends. Mike wanted to visit him, congratulate him, and wish him the best. He called him to make sure he would be there after work. He said "Bill" (at the Metro, he referred to him as Mr. Blake; however, they recently became on a first-name basis.) I heard you are leaving the Metro, and I'm so happy for you. You are too talented to waste yourself there."

"I don't know about that, but I'm so relieved to leave here. You and Summer weren't just my best tenants, and you were the only worthwhile tenants. Although I'm relieved that you both left here, Summer had too many close calls."

"How well I know it. I wasn't a good husband to her when Earl attempted to attack her. I'm sure more protective of her now. Anyway, I want to come over tonight and congratulate you if it's ok."

"It's more than ok. I've missed you and Summer both, and I don't when we can see each other again, so please come."

"I'm coming from work, so please forgive my appearance. Summer is out of town at her folks."

"Mike, I'm always glad to see you no matter the appearance. You forget I used to see you daily coming home from work. " They both laughed, and Bill mentioned her would miss seeing Summer. However, Mike couldn't wait to get off from work to see Bill one more time, for a while anyway. He didn't mention he thought about taking him out to dinner; only then would he have to clean up and dress for the occasion. Bill was staying late as it was, waiting for him. So, his best wishes would have to do for now.

When Mike arrived at the Metro, he couldn't believe what he saw. Earl the "beast" Mason had returned from Tijuana, Mexico. All Mike could think out was how he had threatened Summer. Now he was back, and Mike intended to make sure he never came near Summer again. Bill was busy in the office, unaware of Earl's presence. The man was looking forward to meeting with Mike, and Bill had ordered Chinese for the occasion. He looked out and saw Mike approaching Earl with rage in his eyes.

Chapter 7

Bill immediately ran out to Mike, but before he could get there, Mike had already punched Earl in the face, followed by many other blows. When Mike knocked Earl across the floor, Earl had time to brace himself to pull out his knife and plunged it into Mike's abdomen. Mike looked down and saw pools of blood seeping from his stomach.

Bill called 911 and then got behind Mike and held him in his arms. "Hang in there, Mike. You'll be ok."

Mike replied, "I didn't hold to Jesus. Tell Summer I'm sorry I messed it all up. But I'm with Jesus now." With that, Mike breathed his last.

Bill was in denial, shaking Mike and saying, "Come back, Mike, please." Then he looked squarely at Earl and asked, "Why did you come back, you low life?"

Police sirens blared outside, and an officer came in and took Earl away in cuffs. Earl's face looked worse than a prize fighter's; the police still had to get to the bottom of this, as when they arrived, Earl was still holding the weapon.

Summer was anxious because Mike hadn't called her at their usual time. She knew about Bill's new job and Mike's meeting with him, but it was more than two hours past their regular talk time. Summer knew something was wrong. It was past her bedtime, and still no call from Mike. She would call Lynn in the morning if Mike didn't call by then. Then shortly, Lynn had contacted. "Hello, yes Lynn, Oh No!'" Summer screamed and was crying. Lindy asked, "Honey, what's wrong?" I have to get back home immediately." That was all she could say. Lindy could tell

Summer was in shock and crying uncontrollably. Lindy guessed by Summer's reaction; Mike was probably gone. Lindy knew questioning Summer right now was too painful. So, she called Lynn. All the Logans were sad. They had high regard for Mike, and now he was gone.

Larry Calhoun was thinking about his encounter with Summer this past Sunday morning. He knew nothing about her. No one had mentioned her marital status, but someone as young as Summer wasn't usually married. He recalled his recent engagement to Emily Millet Honds. He had crushed on her since kindergarten, and they dated in high school. Then a new kid came along named Trey Honds. The minute Trey and Emily touched hands, sparks flew. There was undeniable chemistry between them, and eventually, they had married.

Larry was a gentleman and had to step aside for true love. But stepping aside was too easy and not as painful as one would think it should be. The rejection was unbearable. It was the rejection that confused Larry into thinking he felt more for Emily than he did. Also, they had mourned Trey's death together, which was also confusing. Larry was glad it was Emily who ended their relationship. She just didn't have the same feelings for him that she had for Trey. There was a missing factor for both of them.

But just this past Sunday, he had found the missing factor with Summer. He hoped to see her in church again if she was still in town. He knew she lived out of city and state; he didn't know where. Larry had thought of Summer as the most adorable little 12-year-old girl he had ever seen. She was so gifted, with acting ability and fantastic singing voice. He remembered ordering the flowers to have given to her backstage. Back then, she was just a talented child. Even back then, he could tell that she would grow up to become a stunning young woman. Now he would pray for God's will and purpose, hoping Summer would soon be his.

Lynn was beside herself with grief. This woman recalled the early days when she first met Summer and how selfish Mike was.

Yet, a month-long separation from Summer matured him rapidly, and she saw the deep love the couple had for one another. When they returned from Minion, she had called Summer's room the bridal suite. When Mike returned from the hospital, he took a few more days off to have more passion and intimacy with Summer. They stayed in the bridal suite almost non-stop. She would bring them food and something to drink. She knocked on the door and left it outside their room. Mike retrieved it quickly and then shut the door. Rarely did she ever see them outside of the room. And now, she would never see them together again. It was so unbearable.

She thought about Harold. She had gotten through losing him, but she never got over it, and losing Mike brought back her loss as well. Now she and Summer had something else in common, bonding them even more. Both of them were now widows.

Kevin and Lindy saw how sorrowful Summer was. She refused food and drink. "You have to eat something, sweetheart, or you'll lose your strength," Lindy begged. But Summer remained silent. She was in a mild state of despondency. This girl would cry privately, but the signs of her tears were written all over her face. How on earth would she even survive now? If she had stayed in San Francisco, maybe Mike would still be here. Why didn't she listen to the premonitions she had? Yes, she had made a promise, but was a commitment more valuable than Mike's life? Now Mike was gone. How could life go on for her? Tears streamed down her face as her parents and Autumn took her to Lubbock International, and she faced the dreaded trip home.

Kevin and Lindy wanted to comfort Summer. They hugged her almost non-stop. Even Autumn was more affectionate to her sister than usual. Now, as she was leaving for San Francisco, they felt a piece of their heart-ripping away from them. Even Autumn felt it. She kissed Summer on the cheek before she headed to the boarding gate. Even amid the most painful event of her life, Summer was touched by Autumn's kindness and returned her kiss. She then boarded her long and sad flight back to San Francisco.

Summer's plane landed, and Lynn met Summer at the baggage check. When Summer saw Lynn, she immediately embraced her. Lynn, her best friend who had been there for her through her many trials. She held her hard for a long time. Lynn spoke, "Summer, he was like a son to me. And you are like my daughter. I'll never get accustomed to this tragic change."

"I know Lynn, you were so patient and accepting of us both. Even when we didn't deserve it, and you're right, things will never be the same again; I'll miss him forever."

After they composed themselves, they made another dreaded trip home. Summer had thought to ask Lynn to place her in another room. Then she thought of how the bridal suite had uniquely bonded her and Mike, and she didn't want to be anywhere else.

Kevin and Lindy had made the flight reservations for all three of them. Kevin asked himself, "why was this their first trip to San Francisco?" He remembered his anger when Summer ran away with Mike. He vented to Lindy, "Why was I so stubborn? I didn't allow myself to know him. He was my son-in-law for two years; that's disgraceful!" Lindy held him close and gave her comforting words. "Please, Kevin, there is no way we could've known what would happen. Just keep the happy thoughts of the warm union the two of you had when he was here. God doesn't want you condemning yourself."

"Oh, Lindy, I want to go back in time. We shouldn't already went on our first trip to San Francisco long before this."

"Let's, please focus on our Summer. She hurts the most."

"Yes, you are right. My poor little girl. She's too young to encounter this kind of pain."

Lindy also had regrets "Kevin, I hurt too; I'll always wish I had gotten to know him better. Right now, though, Summer needs to know how we love him."

"He had a mental disorder; I think he was released from the hospital too soon."

"Kevin, we can find people and things to blame continually, but God wanted him."

"Yes, Lindy, and that's so comforting to know. Thank you. I feel more at peace now." She warmly embraced Kevin, and they clung to each other. Mike's loss was a reminder of how they didn't want to lose each other.

They both knew that staying angry was a stronghold. The couple had to let it go—it was the only way to release the hurt. They were packed and ready for their flight early in the morning.

Autumn was also reminiscing about when she first saw Mike. The girl thought he was the most handsome young man she had ever seen. She recalled how he pleaded his case for Summer. She'd had a slight crush on him, and Summer knew it. Summer told her, "Autumn, Mike has that effect on women. When I first met him at the lake, all the girls there had their eyes on him. I never expected that he would have chosen me." Yes, he had a handsome face, and Autumn felt the deep sorrow that she would never see his beautiful face again, but the most pain she felt was for Summer. She regretted that life robbed her and Summer of their closeness, but they had that closeness now, and she was determined to let Summer know she would always have her love and support. Early in the morning, she and her parents would travel to San Francisco to comfort and encourage summer and say goodbye to Mike.

Mike's parents, Gerald and Susan Hanley, couldn't believe they had now lost their last remaining child. It was painful to lose their only daughter Ruby, but they still had Mike. Now that comfort was gone. They had a strong faith and felt God was telling them Mike and Ruby were now together. This thought comforted them. Expecting a grandchild was also a comfort, a part of Mike surviving. No, Mike didn't replace Ruby, and the grandchild didn't replace Mike, but it was life going on.

In two more days, they would have Mike's visitation with Summer, her family, Lynn, Mike's co-workers, friends, and the church congregation. They wanted to be at the airport to meet Summer, but they knew Summer and Lynn needed this time together.

Losing Mike was a devastating loss for them. It has been said that losing a child is the most dreaded loss. They have lost both their children. The pain of losing Mike had brought back the pain of losing Ruby. They were feeling the compound loss of both children.

Earl Mason was in his jail cell. His face hurt, but not as much as his heart. He was having many thoughts. He had been on drugs since he was 13. He was condemning himself because he had never killed anyone before. Even when he was in the gangs, he would get out of the "killing" initiation. It wasn't him. He did many despicable things, and he had little respect for women; the least dignity he had was that he wasn't a killer. Now that was gone

He knew Mike's attack was about protecting Summer. Angel had somehow gotten word to him in Tijuana. On the phone, he said. "Beast, you owe your life to Summer Hanley. She pleaded with me not to kill you. However, I might not be so gracious if you ever try to hurt her again." He now felt remorse for attacking her. He also remembered the Heavenly Being that had frightened him away. After that encounter, he never again tried to assault another woman. After finding out Summer had saved his life, he thanked her by killing her husband. How could he go on now? He was going through withdrawal, but the shock of his actions knocked the desire for drugs out of him. If he ever did drugs again, it would be one final time with an overdose.

Dr. Thomas was fond of Mike. He'd known he was unique since the day he observed his post-traumatic episode badgering Ernie. Nevertheless, the pastor couldn't believe he would be commencing his funeral. He thought maybe he had discharged him from the hospital too soon, or perhaps they should have had more counseling sessions. Dr. Thomas broke his own rule of not allowing his patients to blame themselves for tragedies; however, Mike was like a son to him. As this family was seeking comfort, he wondered how he could even help them when he also needed comfort.

On the day of Mike's visitation, his family, the Logans, and church members were there. Summer's *Rebel Freedom* group was there to comfort and support Summer. Mike and Summer's Sunday school class members were there, and Mike's coworkers were there. Ernie took Mike's death especially hard. They had attended college together then decided to drop out and go to work. Summer was overwhelmed by the multitude there for Mike, seeing how loved he was. She stayed by his casket, shedding tears. Gerald and Susan immediately greeted Kevin and Lindy. "Well," Susan stated to them warmly. "There are faces that go with the voices, over the phone lines!"

Kevin replied, "You're Susan and Gerald. It's so nice to finally meet you two after two years of talking on the phone. I'm so sorry about your son. I want you to know after we met him, we truly loved him."

"Thank you," Gerald added amiably. "We have adored Summer since we first met her. I know you have to be proud of her."

Lindy joined in, "Summer is so heartbroken, but there's comfort in knowing that possibly there's a little Mike to be among us."

"Gerald and I were thinking that very thing. It is true comfort. Whether it's a little Mike or a little Summer."

The Hanleys' were overwhelmed by the Logans' kindness. His parents were silent for a while when they visited Mike; they stood giving inaudible prayer.

When the visitation was over, Summer couldn't bear to leave Mike, "I love you so much, Mike. I want you here with me. I'm sorry I left you. I needed to be here to protect you. I could've gone to Minion another time. Please forgive me." Lynn saw that Summer wouldn't leave Mike. She began escorting her away from his casket. "No," She wept soulfully, "please, I can't leave him. He's my husband. Please let me stay." All of the families there and Lynn were angry because of the suffering they were all going through, especially Summer's nightmare.

Dr. Thomas delivered a beautiful eulogy for Mike. Everyone could tell it was hard for the pastor/psychologist to speak without tearing up. He did an outstanding job "Mike and I became close friends, and I almost feel like I'm losing a son." Pastor Thomas declared tearfully. "He was my patient, and we became close buddies who would hang out together. He had anger issues, but God used me with his therapy, and he was overcoming this disorder." He just said a few more brief words honoring Mike. He didn't mention the incident with Earl. Dr. Thomas didn't know how much Summers knew about the incident. He just felt Mike's thought at the time was of protecting her. After the eulogy, Dr. Thomas let the family say goodbye to Mike. Once again, Summer didn't want to leave Mike. In tears, she said, "Mike, you are my husband, please don't leave me. I can't bear my life without you. Please, please don't leave me." Summer wept so woefully, and she wouldn't leave his casket. They had to make her leave, and she cried out poignantly for Mike. Many of Mike's friends were taking the family's hand and offering their condolences. Bill Blake came to Summer privately to tell her Mike's words "Mike uttered in the end Summer that he was with Jesus."

"I'm happy he's with Jesus, Bill, but I would much rather he be here with me." She said bitterly. Summer was not going to look forward to mornings for a long time. She still desired Mike, but he was gone.

Angel made a brief appearance to be there for Summer. They had a reception at Mike's parents' house. Many kind people from the church, and many of the Hanley's neighbors, had donated food for the reception. All of Mike's family were overwhelmed by this kindness. They had rarely seen their neighbors and wondered if they cared. This tragedy proved they were there when it counted. Summer clung to Mike's parents now, and they clung to her. Summer's mourning clothes revealed her baby bump. The Hanleys stared at it for a long time. Then the reception was over; Summer and Lynn went home. Kevin, Lindy, and Autumn went home with Summer and Lynn for a brief time. They were staying at a hotel close to Summer and Lynn. They could all tell how drained Summer was, so they embraced her. Lindy spoke, "Honey, you look as though you could use some rest. We won't tire you out anymore. We'll be by in the morning to say goodbye." Then Kevin added, "Baby girl, we're so sorry about all this. Please take care of yourself." And finally, Autumn. "Summer, I love you, and I hurt for you. Let's, please, stay in touch."

Summer wrapped up. "Thank you so much for being here to support me. I love all of you. You mean so much to me. Right now, though, I want to be alone. It'll probably be a while before I return to Minion." She asserted this out of her bitter feeling for ignoring her intuitions.

Then the Logans went to their hotel room, and Lynn went to her room. Summer needed to be alone so she could cry the way she wanted to.

Angel knew he would have to talk to Summer about reconsidering his hit on Earl. She was bound to want vengeance. But the truth was that since he'd canceled his contract on Earl, he hadn't ordered any more hits on anyone. His gang members were calling him soft. But something Summer had said made him think about hell. He even read the scripture about it. Summer's transformation had him thinking about God and salvation.

He didn't want to give up his blood money, but he had asked God about the direction of his life for the first time. He then told God, "I can't change my life; could you please change it for me?" Then he noticed God was making changes in him. The biker didn't know if it was salvation. Angel claimed he wanted to see Summer to discuss vengeance for Earl, but he wanted to be around Summer's faith, to try to understand it. He had been avoiding her for this reason. But now, for the same reason, he wanted to be around this faith.

Angel was fonder of Mike than he thought. He never thought Mike would die in such a violent manner. He saw how Mike had badly beaten Earl. Yes, Earl was protecting himself, but Angel hated how it hurt Summer. His precious Summer didn't deserve this. Mike reacted to his mental illness, so he wasn't to blame either. Yet, here he was, taking the same risks Mike took daily. The man thought about his many of his gang members who were dead.

Suddenly Angel realized what a senseless life he led. What would he do? Could this biker get out of the gang life without risking death? And even if he could, who would hire him for any kind of legal job? And if he could get hired, how could he live on such a small amount of money? Angel was accustomed to his comforts, but did he want them at the expense of being in hell? Then there was Monica, who always wanted a normal life. She even told him from the beginning, "Angel, I would rather you and I make minimum wage if it came to that. At least it's an honest living!" Honesty was important to Monica. He never listened to her before, but he was listening now. Monica was his everything.

Larry had heard about the appalling loss of Summer's husband. He couldn't believe she had married at such a young age. Her husband was only 21 years old. Summer wasn't quite 18. Larry wasn't sure of all the details, except it had ended in violence. He talked to her parents before they left for the funeral. They thought of Mike as the bravest and most humble man they had ever met. They told him how he was forced to plead for Summer to come back to him publicly. Of course, he could understand that—who wouldn't beg for Summer to come back? He knew it was far too premature to try to get to know her, so he asked God to reserve her for him in the future. He was sure he would never have this kind of connection with anyone else. He also prayed for God's will.

Summer was angry about Mike's death, and she despised Earl Mason. She knew Mike was only trying to protect her. She heard a public defender would take Earl's case to get him off on self-defense. This defense was not justice to Summer. She felt Earl should have fought Mike with his fists. To her, he was a coward to use his knife. She made up her mind that she would be present for his court date to make sure he got what he deserved. Summer recalled Angel's preferred form of Justice, but she believed in the law and thought the law should take care of it. And even if the law didn't, she wasn't going to cross that line. However, she did have an immense animosity against Earl and would do all in her power to make sure he paid for Mike's death.

Summer's new attitude, and her vendetta against Earl, concerned Lynn. She called Lindy, "Lindy, I'm so concerned for our Summer," (This is how she and Lindy always referred to Summer.) "She's obsessed about getting revenge. I can understand her anger, but it seems out of control, and she talks about it all the time."

"Oh, Lynn, thank you so much for calling. I taught her from the time she was in grade school that vengeance is God's. I'm going to discuss this with Kevin." Lindy and Kevin were so concerned that they spoke about it to Larry in person, stating, "Pastor Larry, please pray for Summer she's having trouble letting go of Mike's tragic death."

"Of course, I'll pray for her, and we will pray about this together before you leave, then God will let us know what to do."

"I can't tell you how relieved this makes us. Summer backslid once before; we can't let it happen again."

"I'm sure it's not that serious. I know God won't allow that to happen. Summer's roots are strong. She's hurting, but she'll move past it."

"I hope you're right? However, to be assured, let's have that prayer." Then Larry prayed. "Father God, we come before you, lifting Summer to you. You know all her thoughts and her pain. Please lend her your comfort. And help her to make wise choices. We leave her in your hands—Amen." in Jesus' Name.

Larry wanted to jump at this chance to be near Summer. When he prayed with Kevin and Lindy, he told them he would be in touch. The new pastor had to ask God not to be selfish. He prayed, *Lord; you know my feelings for this woman; please guide me in this. If I go to San Francisco, I want to be in Your will and do it for Your purpose. I will wait for Your answer. I know it won't work out if it's not Your will. Guide me, Lord. In Your Holy Name, I pray. Amen.*

The following day Larry heard from the Lord. He did have a purpose for him in San Francisco. He asked Kevin and Lindy to his office. Larry then spoke, "I do have an idea of what may help Summer with her revenge issue!" Kevin and Lindy listened and thought Larry's idea was brilliant, and they prayed he could reach Summer. "Larry, it's only right for us to pay your expenses." Larry had a 401k from his business executive days. Instead of mentioning this, he said. "It's not necessary the Lord has already made a provision."

Kevin said gleefully. "Well, we can't argue that, and thanks a lot."

Larry's 401(k) payments were deducted from his paychecks with a matched amount from the company. On many occasions, the company double-matched the funds. Larry sacrificed much when he went into the ministry. He was next in line for a CEO position, which would have become available within a year because the current CEO was about to retire. Larry used some of his 401k for Bible University. He had received a master's degree in theology. When Larry had subtracted his educational expenses, he was still in good financial shape, investing a sizable amount of his 401(k) into a municipal fund. In a few years, it had almost tripled. He kept reinvesting, and the money kept multiplying. So, money wasn't an issue for his trip. He justified it to himself by declaring he was due a vacation anyway.

The Logans told him, "She lives with a woman named Lynn Rothberg; she owns the dwelling at the address we gave you."

"I'll call to let her know I'm coming."

He wondered, however, how Summer would feel about it. He was about to find out because he made his reservations. The next day, Larry flew out to the city of the Golden Gate.

Summer had returned to her job at Glad Tidings this week. She was at work when Larry arrived at Lynn's. Lindy had told Lynn their plan, and Lynn agreed that Larry could reach Summer. She had offered to pick Larry up, but he rented a car, as he was staying at a hotel. He drove to Lynn's about 30 minutes before Summer arrived home. What was he going to say to her? The last thing this man wanted was to reprimand her. Instead, he prayed and asked God to give him the words. He told Lynn, "I've come to share my testimony. Summer had heard it many years ago, but I left out an event because I was too ashamed. This event was the most potent part of the testimony. It involves a violent incident I caused, similar to Earl's incident with Mike. I know Summer looks up to me, but she may change her mind after hearing my story. But God has convicted me that I've stayed silent about this for too long."

Lynn was admiring Larry and couldn't help but notice how devastatingly handsome he was. The woman was extremely moved by his message and was anxious to hear his story. First, however, she had to dismiss her thoughts of what a perfect match he would be for Summer after she had a proper mourning period.

Lynn never had an opportunity to prepare Summer for Larry's visit, so Summer was confused when she arrived home. She thought, *Why is Larry here?* The girl tried not to stare at him. She wanted to hide the attraction she felt for him out of respect for Mike's memory. How did this happen? She had forgotten her long ago prayer for Larry. Did God answer it after all? It didn't seem likely, as she was a new widow. Summer was confused, and Larry's presence made matters more confusing. But then, God had gotten her attention, letting her know she needed to listen to what Larry had to say. Larry greeted Summer, "Summer, so wonderful to see you." As devastated by her as he was before, he noticed her baby bump; he wasn't surprised. He was happy she had a living part of her husband. Finally, Summer replied. "It's good to see you too, but I don't' understand why you're here?"

"Your parents have confided in me of how concerned they are about some adverse feelings you're having about your husband's killer. You know revenge is never God's way."

"Lynn, did you fink on me?"

"Honey, please understand that your parents and I are concerned that you're hindering your relationship with God. Therefore, this vendetta is ungodly."

"Is wanting justice ungodly, Lynn? I just want justice!" Summer's unpleasantness was Larry's cue to address the matters at hand. And to come to Lynn's rescue.

"Summer, do you remember that day at Word of God when I gave my testimony?"

"Yes, Larry," she said. "I remember that day well. "

She was trying hard not to blush. Lynn noticed, though; she could tell there was strong chemistry between them.

Larry then regained command. "Summer, that day, I failed to mention an essential part of the story because it involved someone else, and I was humiliated. It concerned my brother's wife, who was his girlfriend at the time. I was heavily into drugs, and my mentality was obscured. There was no excuse for a dangerous incident that I caused, but at the time, I was afraid of going to jail. So, my brother Eric and his then-girlfriend, Cecelia Sparks, convinced me not to mention the incident when I gave my testimony, even though it was the most powerful part of the testimony.

"Eric had thrown me out of the house, administering tough love. I also was put on leave from my job, pending mandatory rehab. I had 60 days to admit myself, or I could be fired and lose all my benefits, including my rehab insurance. I lived in a three-bedroom house with 20 other people to pay less rent to afford my habit. I was losing, but I didn't care. I felt sorry for myself. I hurt over the losses of Trey, my parents, and the breakup of Eric and his girlfriend Trudy. She married someone else, but she was like a big sister to me.

"I resented how close Cecelia was becoming to Eric. Maybe I was jealous. I don't know, and it doesn't matter now. One night, I was broke and desperate for funding my habit. I knew Cecelia would be counting Eric's money, and I went to his office to rob him. Cecelia must have known because she was putting the money in the safe at that moment, and she locked the vault. Her quick thinking in protecting my brother's money angered me, and I pushed her hard. She hit her head on the corner of the coffee table. I saw blood seeping around her head. I called 911 and was about to leave the room when I heard Eric turn the doorknob. I hid in the closet. Eric attended to Cecelia immediately. The ambulance arrived to take Cecelia to the hospital. Eric followed the ambulance.

"I hated not knowing her condition. It was my wake-up call. I then called my job to arrange for my rehab. In ten more days, I would have been fired and couldn't have filed the claim. The losses I experienced due to this addiction make me shudder. I went to see Eric and told him what had happened and asked how Cecelia was. He said she was a little damaged but ok. What I said baffled him because Cecelia had told him she lost her balance and fell. Why on earth would she want to protect me? But Cecelia had the first-hand experience with addictions—her father, Jim, was an alcoholic. When he became free of his addiction, he founded the recovery ministry at his church. Cecelia introduced him to me, and I went to a camp that helped men with addictions. I don't know what I would have done without Jim. Rehab only solved this problem temporarily. After that, the desire for drugs would return. But Jim's ministry gave me a new lifestyle with Christ at the center. I lived at the camp for 90 days. I could've lived there longer, but my insurance didn't cover it. But it was enough. I then attended addiction recovery meetings every week at Word of God. God completely changed my heart and my life."

Summer was utterly dumbfounded. She could only wish this would change her feelings for him. She said, "But, Larry, you did the right thing and called for help. Earl couldn't care less."

"Do you know this, Summer? I think instead of predicting what Earl feels or felt; we should go talk to him."

Summer made a face as though Larry had lost his mind. "Larry, you have to be kidding! I'm not going to see him unless it's inside a courtroom for his conviction."

"Summer, as Christians, we have a responsibility to minister and show kindness to people like Earl. You know Matthew 6:14-15. God forgives you when you forgive others. If you don't forgive others, God won't forgive you. If you want forgiveness from God, then you have to forgive Earl."

"It's about justice. Earl stabbed Mike when he didn't have a weapon."

Lynn had to butt in. "Summer, I talked to Bill Blake. He wouldn't tell you this, but he witnessed what happened and said he honestly didn't feel Earl could have stood another blow from Mike. His face was completely black and blue. Bill also said if he were subpoenaed, he would take the fifth because he wasn't going to testify against Mike."

Summer began to cry. "It's my fault, all my fault. Earl tried to assault me a few months ago, and Mike thought he was protecting me. I should have been here. But, oh, why wasn't I here? Mike's dying words were to tell me he was sorry for messing things up." Summer then knew she had to go with Larry to visit Earl.

Chapter 8

When Larry and Summer arrived to visit Earl, an official told them. "Earl has attempted suicide; a guard found him attempting to hang himself with his shirt. He's been placed in solitary confinement for suicide watch." Then Larry said, "I am of the clergy, and I think given the circumstances he may want to see. me." The guard couldn't argue, but he was also fearful of Earl being pressured. The officer replied, "Only if Earl approves." The officer went to tell Earl about his visitors. "Earl, there's a preacher here to see you with someone named Summer." He was euphoric to learn it was Summer, although he felt she was here to vent her anger at him about her husband. But he didn't care. It was what he deserved. "Please," He replied. "Send them in." The guard learned he was wrong. He didn't expect that Earl would be pleased. Earl's long face then shined bright. The guard then escorted him to the visitor's booth.

Larry and Summer's wait was surprisingly short. Earl came to the inmate booth and told the guard, "Can I speak to Summer first." Earl and Summer picked up the phones to speak. She noticed the severity of his facial injuries, so she then knew it had been self-defense.

Earl began speaking first. His voice was choked up, and he was tearing up. "Summer, I can't tell how sorry I am about everything. I owed you my life, and then I go and kill your husband. I just don't want to go on anymore. I should have let Mike finish me off, and I knew he was protecting you."

"No, Earl, it's not right for you to feel like that. Mike wasn't himself. This man was never the Mike I knew. He was probably released from the hospital too soon. No one is to blame, Earl. You certainly aren't." She then motioned for Larry to come over. "Earl, this is Pastor Larry Calhoun, and he wants to tell you his testimony. I know this will give you a lot of comfort."

Larry then picked up the phone. "Hello, Earl," he said and began to tell his story.

When he had finished, Earl looked at him in total bewilderment. "I never in a million years would figure you would be a junkie!"

"Yes, Earl, I was no different than you. Jesus loves us unconditionally. I felt worthless after I hurt my brother's girlfriend; I also knew I was out of control. Give Jesus the wheel, Earl, and you'll see how more stable your life will be. I will be here for a couple of days. If you want me to, I can arrange for you to have counseling with Chaplain Neal Andrews."

Earl agreed to the chaplain's visit. Larry gave the chaplain his phone number and address for Earl to correspond with him. He told him, "Please keep me posted about Earl." Then, Summer spoke briefly to Chaplain Neal. Larry could tell that they knew each other, but Summer and the chaplain kept silent about the days of Diesel Hamilton. Larry didn't know Summer well enough to pry. He and Summer then left the jail.

Both Larry and Summer were hungry, and they went to The Cable Car Diner for lunch. Larry said, "Let's go in for some lunch." They ordered hamburgers, with everything on them (except Summer omitted the onions), and French fries. Larry asked, "Summer, how long have you lived here."

"Almost two years. I met Mike at Buffalo Springs Lake, and we flew out here together. Our first stop was San Mateo visiting Mike's parents."

"I've heard many good things about San Francisco. Maybe sometime when I can have more time off, you and Lynn can show me around." Summer's heart skipped a beat, and she immediately felt guilt. Then she admonished herself for having a big ego. *His asking doesn't mean he's interested.* She responded.

"Maybe so. It has beautiful sights." She told herself, *"I'm not worried he has no interest in me anyway."* Then Larry commented. "Penny for your thoughts" Summer's Insecure thoughts never let her think he was flirting with her.

"They're probably not worth that much."

"When is your baby due?" Summer felt shy telling Larry about the baby. She never talked much about her pregnancy; she knew he noticed. "Sometime in September." Larry saw how awkward Summer was being and wondered if it was because she had feelings for him. He knew there was a powerful chemistry between them at church on that Sunday. He also knew it took two to have chemistry.

Then Larry started thinking more about Summer's baby. A baby who's going to grow up and never know their father. It made him sad, and his sadness would always encourage him to tell jokes. So he began telling his favorite Pastor Joel Osteen jokes. "Summer, did you ever hear Joel Osteen tell jokes."

"I've heard of Joel Osteen, but I don't recall his jokes. Are they funny?"

"Let me demonstrate a couple of them." He began with the one about this man at a restaurant telling blond jokes. "There was a man at a restaurant sitting next to a blond lady. He asked her if she would like to hear a blond joke. She told him, 'Ok, but before you begin, you must understand that I'm a professional bodybuilder. The blond next to me is a professional wrestler, and the blond next to her is the kickboxing champion of the world. Do you still want to tell your joke!' 'Not if I have to explain it three times.'"

Larry was funny and knew how to tell jokes. He was like a standup comedian. She couldn't remember ever laughing this hard. He said another one about the little girl who asked about the origin people. "She asked her mother, and her mother told her about how God made Adam and Eve. Then she asked her father, and he told people are derived from monkeys. She went back to her mother, confused, repeating what her father said. Her mother then said. "Well, honey, he told you about his side of the family, and I told you about mine."' Larry went on and on telling one joke after another, and Summer was in tears. Larry was in love with Summer. He loved everything about her. He knew he had to give her an appropriate time to mourn Mike, but he was also afraid that someone else could win her heart since they were so far apart. But God would always remind him that all things had to be according to His will. If Summer was meant to be his, he didn't have to worry.

They were finished with lunch when Larry decided to leave the restaurant. It was challenging for Summer to contain her laughter. However, she pulled herself together, and she and Larry then began sightseeing.

After lunch, they walked around San Francisco. They ran into Angel, and Summer introduced them. "Angel, I want you to meet an old friend of mine from back home. Angel, meet Larry, Larry, Angel" Angel was curious about this man with Summer. He was dressed as an FBI informant, so Angel was skeptical and careful. Larry was highly impressed with Angel as he had never met a gang biker before. He could sense Angel's skepticism, then started speaking the same street lingo. "Bro!" Larry began, "What's up."

"Ok, Bro, maybe, the same as what's up with you! Where's your matches."

"You mean you for me, Bro!"

"Or, me for you." Summer then butted in and said, "Will somebody please speak English!" They all laughed. Angel had developed an immediate fondness for Larry. He thought he was cool. However, the biker did notice there was chemistry between him and Summer. Since Larry was closer to his age than Summer's, he felt he was too old for her. He also felt Summer was too vulnerable after losing Mike. Then Larry mentioned, "I'm enjoying the city, and I hate to leave. However, I do have to get back to Minion." "Summer's stomping grounds? I think she said it's in Texas. Is that right, Summer?"

"That's exactly right," Summer replied with humor in her voice. Angel could tell Summer was happier than she's been for a while. However, if Larry lives in Texas, he had the wrong idea.

Larry confessed, "We were at the courthouse earlier visiting Earl." Angel was staggered. What Larry said threw him for a loop. He was curious, why had they visited Earl? He thought maybe he should see Earl. They spoke a few more minutes then went their separate ways.

Lynn was waiting for Summer and Larry to return. She wasn't trying to meddle, but she could tell Larry and Summer had feelings for each other. The woman knew it was none of her business, except for her concern for Summer's vulnerability. She didn't know Larry, except he seemed like a wonderful person. She was impressed with his testimony. Summer had never talked about him, so she was curious about how they had met. She was going to ask Summer after Larry was back in Texas.

She heard the doorknob turning as they returned from visiting the jail. Summer and Larry were laughing. She saw that Larry was comedic funny; he knew how to tell jokes, and his hilarious facial features made the jokes even more comical. Lynn joined in the laughter. She didn't want to appear cruel, but she'd never seen this trait in Mike. Maybe it was because of the tragedy in his life.

It was so good to hear Summer's laughter. She hadn't heard Summer laugh much since she had known her. Larry also reminded her of her Harold, who also had a profound sense of humor. She admired Larry now. Yes, summer needed a mourning period before another relationship. However, the girl was too young to be alone for too long. And from what she could tell, she knew Larry would be compatible with Summer.

Summer went with Lynn to see Larry off on his flight. She never saw him on his last two days in the city, and she missed him. Larry had turned in his rental car the day before; because Lynn insisted on taking him to the airport. He didn't expect Summer to be with her. It was a pleasant surprise; he looked at them

SOUL WOUND

both. "I guess this is goodbye." And Summer felt an instant sadness as he was leaving for his boarding gate. He also thought he had left a big part of himself behind. He loved everything about Summer. The part he loved the most was hearing her laughter. He had strained his brain to keep thinking of jokes to keep her laughing. He would also miss Lynn.

He was so glad Summer had such a wonderful and caring friend. He was relieved Summer didn't hold his attack on Cecelia against him. He had feared it would come between them. Summer tried hard to conceal her feelings from him, and she did an excellent job of it. But the couple couldn't hide their chemistry, and the chemistry between the two of them was powerful.

Moreover, he knew he had to remind himself she needed time to mourn her husband. He would be inquiring about her from her parents. He gave her his phone number should she ever need him, and he had to confess he was hoping she would use it from time to time.

Lynn and Summer returned home after seeing Larry off. Lynn saw a familiar glow on Summer's face. Yes, she had the beautiful glow of a pregnant mother and combined with the glow of new love. She could tell Summer had it for Larry; it would just be a while before she admitted it.

Summer was unaware that she was smiling all the time. She was happier than she had been for a while. Yes, Mike made her happy and kept her fulfilled, but things were different with Larry. She loved the time they had spent together. The girl called him her mentor and tried to convince herself it was nothing more. Yet, she couldn't deny how much she missed Larry and the void she felt without him.

Angel finally persuaded someone at the San Francisco City Jail to allow him to visit Earl. It was Earl who gave consent. Earl was different and wasn't afraid anymore; he had Jesus now. He and Chaplain Neal said the sinner's prayer together. He was writing a letter to Larry, as he was so glad to have someone to communicate with. He stopped writing when the guard told him, "You have a visitor, Earl." He expected it to be Angel because the guard had gotten his consent. He just couldn't imagine what Angel wanted.

He saw Angel on the other side of the inmate booth and picked up the phone.

"How's it going, bro?" Angel asked.

It was an odd thing for Angel to say, as the two of them hadn't been in touch for a long time. Then, Earl decided to testify to Angel; he replied, "I have Jesus in my life now, and my life is going in a better direction. Have you ever thought of accepting him into your heart, Angel?"

Angel was experiencing some jealousy. Summer had gotten to Earl, and he wanted to answer *Yes, well, you know I heard this from Summer before you did.* But he knew that would sound petty, so he said instead, "Hey man, that's awesome. Summer got to you, huh?"

"Actually, no, it was Summer's preacher friend. Did you know he used to be a junkie? I was just writing him a letter."

Angel was flabbergasted. Never did he expect someone as strait-laced as Larry to be an addict. Earl had to be mistaken or lying—he *was* a pathological liar. "You are starting up with your lying again," Angel said. "No way was that straight man ever an addict."

Earl expected this of Angel and didn't argue. He only said, "Ok, Angel, have it your way."

Immediately, Angel knew a transformation had taken place in Earl. The Earl he knew would have argued with him nonstop. Angel was envious and wondered why Summer's friend hadn't offered salvation to him.

He cut his visit with Earl short and saw summer at her job because he stayed clear of the Avenues, where she now lived.

(Monica's parents lived there, and he tried to avoid running into them.) He liked Dr. Thomas and vice versa, so he knew seeing her at Glad Tidings wouldn't be a problem. However, he felt a sense of betrayal. He felt Earl was more favored than he was. He entered Glad Tidings and saw Summer behind the reception desk. The biker noticed she had a glowing smile. He was happy to see her but needed to get to the business at hand.

"Hey, Summer. What's up, baby girl?"

Summer was glad to see Angel and hugged him.

The hug only invited Angel's protest. "Yes, baby. you hug me, yet you don't share with me as you do with Earl." Summer saw the hurt expression on Angel's face. She then began praying herself out of hot water. Why on earth didn't she and Larry witness more thoroughly to Angel. God loves you was all they said to him. All she could do was apologize. "I'm so sorry, Angel. I know I was wrong."

Angel said, "No, Summer, you need to give this message to your preacher friend. Earl thinks the sun rises and sets on him. He's writing him letters. Why can't I be writing him letters?"

Summer was dumbfounded; she was also overwhelmed by Angel's curiosity about Jesus, yet Angel was impressed with Larry. Summer had wanted to limit her contact with Larry out of regard for Mike's memory. Finally, however, Summer promised Angel, "I'll contact Larry immediately. I know you have favor with him." Angel's dilemma meant she was going to have to contact him and let him know.

"Then I need to hear him say so," Angel said in slight hostility.

Angel gave Summer his number so Larry could reach him.

Larry had been home for a couple of days. He missed Summer severely. But the man knew he had to be patient and give her space. He knew she was off today. He wondered what her plans were? What things did she do, and where did she go on her day off? He was deep in thought when the phone rang, he answered, and to his complete surprise, it was Summer. "Summer! What a pleasant surprise." Mike was heavy on her mind, so she cut the conversation as brief as possible, getting down to the business at hand. He listened, "Larry, I'm afraid there's a problem. It seems Angel felt left out when he found out Earl is writing to you. Can you please fix it?"

"Oh, sure, I don't think that'll be a problem. Do you have Angel's phone number?"

"Yes, it's area code 415-677-7777. I have to go, Larry. I just needed to give you Angel's message." He didn't know what to make of Summer's abruptness. He sensed coldness and distance was in her voice. She knew he was only offering his friendship so that he could see a reason for this treatment. She seemed too defensive around him, and it hurt because she made him feel pushy when he was trying to be the opposite. But all he could do was pray and let God have it. At the moment, he needed to talk to Angel. So he dialed the number Summer gave him.

It rang a couple of times then Angel picked up. "Hello."

"Hello, Angel, my brother, how are you?"

Angel immediately began to vent "Bro" was all he could express. Larry immediately began appeasing Angel.

"Bro, I'm so sorry; I apologize for my unfairness. Please forgive me," Larry began, this soothed Angel, and he didn't give the admonishment speech that he rehearsed.

Angel said instead, "You know, bro, you can always make a trip back to the Bay City, and I will buy your dinner. I can even cover your flight and expenses."

Of course, Larry knew Angel's money wasn't legal, and he could never accept his favor. "You know, bro, I just got back to my congregation, so I need to stay put for a while, but write me, man. I promise to write back. I'll give you my phone number too. So let's, please, stay in touch."

They wrapped up the call and said their goodbyes. Angel felt much better and less hurt. He'd made a new friend who was different from those he was used to hanging out with, but it was a friendship Angel treasured for some reason.

Summer was in severe mourning. Keeping busy helped some, but the pain wouldn't go away. She mentioned this to Dr. Thomas. "Dr. Thomas, I hurt all the time for Mike. Some days I want to give up. I don't feel I have any purpose."

He told her, "Try helping others is comforting. You'll find it's what we are designed to do. Sarah can give you a list of ministries that you can volunteer for."

"Thank you, Pastor Thomas. I'm going right now to look them over." Sarah went over the list.

"This one is an inner-city program to keep children from joining gangs. Children seem to become gang members at earlier ages."

"Yes," Summer retorted. "I'm going to give this one a try. I love children, and I hope I can make a difference for them."

Sarah expressed, "I'm so glad you made this choice, too many avoid it, and the ones who respond don't participate. It's like they're not there." This choice gave Summer an incredible feeling of accomplishment.

The church had a high-energized rally every other Saturday morning. They had incentives and received rewards for an average grade point, higher rewards for a higher grade point. The alternate Saturday mornings were for recruiting children to attend. They not only recruited new children, but they also made sure the children in attendance stayed involved. It was successful, as the children loved modern and high-energized praise music. They loved dancing, praising, and worshipping.

They performed dramas based on the popular TV western *Gunsmoke*. They had a Marshall named Marshall Bob and a deputy named Deputy Dan. They called the town Dodge Town instead of Dodge City. They had terrible villains; the children booed them. The skit began, "Howdy Marshall Bob. How are things?"

"Not good, Deputy Dan, that villain Bad Barney is harassing the city folks again, and I can't seem to catch him in the act." Some of these skits were serial skits. It may take weeks to catch Bad Barney in the act so Marshall Bob could arrest him. They would always use this analogy, showing how people think they're getting away with their sin because they don't get caught. God sees our sins, we don't get away with them, and He always catches us in the act

Marshall Bob and Deputy Dan also had powerful testimonies about their villain days. Then they saw the sinister villains accept Jesus into their hearts. Marshall Bob stated, "Deputy Dan, it was wonderful to see Bad Barney's brother Lester accept Jesus into his heart."

"Yes, I hope he ministers to his brother because Bad Barney can sure use a taste of Jesus."

"I don't know about you, Deputy Dan, but I was once a scoundrel just like Bad Barney. No, I never broke any laws, but I broke many of God's laws. So it's never fun being in trouble with Him."

"Wow, Marshall Bob, maybe you can be the one who can reach Bad Barney."

"Maybe so; Jesus is the one who saves. I'm just a tool."

And that's how the skits would end. The children are coming each week hoping to see Bad Barney get caught in the act or see him saved.

Summer was amazed to see tears pouring out of the eyes of these hardened children. There was a nine-year-old African American child who had a significant crush on Summer. His name was Traye Washington. All the children adored Summer; she was as energized as they were. This ministry was Summer's greatest source of comfort. Many of the young boys crushed on Summer, but none like Traye. Summer was sensitive to him since she was once a child crushing on an adult. Yes, this was another reminder of Larry. It seemed at every turn; there was a reminder of him.

Earl's court date was coming due in a week. He couldn't afford an attorney, but Public Defender Jake Grey was assigned to him; he was determined to get him off on self-defense. He was tall, with a medium build, green eyes, and striking features. The DA, Mark Stevens, was a middle-aged, heavyset-man This D.A. was ready to throw the book at Earl.

He met with Earl's attorney to discuss a plea bargain. Jake began. "You know Mark; this is a case of self-defense. You saw Earl's pictures after his assault."

"The man was standing over the victim with a deadly weapon. There wasn't a weapon in the victim's hand. So it's not self-defense!"

Jake took an envelope out of his shirt pocket. "Summer Hanley, the victim's wife, gave me this letter. Would you care to read it?"

"Mark took the envelope and began reading."

Dear Mr. Stevens,

I'm Mike Hanley's wife, and I want to plead with you to please not prosecute Earl. My husband had anger problems, and I don't want to see him exploited. I don't want this matter to go to court and become public. I want my husband's memory to have dignity

Mike had a mental disorder; please let him rest in peace. I know this is what my husband would want. He wasn't himself when he attacked Earl.

Please answer my plea. I thank you very much.

Truly
Summer Hanley

So, Stevens went to the judge. "I received a letter from the victim's wife. A plea to keep her husband's dignity." Earl and his attorney were present. He handed the letter to the judge. The judge replied, "It would serve no purpose to have a murder trial.

We don't want this woman or anyone else to be hurt. Also, I don't think Earl's actions were intentional. He, at the time, was assaulted himself. However, illegal drugs were found on him, and I want him to be committed to a rehab center. I also want him to do 500 community service hours. He can do both at the Rescue Mission."

Earl thanked God. He didn't feel he deserved a second chance, but he was grateful for it. So, Earl walked out of San Francisco County Jail a free man in more ways than one.

Angel learned Earl was out of jail. He was annoyed at his newfound relationship with Summer and her preacher friend. He found himself writing to Larry about two or three times a week. This venture was like a competition for him. He was determined to be the favored one. It was as though he wanted Earl to stay in his bondage because his bondage wasn't the threat; Earl's new alteration was. If only Angel knew the same transformation could be his just for the asking. He also couldn't see that it was Jesus who had made these changes in Earl. Earl did, God opened his eyes, and he knew he had a lot of praying to do for Angel.

Larry was in Minion, and he tried to keep from constantly asking Summer's parents about how she was doing. He cared about her and, at times, wished she would leave San Francisco. Larry loved the city but knew the dangers. He also knew he had to trust God because he had to give her space. So, this pastor wouldn't impose his worries on her yet. However, he had made up his mind about a future for them. He never had feelings for anyone like he had for her. Though she wouldn't admit it, he could also tell that she shared the same mutual feelings. He wanted it to be as soon as possible because Mary Franklin had expressed her devout interest in him. He was trying to spare her feelings, a problem Larry could solve if he was claimed.

Summer was getting ready to retire for the night. She was about six-and-half months along in her pregnancy. She had the sonogram, and her doctor and staff knew the gender of the baby.

However, to Summer, knowing the gender was like opening a package before Christmas. So, she told the clinic staff she would wait until delivery and be surprised. The staff told her to call and ask for Candy anytime she wanted to know.

She was in bed fluffing her pillow, trying to be comfortable, then the baby moved with tremendous force. Summer just laughed and said, "You must be a boy because you can definitely be a football player." She then got comfortable and went to sleep.

Chapter 9

At 3 a.m., Summer was up screaming and holding her stomach. Lynn immediately responded and saw that Summer's breathing was shallow, and she was becoming pale. She called. "911, what's your emergency."

"Please send help fast. I have a young pregnant girl here who's barely breathing and crying out in severe pain."

"I have someone on the way. Is 3020 4th Avenue your address?"

"Yes, and please hurry. She's barely holding on."

Summer was sweating profusely. She let out screams of pain. Lynn became frightened and concerned. She began to pray, holding Summer's hand, speaking to her gently, saying, "Hold on, my sweet girl. You're going to be ok. Please, Dear God, let her be ok. Please spare her and her baby."

Alarmed, Summer cried out, "My baby, oh my baby."

Lynn saw a look of fright on Summer's face and immediately offered comfort, saying, "Your baby is going to be ok too, honey. Just hang on, baby; it's going to be alright. God will take care of this." Lynn was praying, but she was unsure of her confidence. "Please, Father God, give me the faith I need for You to help Summer and her baby."

The ambulance sirens sounded, and the EMTs were inside attending to Summer, applying oxygen, and loading her onto a gurney. Summer had passed out. They moved swiftly, and the ambulance took Summer to Mount Zion Hospital. Lynn immediately called Kevin and Lindy from her cell phone. Afterward, she called the Hanleys.

It was almost 6 a.m. when the phone rang. Lindy was already alarmed. Kevin answered, "Yes, Lynn, is Summer ok?"

"I don't know what's wrong, but she's been taken to Mount Zion hospital in an ambulance. Please try to take the fastest flight out here." and when he turned to Lindy, she already knew, "We have to have to take the next flight to San Francisco. Right?"

"Yes, and I'm calling Pastor Larry; we need all the prayer we can get."

Larry said, "Of course I'll pray." He was shaken up but trying not to sound too alarmed. Kevin and Lindy needed him, and he had to keep it together. Larry was trying not to be obvious; he had to go and be near Summer. "Kevin, I would like to go with you. I can lend spiritual support."

"No, we would love for you to come; your offer is far too generous. You have a congregation to take care of."

"When I visited Summer a short while ago, I found a have a couple of sheep in San Francisco, and they'll need me. So, I can leave the ninety-nine. My associate pastor can take over for me." Larry felt desperate to see Summer, so he had to convince Kevin that he needed to go.

"I will be so relieved for you to go; I need all of the God that I can take with me. I need Summer to be ok."

"Me too," Larry confessed, and he said to Kevin in his head, *"More than you know Kevin, more than you know."*

"Ok, then, I'll book a flight for all four of us."

"Thank you so much, Kevin; just let me know what my share is to pay you back."

"Larry, you helped Summer out a few weeks ago. Let me compensate you for this one."

"I'll take a rain check this time, but when I'm in dire need, I'll let you know. I can't take advantage of you now." Kevin didn't argue. He got off the phone and called the airport.

Larry called pastor Jeremy Collins to fill in for him. Kevin was glad Larry was going because he needed the support of his

Pastor in this trying time. But, little did Kevin know; it was also a trying time for Larry.

Kevin booked a flight for all four of them. They also booked hotel reservations close to the airport. It was a suite with two separate rooms—a room for the Logans and Larry. Larry prayed and expressed to the Lord his concern for Summer. He prayed harder than he ever prayed in his life. It was a long flight for them all. Autumn prayed too, she didn't have her salvation, but she knew she had nowhere else to turn but to God, for Summer. Autumn thought about how mean and spiteful she had been. It seemed so important to her to make it up to Summer. She didn't want to lose her sister or her niece or nephew. *She prayed Please, Dear God, I need for you to spare my sister. She's been the best, and I can't bear to lose her or her baby. I want to know this baby, and I want this baby to know me.* They landed at San Francisco International, went to their hotel rooms to unload their luggage, then went to the hospital.

Lynn had called Dr. Thomas, and he arrived at the hospital swiftly. He went right to Kevin, Lindy, Autumn, and Larry exclaiming. "I know these times are challenging, yet, it's so important to remain faithful and always put God first the way Abraham did." Kevin thought about the sacrifice Abraham made. He was giving up his only child. The bright side to Abraham's sacrifice was that the angel of God intervened, and Isaac was spared. It gave him optimism that God would also spare Summer. Pastor Thomas had prayed with them all.

He could see faith wasn't a problem for Lindy, as she showed a strong determination in her prayers. That gave him hope because he knew the power of a mother's prayers. He recalled the many dangers his mother had prayed for his safety.

Word spread to Angel about Summer being in the hospital in critical condition; he wasted no time and was there before anyone knew it. When he arrived in the waiting room, Larry greeted him warmly. "It's so good to see you, Angel. How did you know?"

"Word about anyone I feel close to spreads like wildfire to me. I have to be with little sis."

Kevin couldn't hear them but stared at the two. He couldn't get used to seeing Angel's gaudy biker attire, but he tried not to judge. After all, he must be one of the sheep Larry spoke about, and the man was here because he cared about Summer. That counted a lot with Kevin. Larry then introduced the two. "Kevin, I would like you to meet Angel. Angel, Kevin." Kevin gave Angel a warm and firm handshake. Larry had mentioned to Angel, "I don't think anyone told Earl. Earl would want to know." Angel offered, "I'll make a call, and the word will get to Earl and in no time." Angel went out of the room holding his cell phone, about to punch in his number.

Earl was on the phone with Angel's contact. "Thank you, man, for sharing this information; I'll try to be there as soon as I can." Earl was under strict supervision at the Rescue Mission, so he needed consent to visit Summer in the hospital. He also had to have an escort. So he went to get permission from Pastor James Marvin, the head of the Mission. "Sure, Earl, I'll take you to visit Summer."

"I hope it's not putting you out; I think one of the volunteers may be free to take me."

"Nonsense, Earl, I pray that Summer will be ok. She's a faithful young lady. She's always been here for you. So you have to be there for her."

"Thank you so much, Pastor Marvin; I not only want to be there for Summer, I have to be there for her."

Earl was saddened to hear about Summer. He was happy he could be there for her. The man was new to the caring game; he had never cared about anyone but himself. Earl had formed few attachments throughout his life. He had been a loner. His prayer was that the heavenly being that had once protected her from him would be with her now. He also knew Mike's parents would be there. He was apprehensive about seeing them because of Mike's death.

The Hanleys were there. This couple was praying so hard, asking for the faith of Job because it seemed their losses were so many. Summer was like their daughter. She would visit them at least once a week. And then there was their only grandchild. Susan sobbed and kept saying, "Gerald, we've lost so much. When will it end? "Gerald tried to comfort her, but it seemed pointless. It was a long and tiresome time. They wished Summer had asked to know the gender. Knowing this seemed important to them now. The truth was, no matter the gender, the pain would be the same. First, they lost a daughter and then their son, so it shouldn't matter.

The attending physician was Dr. Edward Giles, a tall, slim man in his forties. He called the family together to explain what had happened to Summer. "When Summer came, she was having premature labor pain, but we managed to get those under control. Unfortunately, her blood pressure is extremely elevated, and we're now working on getting that under control. Her symptoms appear to show signs of preeclampsia, and her condition is very critical."

After hearing the doctor's news, Larry knew Summer was in critical condition. He prayed and wondered, should he even be pursuing Summer. Had he ever prayed about what God wanted? Was this another wake-up call, and was God trying to get his attention? Larry had to reflect on the answers to these questions. He only wondered if Summer wasn't a part of God's plan, how could he ever overcome the sadness?

The Logans, Lynn, and the Hanleys sat together on one side. Across from them were Larry, Angel, and Earl, escorted by Pastor Marvin. Although the Hanleys looked at Earl, they tried not to have animosity in their heart, even though they knew the fault lay in Mike's illness. They just had to pray about Earl being there because seeing him was painful.

The waiting seemed so long and drawn out, they were all praying for a complete recovery, and they also knew this would take time. If Summer survived, she could be on bed rest for the remainder of her pregnancy. Lynn was willing to take care of her. As long as she survived, nothing else mattered. Dr. Thomas had left after praying with the family. He gave Kevin his card with his contact information and said, "if anyone needs anything, please have them call my office, and I will be here as soon as I possibly can. The church congregation adores Summer, Glad Tidings, and most churches in the area are praying for her." Kevin thanked Pastor Thomas.

Summer was entering a gate, then noticed the greenest scenery she had ever seen. She looked and saw Mike, and a beautiful teenaged girl was with him. She was beautiful, tall with a fair, perfect complexion. The girl also had dark hair, auburn highlights, and emerald green eyes. She determined the girl was Ruby, who would be almost 16 years old. She resembled the picture she had seen at the Hanley's house. She decided that Mike had incredible peace and joy, seeing his sister and being with her again. Summer asked him, "Mike is that Ruby?"

Mike approached Summer quickly and embraced her. She was glad to see him but sad to leave everyone else, especially Larry. "Mike, I have missed you." Then asked again, "Is that girl you were with, Ruby?"

"Yes, Summer, it is."

"It gives me such comfort to know that the two of you are finally together."

"It is joyful for me to be with her. This place is so joyous and peaceful, Summer; you are here because I have a message for you." Summer couldn't imagine a message from God, no doubt. She was excited yet also afraid.

Mike began by Saying, "Summer, I have a window to look out on the earth. I was sad; I couldn't reach you when you were suffering and having animosity toward Earl. And when you finally forgave him, I was so proud of you. I don't have a lot of memories of being on the Earth; I do remember how wrong I was to harm Earl."

"It would have helped to know that it makes me feel more ashamed."

"Don't accept God's forgiveness. I am happy here, Summer. I didn't want to leave the earth, but now I never want to leave here. My life is here, and yours is on the earth. So please, do what makes you happy." She was surprised, wondering if he knew about Larry. Mike said, "Summer, I know I wasn't your first love." She'd never thought of it before, but Larry was her first love. Suddenly Summer embraced Mike, apologizing for her feelings. "I'm so sorry I want to be faithful to you. I'm not letting anything interfere with that."

Mike said, "Summer, you don't have to apologize for anything. I appreciate your loyalty, but this loyalty to me doesn't mean you can't love someone else." Summer was surprised, as she thought Mike would want her faithfulness. Mike continued, "Things are different here. I don't hold to the sentimentality of the earth anymore. In my window, I saw you with your first love. A wonderful man, I saw how he helped you overcome the bitterness you held against Earl. I was an extremely jealous man when I was on the Earth, but things are different here. I'll always love you, but my message for you is that you have to move forward with your life. Being with this man is fulfilling God's destiny."

"Oh, Mike, I can't betray you!"

"It's not betrayal anymore, Summer. Please understand the transformation I encountered when I arrived. Ruby told me how sad she was when she observed me from her window; she hated her death tormented me. I wouldn't have been having known she was in a more peaceful place. Summer, I don't want you to torment yourself either because I am happier here than I ever was on the earth, and I don't want to return to the earth after being here." He told Summer, "I love you and always will, but my love is different now. There's not a place for egos here; I accept that Larry is your first love. However, honey, you have to move forward and let go of us." These words immediately set Summer free. She let go of her feelings of apprehension for Larry and accepted the feelings of love she had for him. She couldn't wait to tell him.

Summer asked Mike, "Could I please meet Ruby?"

"You could if you were going to stay here, but God still has a purpose for you on the earth. Still, I will ask His consent."

He prayed, requesting God's consent. "Father, I fulfilled the purpose for Summer, but she requests to meet Ruby. I come to ask you to grant it humbly." He looked at Summer, stating, "He's given his consent." Instantly Ruby appeared, Mike introduced them. "Ruby, this is Summer. Summer, this is Ruby." They talked briefly, each saying to the other, "How beautiful you are." Summer added, "Ruby, you are so radiant, and so is Mike. The illumination here so much brighter." God allowed these extremely brief encounters. And as fast as she arrived, Ruby was gone.

Mike then walked Summer back to the gate. He told her, "Please give my love to our daughter." Summer was sad, and she knew then how different things were. He said "our daughter," and not number "three," as he stated before. However, she had to ask. "How did you know it's a girl? I didn't even know that." He said, "Things here are hard to explain. I've known about her since I've been here," Then he and Summer had one final embrace.

The doctors saw the rhythm on Summer's heart monitor fading fast. The cardiac team was standing by. Summer's face turned blue. The rhythm went from fast atrial fibrillation to a flat line. Immediately, the cardiac team applied resuscitation. They made several attempts but had to give up. The plan now was to save the baby. Before they could execute this plan, they heard the heart monitor return to a normal rhythm. The color returned to Summer's face. It was an amazing miracle witnessed by the entire medical team. The doctor did a complete examination and found Summer and her child's complications had disappeared, and they were completely normal. Dr. Giles came in with a puzzled look on his face and gave the news to the family. He said,

"I've never witnessed such a miracle; I would call anyone else a liar if they described what I witnessed. I've never been a believer, but after witnessing this girl's return from death, I have to believe" After Larry heard this, bargained with God to stay away from Summer until Larry heard from Him. It was the hardest decision for him to make, but he had to keep it.

Earl attempted to hug Angel. Then Angel gave Earl a funny "you better not" look, then extended his hand for a handshake. Earl then extended his hand. Larry observed the two and immediately came between them. "Come on, you guys," he first hugged Angel, then Earl. He told them, "Real men can hug each other." Angel and Earl hugged, and then Larry joined in a group hug. Larry then asked, "what did that hurt? Let's 'all join hands and give thanks for Summer's recovery." They joined hands, and Angel could see a difference in Earl. He wanted what all of them had; life was too short for one not actually to know his destination. Kevin then asked the doctor, "When can we see my little girl?"

"You can all visit two at a time, except for Summer's immediate family; all three of them can visit."

The Logans went on in. Summer's color was normal. Autumn broke down and cried, telling Summer, "Summer, I am so sorry for being such a bad sister. I talked to God. I promised Him; things will be different, I promise you too, they will be." She was embracing Summer, who woke up slightly and returned Autumn's embrace. Kevin and Lindy joined in the embrace. They felt extreme joy seeing this beautiful union between their daughters. Their visit was brief, and it was time for the next visitors.

The Hanleys went in next; since Lynn was by herself, Dr. Giles let her visit with them. Susan stroked Summer's hair and part of her face. "Summer, honey, I was thinking about the time I first met you. You captured my heart, sweetie, even then. I know things weren't easy, and Mike and Gerald fought all the time. After we lost Mike, you never forgot us. You have been the most wonderful daughter-in-law. "My daughter.'" She didn't mention her thoughts of Earl, who was just outside waiting to see Summer too. She was in deep pain and had to ask God's help; to forgive him. However, she thanked God for another chance with Summer and their precious grandchild.

Gerald just stood over Summer and said some prayers. "Father God, thank you for this miracle healing for our precious daughter." He and Susan stepped aside for Lynn, and Lynn spoke to Summer in a soft voice." "My sweetie, I'm so glad you're ok; I need you so much." In less than a whisper, summer looked at Lynn and said, "you saved my life, thank you." She was in and out of consciousness, so she was aware of all her visitors. The one she anticipated the most was Larry. She planned on telling him everything she felt if she could only be alert long enough.

Angel and Earl stepped out of the way for Larry to visit her, "no thanks, guys, I'll wait for you two." He wanted to be last, to have a final look. Yes, he would see her when she came to visit her parents in Minion, but this could be a farewell to his dream. Even if it was torture, he had to see her; he had to see for himself that she was ok. He watched as the Hanleys and Lynn came out, then Angel and Earl went in. Pastor Marvin told Earl, "After your visit, we have to go back to the Mission." Pastor Marvin waited and decided not to visit. He was just happy she recovered.

Angel jokingly told her, "Baby girl, you can't do old Angel this way. I'm not as young as I used to be."

Summer gave him a big smile.

Then Earl said, "You know, Summer, there are things I have never mentioned; I will never forget the Heavenly being who frightened me away that day. I was so ashamed of what I tried to do. But I know he is always with you, and he's the reason you are here now."

Summer wanted to tell them the whole purpose of this hospital visit, bout being in heaven to visit Mike and Ruby. She felt she needed to conserve her energy, to tell this to Larry, and declare the love the girl's had for him since she was 12 years old. Their time was up, and now it was Larry's turn to visit.

Angel and Earl left and returned to the Mission with Pastor Marvin. Pastor Marvin and Earl left in the Mission Van, and Angel followed behind on his Harley.

When Larry walked in, Summer was fully alert yet, somewhat weak. She looked so beautiful—no makeup, with her hair a total mess, yet, completely beautiful. He almost wished he hadn't come. Seeing her looking so angelic deepened his pain. Only he was here for her. He was surprised when he heard her speak.

"We'll have to skip the small talk, Larry; I don't know how much strength I have. I have treated you terribly."

Larry tried to comment, but Summer gently put her fingers to his mouth to silence him.

"Don't be kind, Larry. I was rude to you. I went away for a while, and I saw Mike and Ruby."

Larry then spoke, holding back his tears, "I am so sorry about Mike, Summer. I don't think I ever really expressed this to you. I am so glad you are ok."

Summer felt some of her strength leaving and decided to declare her feelings. Abruptly she began, "Larry, I love you, and I have since I was 12 years old. I can't keep it inside anymore. I love you so much and so deeply."

Larry was ecstatically happy and about to forget his promise. Summer saw a beaming look on his face, and it thrilled her. Then she looked at him one more time as she rapidly fell asleep again. Larry was holding Summer's hand and then couldn't recall who initiated it. Larry knew what he would have to do, but since Summer was weak yet, he would stay by her side for now. It didn't seem fair, as this was what the man had anticipated. He then asked the Lord to please answer him speedily. He stayed and held her hand throughout the entire visit. Then the time was up. Larry yearned to stay with her a bit longer, yet, he couldn't stay because holding her hand told him he couldn't hide his feelings from her. He just had to leave to see Jim Sparks, his spiritual father. He had to find out what to do next.

Visitation was over, so Larry walked out. He overheard Kevin talking to Lindy.

"You know," Kevin said, "this was a living hell for me, yet, you seemed to have everything under control. So what's your secret?"

"Being a mother, I guess I don't have time to fret. It's hard to pray and fret. So I chose to pray, and God gave me his assurance that Summer would be okay."

"Well, instead of going through all this hell, I should have consulted you."

"You certainly should have," Lindy stated emphatically.

Larry then realized the corporate prayers of everyone had caused Summer's miracle. Not only here, but all the churches and the online requests. He began to believe; Summer was meant to be healed. Maybe he didn't have to make his bargain. Yet, he already had, and he was desperate to hear from God.

Everyone left the hospital. Then Larry and the Logans returned to the hotel, and Larry announced, "I have to leave and go back to Minion." He did not explain, and the Logans were baffled. "However, before I leave," he gave Kevin an envelope. "It's for Summer's baby." Kevin didn't ask questions; Larry may have been called home for a confidential matter with a church member. He said, "Ok, Larry, thank you so much for your love and support." Larry then went to his room and packed. He was gone to the Airport in a matter of minutes.

Lynn had previously contacted the Logans about giving Summer a baby shower. Lynn preplanned the shower before Summer was in the hospital. She called Larry in Minion and told him about it. The following day, everyone except Larry was told Summer would leave ICU and go to a room, probably only for a day. The shower is why Larry already had the gift. The shower would be a surprise on the day she returned home from the hospital. Lindy told Lynn, "Larry had left abruptly last night; I don't know why."

"I hope everything is ok with him and Summer?" Lynn replied back

"Aren't things ok with them?" Lindy asked suspiciously

"Sometimes I think there is, but I don't know for sure. I can tell they're happy with each other."

"Or maybe you're a matchmaker."

"Maybe so!" then two changed to Summer's shower plans.

Kevin had previously asked Dr. Giles' consent to have Summer's baby shower. The doctor said, "I think this will be the best medicine for Summer."

Everyone was preparing for her shower. Dr. Thomas and all the staff who worked with Summer would be there. They knew Summer had her life insurance claim. So, the staff and I took up a collection for Summer to have severance pay. Dr. Thomas exclaimed, "This policy should be for Summer's future, for her child, or emergency expenses. She has proved to be a valuable worker, and this was our gift for her." All the guests applauded.

Kevin, Lindy, and Autumn bought a crib, baby chest, bassinet, and plenty of baby clothes. Autumn had babysitting money, and she gave it to her parents as a contribution to her share. The bassinet was considered her gift. They chose yellow and other neutral colors, as no one knew the child's gender. Lynn purchased a baby swing and a rocking chair for Summer. She also made sure the baby had many boxes of disposable diapers. There were going to be many attendees at the shower, and many would also give disposable diapers. Everyone met every baby's need, and now they just had to wait for Summer.

Kevin picked her up from the hospital. Since it was a shower, mostly women were in attendance. Angel and Earl left their gifts, which were a beautiful walnut high chair and bibs. Lindy, Lynn, and Susan stood back, looked, and Lynn mentioned, "What a wonderful start for a blessed child." Gerald and

Susan bought many gifts. They also put a sizable down payment on the house next door to Lynn. They wanted Summer to have Mike's savings for other expenses. Lynn wouldn't accept any house payments from Summer until the baby, and she had a more stable financial security. All of Summer's income would go for the baby, plus other household expenses.

Summer was eager to go home; she should probably be restless or anxious about her close call. However, to Summer, this was a blessed hospital stay. She had seen Mike again and met Ruby. She knew she was never in jeopardy. Summer now put life her life into perspective. She was free for Larry. Her heart was free. She would always miss Mike, and they had a whole life together. Moreover, she was now ready to fulfill a destiny.

She had prayed for Larry when she was 12. It was a moving and heartfelt prayer. She knew when "you have not, because you ask not." But she had asked, she could see, that she and Larry would have a future. She was daydreaming about their future; she hoped he was coming with her father to pick her up.

Yes, in ICU, she recalled taking Larry's hand; she fell asleep briefly and woke up in short intervals, with Larry still holding her hand. All the feelings of love within her were powerful enough to charge up electricity for Minion. She had everything packed, and Kevin had just arrived, but not Larry. Then Kevin hugged Summer and helped gather up her belongings. He and Lindy had taken almost everything to Lynn's house last night to save time today.

Summer had noticed Larry didn't visit last night either; only she just thought he had a reason. She still had to ask her father, "where's Larry?"

"He must've had an emergency of some kind because he left to go home."

"*Left to go home,*" Summer thought, repeating her father's words. *But Why? Was I too free with my feelings? Did I scare him away?* Summer was trying hard to hide her hurt feelings. No one knew she had feelings for Larry, which made matters worse because she couldn't confide in anyone. No one but the Lord. *Why, Lord, has this happened? He was holding my hand. Did I mistake his intentions? Did I assume our feelings were mutual? She felt so foolish now that she thought, "why would Mike push us to have a relationship?* "too many things didn't add up. She knew God had the answers, and she wanted the answers. She then went with her father to Lynn's house.

Summer wondered how Lynn's house contained all the people who had gathered there. There was Dr. and Mrs. Thomas, all the women from Rebel Freedom, the female leaders of the Saturday morning Pre-gang rallies, many other church members, and her family. She exclaimed, "Wow, what a crowd. I'm overwhelmed." Tears of gratitude were in her eyes. And she saw more baby furnishings and necessities than she could imagine. There seemed to be enough diapers for the child's entire infancy. Then Susan, Gerald, and Lynn called her over, holding up keys" Lynn then said, "These are to your house."

"No, she cried. This kindness is way too generous." Then Lynn told her, "I've decided that you won't have to make a house payment until you have a steadier income."

"Lynn, that could be for a good while. It will be some time before the doctor releases me to go back to work."

"Please, honey, don't worry about these things. I won't put you under any pressure, so please don't pressure yourself." Lynn had thought there wasn't any hurry for her to move, and she preferred that she lived with her until the child was old enough to sleep through the night. In addition, she wanted to help with the child since Mike couldn't.

Summer was so stunned; it was such an abundant blessing. However, before they took her over to look at the house, Kevin gave her the envelope from Larry.

Kevin commented, "Honey, Larry left this for you." At first, she thought it was a goodbye note. Then she saw the words "Summer's baby" and knew it was a baby gift. Probably a tiny check or gift card. Though when she opened it, to her surprise, it was a small booklet with an entry of a large sum of money. It stated it was a trust fund with a payment for the child's educational account. Summer would have never guessed Larry could have this much money, let alone part with it. It should've confused her, but she knew Larry wouldn't have given a gift like this if he had thought of her casually. Summer knew he had to be in love with her. Yet, he was still gone, and she didn't understand. So again, she turned to God, praying and still seeking answers.

She headed next door to take a look at her and the baby's new house.

Chapter 10

Larry was at his spiritual father, Jim Sparks' house, who lived in Lubbock. Jim and his wife Beverly lived in the same place during Cecelia and her two brothers. A small, modest, three-bedroom, two-bath home. Jim was tall with a slim build, light brown hair, and hazel-colored eyes. He was extremely handsome. Beverly was petite, though somewhat heavyset, and had blonde-brownish hair and blue eyes, and she had attractive features. Jim was keeping Larry stable. Larry had a spiritual dilemma; he was in love with Summer Logan Hanley. The man felt his feelings were selfish. Thus, Larry was awaiting God's Word on this relationship. He was willing to accept whatever answer God had, even if it meant a permanent separation. The pastor thought, *What was it like for Abraham when this father went to sacrifice Isaac?* Because Larry felt he was placing Summer on that same altar. However, he had to show God He was number one in his heart, the way Abraham had to at the time. He was glad Jim was with him to keep him from despair.

He wondered what Summer must've thought. Did she feel pain and rejection? Did she think I abandoned her? But, on the other hand, she had given him her complete heart, so she had to feel she made a fool out of herself. Then he recalled she said she saw Mike and his sister. He knew this bore a considerable significance, and he prayed it would be part of this revelation. If not, he hoped maybe he could ask Summer about it. He anticipated a "yes" answer from God.

Summer tried to pick up the pieces of her broken heart. It was Saturday morning, and she was meeting with Gladys Miller to recruit some children to attend the Saturday morning rallies. "Are you ready to go, Summer?" Gladys asked

"Yes, mam," Summer fired back. "More than ready." These Saturday mornings' volunteer work took Summer's mind off Larry and any other problems she had.

They kept track of all the children in attendance. She was looking forward to seeing little Traye. The little boy was so energetic, and he kept her energized. She had met his grandmother, Brenda, a small, African American woman. She was still young, about her late 40s, and looked somewhat haggard for her age. Years of strife and pain had shown on her face. She was rearing, Traye and his older brother. There was no mention of his mother, so Summer was unfamiliar with that situation. She wondered, however, if she were living or dead. Gladys and Summer were arriving when they saw Traye's grandmother. She looked as though she had been crying. Summer knew right away, something was tragically wrong, and she dreaded finding out what it was.

Angel and Earl stayed in constant contact with each other, Angel hadn't officially left his gang, but he didn't spend much time with them either. He attended Glad Tidings on Sundays and Wednesday nights. He even participated in Rebel Freedom's group sessions. Earl had participated in these events too; all the Rescue Mission men did. But instead of *Rebel Freedom*, he attended the *Freedom from Addictions* class. He worshiped with Angel on Sunday mornings.

Last Sunday, Angel attended with his wife, Monica. Earl noticed Angel was different; he seemed calmer and possessed kindness for other people. Even Monica seemed different. Earl remembered the shame he felt, for once lusting, for Monica. Then Jesus reminded him, his past was behind him, and this man needed to leave his indignity behind as well. He stayed amazed by the God of second chances and many chances.

Alfred was becoming concerned for Angel. It wasn't his nature to be as neglectful with his activity. But, he was slowly seeing Angel's decline. For months now, he was ordering the drug runs and recruiting new customers. In the beginning, he felt honored that Angel had such confidence in him. But, he also noticed changes taking place in Angel, and Alfred realized the gang life was no longer holding Angel's interest. Alfred thought, *How could this be? This biker is a man with a lifetime of gang activity. What is his other interest? Does it have more pay and benefits?* Alfred knew from the expression on Angel's face; it was nothing illegal. He dreaded this, but he knew he had to talk with Angel. Yes, the younger biker was Angel's little bro, and Alfred has never felt Angel's wrath, but there was a first time for everything. However, he was going to confront Angel anyway.

Summer and Gladys were comforting Brenda, Traye's grandmother. But Summer was in a state of shock. *How could this be? Traye was mistakenly shot and killed in a drive-by.* The intended victim was Traye's 16-year-old brother, Marcus. He was out playing like any other child his age. Traye adored Marcus, and when he saw him, he ran to him. However, he was in the way of the bullet intended for Marcus. Marcus then cried out loud. "No." The car then sped off with screeching tires and leaving tire tracks. Marcus held the lifeless Traye in his arms, "I'll get them back!" he cried. "They'll pay for this!" His grandmother heard him and then called the police to place him in protective custody.

Summer had heard all of this, and her first thought was she didn't blame Marcus; she felt the same way about Mike's death. But then, she was reminded that revenge was wrong. So she asked Gladys, "Do you think it would be a good idea for me to visit Marcus and share my testimony? My husband was also killed violently. He was in a fight, and I wanted vengeance. If I show Marcus my empathy, maybe I can reach him."

"That's possible and worth a try; just let me look at my schedule." Gladys didn't want any of her volunteers going into neighborhoods or jails without being in the company of other volunteers, and Summer's volunteer friend wanted to escort Summer personally.

She made a quick call to Chaplain Andrews, and they visited Marcus that day. Neal was a good friend of Warden Sam Jackson, so Neal helped make it possible for the two to see Marcus. He just hoped Marcus would agree; the problem was, he didn't trust anyone. Though he did fear his grandmother, and since the two ladies were her friends, he gave his consent.

He picked up the phone to speak to Summer, and he remembered how Traye had a crush on her. She was beautiful, no doubt, but he never trusted white people, so he stayed quiet as she spoke.

Summer said, "I know you don't know me, but my name is Summer Hanley; my husband was Mike Hanley, and now he's dead. I had an outlook like yours, and I wanted vengeance for his death. The only difference was, I tried to use the law for my revenge. It was self-defense. My husband at the time had a mental disorder, but I didn't care. I no longer had my husband, and I wanted someone to pay for it. Vengeance never felt good, I could never admit this, but it was a bitter form of hatred.

"A longtime friend had ministered to me. He had harmed another person once. He pushed his brother's girlfriend, and she hit her head on the sharp end of a coffee table. She didn't die, but she could have. The shock of what he had done made him realize he needed help. He was a drug addict and had hurt her in his desperation to obtain drugs. She was kind and protected him and called her father to help him. It was through her father that he accepted Jesus into his heart. The man who killed Mike was also a drug addict. My friend and I went together to visit him, and at that time, he received salvation, and I forgave him.

"Marcus, I know the pain of losing someone you deeply love. But vengeance will not take away the pain. It only creates more hatred. Even if you do kill this person, the pain will not leave. You will then have this hatred for others. It spreads like cancer, and only Jesus can control it. So please, Marcus, accept him into your heart."

Marcus was shedding tears, primarily for losing Traye; summer had hoped some of those tears were of repentance.

He didn't speak much but to say, "You know, Summer, you are pretty cool!"

Summer was hoping for his salvation, but she had to be patient. Finally, she said, "You know, Marcus, I loved Traye. He will always be special to me."

"He loved you too. He said he was going to marry you. I know your love is different, but it's love, and that's what matters. I know because of you, Traye is in heaven."

"And you can be there with him someday." These words came out of Summer's mouth before she knew it. She wondered if she should call them back. But she didn't want to be too assertive. Marcus was crying uncontrollably; Summer only hoped it was a good sign. Then their time was up, and Summer began to pray for Marcus silently; the young man never verbalized that he wanted prayer. Gladys spoke to Marcus briefly, expressing his grandmother's concern. "Marcus, honey, your grandma is so worried about you; please do what it takes to stay safe."

"I promise, Ms. Gladys, I Will."

Then the entire visit was over, and both Gladys and Summer left.

Larry and Jim were having a prayer meeting; Larry was trying to get as close to God as possible. The minister knew seeking him first, and putting him first, was the only answer. He tried putting Summer out of his mind; he focused on reading the Bible and other spiritual books. He mainly read Daniel and Revelations, as a revelation was what he was seeking. He prayed to have the focus John and Daniel had, Daniel fasted and prayed, the Angel of God told him Satan blocked his path, but Daniel's prayers had unblocked the way. The Angel thanked Daniel for his soulful prayer, then gave him the message from God, about how much he loved him, for his faithfulness.

Larry knew God alone had the power to come against Satan without Daniel's help. He doesn't need our help, but in the book of Daniel, it showed God and Angels need love and caring too. Man's fellowship is God's only need, so Larry was trying to fulfill it. Jim was fulfilling it with him. Jim was devout in his faith, but he had to admit he was learning something from Larry. He then asked himself. "Can any person ever be faithful enough?" So, day by day, he and Larry studied and heavily meditated on the Lord together.

Summer felt accomplished speaking to Marcus and giving her testimony. But she grieved heavily for Traye. *Why did this happen?* She thought, *Why do these precious children have to live on a battlefield each day? Can a child not even go out and play without the risk of harm? Why do we lay hands and pray over them if it can end like this?*

Lynn could see Summer was in deep thought. She usually asked about her pre-gang children, and she knew how heartbroken she was over Traye. The woman had wondered if her young friend was also heartbroken over Larry. She and Lindy had talked about it. They knew Summer needed to mourn Mike, but they both felt Larry would be suitable for her and the baby. At the hospital, Summer had asked about the child's gender. So, everyone but Larry knew it was a girl. Summer named her Ruby Destiny, calling her R.D. for short.

Angel was with Alfred, and the former biker saw a puzzled look come across Alfred's face. The older biker asked, "Alfred, my man, what's up, little bro?"

Alfred took his time answering, but he finally said, "Man, Angel, why are you so different? I'm doing all of your work." Alfred wondered after he got it out if he needed to duck.

But, surprisingly, Angel was meek and mild. He said, "Little bro, you can have it all if you want it. I don't care about it anymore. I'm just trying to figure a way to get out."

Alfred couldn't believe his ears. He knew for Angel to get out was impossible, but he had to understand why. So he asked, "What is this change in you, man? You are too different."

Angel said, "It's Jesus, little bro. He's been changing me for a while. I thought I was Superman, but the time came I was unable to protect someone important to me, and God did it for me."

Alfred knew he meant Summer. However, he knew Summer was also different, and it angered him. The younger biker felt Angel was brainwashed by Summer.

Marcus cried off and on for hours after Summer left. He hated to admit it, but he knew Summer was right. He was here because his grandmother wanted him protected. And the last thing Traye would want was for him to risk his life. But the pain was so unbearable. He had always looked out for Traye, and this time he couldn't. He recalled when he was eight and Traye was one. His mother, Keisha, was an addict. Most of the time, she would take Traye and him to Grandma Brenda's. However, sometimes her brain didn't function enough to remember to do that. During one of these times, he and Traye were left alone for two days. He tried his best to take care of Traye. He would shoplift groceries, diapers, and other baby necessities for them. He put them in a backpack he always carried. He was cautious not to get caught. Little did he know he was caught on camera.

Instead of calling him to the side to give him a lecture, the manager followed him home. He was curious about the baby stuff. He saw that Marcus and the toddler were all alone and called Child Protection. Gladys Miller answered the phone "Child Protection Agency to whom am I speaking?"

"Let's just say, an anonymous citizen reporting a child abandonment." The store owner retorted. Gladys took down all the information and went to the address the citizen gave her. Along with the Child Protection Agency, the police came and took them to a temporary place to live. Gladys asked, "Do you have a family to come to get you."

"Yes, Gamma," Traye cried!

"Do you know where she lives?" Marcus remembered his grandma's name, but he never learned her address or phone number, yet, they somehow located her, and she was coming to get them. Marcus and Traye hadn't eaten yet, so Gladys took them for a hamburger while waiting for their grandmother. He ate three burgers, and Traye ate almost two.

Marcus was one of the first children in the pre-gang rallies Gladys founded. He loved to attend these rallies and had accepted Jesus the first year. *What changed? Why did I leave?* He knew God would protect him.

Nonetheless, he still joined the gang. He did despicable things, like drugs, and robbing, people. He never was hooked on drugs because a frightening encounter took the desire for drugs from him. He did, however, drink. The gang had required him to do that, to be accepted by other gang members. However, he never enjoyed it, so he never became addicted. He just did what he could to be convincing and faked the rest.

He always wanted to have his head on straight, for Traye, because it had been that way from the beginning. Keisha's head was never on straight. Two years after he lived with his Grandma Brenda, he learned, his mother had died of a drug overdose. The news broke Brenda's heart; Keisha was her only child. Now, Traye was gone. Traye loved Jesus; he talked about him all the time. Later, when he was four, he learned his mother had died, he insisted she was with Jesus. He told Marcus. "Guess what?"

Marcus said, "What squirt?" Which is what he called him most of the time. "I know something you don't know."

"And what that be?" Marcus said.

"Mama's, in heaven." Severe pain was always inflicted on Marcus at the mention of their mother. But he always had patience with Traye. If Traye believed Keisha was with Jesus. He wouldn't dispute it.

Not long before Traye died, he mentioned he was going to see his mother in heaven. But, then, in Marcus's mind, he felt, if he saw Keisha, it wouldn't be for a long time. *Did Traye know his fate? Was he right about Keisha?* These questions never seemed as important as they did now.

He then thought about Don, a member of his gang. They were friends once, but now he was out to kill him. And he thought he had killed Traye, though he didn't know. Someone had told him Marcus was trying to leave the gang. It wasn't true, but now Traye was dead, and Marcus wanted no part of the gang life now. Thoughts of revenge still consumed his mind. He wanted Don dead. He had to pay for Traye. What else was there? Then he thought of Summer's words. She lost her soul mate. How could she forgive that? Maybe she didn't love him enough? Then he remembered she said she did have thoughts of revenge. She never had peace until she forgave the man who killed him. Marcus then told the jailer, "Could I please speak to Chaplain Andrews?"

It had been three weeks since Larry began his extended leave. He was grateful to Jeremy Collins for taking over for him. Jeremy had said on the phone, "The congregation misses you; I told them you had to go, shut yourself away with God. No one felt an explanation was necessary."

"How are Kevin and Lindy. Did they say anything about how Summer was?" Larry had been concerned because he left San Francisco without knowing any follow-up on her condition.

"Yes, Summer is gaining more strength every day. The Logans are extremely relieved." This news relieved Larry too. Then he asked about the congregation. "Is everyone in the congregation okay?"

"There are some who are sick, but nothing drastic."

"Thank you, Jeremy, for updating me on all the happenings. I miss all of you. Jim asked consent from the church board for our leaves of absence."

'Well, the congregation is satisfied, and church attendance stable; there should be no problem."

"Thank you so much, Jeremy, and I'll remember you when you need any time off."

Larry still hadn't heard from God. He felt he had his entire focus on him, but still no word. The minister didn't want to be impatient, only waiting was becoming difficult. He had to have an answer, even if the answer was no. He missed and longed for Summer. Did she miss and long for him? Or had she made up her mind to give up on them? Summer's forgetting him was one of Larry's worse fears. Usually, though, when Larry was in this kind of dilemma, Jim, reminded him "Let's keep our focus on God, he has the answers, and we need them. We need to put God first." But, Larry still wanted to know when His answers will come.

Summer was in compounded pain. She hurt and couldn't understand the tragedy of Traye. *Why would this happen? Every week we lay hands over these babies for protection, and then this happens. Why Lord? Why? Am I selfish because I want to keep seeing that sweet little face?* And where was Larry? He's the one who could lend comfort. She hurt the most for him. She missed him. The love she had for him wouldn't die. She prayed, *Lord, I have to know. Is this an empty dream? It's been almost a month, and no one has heard from him. Yes, Lord, he is on standby for his congregation, but what about me? Will he be there for me?* There wasn't a reply, so Summer knew she still had to wait. Or did He want her to give up? That thought was too painful. So, Summer had to wait on God's answer.

After six weeks, Larry's revelation had finally come in the form of a dream. He and Summer were in a world of gladiators. He was fully skilled, and Summer was partially skilled. They are battling enemies that had different forms, but they were Satan and his demons. He warred with them and defeated them. The demons shouted, "You won't succeed; you will fail. You have no chance against my kingdom!" They repeated this chant over and over. Finally, Larry's power was too strong for them, so they left him alone and came against Summer, as she wasn't as skilled. "She'll be ours," they chanted. Larry then knew he had to go against them to protect her. "Leave her alone!" he shouted in a voice so loud it left an echo. The dream had become extremely intense, and Larry awoke in a cold sweat. God spoke to him, saying, "*This dream is a revelation of a ministry ahead. A ministry that you and summer will create. I answered the childhood prayer of her desire for you. The battle in the dream represents Satan's bondage over hurting people. Summer's, and your, revelation will be to set them free.*"

Larry was euphoric, and he ran and hugged Jim and his wife, Beverly. "He answered," he cried. "God has finally given me my answer. Summer and I are destined to be together to serve His purpose." Larry immediately called Pastor Jeremy and requested more time off. And Pastor Jeremy was happy to oblige. At least now, he had a time frame to give his congregation.

Summer was more than eight months into her pregnancy, her hormones seemed to be running rampant, and she had intolerable mood swings. Lynn was being incredibly patient but wished Summer would have the baby. She'd never been pregnant, so she didn't know stress occurred close to the due date. The doorbell rang, and Lynn saw it was Larry. "Larry, so good to see you. How are you?" Larry was glad to see Lynn but highly anxious to see Summer. He replied. "I'm glad to see you too. I know everyone has to be confused, and I'm sorry. Could I please see Summer?"

"Of course," and she called out to Summer, she was happy Summer had another focus. Lynn then left the room to give them some privacy; she could tell the couple wanted it. With Summer's mood, she didn't want Larry to be embarrassed by her presence if summer had a "swing."

Larry entered the room where Summer was, and she was speechless. Larry began awkwardly, "Summer, I know how things appear. You declared your love, but I didn't feel free at the time to declare mine. I made a bargain with God when you were close to death. I had to go where I could hear from Him, and I have. I believe our life is going to be together, Summer."

Summer was in her anger mood and cried out, "Larry, I was going through some tough challenges, and I needed you to be here. I guess there is a lot I don't understand."

Larry realized he never took a good look at Summer. She was great with child, but she was more glowingly beautiful than he had ever seen her. She was still complaining, but she was so irresistible. He immediately stopped her protests by holding her in his arms and kissing her passionately. Again, she was shocked but, again, at a loss for words.

Larry pleaded, "Does it even matter, Summer? Does anything matter but this moment?" He told her, gently touching and stroking her face with one hand.

Impassioned, Summer immediately said, "No, nothing else matters," and kissed him back with increasing fervidness.

Lynn came in and said, "Wow, looks like I came just in time, looks like the two of you need a chaperone."

Larry and Summer laughed, and Summer blushed. Lynn was jubilant and surprised. She and Lindy had hoped for this, only they didn't know Larry and Summer were so engrossed with one another. Lynn did recall some tension and chemistry in the room when they were together.

Larry and Summer were still embracing when suddenly both of Summer's hands went to her stomach. She was in pain as she told them, "I think it's time for R.D. to arrive!"

Larry mouthed, "R.D.?"

Lynn said I'll explain later," and immediately called 911.

Chapter 11

Lynn was on the phone with the emergency dispatcher, who explained, "Yes, Mrs.Rothburg, we have a dire emergency at the moment, taking up our crew. We have most of our emergency crew attending a bus collision, with at least a 17-car pileup. Our available crew is taking care of the most critical emergencies; first, please leave her name and birth date so that they could find her chart for triage placement. It sounds like her contractions are far enough apart that it's not an extreme emergency." Lynn it was, and she considered driving her to the hospital, but if the interstate was tied up, Summer might have her baby there; going another direction would also pose delays.

Lynn was trying to consider what to do when a nurse, Cindy Miles, called from Mount Zion. She said, "Mrs. Rothberg, Mrs. Hanley's chart is showing a normal pregnancy and delivery. All our hospitals are on standby for accident victims, and Mrs. Hanley is very low on the triage list. So we're looking to arrange a midwife to go to her as soon as possible." Lynn, of course, had no choice but to agree. Only until the midwife arrived, it was up to her and Larry.

Larry was a nervous wreck. He wasn't trying to be comical, but he kept saying over and over, "I ain't never birthed no baby!" Much time had passed, and a midwife hadn't arrived; Larry called Angel, who said, "I know a midwife bro, and she lives close by; she'll be there before you know it, so take it easy." Angel could tell Larry was tense. Summer's contractions were becoming closer. Finally, the doorbell rang, and Monica arrived; Angel was right; she must live close. Lynn was happy it was

Monica; she remembered meeting her at church; Lynn began, "Thank God for a familiar face. I had no idea you were a midwife."

"Yes, and I'm here to take over, so please give us some privacy; I'll call you when I need anything."

Larry was apprehensive, and he loved Summer so much, he hated that she was in pain.

Monica found the baby's head crowning, and it was close to the time for Summer to begin pushing. She said, "Summer, I am going to let you know when I want you to push; when I say to stop pushing, you need to stop." Summer nodded her head and followed Monica's instructions; she pushed after several contractions, breathing hard in between. Summer was exhausted, but she stilled obeyed Monica.

It seemed to them all like a lifetime. Yet, finally, baby R.D. arrived. "Oh, so beautiful!" Monica said, admiring the newborn. Summer looked at her as Monica cut the umbilical cord. She kept saying, "She is beautiful, so beautiful!" Finally, Monica took the baby to Lynn and said: "They have me extremely busy today; I need you and that young man to take over. I appreciate it." Larry picked up baby R.D. and took her to the sink, "come, beautiful baby, I'm going to take care of you." R.D.s cries were sharp, but Larry was patient. "It's ok, little one; I hope you're not hurting." Larry was quickly bonding with R.D. although the infant continued with her sharp cries, Lynn brought him her diaper, cradle shirt, and blanket. He kept trying to console the crying infant, but R.D. kept crying nonstop. Finally, the minister dressed her and immediately took her into Summer. When he handed R.D. to Summer, her cries stopped immediately.

Larry play-acted that he was offended, stating, "Ok, Miss Ruby Destiny, I see who you like the best!"

Summer draped another blanket over her breast for privacy, then began nursing her, then she told Larry, "don't be upset, Larry, it's her food she likes the best, at the moment." Larry kissed mother and child on their foreheads, then left to give them privacy. Then Lynn called Lindy and Kevin with the news of R.D.'s birth. Kevin said in enchantment. "I'm a grandpa and have a granddaughter. Thank you, Lynn. Lindy is by my side and ecstatic. Tell Summer to please treasure her."

"Oh, I don't that will be a problem at that all; Summer's close call has made her appreciate her tiny daughter. I'll let Summer tell you her name and all the other details; it's the infant's dinner time right now."

"That's ok I can wait; I bet you want to speak to Lindy!"

"Oh please!" Lynn said enthusiastically. Lindy came on the phone. "I heard Kevin say we have a new granddaughter."

"Yes, Kevin, and you are so lucky!"

"And you too, the baby is just as much your granddaughter," Lindy exclaimed

"How generous." Lynn replied, overwhelmed, "Thank you so much because I do feel like her grandma."

"Lynn, you are her grandma. I've never told you how grateful I am for your being there for Summer at the times I couldn't be. And you are my best friend."

She and Lindy spoke on the phone for a long time. Then she talked to Summer with info on the child. Lynn told Lindy all about Summer's and Larry's new love for one another. Lindy applauded. When Summer hung up with Lindy, Lynn then called the Hanleys, giving them the news, "Susan, it's Lynn, the time has arrived, and you and Gerald are new grandparents."

"Lynn, thank you so much for calling and letting us know. When can we see our new family member?"

"Whenever you wish."

"I'll talk to Gerald now and get back to you. And thanks again."

"You are welcome." Then she finished their conversation.

Angel and Earl were at a department store to pick out a beautiful christening gown for the baby. The two noticed that many infants dedicated to the Lord were wearing the beautiful gown at church. Angel and Earl gazed at the tiny gown, seeing how much it resembled an infant version of a wedding gown.

Earl said, "I guess that's fitting, being dedicated to Jesus first."

Angel answered, "Yes, and it's such an honor to partake in such an event." Angel was thinking about the role of Godparents, he remembered, at the Catholic Church. They took on the role of making sure the child was endowed spiritually. They would oversee everything from christening to college. So, he thought, who could be suitable Godparents for little R.D.? Angel recently had many thoughts of the spiritual realm. He and Monica had even discussed renewing their wedding vows. However, his life was so complicated. He wasn't sure he could have his freedom. That is if he even survived, leaving his gang life behind. However, Angel was sure he had to leave it, and he also had to give up his blood money.

Angel planned to speak to Dr. Thomas, inquiring if the church would accept a massive donation of tainted money. Then, maybe, it could help with the church missions. First, though, he had to wonder if it would be sinful to give it. He thought *if people were forgiven, why couldn't money be? If no ministry accepted the funds, what would become of it? Would it be confiscated by the police and later distributed among the staff? Would he have any choice about where the money went?* These were the questions he wanted God to answer.

Another change in Angel was his reluctance to visit the Avenues. Monica's parents lived there, and there was bad blood between them and him. They just didn't understand him. Angel felt they judged him because he was different, but now he understood them. Angel put himself in their place, imagining having a daughter dating a violent gangster. He could see their position and now agreed with them. The former biker was hoping now;

he could earn their trust and convince them he was a changed man. He didn't avoid the Avenues anymore. Monica had lived close to her parents for a while. Now she resides in Twin Peaks, in an apartment close to Angel.

Monica was visiting her parents when Angel called her on her cell. "Monica, my friend Summer is about to give birth and needs a midwife. Can you please go to her?"

"My job has called to another location, but let me call my clinic and ask the dispatcher if it's ok. My other call is not as far along as Summer." Summer was just a short walking distance away. Monica contacted the emergency dispatcher; she mentioned to the dispatcher, "I have another emergency with contractions closer together. Can I please attend to her first?" "Of course." the dispatcher replied, "as long as you can get to our other patient in time." And Monica was able to deliver both babies that day. She worked for an obstetrician and had her patients. This midwife did prenatal examinations and post-natal care, and her patients trusted her and relied on her. However, if the pregnancy became complicated, she would have to insist the obstetrician do the delivery. Again, her patients preferred her but trusted her referrals.

R.D. was in her bassinet sound asleep; Summer was also about to sleep when Larry walked in. Larry thought she was sleeping, so he was about to leave and stirred Summer up. Since they were alone, she asked, "Why did you leave, Larry? You were away for so long, and I wasn't sure you were coming back."

Larry knew this was coming. So he replied, "I never wanted to leave you, Summer, but I had an arrangement with God on your behalf, and I had to go to meet with him."

Summer wasn't sure she understood. She'd never told him of her Heavenly experience and felt if she had, maybe he wouldn't have left her. Instead, she said, "I have missed you for way too long."

Larry wasn't sure if she meant when he went away to Texas or since she was 12 years old. He remembered her telling him she had loved him for that long. Larry knew for sure he had loved her since his premiere sermon at Word of God Church. He said, "I had loved you, Summer, since our encounter, when I preached my first sermon in Minion. I just didn't know then that you were married. I never knew until you were widowed; you are so young, Summer."

"I know, and I didn't marry for the right reason. I learned to love Mike, but he wasn't you. So I don't know why I didn't wait."

"I still believe it is still part of God's plan; you were meant to be with Mike too."

Summer believed that because she was happy with Mike, especially toward the end. But it seemed the chemistry was more intense with Larry. She hated herself for making these comparisons; then she remembered that Mike knew this and accepted it. He had set her free to give Larry all of herself. To her, it was the greatest gift she had ever received. She wanted Larry to know but feared he wouldn't believe her. So many people didn't believe her experience in the heavenly; she hoped Larry would. However, that would be for another time; she wanted to enjoy her time with Larry now.

Lynn answered the doorbell, and it was Angel and Earl; they came in and embraced Lynn. "Lynn," Angel said with enthusiasm. "How are our patients? how is the little one?" Lynn was happy to see them and bragged extensively, "You mean my grandchild."

Angel yelled, "What?"

"I am the grandma, and I have consent from Summer and the other grandparents!"

"Ok, I believe you," Angel said laughingly

R.D. was asleep in her bassinet; Angel told Summer, "Monica tells me that R.D. is the most beautiful baby she had ever delivered, and this newborn has her wanting children; after looking at this beauty, I can't wait for one of our own."

Larry then told Angel, "Bro, before you enter parenthood, shouldn't you tie up your loose ends with your gang activity?

You have to take a stand on this." Angel explained to Larry, "That could be dangerous, man."

"Angel, you have to believe God is your protector. Get with some other born-again bikers, hear their testimonies." Larry knew many bikers had testimonies of how God had gotten them out of their gang lives safe and sound. Their key scripture was Zechariah 4:6: "'Not by might nor by power, but by my Spirit' says the Lord." This verse was monogrammed onto their biker jackets. Many of these bikers repeated this scripture repeatedly, as their old gang members were coming after them with their knives and chains. The predator bikers knew a more powerful presence was around, and they threw down their knives and chains and ran. They also would flee from them whenever they ran into them publicly. Larry also reminded Angel, "God is no respecter of persons, and He will protect you too. And if you want a stable life Angel, with your wife, and with children, you will have to place yourself under God's protection." Angel knew this to be true. And he was ready because he wanted a more stable life. Earl remained silent all this time. Larry and Lynn wondered if he was still here. Larry couldn't resist and asked, "Earl, does the cat have your tongue!"

"I don't see a cat," Earl said amusingly. "I'm just too enchanted by this newborn angel." He was holding his gaze on R.D. Angel had to remind him, "It's that time, Earl." Then Angel and Earl presented Summer with the beautiful dedication gown for R.D. The gown took Summer's breath away. It was pure white, made with traditional silk with fringes of nylon embedded with tiny beads. Summer exclaimed, "I've never seen anything so beautiful. When Pastor Thomas comes, I'll have arrangements made for her baby dedication. He's going to visit early this afternoon. Thank you so much, Uncle Angel and Uncle Earl." They officially become R.D.'S uncles. Larry then expressed. "I am spellbound, Angel. How did you and Earl know about dedication gowns."

Angel told him, "I know more than Earl. I've seen many babies christened, wearing these beautiful gowns, I've never forgotten. But, you know, although I can't remember, I have been christened myself."

Larry laughed and said, "Yea, that was a little sprinkle of water. Soon you will have a full-dunk baptism."

Angel gave Larry a funny look. "Hey, man, don't be bringing up the baptism. I don't look forward to it, and I almost drowned once. Only for Jesus will I do this!"

Everyone laughed as Angel's face looked pale.

Then Larry said, "Don't worry, Angel. You know I will be there with you."

Summer thought it was funny that Angel, this brave and bold guy, was afraid of a bit of water. Angel and Earl spent a little more time with Summer, the baby remained asleep, so they never had an opportunity to hold her. They just didn't want to tire the baby and her out. They also knew she would wish for privacy when Dr. Thomas came to visit.

Dr. Thomas and his wife came by as Angel and Earl were about to leave. They greeted one another, shook hands, and spoke for a minute. Then Angel and Earl left. Dr. and Mrs. Thomas entered the room where Summer and R.D. were. R.D. had awoken. It was changing and eating time. The couple gave Summer privacy, and the pastor and his wife talked to Larry.

Pastor Thomas asked Larry. "How do you like San Francisco? It must be quite a change from the small town where you are from."

"Yes, quite a change. I haven't had a tour of it yet, just the small areas Summer and I visited. I'm hoping to see more of it soon. This time will be brief; I'm going to visit Summer and R.D. for a little while longer, then I'm going back to my congregation." Larry didn't know how to explain to them about Summer and him. When he and Summer began dating, he decided it would be better to let him know their plans, including marriage. Then Larry wanted to show him the beautiful dedication gown, but then decided it was Summer's place to present it. Larry told Dr. Thomas, "I look forward to visiting Glad Tidings Sunday."

"We'll be glad to have you." They had talked about everything from fishing to sports and a lot of Jesus in between.

Lynn told them, "Summer would like to receive see you and your wife now." Larry decided maybe Summer would like privacy with them. Dr. and Mrs. Thomas were with Summer for a short period, and Summer showed them R.D.'s dedication gown. Mrs. Thomas expressed, "What an exquisite gown, on an absolutely beautiful baby" The couple began to dote on R.D.

Pastor Thomas added, "Yes, but that infant is so small for it. In about two months or so, we will arrange for her dedication."

The time frame gave Summer relief. She was still feeling the fatigue of childbirth and wanted a lot of recovery time to enjoy the dedication. Two months is perfect. She would be better by then. The Thomas's stayed a bit longer, then announced, "It was so lovely to see you, Summer and your little one, you too Lynn, and nice to meet you, Larry. However, we have to get back to the church to help the staff create the calendar of events. So we had just taken a little break." Summer expressed, "We appreciate you taking this time out of your busy schedule to see our little bundle."

Lynn added, "Yes, Pastor and I look forward to seeing you and Mrs. Thomas Sunday,"

Finally, Larry replied, "It was wonderful to meet you, and I also look forward to Sunday." The Thomas's departed, then Summer, Lynn, and Larry had the joy of again being alone with R.D.

Alfred had taken over Angel's leadership of the gang. The gang members were suspicious; they knew Angel had probably gone straight. The gang knew this often happened; with older bikers, they wanted to get away from criminal life to begin a new one. However, their gang members had trouble trusting them because some former members gave up the confidence of their gang activity. They said they wanted a more stable life and promised not to rat them out; then, they dealt with the law for their freedom. The gang knew the law could lock Angel up and throw away the key. The problem was, they loved Angel and were loyal to him.

Alfred also loved Angel. He was angry at first, but then he thought Angel was entitled to live his life; however, he wanted to live it. Alfred had a lot of thoughts about God himself lately. Angel had been his influence from the beginning. If he'd found a better way of life, then Alfred felt he had to give it at least a try. First, he had to set up a drug deal. Only then the younger biker would have to face the gang members too. No matter the cost, he was going to protect Angel. Although for now, Alfred knew it would be business as usual. He just wasn't aware; the opposing gang was there and had set a trap for Angel.

The gang told Alfred that the plan was that the jokers would supply drugs in exchange for weapons. But the opposing gang was behind the guns, and they fired, thinking it was Angel.

Marcus was out of jail. He had visited with Chaplain Andrews, but his heart wasn't in favor of leaving gang life just yet. The young gangster had revenge in his heart for Traye. He wanted to hunt Don down and kill him.

He was in the vicinity of the gunfire. He knew it was the leader of the Red Vipers, who was one of Angel's opposing biker gang. They were an Italian gang. Marcus's dream was to one day be in Angel's gang. Alfred was like his big brother. He never wanted to kill, but all that changed with this vengeance in his heart.

He approached the opposing gang with caution and saw Alfred on the ground. He knew he was dead; he then picked up Alfred's gun, took aim, and emptied the chamber on Antonio, the leader of the Red Vipers. Marcus had never killed before. He had never desired to kill until the day of the driveby and Traye's murder. Before that, his gang had never pressured him to. Everything happened so fast. He was despondent and shocked by his action. The Red Vipers couldn't see who had hit Antonio, then the police sirens sounded, and the Vipers fled.

Marcus became unnerved when he saw Antonio's lifeless body staring at him. The young gangster then knew Summer had spoken the truth about revenge. His heart wasn't as satisfied as he thought it would be. He used Alfred's phone to call Angel to let him know what had happened.

Angel had again stopped by to visit Larry and Summer; he was there when Marcus had called him. When Angel saw Alfred's number come up on the cell phone, he answered, "What's up, little bro?" He became confused when he heard Marcus on the other end. He was hysterical, and Angel couldn't understand him. He understood the part "Alfred is dead. He also told him, "I --- Antonio." Finally, he could bring himself to say the word killed.

Angel was in deep pain about Alfred, but he had learned to hide it. However, Larry could see by Angel's body language something serious had happened. So he waited until he hung up his phone and then said, "Are you, ok Angel."

"Bro, I have a private matter to take care of." Larry didn't want to intrude on Angel's privacy, but he had a hunch he needed to be with him. He said emphatically, "Angel, I know you're used to handling your hurts, but something inside tells me you need me. Please let me go with you." Angel could see Larry would not cease until Angel gave consent. Angel thought to himself that Larry didn't miss his calling if he could persuade him to relate to him. He confessed to him in private, "It's my best friend, and I think he's dead. I love you, bro, and I don't want you involved; I couldn't bear for anything to happen to you." But Larry was determined and stated, "I love you too, and I won't let you face this alone."

"Marcus is in shock, talking mixed up and funny, and I don't know if it's true. Ok, man, let's go." Then they went in to announce they had to go and take care of this urgent matter. Summer was concerned for Larry; she said, "No, Larry, please don't go. The gangs are dangerous; please stay." Summer had seen some casualties of the gang wars. But Larry had to remind her, "You have to trust God, I have to be with Angel, should he find out the worst about his friend." They then left, and Summer remarked to Lynn, "I hope Marcus didn't take revenge for Traye. I don't want him to get in trouble."

Monica was leaving work. She had been a Certified Nurse Midwife (CNM) for a few years. The nurse-midwife was in grad school when she had met Angel. She was from an educational background. Her family never approved of Angel, and if they hadn't been so adamant about showing their disapproval, she might not have been so influenced by him. Yet, it was more than that; Monica seemed to see the real Angel, the one with the kind heart. He was always caring and gentle with her. It was challenging to keep Angel's biker history a secret from her family. She would have him wear regular attire, with long sleeves, to cover up his tattoos. This deception was unusual for Angel, as he never wanted anyone to change him. Angel was an honest person, and he soon got tired of pretending, then he told her, "Monica, either your parents accept me or not. I'm not pretending anymore. And if you're ashamed of me, you too can also make another decision about me." Monica never could resist Angel. When an opposing gang member tried to hold her at gunpoint, she had to witness Angel defending her in a shootout. This woman went to school to become a nurse to save lives. She detested witnessing death, principally senseless death. When her family learned the truth about Angel, they were highly concerned. They did notice, however, that Angel did go out of his way to protect her. They knew he would also give his life for hers. But they wouldn't let Angel or Monica know they harbored this admiration for him.

Monica, like Angel, was an only child. Their parents had never met. But, Angel's parents were as concerned for Monica as they were for Angel; they loved Monica and hoped her influence would free him from this insane gang life.

Angel and Larry arrived on the scene and found Marcus crying uncontrollably. He cried for Traye and Alfred and cried because he had finally killed someone after all the years of gang life. Marcus wanted revenge for Alfred and Traye. But when it came, he knew what Summer Hanley said was true. His tears were uncontrollable, and he was now calling out to God. Larry had ministered to him and saw he was so young. "Hey, young man, it's going to be all right. God has it all under control." Marcus clung to Larry as a baby clings to its mother. He held to his words of encouragement.

Angel then bent over, holding Alfred's dead body with tears in his eyes. They had been together as gang members for 14 years. He was telling him, "Little Bro, why didn't you tell me you were coming here. I would've been here for you." Tears were splashing down his face as he thought to himself, *why wasn't I here?* The ambulance then came to remove Alfred. Angel could barely contain himself, and he was slow to let go of his corpse. The police had taped off the crime scene, trying to get answers from Marcus. Larry and Angel never thought to take the gun out of his hands, or perhaps, it had been out of sight. The police believed Marcus was possibly defending himself in a shootout, as they also saw Alfred, except without answers, they weren't sure. They would have to take Marcus to the precinct for questioning. The police knew Marcus as a teen gang member, and he didn't seem to have the rap sheet many gang members had. Also, the officers were fond of him. He probably owed his low-profile arrest record to his Grandma Brenda. She seemed always to know when to call, to keep him from getting into too much trouble.

Larry and Angel went to the police station with Marcus. The police made them wait outside the interrogation room as they interrogated Marcus. Larry and Angel both advised him, then

Angel stated, "Marcus, you don't have to say anything without an attorney present." The police, however, felt they had to get to the bottom of this sordid matter. They said, "Marcus, we have to have answers. You were holding a gun, and a man is dead. Was it intentional?" Marcus was despondent. He merely wouldn't, or perhaps, he couldn't speak. Larry had Angel call an attorney. He called Charles Henker, "Charles, please come to the precinct." He gave the location. "I have a friend who needs your services."

Charles had gotten charges removed from Angel many times. However, now that Angel had made his commitment to Christ, he wasn't sure about him. The former biker wasn't even sure he should have been a free man on the many occasions Charles had represented him. He wanted Marcus to be free, but he wanted the truth to be known more than that. Truth had always mattered to Angel; he just wanted his freedom more. Charles had to be the one because Angel knew of no one else. His repentance had him thinking about his contracts on opposing gang members and leaders that he had wasted. Angel never understood this was leading these culprits into hell. He had been thinking this over lately. The former biker was going to turn himself in, along with his blood money. But, first, he wanted to seek spiritual counseling. He was going to set up a session with Dr. Thomas as soon as possible, and he also wanted to talk it over with Monica.

Charles Henker arrived at the precinct. It was apparent he didn't like cops. He said to the attending officers, "Do we now abuse children?" as he looked firm at Marcus.

Officer Jones was just as arrogant in return as he said, "ask this boy's grandmother if we abuse him. She always calls on us to protect him, which is what we are trying to do. He won't explain why he used Alfred's gun on the Red Viper leader, Antonio. It could be self-defense, only he isn't saying so."

"Man, the child by himself, against that vicious gang, should tell you that. If you guys hadn't arrived when you had, I'm sure Marcus would have been another corpse."

"Then the boy needs to say so. That's all he has to do. We aren't interested in throwing the book at him."

"If that's true, you need to go ahead and call the prosecutor's office and tell them it's self-defense."

"We would if it were easy. But, unfortunately, there are just too many unanswered questions, and we need the answers."

"I am advising my client to exercise his right to remain silent, and he is to talk to me only. But I guarantee you will have to let him go. Otherwise, you will look like total fools. Do you think a young boy like this would take down a kingpin without fear for his own life?"

"Then he needs to say so; if he does, we will help him in every way we can."

"The only thing he needs to do is to confide in me first; it's his right."

Angel had offered to post Marcus' bail. Posting bail is usually set for adults. If charged as a minor, he would go to a juvenile correctional facility. The police planned to investigate self-defense first, and if it were not self-defense, the DA would be involved. They let Marcus go, but Officer Jones told Marcus, "We are still investigating, and we don't want you to leave town, is that understood!" Marcus nodded his head then left with Charles.

Larry thought it would be good for Marcus to go to the Rescue Mission for his safety. He would also request that the court allow Marcus to stay at the Rescue Mission instead of a juvenile correction facility. The Rescue Mission was strict and kept a watchful eye on the people in residence. The security was the same as a correctional facility. The court system had many inmates sent to the Mission—boys from 16 to adults.

Sergio was the next in line for the kingpin of the Vipers. This man wasn't as angry about losing Antonio as the other gang members. On the contrary, he was happy about his new position. However, he had to satisfy the other members, so he ordered another contract on Angel. The Vipers believed Angel called the hit on Antonio; they had fled fast, running from the law. They couldn't afford to be caught with the stolen drugs and weapons supposedly brought to the table. They had a particular plan for Angel now. They were satisfied, Angel lost his best friend, but that wasn't enough. They wanted to kidnap Monica and get blood money from Angel. They were broke, so they needed the finances; otherwise, they would have been happy with only their revenge against Angel. The problem was whenever they stalked her. There was never an opportunity to grab her. But, they wouldn't give up because, at some point, an opportunity had to present itself.

Marcus left with Charles to the attorney's office. Charles began his questioning, "son, can you tell me what happened? I'm your defense attorney, and I will do what's best for you." Marcus began, "I can't believe what I did. The police freed me from jail; I wanted revenge for my baby brother, who my gang killed in a drive-by at my place. I was looking for his killer. I heard a gunshot and saw my friend Alfred dead on the ground. I had so much rage in me. I looked and saw Antonio holding the gun with an evil smirk on his face; I couldn't control myself. I aimed and fired. Once I started firing, I couldn't stop myself; then it was all over, and I hated myself for killing another human being." Charles could tell Marcus's mind was still in a state of shock. He knew a psychiatrist had to be involved, as he was more than sure Marcus' defense would be temporary insanity.

Angel had once briefly met Alfred's parents, Pedro and Maria. The former biker was feeling remorse about everything, especially about involving Alfred in gang life. Angel attended his funeral but viewed it from a distance, as he wasn't ready to face Alfred's parents. He covered the burial expense because he didn't want these people to have that burden after suffering the tragic loss of their son; their finances had already burdened them. Angel requested that the funeral home director let this gift be anonymous. Angel wanted to lavish them with money as a guilt offering, but he knew this would only offend them. Angel also knew that he could no longer give away tainted money. He had legal money besides, thanks to Dr. Thomas. He had a talent for determining the stock market; he knew when it was safe to invest and when it was time to remove the investments. Dr. Thomas had many financial advisors, who were church members, and he informed them about Angel's gift. Angel lacked the education to be a financial advisor, but a firm of FAs had offered to pay for his education. They also paid Angel well for his stock market findings. Angel didn't want to work nine to five right now, but he agreed to email his conclusions. The FAs paid him well for this. He also looked forward to going to school. He took an adult education course and learned rapidly. He then took the high school equivalency test and passed it. He also took the college entrance exam and passed that, as well. He had saved the money the FAs paid him and made his investments, which quickly multiplied. He was on the verge of becoming a millionaire.

Angel had kept this money separate from the blood money. He obtained more increase from this in a short time than in his whole tenure in the gangs. However, Angel never gave the blood money away because Dr. Thomas advised him to pray about what God would have him do. The funeral was wrapping up, and Angel stood and prayed about facing Alfred's parents and offering his condolences. He didn't want to, but he felt it was time to grow up, be responsible, and do as God would have him do. He then walked up to Pedro and Maria. When the couple saw him, they thought about Alfred's adoration of him. They embraced him, and they all cried uncontrollably. Angel tried to confess, "There's something you need to know." Angel began. But Pedro stopped him. Seeing the pain on Angel's face told him what he was about to say to him would bring about more pain. "You can tell me later, Angel. There's enough sadness. Let's, please don't invite more." Angel was suppressing his hurt and needed to cry; however, he honored Pedro's request.

Angel's heart was in pain for the Dominguez's, so he attempted to give them a cashier's check anonymously. Although it was a considerable sum of money, when the Dominguez's saw the check, they instantly knew it was from Angel. They felt that the money was illegal and probably guilt money, yet, they had never once blamed Angel for Alfred's death. They knew that Angel had ignored the gangs for months while Alfred remained in the gang. They didn't want the money because they felt they had brought a curse on themselves by accepting Alfred's money without question. They believed losing Alfred was a part of the curse. So, they phoned Angel. "Angel," Pedro began, "We need to meet with you. Please come to the house today for lunch if you can." Angel replied, "Sure, give me the time."

"Any time after eleven,"

Angel dreaded the meeting with the Dominguez's; he knew they had figured out that he was the one who gave them the check and that they wouldn't accept guilt money. However, he loved them and wanted them out of poverty. They met at Pedro's house. Angel then rang their doorbell, and they invited him in. Pedro began, "Angel, thank you so much for coming to Alfred's funeral; you didn't have to keep your distance, no one's angry with you." Angel was still trying to hold back his tears, and it was becoming more difficult. "You are just too kind," Angel said. Pedro then came to the point. "Angel, we can't accept your money. Please don't get the wrong idea; we know you're showing compassion. The truth is, we turned a blind eye to Alfred's illegal money; we now believe this is why we lost him. We can't accept money from you because we don't want to lose you too."

Their kindness was too much, and he broke down and cried uncontrollably. He vented his guilt. "I never should have involved Alfred in gang life. My life is so unbearable without him—he was like my little brother, and I miss him dreadfully." Tears were now streaming down his face. The Dominguezs' heart went out to him, and they embraced him and held him hard for a long time. "Angel, it's no more your fault than ours. Our son adored you. Angel, we know you haven't been involved in the gangs for months. Alfred was. We don't blame you. Please don't blame yourself." Angel then knew he had to tell them about his legal job. "I have a legal job now that pays me handsomely. I wouldn't offer you illegal money, God is my provider now, and I believe He wants me to contribute some to you."

"We still can't take it. We're trusting in God more. It's what we learned from losing Alfred."

"Please, I must insist that you take it. It's not just guilt. I love you, so please accept this in Alfred's memory." That's the only way they would accept it. Then Pedro told Angel emphatically, "I'll accept your gift, but please come around more often" Angel agreed; Juan and Carmen often visited them as well, and often, with Angel. Pedro felt that this was their extended family; God had given them comfort for the loss of their only son.

Monica had finished up with all of her patients. She left the clinic and had just locked the door to the office when a hand reached out and covered her mouth. "You better be quiet, pretty lady; do you feel this gun against your head." She nodded her head in fright, wondering what was going on. At least three people had abducted her. She was terrified, and her life flashed before her. They were taking her to their secret location at their warehouse.

She was praying hard, especially for Angel, as she believed he was the one this gang wanted. They were deliberately rough with her. But, somehow, she knew it could have been worse for her if not for her prayers.

They transported her in their GMC SUV to their safe house, then presented her to Sergio. Sergio was short and stout, handsome, with dark hair, olive-colored skin, and dark brown eyes. He feasted his eyes on Monica's beauty. Then, he ordered the gang, "Please remove the tape from her mouth." They obeyed him. Sergio appreciated women's beauty; therefore, he would not allow the gang to rape her. Still, he had to kill her. Angel had to pay somehow. However, he would shower this beautiful woman with gifts, for now, make sure she was comfortable and got the best he had to offer.

He talked to her, "I know you are frightened, my rare beauty, but rest assured my colleagues will not harm you in any way." He showed her his gun. "This is insurance that they won't," Monica said nothing; she was relieved and believed Sergio was telling the truth. She was grateful for the favor she had with him. The favor came from God. Only she didn't favor the other gang members, even though Sergio gave his assurance; if the gang were desperate enough, they would commit mutiny to have their way with her. Monica could only pray. She and Angel were abstaining from each other to renew their vows and enjoy a honeymoon together. *Please, Dear God, don't allow these men to take what is Yours and a pure gift to be given to Angel. It's so sacred. Please, Dear God, don't allow it.* Sergio had his weapon drawn as the gang members flocked all around, staring at Monica with hungry eyes.

Chapter 12

Angel was late meeting Monica at Don Pistons Mexican Restaurant on Union Street. The man looked everywhere. Sometimes Monica would get detained at her parents' house, which caused her to be late. The former biker wasn't concerned until he had waited almost two hours. He hated to call her parents because he wasn't their favorite person, and sometimes, Monica's father gave him the third degree. However, it appeared he had no choice, so he made the call.

Joseph Lewis, Monica's father, answered the phone, Angel's heart fell to his feet. Angel was bold and courageous, but Monica's parents had always intimidated him. He recalled when they had first met. Although they were unaware he was a biker, Angel insisted they know the truth when time passed. With Angel, one either accepted him or they didn't. Angel could live with either decision. However, the hardest one he made was when he told Monica she had to accept him. The former biker would have felt a significant loss if she had abandoned him. He was genuinely grateful he never had that experience. Nonetheless, now he had to know where Monica was, so he asked, "Mr. Lewis, is Monica over there?"

"No, Garcia. Why do you ask?"

Angel was disturbed now but didn't want to alarm Mr. Lewis until he knew a reason. So he replied, "No reason, just wondered. She's a little late for our date, but I'm sure she'll be along soon."

"Yea, Garcia. You better be right if you know what's good for you." Mr. Lewis hung up on Angel before saying goodbye.

This abruptness had once offended him, only now he made changes in his life and had developed more patience. ; Angel wanted a relationship with them now, when before he didn't care. He never told Monica to choose between them, though he wouldn't visit them with her. However, the past years were a waste. Her parents thought they had already separated. Again, he recalled the time he had to take out an opposing gang member for holding Monica at gunpoint. Monica had separated from him; briefly, Angel wished he hadn't pursued her, he just loved and wanted her too much, and Monica felt the same way. From that point on, for her safety, they had to meet in secret. All her parents and everyone else knew was that they had separated but never divorced.

Angel was sure that something had happened to Monica. He had nowhere to turn, but to God, he fervently prayed, *"Father God, please remove this alarm and concern, replace it with peace, and please assure me that Monica is safe."* It appeared God was letting him know that he wasn't going to be hearing from her right away. Nonetheless, God promised him that she was safe. So he kept praying, and God was providing him, His peace.

Monica remembered her date with Angel. She thought. How worried and concerned he must be. *Will he retaliate? Angel is a different person now, and I know this could be a test. Can Angel pass it?* She was fearful for herself but more concerned about Angel's reaction. She began her prayer, again, *"Please, Lord, be with Angel. Guide him and don't allow him to react in anger. Let him be wise and seek you. Let him confide in Larry, who will give him knowledge and wisdom about what to do. Bring someone to my rescue so Angel and I will spend the rest of our days worshiping and serving You. I trust You, Lord. I know You have the best for Angel and me."*

Sergio had most of the gang members controlled; he threatened to hold on to their ransom share. However, there is a gang member named Mario who doesn't follow the rules. Antonio had kept him around because he had shown himself an expert with weapons in the past and brought in a lot of revenue from drugs and weapons sales. However, Mario had embezzled much of the gang's money and was clever and careful not to get caught. Sergio didn't trust Mario. Antonio had an elaborate lifestyle. So, between Mario's cheating and Antonio's splurging, the gang's finances were dwindling. They would have killed Angel for nothing, but they honestly needed his money. So that's why they would demand a ransom, and Sergio makes sure it didn't fall apart. He knew Monica had to be unscathed, so he repeatedly told his gang members, "You won't touch her if you want to see a payday." Mario, however, seemed to be deaf to this order, as he had a secret motivation to molest her.

Earl missed seeing Angel, he sensed something was wrong, but he quickly learned God solves problems were more efficiently through prayer. He also felt whatever was happening with Angel was somehow gang-related. Angel had high favor with his gang, and Earl prayed for God's favor to remain, when Angel announced he was leaving the gang, for his faith, giving up ways of the world, was a kinder way to identify it than to call it criminal activity, which is what it was. However, Earl and Angel wanted to reach these gang members, so they had to be careful with terminology and not appear judgmental.

Earl now had freedom at the Mission to mobilize on his own He had completed his community service hours. Therefore, Pastor Marvin had given his consent for this freedom and had the courts approve it. However, Earl still had to be in rehab until the courts released him. He loved giving his testimony at all the services; he had a hunger for the things of God and strongly desired to serve. He was assigned by the courts to live there, be in rehab, and donate his community service hours. The former addict's hours had been completed. He loved his service to the Mission and planned on serving, even after completed his mandate for the court system. Earl thought of the place God brought him through—a place of bondage. He was a slave to addiction and sin. Yes, he hated his past sinful life, even though God made a beautiful testimony out of it. Earl had learned fast to rebuke the devil, as Satan loves reminding us about our pasts; however, God uses our history to our benefit. We don't have to be ashamed of it, though; we shouldn't be proud of it either. It's there as a reminder to never return to it. Earl thought of himself as the chief of sinners, who had become one of Christ's most dedicated followers.

Larry and Summer had toured all over the city; Larry had rented a 2003 Mercedes Benz E class although Summer had lived in luxury; she had never experienced the elegance this car had. She knew it was the same model as Larry had in Minion; however, Larry's heart she loved the most. Although the young woman did like the idea of his being financially sound, it wouldn't have mattered to her if he was a blue-collar worker, making a modest wage and driving a modest preowned economy car. Instead, it was the man she adored. God had given her a complete blessing with Larry. She recalled his testimony; it was a perfect example of how God had raised beauty from ashes. Larry had almost lost it all, and if nothing had changed, he eventually would have lost his life.

She wondered what would have happened if she had waited for Larry. But then, she thought of what wouldn't have happened, and that was Ruby Destiny. Yes, she couldn't deny she was happy with Mike. He had led her to Larry. But, this destiny only would've occurred by marrying him. She had witnessed God weaving the whole picture before her; everything that had happened in her life was shaping her future. Even the unhappiness in her childhood had made her the person she was—a person God wanted and needed to use. She never thought she would ever praise Him for the unhappiness of her past, but that was what she was doing. She looked again at Larry behind the wheel and smiled as they began their tour throughout San Francisco.

Charles had decided to involve Psychiatrist Dr. Craig Williamson in Marcus' case. First, he would have Dr. Williamson determine his mental capacity; when he shot Antonio, Marcus knew this man's determination could change his life for either incarceration or freedom. Second, he knew Dr. Williamson was a potential witness for his defense, but what if his diagnosis showed he was mentally sound when he shot Antonio? Then the good Doctor could become a witness for the prosecution, and the case Charles was creating on his behalf, could backfire.

Larry had advised, "Marcus, please stay positive no matter what. You have to believe for the best."

Marcus declared, "I'm trying, really trying." But the truth was Marcus's life hasn't been positive. He felt he didn't know how to be positive. Then the boy remembered prayer was the secret. Where was God when Traye and Alfred were murdered? If God was good, why did tragedy always have to occur? Why couldn't his mother have been a mother to him? Why was she on drugs? And why did she have to die? Why couldn't he have known his father? And why couldn't God talk him out of killing Antonio? He wanted answers to these questions, and maybe, when he had these answers, he could be positive.

Charles could tell by the look on Marcus' face that he was having doubts; Charles wasn't a Christian but believed in positive thinking. The attorney always advised his clients to believe the best would happen. The attorney also thought that when he lost a case, his clients weren't positive enough. He was a free thinker. God was the only one who could judge him. He believed accomplishments, even spiritual ones, were achieved from his power. Charles also thought he could solve his problems, regardless of their enormity. Though he had to confess, there were many pressing problems he couldn't solve. He just had to live with them, no matter how burdensome. He noticed, however, how free Larry had seemed as he claimed, that he gave all of his burdens to Jesus; Charles had to admit, it would be nice to be free of burdens.

Charles was now 42 years old, but he had been a street person since he was 15. In his family were his father Richard, mother Marge, and younger sister Jenna. He would see his sister from time to time, but she lived far away in Wisconsin. She hated the fast life of the city, so she chose to relocate there. She lived with a man named George Olson, and they had a 10-year-old son named Alex. Alex and Charles were close, but he never knew about Charles' past life of hustling drugs, and weapons, to make a living. He was extremely wealthy from his activities. He was never a member of a gang, but he liked making money from many different gangs. The gangs also found him to be helpful. His father's dream for him was to have a higher education, and Charles's lifetime dream was to become a lawyer. He was inquisitive and diplomatic, so he was equipped and qualified for this position. His family wasn't incredibly wealthy; however, they saved for his education. Charles had a massive revenue from selling drugs and weapons. Since his parents funded his education, he had saved a lot of money to have his practice when he was out of law school.

He was glad when he passed the bar exam. He was relieved he longer needed to sell drugs, or participate, in any other gang-related revenue. Instead, he planned to represent the gangs legally. Why not? They had extreme wealth and paid generously. When he opened his practice, he had many clients involved in gangs and crime, and he had many legitimate clients. Many of them knew about his nefarious activities, but Charles was the best, and they wanted the best. The only thing people didn't like about Charles was his frequent personality changes and demeanor, as he would be good at times, bad at times, and even ugly. However, because of his reputation for success, that didn't matter to his clients. They wanted a winner, and Charles was a winner.

Dr. Williamson had talked to Marcus, he had always been a tough street kid, but now he was like a scared little boy. He asked him questions about his past life. "Marcus, I know you live with your grandma, and you lost your little brother. Can you explain to me why you chose to join a gang?"

"I guess I don't know, and there was a lot about the gangs I hated. However, they did make me feel like I was a part of their family."

"Can you tell me about your childhood?"

"I lived most of my life with my grandmother and my brother, and I only remember a few things; my mother was on drugs and left Traye and me alone a lot. So I had to take care of him, and I made sure we had food and whatever else we needed." This fact convinced Dr. Williamson that Marcus had to steal for his and his brother's survival.

"Do you remember anything else in the time before you came to live with your grandmother?"

"No, not very much." Marcus didn't remember much about that time. However, he did seem to have a few flashbacks of his father. The boy recalled the pain he felt when he was told his mother died when he was ten years old and Traye was three. His Grandma Brenda had mourned her, the woman had blamed herself, she never told him how she died, but Marcus knew she was on drugs, and he knew people died from overdoses.

He helped raise little Traye, and he was glad about the Christian rally he became involved in because he never wanted Traye to become entangled in a gang. That thought brought about deep pain, and Marcus stopped answering the doctor's questions. Dr. Williamson knew it would take some time for Marcus to have a breakthrough; he had to give him time. So he called and told Charles, "When you talk with prosecutor Wilshire, please have him call me. I can't make any decisions about a court date just yet, because I must continue assessing Marcus." After the call, he addressed Marcus, "ok, Marcus, that's it for today. We'll continue tomorrow. Please think hard and try to remember the time you lived with your mother. Can you do that?"

"I'll try my best." But, the truth is that reflecting on the past was painful for Marcus, especially with Traye gone.

Dr. Williamson suspected there were painful occurrences in Marcus's childhood and had Marcus's court date moved up. "Hello Pete, it's Craig; I need a later court date for my patient. He's experiencing flashbacks and has a bad memory lapse. So I have to have more time with him for his trial to be fair."

"I understand, Craig," Pete replied. "But it can't be indefinite; I have too many cases on the docket."

"Yes, Pete, I understand, and I only want enough time to decide the proper placement for his treatment. However, he does need treatment, and I'm already certain incarceration is not the answer."

"Ok, then I'll notify his attorney and the prosecutor that there'll be a delay."

"Thank you so much, Pete. I owe you."

"Well, if you insist on a payback, give me the chance to beat you in a round of golf when court is over." Craig just laughed; Pete has never beaten him in golf.

Charles was glad for the delay. The defense accepted Dr. Williamson's request immediately, Robert Wilshire was a tough prosecutor, but he respected whatever Dr. Williamson recommended. Robert was also self-confident about his case, believing nothing would keep him from prosecuting Marcus. Marcus was only 16, so Wilshire knew he would have to cut through some red tape to charge him as an adult. Charles hoped that wouldn't happen. Charles didn't respect the Red Vipers, and he would never handle any case for any of them. He would have to fight hard for Marcus because tried as an adult, his name would be in the newspapers, and then the Vipers wouldn't rest until they wasted him.

After Larry and Summer toured the city, they once again patronized The Cable Car diner. "We'll call this our place." Summer remarked, "only until I have the opportunity to take you to a more elaborate cuisine." Larry replied

"Wherever you take me, this will always be our first place. It's also kind of our first date. The last time we were here doesn't count." Larry said, changing the subject, "We want lunch to be light; Lynn is preparing roast beef, with all the trimmings for dinner." They then ordered roasted chicken subway sandwiches on wheat bread garnished with spinach, tomatoes, extra dill pickles, and extra mayonnaise. Chips also come with the order, but they decided to share one small bag of chips. After they ate, they headed to the Rescue Mission. Pastor Marvin and Earl greeted them. "It's so good to see you, Larry. I'm glad you stopped by. Let me show you around," Pastor Marvin stated.

"Is Marcus here?" Summer asked.

Pastor Marvin answered her, "A psychiatrist is assessing him for a legal decision on his case. It'll be later this afternoon before he gets back. I want to thank you, Larry, for your recommendation. When minors come to us, we can work with them and rehabilitate them before it's too late. Marcus shows promise, and he'll be here until a decision is made on his case." Pastor Marvin's optimism gave both Summer and Larry peace of mind. Larry then went with Pastor Henry to view the mission. Larry had never seen such an organization; it had three quarters—one for single men, another for single women, and the other for families. He was surprised because he had expected to see run-down old houses; it was a newly built, extravagant building with modern conveniences. The quarters for the singles served the meals, but all the residents had to contribute to the meals with job assignments, such as helping with food preparation, cooking, serving, and cleaning up. The quarters for the families had three kitchen areas, allowing a parent or older child to cook the meals. Larry was highly impressed. "Summer, this reminds me very much of the camp I stayed in when I was in recovery. Let's, please, stay for the meeting." Pastor Marvin added, "we also hold weekly meetings at Glad Tidings to prepare this group for graduation from the Mission. They will be allowed to stay here until they are employed and stable." Larry was impressed at all the benefits the residents had. "Far more is being done than when I was in recovery; these men, women, and their families have a brand-new start." Pastor Marvin told them, "There are organizations who supply professional attires, interviews, and wardrobes when the residents receive the jobs. Many employers hire these residents because the Mission gave them a great reference. Larry decided to volunteer at the Mission for two or three hours every day, and he extended his stay in San Francisco. He saw a massive need in the ministry for young people. The time had passed, soon, so this pastor would return to Minion. However, he wanted to take a day to pray about being in the ministry here. He felt the tug of God calling him, but he wanted to give time in prayer and be sure. Larry also learned Glad Tidings owned the Mission.

Summer remained silent; she was surprised that Larry was considering a ministry here. Larry didn't seem to notice she never commented; he was too enthused. The young woman now felt ready to return to Minion; Larry's job was there. She no longer wanted any part of the fast pace of the city and wanted to go back to living in a quiet little town; she had to pray though, this could be what God called Larry to do; she knew she had to respect, whatever decision Larry made. However, she didn't want to risk losing him again; Summer was insecure, it was still hard to believe that Larry wanted her. She recalled having some of these issues with Mike; however, losing Larry would be more devastating.

She recalled the year when he left for seminary; she missed him for what seemed like an eternity. But, time did heal, and she moved on, or at least she thought so, until that day at his church when she and Larry had the electrifying handshake that shook her world. She had been thinking about him ever since. And it appeared their feelings were mutual. Her mind lingered on the kiss they shared when he came from Lubbock and united with her. He had occupied her mind ever since. Her hope now is that they'd become engaged. She also believed that this would release her insecurity.

Sergio was trying to put his plan together. He didn't trust Mario; he caught him three times, him coming near Monica, glaring at her with his lustful eyes. He continually let him know, "You will not have a share in the ransom if you don't leave this girl alone." All he could do was warn him and have Monica watched at all times. The biggest issue was Mario had money; it wasn't a big deal for him to lose in the ransom. He had been abstemious with all the money he had confiscated. Sergio also knew whoever he commanded to guard Monica could be bought by Mario. He had always suspected Mario of skimming off the top. However, he never had proof. With Antonio, Mario was never the problem that he is now. Sergio only knew that he had to watch Mario like a hawk at all costs.

Charles had never cared for a client like he did Marcus; Angel had paid him a handsome fee, but, truthfully, he knew he would serve Marcus pro bono. Charles favored Marcus couldn't figure it out, as money was his primary motivation for existing. He never married but had a relationship once, actually an engagement. However, it ended because of his illegal activities.

Her name was Marguerite Larson, and she was the epitome of beauty in his eyes; she was petite, had fair skin, long, reddish-golden hair, and emerald green eyes. Her devastating features kept him entranced. They had met when he was in college; she was so honest and sincere that he was naturally deceitful about his past and present career. Only she found out anyway and confronted him, "Charles, why have you lied to me? Our whole relationship is a farce. I don't know who you are!" He couldn't explain, and the truth was out. However, he chose to justify his actions instead. "You don't understand; you were born with a silver spoon; I had to struggle to survive. I couldn't keep struggling when there was another way."

"Even if I weren't born with a silver spoon, I wouldn't break the law and hurt people to get ahead. I have to break up with you; I won't let myself become like you." She then took off his ring and gave it back to him.

"Fine then," was all Charles could manage. He had spoken in a detestable manner.

This painful memory ripped out his heart. He tried to never think about this woman or their horrible fight; He tried not to envision the unstoppable tears in Marguerite's eyes or the pain in her face when she sadly announced they were over. He often wanted to find her and reconcile. He even thought about stopping his defense of criminals and becoming a more honest man. He had enough legitimate clients. He had enough money to start a new life together. However, Charles chose to cling to his pride. He had made his choice; he had to suppress the heartbreak he would forever have over losing Marguerite. The attorney learned throughout the years to dismiss her from his mind. And he did it daily and at many times during the day. He did keep track of her. He knew she never married anyone else, nor did she have any other lasting relationships. This knowledge gave his heart a certain amount of peace and comfort.

Marcus thought himself to be such a rigid gang member, but he was always different from the other members. He never liked the violence. At twelve, Marcus had the experience of stealing, but that was for survival, for Traye and him. He always had a conscience about it, and he never wanted to participate. However, to be initiated, Marcus had to be a thief at least. He only stole because he would instead do that than kill; it was a true miracle that this gangster could get out of killing; as a member, to be initiated, he was required to shoot someone. But Marcus stood his ground about that. He said, "I will steal as much as you want me to, but I'm never going to kill anyone."

"Ok, man, from now on, you will do all the stealing." Darien, the gang leader, said. Marcus was relieved. He didn't realize that he took Darien, and the other gang members, off the hook. When the times came, and he'd get busted, the other members wouldn't be around. However, he still wouldn't snitch on them; Marcus took all the risks, which pleased Darien. Dr. Williamson could see Marcus was suppressing a lot of pain. He dreaded the excruciating pain he was about to encounter; however, the pain was necessary for his recovery. The doctor knew the source of the pain involved Traye's death and even Alfred's, but something deeper had to emerge. Marcus would get to the point about his mother and father and then clam up. The psychiatrist considered that Marcus was suppressing a painful memory. He could dismiss this pain and take his mind somewhere else. It would always go to Traye, as those were some of his fondest memories. It often took many years for some patients who suppressed painful memories to break through. Sadly, Marcus was about to face court, and the court wouldn't wait. Dr. Williamson believed Marcus was temporarily insane when he shot Antonio, as he showed immediate remorse, and shock, in the question, *"What have I done?"* And Dr. Williamson believed Marcus wouldn't have done it if his frame of mind wasn't so fragile, yes, Marcus was temporarily insane, but Marcus also had another pressing mental issue. There was a good Mental Health unit in the juvenile correctional facility. He was going to inform Charles, the prosecutor, and the judge that Marcus remains under his care.

He prayed all parties would agree because this was indeed the best placement for Marcus.

Dr. Craig Williamson was 55 years old. Craig was married to his wife, Shirley, who was two years younger than him. They had been married for 30 years. They had two grown children—a son, Josiah, 27, and Melinda, 24. They each lived in different states—the son in Nebraska and the daughter in Colorado.

Dr. Williamson had some severe problems growing up and decided to become a psychiatrist to help people. He had his practice, but he also volunteered two days a week at the Mental Health Clinic; Craig believed lack of finances should never be an issue in mental health. When society ignores mental problems, they become society's problem. He also cared about people, and he knew God was the healer. Craig always prayed, for his patients, before he treated them. This man always consulted God for all diagnoses and treatments; Craig relied on God heavily. The doctor knew Marcus' treatment could be chronic, he wasn't mature enough to be tried as an adult, and he did show remorse for the killing. The boy never had a lengthy juvenile rap sheet. He knew Pete Mate would be the judge, and he and Pete played rounds of golf regularly; Craig was also friends with the prosecutor, Robert Wilshire, who he had invited him to church, and Robert attended often. Yet, he never decided for Christ, and neither did Pete Mate. However, Craig spent much time in prayer for them both. Now they would have to go their separate ways because Marcus's case involved them all and could cause a conflict of interest.

Sergio was considering asking for a ransom; he knew Angel could come up with $400,000 easily. However, he had to view all the risks and consequences; Monica was a beloved health professional, someone could ask a sizable reward for information about her death. This viper had to consider that he would have to leave the country. He had family in Sienna, Italy, and he knew he would have no choice but to go. He never told the other three involved how much the ransom would be, and he would make a deal, with his confidant Alberto, to handsomely increase his share. There was a condition, Alberto, would be sworn to keep the amount of the ransom a secret. He would deceive the gang into thinking they would get a four-way split of $100,000 when the actual ransom would be $1,000,000. Alberto would have to be the only one to pick it up.

After twenty-four hours, Sergio made a call to Angel, "Finally, the call you've been expecting Garcia, she's unharmed, but I'll let you talk to her. First, let's get down to business; it'll be $1,000,000 for her safe return. Just make sure there's no cops or any other interference, or I'll have her wasted. There's a pervert here who wants her, and if things don't go right, I'll let him do whatever he wants to her. Do I make myself clear?"

"Sure, man, whatever you want, just please don't hurt her. Can I please speak to her now?" Sergio put Monica on the phone. "Angel, are you okay."

"Of course, my love. I just hope you are ok. I hope no one's hurt you."

"They haven't, but please be careful; I love you." She was concerned because she overheard the plot to kill him. She couldn't let him know this, and she could only leave it in God's hands.

"I love you too," Angel replied. He wanted to let her know he planned her rescue. But, of course, he couldn't. So then Sergio came back on the line. "Remember Garcia, no tricks."

"No tricks." Angel lied. He knew they would have Monica killed anyway. The biker also hoped that what Sergio said was true and that that pervert didn't already assault her.

Sergio continued, "well, then, we have an agreement, and I'll have someone meet you tomorrow. I'll call just before the meeting, to let you know where. Nothing better go wrong."

Angel, of course, had to make them believe he agreed to their demands; however, he had to have insurance that she would be safe. He knew the Jokers could get her out safely. Angel didn't want to deal with them; he then prayed about it. He had to go with the Jokers for Monica's rescue, and he asked for God's forgiveness if it wasn't the right decision.

Angel met with the Jokers. "Where have you been. We have missed you." Juan, one of the gang members, replied. Angel merely told them, "I have a different kind of life now. Attending church and all that good stuff." Angel asked for wisdom as he spoke to them. They felt a little angry and betrayed, but they still loved him. It was unusual to let a member out of the gang without violent consequences, let alone a leader; nonetheless, they trusted Angel and believed he would never betray them. They had paranoid thoughts in the beginning, but that turned to favor. The gang didn't understand this. Juan began again jokingly, "Well, I don't have any issue with being the leader now, I wish; however, it was Alfred. We miss him and love him so much. It was losing Alfred that gave us second thoughts about turning on you. We love you, too." Angel's tears began to flow, and he tried to stop them. Juan then said, "we all know how you felt about Alfred; he deserves all our tears; go on and cry, Bro!" Their kindness touched, Angel knew God's hand was in this; only He could move a vicious gang to show grace. Juan began again, "We do need assurance that you will never rat us out. You've never lied to us, and we will believe your word."

"I could never turn you over to the law; I would serve time. But, first, I swear." Then Angel told them about Monica's kidnapping. After that, the gang all agreed to rescue Monica, and Mario owed them a favor to quickly find the safe house.

Mario knew Sergio was keeping a close eye on him; he wanted Monica badly, he was trying to think of a distraction for Sergio. He had paid two other Vipers to distract Sergio so that he could get at Monica. It had to work and be done without Sergio's knowledge. The members involved didn't want to have any confrontations with Sergio. So, one gang member told Sergio, "There are cops outside. We have to be careful." This information didn't sit right with Sergio; however, he went to the front door to look.

When Sergio was at the front door, Mario slipped into the room where Monica was. It had to work.

Sergio noticed earlier Mario had toned down his interest in Monica. He didn't believe it but thought maybe Mario had wised up to the plan and had a greater interest in a share of the ransom. At least Sergio hoped this was the case. Sergio was also aware; this could be a trick. He looked out and observed: Sergio knew his police cars, marked and unmarked, and saw nothing. He went back and saw Monica's door partially opened; Sergio had it under lock and key; he walked in and found Monica with a shattered look on her face, and Mario straddled over her. "You creep, I should have known you were up to something." Mario had a look of fright on his face, Sergio was a powerful man, and he lifted Mario off of her as though he were a feather. Mario had squirmed out of his grasp and ran out the door and escaped. Sergio's instinct was to run after Mario, but he was too close to attaining the ransom, so he had to let him go for now. He wasn't worried, as he knew Mario wasn't going to the law. Mario had too much of a rap sheet. He couldn't worry about Mario because his primary concern was leaving the country and taking Alberto.

Mario then left and went to his hiding place; he met with Angel and his gang. Mario had owed a favor to one of the Jokers, he had helped him on a drug run, and it involved hundreds of thousands of dollars. He was able to keep this score a secret from Antonio and the other Vipers. Angel asked his favor to find Monica. "Have you seen Monica?" He didn't want to respond to Angel. Because of his attempt on Monica. He was afraid for his life. He saw Juan and owed him a favor. He began, "Yes, I'll tell you exactly where she is." He stalled them. "But first, I have an important phone call to make." He has connected the line to find the next plane to Cancun, Mexico. He was sure Monica would rat him out about his advances, and he was terrified of Angel. After Mario hung up, he stalled again. "I have to find someone else to help us; I'll leave you my dearest possession, this St. Christopher medal." Juan knew how much Mario valued the medal. He thought it kept him alive. So, Juan persuaded Angel to let Mario leave. Juan said, "Please, man, he has to be telling the truth; he wouldn't part with that medal."

Angel chatted to Mario in anger, "You are my only chance to get Monica back; if you don't come back, you know I can have you tracked down." Mario did; he knew Angel's reputation of always finding his victims. He groveled, "I know you can have me put to death; I wouldn't betray you, just please let me take care of this one issue, and your wife is as good as in your arms. I owe Juan a big favor, and I won't let you down." He sincerely was glad to oblige Juan. He helped him get the biggest score of his life, and it was enough to leave the country and get far away from Angel and Monica. So, he arranged to be in Cancun, Mexico, by the time they found her.

The look of fear in Mario's eyes spared him from Angel. Angel knew he wouldn't dare cross him

Before he boarded the plane, Mario called Juan "the safe house where Monica is located, by the pier." He gave the exact location. Angel's finding Monica was also his way of getting revenge on Sergio.

Angel and the gang found the safe house and entered cautiously and quietly. They heard Monica's moans. They hid as they heard Sergio head to her room. It was four hours before they were to trade the ransom money in exchange for Monica. They hid, stayed extremely quiet, and never moved a muscle. Angel wasn't a physical match for Sergio, so he had to be cleverer. Finally, Sergio left the room, and Monica was quiet. This alarmed Angel. He then entered the room when Sergio was far away. The Jokers could hear Sergio warning his Vipers, "you will pay a heavy price if you betray me; I have a hitman looking for a traitor who abandoned ship." they knew he was talking about Mario.

The Jokers kept watch and were willing to give everything to help Angel and Monica. Angel had untied Monica, but the tape was already off of her mouth. He whispered as low as he could. "Are you okay, baby?" Monica barely whispered, "Please, Angel, they can't find you." They heard the Vipers talking, and their voices grew closer. Angel and Monica moved as fast as possible to the nearest exit; the Jokers helped them safely. From the house, they heard Sergio yell in a loud voice, "where is she? How did they find her?" He was sure it was with Mario's help. "I'll murder that little creep myself!". Angel's gang was outside the house with their weapons, prepared for a shootout. The Vipers began shooting, and the Jokers returned fire. Many of the Vipers had fallen; Sergio saw too few Vipers left, so he ran. The remaining Vipers also ran. Angel's gang shouted for their victory, "Yeee Ahhh!" then looked on the ground and found Angel shot. They were all as pale as ghosts because they knew this was Angel's third bullet wound. No gang member, to their knowledge, had ever survived three bullet wounds. All the tough Jokers were standing over Angel, with tears in their eyes, watching Monica as she applied pressure to Angel's chest to stop the bleeding. She had called 911 with Angel's cell phone. "Please, please," she said, sobbing desperately, "Come, fast, a man's been shot. I know it's his third bullet wound. Please hurry!" In tears, Monica was praying fervently. As a nurse, Monica knew what a third bullet wound meant.

They heard sirens from a distance; she told the gang, "I know you want to stay, but you must go. I appreciate what you risked for me, but Angel wouldn't want you to get arrested. Please go!" They left, but Monica could see they didn't want to leave Angel. It's true the law rarely investigated gang wars, but it was never a good idea to be present at the scene. They left in the SUV that they had arrived. They went back to their house. They would give their bikes a rest for now until Angel could ride with them once more. Juan told the other jokers. "I've asked Monica to keep us updated, we do know the score, but we have to believe Angel is going to survive. I think we need to talk to his God."

Larry and Summer were about to say their goodbyes. Larry told Lynn, "I'm coming back to stay. I've talked to Pastor Thomas, I've decided to be the Recovery Pastor; the pastor they have now is temporary. So I have to return to Minion to tie up loose ends." He had a few hours before his flight, the phone rang, and Lynn answered; then Lynn came back into the room with a look of shock on her face. Summer immediately asked, "Lynn, what's wrong?" Lynn didn't know how to begin to tell them. "Dr. Thomas called and said, "the paramedics rushed Angel to the emergency room for a bullet wound in his chest. He is in extremely critical condition and had emergency surgery last night to remove a bullet. It had missed his heart, but it was close. So it's touch and go, and they are preventing his hemorrhaging."

Larry immediately wanted to go to see Angel. He even considered postponing his flight. Lynn said, "Dr. Thomas mentioned this too; he asked me to tell you, please go on to Minion. There was nothing anyone can do for Angel but pray." Larry then said, "I will return to Minion, but I want to go to the hospital, to lay hands, and pray over him. Then I'll feel more confident to leave for Minion, leaving Angel in God's hands. Please, keep me posted. If he needs me or asks for me, I'll come back".

He and Summer left to visit Angel. Larry was allowed to go in as clergy, but since Summer wasn't family, she couldn't visit the ICU while he remained in such critical condition. Monica would never leave Angel's side. The nursing staff tried to convince her to take a break, then she saw Larry go into the ICU, "Larry, I'm going to give you and Angel some privacy."

"That's not necessary," Larry pleaded, "There's nothing to say that you can't hear."

"I need a break anyway, please Larry, ask God to please spare him. We've been through so much, and I can't be denied my new beginning with him."

"Monica, God will answer your prayer. Angel means a lot to many people. He has so much to offer. But, I have to believe that God will spare him."

Summer embraced Monica and tried to comfort her. However, comforting Monica now was almost impossible, except that she never gave up hope, as long as Angel drew a breath. It was a miracle for Angel to be alive. According to statistics, he should have died instantly. This fact gave Monica more hope. It also increased her faith. Monica never ceased praying for Angel.

Juan and Carmen, Angel's parents, were still in the ICU, and they introduced themselves to Larry. "We're Juan and Maria, Angel's parents, and you must be Larry; Angel has spoken very highly of you."

"It's so nice to meet you. A large chain of prayers is going out for your son. I believe God will work a miracle."

"That's so encouraging to hear. Angel's our only child. We pray hard God will give our son back to us if it's his will." Larry appreciated this attitude. Larry knew the pain of death; he had lost his parents and his best friend. It took a long time, but Larry had to accept that these losses were God's will. He knew even with powerful prayers, and people died anyway. However, Larry couldn't give up hope as long as Angel had breath in him. He then laid his hands-on Angel, asking if it was God's will to please give Angel a speedy recovery. First, he read to Angel a scripture about healing. It was John 11:1-44. Lazarus was already dead, and his family thought all hope was gone. Then Jesus raised him from the dead. His prayer began, "Father God, I place Angel in Your hands. We ask that you heal him and give him a complete and fast recovery, and we also ask for your will. I release my precious brother to you. Please give peace and comfort to his wife and all of his family. I ask this in the name of your son Jesus Amen." Juan and Carmen also prayed. As the couple was

SOUL WOUND

devout Catholics, o Larry's ways seemed abstract to them, though they couldn't deny the presence they had encountered, with Larry's laying on of hands. They spoke as Larry was leaving.

"Larry, thank you so much for your prayers; your style is a little different from ours; however, we are very impressed."

Dr. Williamson debated with himself about giving Marcus the news about Angel; Marcus' condition was fragile. He knew he couldn't keep the information from him indefinitely, but he didn't have to tell him immediately. The doctor had to pray about it. He kept hearing in his mind, *The Truth Will Set You Free*. If he kept this sad news from Marcus, how could he expect him to let go of a painful memory? He was indecisive. He committed this to prayer. In the meantime, he was still having therapy with Marcus and praying for a breakthrough. He also had to arrange a meeting with Charles, Prosecutor Wilshire, and Judge Pate; protecting Marcus was his priority; he prayed there wouldn't be any controversy about his decision.

Juan and Carmen said their goodbyes to Larry. Carmen said, "Larry, we have just met you, and we miss you already. It's easy to understand why our Angelito loves you so much." Then she spoke to Summer. "Summer, as Angel calls you his little sister, that must mean you are our daughter," Juan stated, jokingly. They all laughed, then they all hugged, and the Garcias went back into intensive care, praying wholeheartedly for Angel.

Juan and Carmen had extreme faith and believed tragedy meant it was God's will. Although they, of course, prayed for Angel to survive, they didn't want to mourn for him, but they had to put God first.

Lynn was also at the hospital talking to Dr. and Mrs. Thomas. Finally, summer announced, "It's that time."

Lynn then said goodbye to the pastor and his wife. "Dr. Thomas, please keep us posted about Angel. I have to leave and take Larry to the Airport."

"Of course, I will," Dr. Thomas said, giving Lynn's shoulder an affectionate squeeze.

She followed Summer and Larry to the airport. When Larry left, Summer would return home with her. Larry's one-week trip had turned out to be for three weeks. But he was due a vacation, as he had never had one in his two years of ministry. Summer felt sad about Larry's leaving, and she was already missing him. They would speak on the phone every night, and Larry would plan a visit from time to time. Before he would resign, he had to give his church enough time to find an appropriate replacement. Larry felt that was the least he could do.

He and Summer embraced and kissed at the security gate. "My sweet angel," Larry said with enthusiasm, touching and stroking her face. "How I'll miss you and our new little angel."

"Summer then spoke, "I know she's very young, but I'm sure R.D. misses you; Mike's parents have never spent time with her and request that she come to their house. I couldn't deny their request."

"I understand, R.D. needs to know them too. That baby as my heart too." I was just glad I could kiss her goodbye before she left.

"She's the only woman I'll share you with." Larry left Summer adoringly, looking at him, as he left for the boarding gate. He felt lonesome for her, and R.D. Larry loved the time spent with his baby girl; he couldn't have been anymore attached to her if she were biologically his. He never knew Mike, but he felt it was an honor to raise his child, and R.D. deserved a loving, devoted father like Larry.

Monica's dad, Joseph Lewis, was tall with a medium build, brown hair, hazel eyes, and striking features. Lisa Lewis was petite, with dark brown hair, blue eyes, and attractive features as well. They were considered family by marriage and attempted to visit the hospital; they loved Angel. However, it was as though they kept it a secret from Angel and Monica. Should they confess it now, likely, Monica and Angel wouldn't believe them. The animosity they had shown Angel now brought them deep sorrow in this crisis. They hurt for Monica, whom they greeted; she just blew them off. "So now you approve of him." Monica cried bitterly. "He was never good enough before. What is this? Guilt because you think he's dying? Perhaps you'll be relieved when he does. You know the consequences of a third bullet wound; maybe you'll finally be rid of him."

Lisa protested. "Monica, nothing could be farther from the truth." Monica then lit into them.

"Stop being hypocrites; you have never been anything but rude and hateful towards him; I want you to leave, and please don't come back. I never want you to be here again. If you try to return, I'll make sure the hospital bans you from here." They had no choice but to leave peacefully. They weren't Christians but turned to God, not only to repair their broken relationship with Monica but also to pray for Angel's healing. They did know the consequences of a third bullet wound, and they were terrified for Angel.

Juan and Carmen kept Pedro and Maria updated on Angel's condition. They weren't allowed to visit him in the ICU, but they were grateful for the consistent contact with the Garcias. "You heard from the Garcias'" Pedro asked Maria

"Yes, we have to pray. But, we can't lose you, Angel; we just found each other." Pedro prayed for God's will but wouldn't mention it to Maria because His will could mean taking Angel home. That very thought was painful.

They prayed long and hard because Angel was like another son to them. They had boundless faith and felt God's peace that

Angel would make a full recovery. They wanted to see Juan and Carmen, but they understood they had to stay at the hospital for Angel. It was a long, drawn-out process for everyone.

Angel was in a coma and a deep sleep, conversing with God. He was aware he was shot, and he also knew it was his third bullet wound. However, Angel felt a power and a presence that defied all odds. And he felt love—a love more powerful than any he had ever experienced. Angel never thought he fulfilled his purpose was on earth; he had a disregard for life. He judged and tried to place a value on life. He tried to justify his hits, declaring, these people were a waste. He felt the same way about the addicts, who overdosed, and died from the drugs he dealt. He had recurring dreams, and it was as though God were asking, "Angel, why did you take these lives? I am the Author of Life; you defied me."

This experience reminded Angel of Paul's Damascus Road (Acts 9:1–19) experience when Jesus asked Paul why he was persecuting Him. Angel knew then; his repentance wasn't genuine. Although he was attending church faithfully and abandoned his gang activity, he was only going through the motions. The last thing he wanted was to be in trouble with God. However, Angel thought he was in control of his salvation; he never thought it was as simple as accepting Jesus into his heart because nothing was ever simple for Angel. He was a criminal; he worked hard at it; he thought nothing worthwhile could come without hard work. He thought the same was true with his salvation. So, instead of accepting Jesus into his heart, he tried to work at being righteous, being involved in church, and no longer committing crimes. He didn't know this didn't erase his sins. He was conversing with God, asking him, "Please tell me when these nightmares will end."

Marcus was fighting his breakthrough; he had flashbacks and memories about his parents when he was about eight years old, only his mind refused to let him visit this place in his past. Though, somehow every tragedy seemed to carry him there. He recalled how Traye's death had brought much to the surface. He would see his mother's face with a look of horror and his father leaning over her with a look of rage. Marcus was able to suppress this recall deep in his subconscious, and he was able to keep the memory from rising to the surface. But, miraculously, Dr. Williamson was making matters difficult for him to control. Marcus didn't want any more sessions with Dr. Williamson. He tried to talk to Charles; he felt Charles had his best interest at heart. Then the boy remembered that Charles had told him his only chance, to get off, was temporary insanity. All he could see was that the search for temporary insanity led him to permanent insanity, and he was terrified of the outcome.

Robert Wilshire had met with Dr. Williamson, who was also his friend Craig. "Craig, when do we expect a trial date?"

Craig replied, "I will keep everyone posted, I promise, but Marcus's well-being is my first concern right now." But, Robert told him, "we can't decide a case not knowing the state of this young man's mentality."

"It won't be long; I will be having a meeting with all of you. Just please wait until that time." He sensed Craig was about to have some critical sessions with Marcus. Robert had read his history; he knew his tragic story. However, Marcus wouldn't answer questions the police had asked him. Maybe he had something to hide. Of course, the assistant D.A. knew that Charles had insisted, Marcus, not answer their questions. He didn't believe Marcus to be temporarily insane. He could sense he had a crucial mental health issue that could require him to be committed, to a behavioral medicine facility, for a long time. Robert didn't care. He just wanted to prove he was a danger to society.

He had every confidence he could win this case. He knew Pete Mate was a fair judge. He felt he and Pete agreed; only Craig seemed to have a knack for everything to go his way. Robert thought Craig's patients t should have incarcerated when Craig committed them to a shorter term of mental care. He knew this was his plan for Marcus, and Robert also knew he would try to get himself and the judge to agree. Then there was Charles, the defense attorney; The prosecutor admired Charles' cleverness as an attorney; only, Charles dealt with shady clients and had always managed to get them off entirely or with a mild sentence. So, yes, Robert did believe this to be a winnable case for himself, if he could get Pete to agree to try Marcus as an adult, and if the case went to trial.

R.D. was three weeks old and already sleeping through the night. Lynn loved having the baby around; she would keep her whenever Summer went out. She had promised Summer she could live in the house next door. The woman was now attached to R.D and hated being separated from her. Since Lynn never had a child, she bonded with Summer and loved her as a daughter. Currently, Lynn emotionally adopted R.D. as her grandchild. She didn't want them to leave her home because then it would feel empty. She had so many memories—memories of Summer and Mike, Summer and R.D; now her memories included Larry.

She didn't like making comparisons, but she couldn't help but notice Larry's maturity. She felt he was the perfect match for Summer. She recalled how heartbroken Summer had appeared when Larry took off suddenly for Lubbock; only Larry's assistant Pastor knew his whereabouts. She didn't understand why he had to leave; she only knew he had returned to pursue Summer. She was praying for a wedding in the future and the best, loving father for R.D.

A week had passed, and Angel was still in the land of the living. This miracle could only be an answer to many prayers. Monica was amazed. Already the odds were stacked in Angel's favor; surely God wouldn't give Angel all this time to have him die by the wayside. Monica had vowed to praise God, no matter what. She had declared God was first in her life. Monica decided to take time off from work to be in ICU. Angel didn't look any worse, but he didn't look any better. Her husband was getting IV fluids, which kept him alive. He also had fair brain and heart activity; Monica gave him personal care; she was his wife and a nurse, so she knew how to be careful with him. She didn't want anyone else to take care of him. Angel's great care was helping him recover, though it was still touch and go, as the medical team felt he could still hemorrhage to death. His past bullet wounds made his condition massively fragile. Monica and all the hospital staff noticed how deep into a coma Angel was. They saw an angelic expression on his face, as he was possibly communing with God. Even doctors and staff who claimed to be atheists noticed this. Angel's parents tried to figure out did it mean God was about to take him home. They never said it out loud because they knew it would upset Monica. The true miracle was, Angel was still here.

Earl had also been visiting Angel; Monica could get him special permission; he couldn't believe he was shot and in critical condition. His heart was heavy and in excruciating pain. He recalled the days when he and Angel had stayed at odds with each other, only, now they were both different people. Angel had been faithful to visit Earl, both in jail and at the Rescue Mission. They had become best friends. At first, they had been rivals for Larry's attention, but Larry had persuaded them he didn't play favorites. While Larry was in Minion, Earl and Angel bonded as best friends; Earl prayed and told God he wasn't ready to lose his best friend. It took too long for them to gain this special friendship.

Angel still conversed with God while in his deep coma. God forgave Paul immediately of his crimes against Christians; God also forgave Angel of his. He said the sinner's prayer with Jesus. He repeated, "Father God, I am a sinner saved by grace, please forgive my many and horrific sins. Forgive my destructive action on humanity, and help me to move forward and have self-forgiveness. Thank you for this generous grace; I am ready to take my place either on the earth or with you. I love you and thank you for your unconditional love, a love I don't deserve. I accept your Son into my heart; He is the only way to salvation. In His Holy Name Amen." The nightmares he had encountered frightened him. He cried out to God, who showed him mercy. Angel would also be silent and embrace God's presence. He was becoming closer to God. Angel couldn't sing, but he was singing praise and worship to God in a musical tone. He was singing "It Is Well with My Soul." He was truly joyous and happy and honestly never wanted to leave. Angel wanted to fulfill his destiny and serve his purpose on the earth; that was Angel's choice; however, it was up to God to give him more time on the earth because maybe it was enough for Angel to desire righteousness. Maybe God's plan was for Angel to rest from his earthly burdens; God had already given him more time on the earth, God could have taken him away in an instant, Angel loved this particular time with God now—a time no one else on the earth had ever experienced. He didn't want to think about the earth or eternity; he only wanted to embrace this particular time in his presence and enjoy it while it lasted. He had requested never to lose this precious memory, no matter where God placed him in the end.

When Larry returned to Minion, he had left his heart and his mind in San Francisco. The pastor missed Summer. The closeness he had with her was one he had never experienced with any other woman. He knew the thought was early, but he wanted to be married to her. He also knew she felt the same way. Most counselors always advised couples to wait at least a year in courtship before deciding on marriage. And Larry was a counselor; however, there had to be exceptions to this rule, such as a small infant girl needing a father. Larry and Summer felt they knew each other well. Testimonies were another way to know someone, and they both knew each other's testimonies. He was going to spend time in prayer and await God's answer.

It was almost time for him to leave work; he would go home, eat his crockpot supper of chicken corn chowder, then call Summer. Larry made this their routine every night—the particular time they both relished. He was thinking of how he could soon plan to fly to San Francisco for a long weekend. The church board had approved for him to take frequent weekends for his newfound courtship. His assistant clergy could cover his sermons. He also had guest speakers lined up. He was going to talk to Summer about it tonight for the following weekend; Summer replied to Larry, "Honey, I miss you so much, but R.D. has a fever, and I need to take care of her."

"Summer, we will have the rest of our lives to spend together. Please take care of our precious bundle." Summer loved when Larry expressed his affection for R.D. She knew she'd never find another man with his vibrant character. She told him, "Larry, there's only one like you. And R.D. and I are the most fortunate people in the world having you pursue us. I hope next weekend we can all be together, maybe even go to the zoo."

"Sounds so wonderful Summer, I love the both of you with all my heart, and I miss the two of you." Once again, Summer was delighted that when Larry spoke, he always includes R.D. Then Larry asked, "Can tell me, how is Angel?"

"He's improving slowly, but not out of the woods yet; Monica calls every day, the fact that 's he's still with us shows God's answering our prayers."

"He is indeed!" They spoke for over an hour. Larry was disappointed not to make the trip, but he understood Summer's complete focus needed to be on the baby.

Charles wondered why Dr. Williamson's assessment of Marcus was taking so long. Maybe the doctor found the boy had a more severe problem. If that were the case, it would keep Marcus from prison; the decision could be to try Marcus as a juvenile. Charles knew the doctor was close friends with Judge Mate and Prosecutor Wilshire; he also knew the doctor to be fair. He was a juvenile psychiatrist and an adult psychiatrist, and Marcus couldn't be in any better hands. Charles knew if the prosecutor had his way, Marcus would be doing hard time. And it wouldn't concern him one bit if Marcus turned up dead in an adult jail cell. Charles was fighting as hard for Marcus' life as though it were his own. He had made his mind up he was going to visit Dr. Williamson Monday.

When Dr. Williamson graduated from college, he didn't believe in hypnosis. He had thought of it as a form of witchcraft. Many Christian psychiatrists and psychologists still believe this. He prayed passionately about this, and he felt the Lord revealed to him hypnosis in itself isn't evil if used responsibly. He thought it to be a valuable tool to unlock painful memories. It was a better choice than truth serum meds. However, it couldn't work if the patient didn't believe it would work. Marcus's belief was the obstacle to overcome. Even if Marcus consented, would he believe? Dr. Williamson decided he would fast and spend much private time on his face with God. He only wanted His answer.

Emily Millet Honds was present at Word of God Church, to Larry's surprise. She attended his Sunday morning worship service. Larry and Emily never had strong enough feelings for each other for marriage. Emily was the first to notice this and had broken off their engagement. Yet here she was.

Summer missed Larry and decided to go to Minion to surprise him. It had been over a month since she had seen him. They talked on the phone every night, but obstacles seemed to get in the way of them visiting—things like R.D. being sick or Larry's pending church matters. Summer anxiously awaited her flight. The Hanleys had R.D., and Lynn waited for Summer to get ready, and then she dropped her off at the airport. Lynn always prayed for Summer to have a safe flight. She left Summer as she was heading toward her boarding gate.

Summer's heart was light and singing one love song after another traveling to Minion—songs like "What a Difference You Made in My Life." *"What a difference you made in my life, what a difference you made in my life my sunshine day and night, what a difference you made in my lif*e." by Ronnie Millsap or The Righteous Brothers' "Unchained Melody." *"Oh, my love, my darling, I've hungered for your touch, a long lonely time, but time goes by so slowly, and time can change so much. Are you still mine? I need your love; I need your love, God speed your love to me."* She would not make it for Larry's sermon, but she had a good chance of arriving after the church had ended. She wanted Larry's face to be the first she saw when she came.

After his sermon was over, Emily greeted Larry. They hadn't seen each other for months. Larry was merely curious. He knew Emily couldn't have changed her mind. And if she had, he was praying he wouldn't have to hurt her feelings because his whole heart was Summer's. Then Larry could tell the woman had some news to share with him. She had a broad smile on her face.

From a distance, Summer saw them together and watched as they embraced. At that moment, every love song in Summer's heart vanished. Larry and Emily never saw her, and she made sure they wouldn't. She left the church. The girl didn't want to go to her parents' house, but Summer knew it was only appropriate to put in an appearance. Then she would leave Minion as fast as she had arrived. *What happened? Had Larry never gotten over Emily? Why on earth didn't he tell her?* So many questions bombarded Summer's mind. She had to pray for God to calm her heart to have a peaceful but short visit with her parents.

Kevin and Lindy were surprised to see Summer. They had just come from church. Many Sundays, Larry had dinner with them after church, but not this Sunday. They had seen him with Emily and wondered if they would be going out for dinner. They weren't trying to speculate, but Emily's visit seemed to be a surprise for everyone. Of course, they decided not to mention Larry at all for Summer's sake. They knew there was a good reason for Emily's visit. But for now, they were going to give their attention to Summer. For Sunday dinner, Lindy had chicken and dressing with fried okra, sweet potato casserole, and cranberry sauce. There was banana pudding for dessert. Lindy made dessert only on Sundays. It was all Summer's favorites, but she didn't have an appetite. She tried to eat as vigorously as she could, but Lindy could tell her appetite wasn't up to par, especially for chicken and dressing.

After dinner, Autumn invited Summer to her room. "Summer, let me show you my electronic layout" They toured her room, showing off her computer and entertainment system of television and music players. "Wow," Summer exclaimed. "This is awesome, and I love the CDs. These are all my favorite bands." Summer was relieved, as it took her mind off Larry. Autumn and Summer had been telephoning each other two or three times during the week. Her flight was in the morning, and, of course, her family was curious about why her visit was so short. Lindy seemed to know whenever something was wrong with her children. She would then make sure the rest of the family didn't ask questions or pressure her in any way. After a two-year separation from Summer, Lindy just relished Summer's visits, even if they were cut short. "Summer, your room is ready," Kevin mentioned.

"Thank you, Dad, but I'm going to be a while with Autumn. I don't have my music in my room anymore, and I need to listen to it." Music was always therapeutical to Summer. Especially Christian music. She identifies with many of the songs. The songs gave her comfort and peace.

The words and melody seem to speak to Summer's hurt.

The following day, Lindy had to go to Lubbock for a staff meeting of her home design company, so she dropped Summer off at the airport.

"Well, Summer," Lindy began, "It was a concise visit, but we are always happy to see you." Summer then felt guilt for cutting her trip short. So she replied to her mother. "I'm sorry about the trip. But next time, I'll stay longer."

"Yes, and we'll find places to go to for recreation! Ok, sweetheart, I need to scoot on to work, and you need to catch your flight." She hugged her family and parted their separate ways. Summer was happy seeing her family and would have loved staying longer. But she couldn't risk running into Larry or him dropping by. She was surprised he didn't drop by yesterday, then she remembered he was probably occupied with Emily. The pain in her heart was a 20 on a scale of 1 to 10. She never called Lynn; she decided to take a cab home. She and R.D. now lived in the house Lynn had sold to her. She was to be gone for a week. The young woman decided to stay at the house and not make an issue out of her quick return home. She had plenty of groceries. She would take a bus to San Mateo in the morning to go after R.D. She just had to have the comfort of the baby being with her. She was grateful the Hanleys never asked questions. The following day, Lynn ran into Summer as she left the house to go to the Hanleys and asked, "That was a quick trip. I hope everything is ok?" In the affirmative, summer was about to answer, then remembered Larry might call. She stated, "If Larry should call, please don't mention that I was in Minion.!" Lynn knew something was wrong, but she has never interrogated her and wouldn't now. She replied. "Whatever you wish, Summer. I'm glad you told me because I saw Larry's name on my caller ID. I haven't a chance to get back to him." She was relieved Lynn hadn't returned Larry's call. She just didn't make a big deal out of it. She knew she also had to reach her family, so they also won't mention her trip.

Summer was at the Hanleys. Susan said, "Wow, that was a short trip; I hope everything's ok."

"Yes, it is, and I promise I will make it up to you for stealing your time away from R.D. I need her right now."

"Honey, don't worry about that; you are more than fair to us. I appreciate your generosity." Summer always loved Susan. She has been more than kind to her. At one time, Susan seemed to be more of a mother to her than Lindy did. Although Summer has seen an immense change in her mother, her own heart has also changed since her rebel days. While thinking about those days, she asked God to help her always treat Ruby Destiny fairly, even if she had other children. She then stopped herself from reflecting on the past; only it didn't appear her future looked bright either.

She said goodbye to Susan and Gerald. "Goodbye; I'll be back with her next week."

"And we'll look forward to seeing both of you," Gerald replied. To him, Summer was indeed his daughter. R.D. was the apple of his eye.

Summer had a brief visit with the Hanleys. She was in good spirits as long as work and the baby occupied her. However, at night, Summer was broken, she would cry, and it had to be private. She was just grateful R.D. wasn't at the age to ask questions.

Larry had tried to reach Summer Sunday night and last night. He tried both Summer's and Lynn's numbers. Finally, he spoke briefly to Lynn, and she appeared evasive. "Lynn, I haven't been able to reach Summer, is she and the baby, ok?"

"Yes, Larry, they're ok. How are you?"

"I'm ok, but I'm very concerned about Summer. Please have her call me."

"Yes, Larry, and you'll have to tell me about your congregation sometime." She didn't want to ask about his Glad Tidings ministry. She knew Summer was heartbroken, and maybe Larry decided not to leave Minion.

Larry felt Lynn was acting strange. They were trying to change the subject when he referred to Summer. He was becoming excruciatingly worried. Kevin and Lindy also seemed to avoid talking about her. They just said, "Larry, Summer is at the peak of health. You don't' need to worry about her." And that was it; they only spoke about her physical health like something else may be wrong, and they were avoiding what it was. He noticed too that the family would scarcely speak to him. Things just didn't add up, and Larry felt he needed to make a long-past-due trip to San Francisco. He missed Summer, and now something was wrong, and he couldn't put his finger on it.

"I'll agree to hypnotized," Marcus announced to Dr. Williamson. The doc was relieved, and he told him. "I wish there were another way, but I know once we find out what's suppressing your memory, healing can begin." Marcus agreed, although he was afraid, and more than that, he was tired. He wanted it all over. Marcus asked God to prepare him. He had to stop running away, and agreeing to hypnosis seemed to be the only answer. Dr. Williamson expressed, "Let's have a word of prayer that you believe the process will work." This procedure seemed scary and like mind control, but Marcus did trust Dr. Williamson. Marcus wanted to be well from this illness that appeared to be controlling him. He would agree with whatever Dr. Williamson recommended. And he left it in God's hands. They would make a court appearance in a week when Dr. Williamson would recommend treatment at the juvenile correctional center. Marcus trusted Charles; he liked him because he treated him like a son. The young man felt Prosecutor Wilshire was out to get him. And he just didn't know about Judge Mate. But "Doc," as Marcus called him, convinced him he was a fair man. Marcus did go to God. Who else would help him in these dark hours he was facing?

Charles telephoned Dr. Williamson. "Doc, Charles here; when will we meet to discuss Marcus's case?" Dr. Williamson then told him, "I was just about to call you Charles. I plan to meet in Judge Mate's chambers in a few days with all parties concerned. So please don't worry, and I'm going to do everything for Marcus to be healthy again. I'll make sure any legal matters will be in his best interest."

Charles was uncertain of what Craig meant by best interest. But replied, "I'll see everyone in a few days." Charles chose to believe that Doc would be fair and favorable and Marcus would be tried as a juvenile. That's if there is even a court date. He hoped everyone could reach an agreement so a trial wouldn't be necessary. Charles was relieved that the process was almost over for Marcus. He didn't pray to God but asked for Craig to pray for the best for Marcus. Craig, of course, was already praying.

Monica was holding Angel's hand, and she felt a soft squeeze. At first, she thought she was dreaming, but she felt the squeeze again, and it was slightly more robust. She immediately hit the emergency buzzer. The entire medical team flew in. Monica explained, "Angel squeezed my hand." She prayed he would do it again while the team was there." They feared that Monica's call meant it was finally over for Angel. But they couldn't believe the miracle of Angel's complete recovery from his third bullet wound. He was completely alert except that he was weak. The medical staff then knew it was a miracle. That was the only explanation. Dr. Lyles exclaimed, "Monica, everything is back to normal; his vitals and his latest blood work are all completely normal. It has to be God. There's no other explanation." Monica knew that God will always make himself known even to unbelievers.

Angel tried to tell Monica, "Sweetheart, I spent time with God. I had a Damascus Road experience. I have true salvation now." But Monica had to stop him. "Angel, my darling, you have nothing but time now. Tell me when you get your strength back. I'm not going anywhere."

Angel gazed at her with a fantastic smile on his face. He knew Monica was right. But, the former biker did need his strength back, so he rested. Angel was also looking forward to seeing his parents, the Dominguez's—who were also like parents, and his friends —Earl, Larry, and Summer, Dr. Thomas, his church friends, and the Jokers. He prayed especially hard for the Jokers because they had saved Monica's life.

Larry had booked his flight for San Francisco. He was afraid of heartbreak. The pastor wondered if the change in Summer meant a change in her feelings for him; no matter the reason, he had to know what it was. If he had to bite the bullet, then he would. That was better than not knowing. So, with a troubled mind and a heavy heart, he headed out to the city of the Golden Gate again. He couldn't believe how he was shaking as he headed to the car rental.

Summer's allowed Larry and Emily's meeting torment mind. She knew the only way to bring it peace was to confront Larry about his encounter with Emily. She picked up the phone and called him, and the line just rang constantly. He had called her every night, and she saw his name on the caller ID, but she never wanted to answer. She felt he was going to tell her about Emily and break up with her. She just wasn't ready to face that. However, now with no answer, she was more convinced than ever it was because of Emily. She was about to have another cry when she heard the knock on her door. She opened it and saw Larry on the other side. She felt it was all over. Larry was being an honorable man and telling her outright about Emily. When she looked deep into his eyes, she saw a shattered look. It confused her. She blurted out, "Okay, Larry, let's settle this. I was in Minion, and I saw you with Emily!"

Larry was in shock. He had no idea she was in Minion. He was baffled and also wanted to laugh, but he didn't dare. All he did was wrap his arms around Summer and say, "Oh, honey, I didn't know what was wrong. I thought maybe you were feeling differently toward me. You'll never know how scary this trip was for me."

Summer looked at him in confusion. "What about Emily?"

"Honey, you jumped to conclusions. Emily and I have been friends since kindergarten. She married my best friend, Trey. We tried to have a relationship. Not like what's between you and me, or her and Trey, she just came by to tell me she was in a new relationship. I hugged her because I was happy for her."

Summer then felt foolish. She had let her insecurity get the better of her. And it could've cost her Larry. All she could do was apologize. "Larry, I am so sorry. I misunderstood." Larry just kept embracing her and kissed her. Then he said, "Summer, I know this may be soon, but I want you to be my wife."

"Why would you want to marry such a foolish girl as me?" Summer asked. "I could've messed everything up for us."

"I wasn't going to let that happen. But, summer, I would never give up on you or us."

Then Summer let out a resounding, "Yes, yes, Larry. I want to marry you."

"I don't have a ring yet, because I didn't know I would plan this."

"That makes it more romantic and exciting. This is the most romantic collision I have ever experienced. I'm just so glad you forgave my foolishness."

"I may be a clergyman, but I'm far from perfect. You will find out in time if you give me a chance."

"I said yes, and there is nothing else to say except, Larry, I love you!"

"Oh, Summer, how I adore you. You have my whole heart!" Once again, they embraced and shared a long passionate kiss; Summer was holding Larry's face with both her hands.

Lynn chose this moment to visit Summer. She knocked on the door, waited a minute, and then she saw them. She recalled another time she caught them kissing—when R.D. was born. The infant was sound asleep in another room, unaware this couple was planning a beautiful future for her. Summer then told Lynn, "Lynn, Larry, and I will be married.". Lynn was so happy. She had prayed about this for Summer and R.D. She expressed, "Please let me help with planning. I'm so excited." Summer replied, "Lynn, of course, you can help with the planning, only now we need to go to Minion and announce the news to Mom and Dad." They couldn't see waiting too long. Lindy had connections and could probably arrange a wedding in three months.

They would head out to Minion in a few days taking R.D. with them. Her mother would send wedding invitations would out to everyone. Angel was on the mend and would be in full recovery by then. They wanted him and Earl to be a part of the wedding ceremony.

The Sunday before they headed for Minion, they attended R.D.'s baby dedication. When they visited Angel, Larry said, "Angel, I wish there was a way that you could be there. We could postpone it for a few more weeks."

Angel replied hastily, "please don't; by then, her gown won't fit. Bro, it hurts deeply that I can't be there for my little sweetheart, but Monica will keep me posted. Thanks."

Larry had told Dr. Thomas about his and Summer's engagement, so he asked Larry, "I am so happy about you and Summer's engagement. Why don't' you participate as her father?"

"Nothing would give me any greater pleasure, and as for as anyone's concerned, I am R.D.'s father. However, I want to be sensitive to Gerald and Susan. So maybe we shouldn't place too much emphasis on it because, after the service, we are taking them out to lunch to break the news about our engagement. Lynn will be watching R.D."

"Yes, I quite understand." The pastor replied.

Earl was there, and Monica came, appearing for both herself and Angel. She gave R.D. a big kiss. "This little one is from your Uncle Angel who misses you."

R.D. looked precious and sweet and stared up at Monica.

The ceremony was very moving. Dr. Thomas declared, "We are here today to dedicate Ruby Destiny Hanley to Jesus. Will her father and mother bring her to me?" Summer carried R.D. to the pastor with Larry standing beside her. Lynn and the Hanleys also stood with R.D. The pastor continued. "Ruby Destiny, God has a divine purpose for your life. You belong to God, and you're His child. You will serve mightily in the Kingdom because God has an important plan and destiny for your life." He spoke out both her names. "You're Ruby named after Mike's sister, but it's also a precious jewel, Ruby you are valuable to God and his Kingdom. Destiny means that God will take you many places, you will have many challenges, but you will conquer them all." Then he spoke to Larry and Summer. "Hannah gave Samuel to God. (1 Samuel 1:21–28) She gave him willingly, and God never asked her. This child will remain you two for the rest of her life, yet her purpose will be as divine as Samuel's. Never fail to teach her about God, and she will never find difficulty in serving Him. King Solomon said centuries ago, 'Train up a child in the way he should go, and when he is old he will not depart from it' (Proverbs 22:6). I anoint this child to be God's servant, and her parents to train her up. God always be with you." The family stood on the platform with tears, amazed by powerful words spoken over this tiny infant. As they stood there, they envisioned the future that Dr. Thomas had prophesied over her.

Larry had called the Hanleys earlier, inviting them to lunch after the baby dedication. He and Summer wanted to break the news to them of their engagement; of course, lunch was going to be his treat. They planned to meet at the Zuni Café, one of San Francisco's most elegant dining places. The Hanleys were highly impressed. They had dined at many fine restaurants in San Francisco (as the city is famous for its fine cuisine), but somehow, they had missed this place. After they settled in the restaurant, Larry announced, "Summer and I invited you here because we wanted to be the first to let you know that we plan to be married, and of course to invite you to the wedding."

The Hanleys had suspected that Summer and Larry had a romantic interest in each other, so they weren't surprised at their announcement. Gerald replied. "Summer, you are like my daughter, and Larry, I will only tell you, please take care of my little girl. I am happy for the both of you." Summer and Larry could sense the tension and sadness that was in the room. The Hanleys were thinking about Mike. It was bittersweet for them. They were honestly happy for Summer and Larry, only they didn't want Mike forgotten. They had never imparted these feelings. However, Summer instinctively knew and said, "I want you to know we will always remember Mike. R.D. will know that he is her biological father. We will speak about him in honor, and his picture will always be in her room. She may never have any memories of him, but we can present him to her in other ways. She will always want to know about her father. We will make sure she knows he loved her very much." Summer thought she would tell R.D. when she's older about her visit to heaven to see him. She had already told Larry about her visit to Heaven. Larry knew what Summer had said was a part of the revelation that God had for them. Then Larry spoke, "I will also remind R.D. about Mike. I'm not jealous of his memory; I was sad when I heard about this loss. The most sadness I experienced was that the child lost her father. I won't take Mike's place; however, I will honor him by raising her as my own. I believe this is what he would want."

Gerald spoke, "of course, Mike would agree. We all know R.D. needs a father, and Larry, there's no finer man than you, I mean this sincerely."

Larry responded. "Thank you so much, sir. That means everything."

This gathering gave the Hanleys much comfort and peace. It was a pleasant lunch for them all—roasted chicken with a variety of vegetables. They also enjoyed water with lemon, coffee for the Hanley's, and green tea for Larry and Summer. The Hanleys then addressed the ticket, "Larry, please let us get the ticket or pay something on it. You are more than kind." They thought that Larry was paying the ticket out of compassion, and they didn't want to take advantage, only Larry said, "Absolutely not, you are going to have to get used for me to pick up the tab sometimes. It's what family does."

They never felt more loved and welcomed as Larry had made them feel. Unfortunately, they lost Mike, and Larry didn't replace him; however, he was comfort in Mike's place.

On one of Summer's visits to the Hanleys, she told them about her visit to Heaven and meeting Mike and Ruby. It was on Summer's medical record. They believed her because they knew she'd had a near-death experience. What Summer had told them had given their heart and mind total peace and comfort and reduced their mourning. They also fully forgave Earl and greeted him warmly whenever they visited Word of God.

Larry and Summer visited Angel in the hospital. Angel asked how the baby dedication went. Summer answered, "It was perfect, except not as complete with her Uncle Angel." I was looking at the time it was to begin and thought and prayed for all of you."

Summer continued, "Larry and I are going to Minion with R.D."

"Anything we should know?" Angel pleaded

Larry replied, "I'm sure you've already guessed it" Angel and Monica knew they guessed right and that Larry needn't say anymore.

Larry continued, "however, we have to verbalize it to Summer's parents first."

The Hanleys had told Summer, before departure to the Airport, "I will miss R.D.; just remember you owe us a visit."

Summer replied, "I know I owe you, and I promise she will be yours once I return; she just has to be there when Larry and I announce our engagement." Susan agreed.

Lynn wanted to take Larry, Summer, and the baby to the airport. So, Larry turned his rental on the day before. That night Summer told Larry, "I was so happy on my flight to Minion I was singing you love songs."

"Well, I didn't hear them, and now you have to be fair. I want to hear all of your songs. I love your voice, Summer."

"Ok, then, but it may not sound like it did a few years ago."

"Let me be the judge of that!"

Then, Larry had her serenading him until bedtime. Larry remembered the first time he first heard Summer sing. He had attended her Christmas concert with his brother Eric and his then-girlfriend Cecelia. She had a prominent voice for a 12-year-old. He noticed her voice had much improved, and he couldn't hear enough of it. Only it had to end, as Lynn said abruptly, "Lights out, you two, we have a long day tomorrow." Larry replied, "Ok, Lynn, just let me kiss my angels' good night before I head next door."

Summer's house had four bedrooms and two baths. She loved designing the bedrooms. One was the baby's, of course, and she had the others intended for her parents and Autumn when they came to visit. She had a beautiful room for Autumn, designed exquisitely for a teenager. She also had an attractive layout for her parent's room. Tonight, Lynn was rooming in Autumn's room, and Larry would be residing in Lynn's house.

Larry had never made hotel reservations because he was too preoccupied with his and Summer's dilemma. However, Lynn insisted that Larry stay at her house and she would stay with Summer. So, at lights out, Larry took the key from Lynn and let himself into her home.

Angel was getting stronger all the time. Finally, he was out of bed and walking. Finally, he told Monica, "Baby, I'm getting cabin fever; I've been cooped up long enough. I need to get out of this place." Angel hated to be confined. It reminded him of his jail time. He wondered would he be free. He had a lot to account for, and he had made his mind up to pay for his crimes if necessary. His gang friends visited him frequently. They were so happy Angel had pulled through. It was a miracle that led many of the Jokers to Jesus. Juan said, "Angel, you couldn't have been more right about Jesus. I'm ministering to all the Jokers. Trying to get them to repent, then we'll form a bikers' ministry. We'll have to change our name, of course." Juan's remark made Angel smile.

Angel had also gently rebuked Monica for the grudge she held against her parents. He said, "Baby, I know you were defending me, but you were way too hard on your parents. Please remember the fifth commandment."

"Angel, you're right. Although I was hurting and angry that day, I know it's not an excuse."

"I want their friendship. I think that's important to us both."

"They just aren't kind like your parents."

"That doesn't eliminate the fifth commandment. And love, if you want God's forgiveness, you have to forgive them."

"I know you're right. It's just hard to approach my folks now."

"Would it help to know that I understand where they're coming from? If we have a daughter, I will be careful of the men she chooses. I wouldn't want her to date someone like the old me."

"Angel, you have become too wise; I'm not happy with the broken relationship between my parents and myself; please ask God to help me swallow some pride."

Angel had favor with many police officers who had visited him in the hospital. One of the officers said, "Angel, I feel you paid a big enough price when you suffered that last bullet wound. We are praying the courts will grant your freedom." Many of these officers belonged to *Glad Tidings;* another officer said, "We will be happy to speak up for you. We'll do anything that will help you."

"Not all officers feel that way. There some who want me to rot in jail; maybe they'll come forward too."

"I know these other officers would feel otherwise if they could see the change in you. But, Angel, you're not the same person." A third officer said.

"Thank you so much for coming to visit. I have to tell you that I'm just going to abide by God's will. If he wants me in prison to serve, that's where I'll be." The officers had to agree and prayed that Angel wouldn't go to prison.

The officers were particularly happy for him and Monica. They wanted to gun for Sergio and the other vipers for abducting Monica; it was as though Sergio had disappeared off the face of the earth.

The old Angel would have already put a hit on Sergio, and Sergio would be dead. Angel's former vendetta was the biggest reason the gangs feared Angel and wanted him dead. The news was also circulating about Angel's change, and the former biker wasn't feared anymore. The fact was, opposing gang members cared less about him. This favor was God's protecting hand over him. He didn't heal Angel for his enemies to slaughter him. He had a purpose for him, and it was a great purpose. Even when

Monica told him about Mario's attempt, he let it go to God's vengeance. He then found out he would be going home in a couple of days if his last round of lab work was evident. And from the looks of Angel, Monica knew it was a great possibility.

When Larry and Summer arrived at the Logans, Kevin had just come home, and Lindy was already home. She only went to Lubbock for staff meetings or business emergencies. Her staff ran the business efficiently. Summer said, "Larry and I have something to tell you, but we need Autumn to be here." Lindy and Kevin had guessed the news but wanted to hear the announcement. Autumn, however, was at cheerleader practice. But Lindy called her on her cell and told her, "Autumn, you need be here. We have a family emergency,"

"It better be an emergency; I have to work a lot on my technique. But, hold on, I'll be there." Lindy could tell that Autumn was not happy and would probably vent her anger at them. However, Lindy was ready. She was stricter and firmer with Autumn now. More like her mother and less like the buddy that she was used to be. An adjustment that's been hard for Autumn to make.

Larry and Summer were waiting for her. They thought Autumn would never arrive; however, they weren't going to announce anything without everyone present. When Autumn arrived, she was more impatient than anyone. She Vented, "Ok, I'm here. What's this family emergency?" She ranted on and on. Lindy tried to ignore her as she didn't want to discipline her before Larry and Summer. Despite this, the minute she saw Larry and Summer, her annoyance dissipated. Autumn was glad to see them together. She felt something was wrong on Summer's last visit; on this one, though, she could tell things couldn't be righter. She exclaimed, "Summer!" In her excited teenaged voice. She embraced Summer and greeted Larry warmly.

Then the couple had them all sit down as they announced their plans. Summer began, "You know the last time I was here was not a happy time for me." Kevin interrupted, "Naw, I'd never guessed that, especially when you refused banana pudding." That made Summer hungry, she said. "Mom, I don't guess you have any?" Lindy shook her head and scolded Kevin. "Stop interrupting. I want to hear this news."

"Yea, Dad, you need to stop," Autumn added

Summer continued, "Well, I had seen Emily and Larry after the church service. They were hugging. I was pouting and stayed here briefly. I had jumped to conclusions. Poor Larry didn't know what was going on as I refused his calls. Finally, he came to my house, and we resolved our concerns. He proposed, and we want to make plans to get married. Can you help us?"

Kevin let out a huge shout and shook Larry's hand so hard Larry felt his arm would fall off. Then he went to Lindy as the family circled Summer to group hug her. Then they made Larry join in. Kevin said, "If you're going to be family, you had better get used to this!" Then annoyed, Lindy gently admonished Kevin. "Please let me answer Summer's question. Yes, sweetheart, I'll help. I will arrange and make sure your wedding will be when you want to have it and that everything will be going smoothly."

Larry was overwhelmed with affection. He not only had picked the suitable mate, and she came with the right in-laws. They visited briefly and had dinner. Lindy prepared her wonderful beef stew with cornbread. At Summer's earlier request, Lindy and Autumn managed to whip up some banana pudding. After they ate, Summer announced, "Mom, can I please be excused from dishes. We have to go to Larry's brother and his wife's house and announce it to them."

"Of course, I'll excuse you, and I wasn't expecting you to do the dishes," Lindy replied

"That's because it's my turn." Autumn joked. Larry and Summer then left to go to Eric and Cecelia's house.

Eric Calhoun owned Minion's only fitness center. He had owned it once with Trudy Miles, who is now Trudy Harper. Eric He was extraordinarily handsome and physically fit. However, he was also arrogant and conceited. He and Trudy had been a couple, and they had insurance on their business through The Harper and Logan Agency, where Trudy met her husband, Leo Harper. Leo wasn't a perfect build as Eric; in fact, he was slightly overweight. However, Trudy was attracted to his sweet nature. The beautiful woman also loved his sense of humor. She didn't want to hurt Eric, but she realized what they had was just a physical attraction. She had much deeper feelings for Leo. Trudy was afraid Eric would be a sore loser and cause a scene. Only it turned out Eric chose the high road. His father taught him to be a good sport. He learned this the hard way once at an elementary school football game. His father had pointed out the fool he had made of himself because he had a tantrum over a lost game. He was severely humiliated. That incident came to mind when Trudy told him about Leo. He wanted to rebel and act spitefully, except he saw his father's face and then told Trudy, "Honey, I will miss you, and losing you hurts, only I'm happy for you; Leo is a fine man." He was sincere. It did hurt to lose her, and he was happy for her. He also congratulated Leo. "Leo, I want to give you and Trudy my warm congratulations. I also want you to have this as a token of my sincere friendship." He showed Leo the colorful and beautiful down comforter he gave to them as a wedding present.

"This more than generous of you. You didn't have to do this." He wanted to say letting go of Trudy for him was gift enough. But he didn't want to pour salt into the wound.

"That's not all." Eric continued, "Trudy wants me to buy her share of our fitness center. So I decided I would, this way that we can all start over. Plus, I'm sure you could use the money for a special honeymoon. My best wishes to you again."

Leo and Eric became good friends. Eric also kept his insurance policy with Leo and Kevin. Later he met his current wife, Cecelia. She was petite and adorable. She had short, blonde hair, blue eyes, and beautiful features. He discovered he also had deeper feelings for her. He became a born-again believer when

Larry was struggling with his drug addiction. The addiction story was Larry's testimony.

He and Larry had lost their father when he was 20 and Larry was 10. Larry took his death extremely hard because he still desperately needed his father. The man found his little brother sobbing. He put his hand on his shoulder, expressing, "Larry, it's going to be alright. We still have each other and Mom."

"Please," Larry sorrowfully pleaded, "Promise me you won't leave me. I need you so much now." Eric warmly embraced Larry. "Yes, my baby brother, I promise. I won't leave you." Eric's words brought Larry comfort. He moved on and did well in school. He thought of Eric as a father, and he overachieved to make him proud. And Eric was very proud of Larry.

Then if life for Larry wasn't hard enough, they lost their mother to cancer when Larry had graduated high school. Larry was unfortunate, but he kept his focus on making Eric proud. Then when he had his first job after graduating from college, he lost his lifelong and best friend, Trey, to a car accident. At this same time, Trudy broke up with Eric. That was a significant disappointment, and he took their breakup hard. To him, Trudy was like a big sister, and she was irreplaceable. Larry was antidrug in high school. Eric would never have dreamed that Larry would turn to drugs. In the beginning, he didn't pinpoint the problem. Eric thought his brother had a mental illness. He wanted to get help. Then Eric found drug paraphernalia in Larry's room. He confronted him. He was patient at first but firm, "Larry, my baby brother, you are killing yourself. I don't want to lose you; please get help."

Larry lied, "Yes, Eric, please help me. I'm in over my head."

"I will go to Leo's church and find a program for you." Larry hated Leo. He was a homewrecker in his eyes. He immediately protested, "I'm not receiving help from that clown or his church." That was the first time Eric saw Larry's bitter attitude. He knew then he had to play hardball. He harshly exclaimed,

"Larry, you can't live here doing drugs; if you don't want to get help, you'll have to leave."

"Well, if that loser's help is all you can offer, I'll be glad to leave." Larry knew where there was a flophouse for drug addicts. Larry had sold everything he had and was now panhandling for drug and crack house money."

Larry had lived with Eric ever since their mother died. Eric's business was successful, and he paid for Larry's higher education. Larry remained living with him after that; he graduated from college and had his career in business. He began work for the Taylor Foundation, and Larry climbed the ladder rapidly. Larry worked there with his best friend, Trey. It was when Trey died that Larry had his struggles. He had felt the compound effect of every loss in his life.

Trudy had left a job vacancy, and he had to find a replacement for her. Cecelia filled this position. She was also lovely. He had never been shy, but she devastated him. He shyly asked her out. "Cecelia, you have worked so hard; how about dinner and a movie?" Celia knew he was cleverly asking her out on a date. She replied, "I would love to." She couldn't deny her attraction to him. When he found her unconscious in his office, he knew how deep his feelings were for her. He had never in his life been so afraid of losing someone. At the office one day, he had flowers placed on Cecelia's desk. Then he got down one knee and asked. "Miss Sparks, would you do me the honor of becoming Mrs. Calhoun." Eric was clever from the beginning. It was what she found attractive in him. In complete wonder, she replied, "I would be more than honored to be Mrs. Calhoun." They were married at Word of God Church. Larry was his best man. They had been married for six years now, and every day for them was a honeymoon.

They were expecting Larry's visit. They knew he was seeing Summer Logan and wondered if that was the reason for the visit. They were about to find out as Larry knocked on the door. They greeted each other affectionately. They lived close but seldom saw each other outside of the church. Though, often after church, they would go out to eat. Eric was proud of Larry and his call to the ministry. Now he had to know about their visit. He greeted Larry affectionately, embracing him. "Baby brother, it seems I rarely see you these days. It's so good to see you."

"Eric, you know you've always been my hero. And I have some delightful news to tell you. I'm about to be married. Summer is the love of my life. I know this sudden, but we have seen each other for a little while."

Eric and Cecelia were a little surprised, as he and Summer just had a brief courtship. After that, however, they minded their own business. He then said, "Congratulation's baby brother. Summer is lovely." They all hugged, Then Cecelia spoke. "This little Summer has grown up. Larry, isn't this the child you gave flowers to backstage after a church play."

"The only one, and she sings even better now. She serenaded me the other night with beautiful love songs."

"Wow, Summer, you have a fan," Cecelia replied to Summer. Blushing, Summer replied modestly, "Larry's just blinded by love." Everyone laughed and knew Summer's sense of humor indicated how happy she would make Larry. Eric also prayed for God's best blessings for them

Dr. Williamson arranged for the court session to be private in the judge's chambers, with just Judge Mate, Charles, Prosecutor Wilshire, Marcus, and himself. He gave his assessment recommending the best treatment for Marcus. Judge Mate listened carefully, then asked Marcus some questions. Prosecutor Wilshire also asked questions. The prosecutor gave it up because he already knew the judge's decision, and it outranked his. The prosecutor had to hand it to Dr. Williamson for knowing his profession. He did not argue. He just hoped Marcus wouldn't prove to be a danger to society. Court lasted less than 30 minutes, the judge's decision "After carefully looking at the evidence before me I don't believe prison would serve Marcus Washington. I also don't believe Marcus is mature enough to be considered an adult. Given Dr. Williamson's diagnosis, I believe that he was under temporary derangement at the time of the shooting. This young man had lost his brother to a drive-by shooting and held his lifeless body in his arms. Then his close friend who Antonio, murdered. Antonio should by no means be considered a victim, with all the blood on his hands. Dr. Williamson believes Marcus to have promise, and I agree with him. He will have mandatory mental health treatment at the mental health unit of the closest juvenile correctional center, under Dr. Williamson's care until the doctor determines Marcus will be ready to be back in the population. Are there any objections?" Prosecutor Wilshire said, "No objections," and then remained silent. The judge wasn't going to change his mind. The prosecutor then had to agree that Judge and Craig were right. Marcus did deserve compassion and not incarceration.

Marcus was scared but glad to be under the "Doc's" care. Soon he would have his first hypnosis therapy session. The former gangster didn't like any of it. However, he knew something needed fixing, and he wanted it to be finished. Charles agreed and was relieved. He believed this was in Marcus' best interest.

Angel's parents, the Dominguez's, and almost the whole church congregation of Glad Tidings had visited Angel by the time he left to go home. Earl was there to help him pack. Monica had been taking gifts and flowers home each day, so there wasn't a lot to pack. She and Angel weren't living together. Angel stayed away so she would be safe. They were husband and wife, but Monica and Angel felt they needed to renew their wedding vows before consummating their relationship. So, Earl moved in with Angel until the doctor suspended home care. He also ordered Home Health for him three times a week.

When Angel had regained his strength, he and Monica stood before Dr. Thomas at Glad Tidings to renew their wedding vows. It was a simple ceremony of many friends and family (Angel now considered Dominguez's family). Monica's parents were among the guests because Angel had persuaded Monica that it was time to forgive and bury the past. Monica was stubborn at first, but she eventually realized that she had too much to be thankful for to keep holding a grudge. God had also convicted Monica for breaking the fifth commandment, "Honor thy father and thy mother." She had reconciled with her parents, embraced them warmly, and invited them to her and Angel's wedding renewal ceremony. The Lewis's gave their full approval and enjoyed the ceremony, grateful that life gave Angel another chance at life. It was a true miracle. The jokers were also there. Angel had to do some persuasion to get them to come because they weren't comfortable around straight people, except Angel's miracle had made them believers, and many of them received salvation. The entire wedding party had donated money to cater a spread of the couple's favorite dishes and a beautifully designed wedding cake bearing a miniature replica of the wedding couple. The celebration was an incredible reception, which Lynn held at her house, and there were many wedding presents. God was giving them the dream wedding they had always wanted. Summer stood in proxy for Larry, who was in Minion with Kevin and Lindy to prepare for their wedding. R.D. was there, and Angel and Monica took turns holding her. Summer could tell that parenthood was their next plan.

March 22, 2004

Summer looked stunning in Lindy's wedding gown. Autumn was her maid of honor. Summer was disappointed that Ella couldn't be her bridesmaid. However, Taylor and five other former classmates filled this spot. One of them was Mary Franklin, who was a former adversary—one of the mean girls. Seeing Summer again made her ashamed of how she and the other mean girls had treated Summer in middle school. She had been furious when Child Protection Services placed her in foster care. Although she suffered abuse in childhood, all adults were abusive were her thoughts at that time. Looking back, she appreciated her foster family. Their names were Jake and Helen, and they had an eight-year-old son, Joshua. At first, Mary only loved Joshua and thought of him as her little brother. Jake and Helen were very strict and kept careful track of her whereabouts at all times. Mary was initially resentful of this. However, in time she realized she had people who cared about her. However, high school was a challenge because Mary would sneak out to be with Lilly and the wild boys. They had another friend named Marcia, who was Lilly's secret friend. Lilly used her to befriend Mary so they could go out together. However, it was apparent that Lilly never cared for Marcia. Lilly was never friendly, and, at times, she was rude and hostile to her. After a year or so, Lilly found other ways to help Mary sneak out, and she just discarded Marcia. Lilly's rejection had a severe impact on Marcia's self-esteem because shortly afterward, she attempted suicide with an overdose of pills obtained from a dealer at school. She nearly died, thankfully her parents found her in time and sent her to a behavioral hospital for a while. Taylor Miller and other Christian students visited the hospital and befriended her. Marcia then became a believer.

Mary felt immense remorse for Marcia's treatment and realized how devastatingly cruel Lilly was. Around this time, the Holy Spirit began to convict her; only she didn't know how to reach out. She soon realized Lilly wasn't her friend—she just wanted to be in control. When Mary and Lilly graduated high school, one of Lilly's graduation presents was a trip to Europe. She had wished Mary to go with her, except her parents wouldn't include Mary. In Europe, Lilly met and eventually married her husband, Roberto Esposito. Lilly was so engrossed with

Roberto that she rarely visited home. Lily's absence Mary depressed her initially and then began to feel like a bird let out of a cage. She wasn't aware that Lilly's influence enslaved her for many years.

Mary's whole life had then flashed before her. Seeing Summer again caused her to recall her shame for endangering Summer's life by having the apartment, which could have also put her, Taylor, and even Lilly in danger. When she confessed all her torments to Larry, she repented. She visited Sally Ames Chandelier in Lubbock and told her, "Mrs.Chandlier, I'm so sorry for the resentment I had towards you when I was in middle school. I realize now that you were protecting me, along with everyone else." She reflected on everything—not only the near tragedy for Summer but also the blackmail schemes against Taylor and her brother, to whom she had also apologized.

The biggest hurdle Mary faced was forgiving her parents, Hugh and Marge. Hugh began abusing her since she was ten years old, and this continued for many years. When Hugh met his doom in a bar fight when she started high school, she recalled Lilly, and she had celebrated his death. The fight was because Hugh tried to molest the offender's daughter. The man beat Hugh beyond recognition, and the crowd just stood by because they felt Hugh was getting what he deserved. He later died from a severe head injury. The court tried the man and t delivered a verdict of not guilty by temporary insanity. Beating up Hugh was out of character for this man. He had never been in trouble with the law, but the attempted molestation of his daughter snapped his mind.

Since Mary had developed a relationship with Christ, God b convicted her to forgive Hugh and Marge, although she didn't want to. However, God never gave her rest, so she finally went to her mother. She found her mother crying uncontrollably; then she saw Mary and said in remorse. "Mary, please forgive me for your father's abuse of you. He was an extremely violent man, and I was terrified of him. I thank God your friend took you out of that situation."

"Mom, I wasn't in a much better situation."

"Yes, the apartment. Lilly, I know you won't believe this, but I always prayed for your safety when we were at home with Hugh." Her mother's confession touched Mary, and she was compassionate. Forgiving her was easy, but how do you forgive a dead man? Then Mary's mother vented all her hatred for Hugh. "Mary, I despised that man. Finally, he got what he deserved. And I hope he's rotting in the hottest hell." observing her mother, she saw how destructive hatred was. She then embraced her mother and said, "No, Mama, we aren't going to hate him anymore; we are going to forgive him."

Mary was now grateful for the intervention that had prevented tragedy for Summer and all of them. She had asked Summer's forgiveness the last time she saw her at church. She felt lost when Lilly left to travel Europe and met her boyfriend, who later became her husband. However, that was the best thing that happened to her. It took being apart from Lilly for Mary to realize the destructive influence she had on her. Mary had confessed her testimony to Pastor Larry, and her life had started changing when she forgave her mother and Hugh. Unfortunately, Mary had also developed a crush on Larry, but Mary couldn't be happier for Summer. And now, she was about to witness the uniting of Summer to her pastor.

Pastor Jeremy Collins would be performing the ceremony. He was the new senior pastor at Word of God and had been the associate pastor under Larry. He was going to have a new associate pastor, Noah Green. Jeremy had taken Larry's position, and Noah will be taking Jeremy's. Jeremy was young and single. He was tall and physically fit, with highly handsome features, blue eyes, and almost black hair. He's now dating one of the bridesmaids, Taylor Miller, who had worked at God's Temple Church since graduating high school. She had also attended this church for many years. She and her brother Norman started attending there together. Norman was now married and lived in Little Rock, Arkansas. Norman's community service work as part of his sentence gave him a desire to be a social worker. He attended classes in sociology at Texas Tech University, where he obtained a bachelor's degree. He worked for Texas, but when he married, he was transferred and worked for Arkansas. Summer invited him to the wedding, and only he had more pressing matters. When Taylor started dating Jeremy, she spoke to Pastor Brim, "Pastor Brim, I want you to know I love God's Temple, but I'm dating Jeremy Collins, who's becoming the Senior Pastor of Word of God Church, so I'll be attending church with him."

"Well, of course, you will, Taylor. I will miss you. I still greatly miss Norman. Life has to move on, though, and the only thing that matters is that you attend a church that teaches Jesus is the way to salvation; I know Pastor Jeremy teaches that. But, I hope you still stay on here as an employee?"

"Of course, I have over two more years of nursing school left, and I have to have my job."

"Well, it's settled then, Taylor, you are a fine employee, and they are hard to fine. I appreciate you, maybe you, Jeremy and myself can go out to dinner sometime. I've met him, but not as your sweetheart."

"Definitely, and I know Jeremy will be thrilled." Confessing to Pastor Brim relieved Taylor because she had strong feelings for Jeremy, as he did for her. She also needed this job as she still had a few years before graduating from nursing school. And Jeremy was her greatest supporter.

Lindy and Kevin had enjoyed watching the blossoming relationship between Taylor and Jeremy. Summer's other friend, Ella, met a young man in a missionary school. They had known each other for a year. He had proposed, and they continually speak about a future together. Ella kept Summer's parents posted about the events in her life.

Lynn was there, and she felt she was the one giving Summer away. She had become good friends with the Hanleys. They shared visitation times with R.D. and were together witnessing this blessed event. R.D. was there, but she was too young to understand what was taking place. Lynn offered, "Kevin, Lindy, Gerald, Susan, and I all agree that you should have the baby for the honeymoon period. You haven't been with her much, and this is the chance for you to get to know her."

"How wonderful, of course, you can stay longer and spend time with her too," Lindy replied

"No," Susan began, "We have to get back, and we want you to have some privacy with her. We see her all the time.". Of course, Kevin, Lindy, and Autumn were delighted. Autumn wanted her friends to come to see her precious little niece. Lindy was also going to postpone her staff meetings unless she took R.D. along. She wanted to show her off. The infant looked like Summer and Mike. She had Mike's blond hair and Summer's blue eyes. To her and Kevin, she was the most beautiful baby God had made. She also noticed this was how Summer looked at that age.

Angel and Monica were there, "guess what?" Angel said, patting Monica's stomach. It wasn't hard to guess, then Monica shared the news "There's going to a new edition." All the grandparents (including Pedro and Maria) were excited and joked about the child's gender. But all they wanted a healthy baby. Angel and Earl were Larry's groomsmen. His other groomsmen were Larry's four deacons. His brother Eric was his best man. Angel was so grateful for another chance at life. He was different. The former biker didn't take life for granted. He also didn't mind seeing eternity, as he had experienced God's presence. He thought a lot about Alfred. He hated that he hadn't witnessed more to him because there was no opportunity for it now. While spending time with his parents, he somehow believed these people of solid faith had prayed him to heaven. This thought gave Angel peace. He did receive special permission from Dr. Williamson to visit Marcus at the juvenile center. Marcus had said the sinner's prayer after he spoke the prayer. He confided in Angel, "I hated to hear that you had a third bullet wound. You have defied statistics. The doc was trying to protect me, so it was a while before I knew. Then when he finally told me, you had recovered."

"How much longer will you be in here."

"A while longer, I guess. Doc said I had a mental breakthrough, and that can take some time to heal."

"Wow, anything you want to share. That's if you want to." After Marcus had his breakthrough talking about his early childhood experience was no longer difficult. He began, "Yes, it was something I experienced many years ago; I didn't remember, a part of my life went missing. The doc used hypnosis, and everything came back to my memory. The problem is that it's new hurt. I don't know how much time it will take to heal. I know for sure I want to stay here until I feel safe again." Angel was curious as to what happened but didn't want to push it. But he did say. "I am so sorry little brother. But if you ever want to talk about it sometime, you know your secret is safe with me."

"I can talk about it now. It's not as painful as before my memory returned. It was from when my father and mother lived together. I was eight years old; my father had sexually attacked my mother. It was painful hearing her screams. I just stayed in the closet and cried. I was angry, and I wanted to fight him, only I knew I couldn't; I wasn't strong enough. My father then left, and my mother never found me. I just got Traye out of his crib and slept with him. Until now, I couldn't remember. The doc said It explained the hunger I had to avenge Traye and why I reacted to Antonio violently after Antonio shot Alfred. It was weird that a whole part of my life was missing." Angel wanted to cry and embrace Marcus and never let go, all he said. "Little brother, I will always be here for you; you can call my cell phone anytime, day or night. I mean this, please don't ever fail to call me if you ever need me."

"I will, big brother; I love you."

"I love you." And they embraced, and Marcus wept uncontrollably. Even after the breakthrough, he knew he had to heal, and he was happy to have therapy with Dr. Williamson. Angel told Larry and Summer about his visit with Marcus. All except what was confidential. That was Marcus' testimony when he wanted to tell it.

Larry wanted Marcus to attend his and Summer's wedding. Marcus wanted to participate. Only Marcus thought his healing process was more important. He felt safe at the juvenile facility under Dr. Williamson's care. He didn't want to be on the outside again until he thought it was safe.

Angel confessed to the police; he told it in night court with the police chief and Judge Mate. Although Judge Mate hadn't much sympathy for criminal gang members, the ones Angel ordered hits. Although they were also killers, he highly favored Angel because he changed his life and became a person of impeccable character. He then told Angel, "Angel, just give the money to the church, let it bless others." And Angel did just that. Dr. Thomas gladly accepted the money since it became declared legal and also to be church property.

Angel had memories of his last ride with the Jokers. They went on a cross-country ride to Orlando, Florida. They had explored Disney World. They attracted a lot of attention when children asked them various questions about how they survived gang violence. One boy pointed to them when they arrived.

"Look, "one child said. "A real biker gang!"

"Are you a violent gang?" another boy asked

"How did you survive attacks from other gangs?" A third boy asked. Exaggerated violence was what Hollywood projected to these children. Angel and his gang explained to them, "Yes, son" Angel began his testimony. "We were a violent gang at one time only now we are "Biker's for Christ." Biker's for Christ is the new name given by Juan. "I had been a gang member since I was twelve years old; I loved my trophies of knife and bullet wounds. I grew up in the Catholic church with faithful Christian parents. I know that my even being alive to testify to you is a true miracle. I thank God for my parents, who never gave up praying for me. I also had many other believers who prayed for me. I am a survivor of a third bullet wound, and that is considered a medical impossibility." The children's eyes were as big as saucers; these children were mesmerized as each gang member gave his testimony. Then after they all spoke to them, one boy stated. "I don't know about my friends, but I love motorcycles, and when I grow up, I want to be a "Biker for Christ."' The other boys hungrily expressed the same thing. The boys' families then took them to see other events at the park; their parents were also emotionally moved by the bikers' testimonies.

    Earl had never attended a wedding before other than Angel and Monica's renewal ceremony, but that wasn't the same to him. He was almost 40 years old and had been on drugs since his early teens. It was the only kind of life the former user knew. He never knew how to have a responsible physical relationship. He just went after any woman he desired and didn't care if the feelings were mutual. Sometimes they would be, but Earl's first love was drugs. Women were just for using one way or another. He regretted being so disrespectful to women because he felt now ready to have someone in his life. The removal of drugs had implanted many new desires in his life; a wife in his future was one of those desires. He only regretted that his testimony could frighten a potential prospect away. He moved out of Angel's apartment when Angel and Monica renewed their vows. Both Angel and Monica gave up their apartments in Twin Peaks and moved into a house they bought in the Sunset district. Angel had become good friends with Monica's parents and wanted to live close to them. Earl then moved back into the Rescue Mission, worked in the kitchen, and helped other addicts start their lives. Earl felt hopeful about his life and thought he was finally fulfilling his destiny.

    The groups in the wedding party were in place—Larry and Eric at the altar waiting for Summer. The bridesmaids were in beautiful flowing gowns of pink. And the groomsmen were in handsome black tuxedos. They had all made their way through the procession as the orchestra played "Here Comes the Bride." A small girl and boy were the flower girl throwing out flowers and ring bearer, bringing the ring to Eric to give to Larry. Then, at last, Kevin approached, and Summer took his arm and marched to Larry. She was wearing a beautiful white flowing gown with a long train, which was first worn by her mother when she married her father. The gown had a veil adorned with small pearl-like ornaments. The veil hid her face until Larry unveiled her. To Larry, this was equally as exciting as the wedding night. Larry and Summe's adrenaline was felt in the entire room by all the guests.

The pastor asked, "Who gives this woman to be wed?"

"Her mother and I," Kevin said.

Finally, Summer stood before Larry, saying the traditional wedding vows. Jeremy asked Larry to repeat after him: "I, Larry, take thee, Summer, to be my wife, to have and to hold from this day forward. For better, for worse, for richer, for poorer, in sickness and in health, to love and to cherish till death do us part." Then Summer repeated the same vows after Jeremy.

Then Pastor Jeremy said a few more words and pronounced them husband and wife. Finally, Larry unveiled Summer, gently framing her face and giving her a long passionate kiss. The wedding guests were stunned.

Pastor Jeremy then said to the congregation, "I now introduce you to Mr. and Mrs. Larry Calhoun."

They had a beautiful wedding reception with a huge feast at the church's reception hall. They upheld the tradition, placing a piece of cake in each other's mouth, and then they went on to the dance floor. Summer shared her first dance with Kevin, and then Kevin gave Summer to Larry for the rest of the dances. From the reception, the couple headed to the airport for a beautiful and exciting honeymoon in Jerusalem, Israel.

Summer couldn't believe her storybook tale. She started as a teen in a small Texas town who met and ran away with a California boy and lived in the most horrifying district in San Francisco for over two years. They married shortly after. It proved to be a horrific and challenging two years, but God brought them out of the land of horror and into their land of milk and honey. God placed her there and allowed her to meet Lynn Rothberg, who lived in the most elegant part of the city. She and Mike lived with her until he died. Then fate struck her with the tragedy of being a young widow, pregnant with her first child. She then was more overwhelmed that she would reunite with her first love — a love she had never gotten over. And now, here they were in Jerusalem, about to walk throughout the land Jesus had walked.

Acknowledgments and Events that Inspired the Book

This book is a fictional account of my life story. I lived in San Francisco in the late sixties and early seventies, proclaiming myself to be a flower child at the time. I lived in the Tenderloin in a rundown residential hotel. Hippies lived in a communal and a single room that housed as many residents as the hotel staff could board illegally. The hotel owners didn't care about laws or regulations—it was about how much money their greedy hands could grasp.

The residents of these rats- and roach-infested dives were on drugs and stoned most of the time, so they didn't care about the conditions. Instead, they needed to pay inexpensive rent to afford their drug habit.

The fictional character, Summer, liked her place neat and in order. However, since she and Mike lived by themselves, the other residents deemed them as wealthy. Druggies would have robbed Mike and Summer numerous times, except the hotel manager, Bill Blake, declared an immediate eviction for anyone who committed any crime against a hotel resident. The locks on the doors were evidence that Bill meant what he said.

God sent Lynn to Summer's rescue. She wasn't a believer until she witnessed Summer's transformation. Then she prayed intensely out of concern for Summer.

Before September 11, 2001, friends and family were allowed to see their loved ones off at the boarding gate. However, today, only the passenger is allowed at the entrance. Before the new laws went into effect, Autumn saw Summer at the San Francisco boarding gate but did not tell her family. She was loyal to Summer and knew she didn't want her family to know. Autumn also liked being an only child. She became a little jealous when she witnessed the concern their parents showed Summer.

It was through media sources that Autumn discovered that San Francisco was a dangerous place for young women. Blood was thicker than water, and she had to tell her parents, even though it meant punishment. Her coming forward helped Andrew Marks find Summer and apprehend a dangerous killer— the same man who had killed his daughter and shortened his wife's life.

I knew a biker named Angel in San Francisco. But the character in this story is fictional. The real Angel had a wife. She separated from him because of his lifestyle. Although he also had numerous girlfriends, he told them they had to accept that he would always be in love with his wife. The bikers' chicks never had much self-esteem and would settle for whatever crumbs a biker threw at them. If only they knew that, with God, they could have the best of everything. They would have a mate who respects them and loves them as Christ loved the church.

Many bikers became part of the Jesus Movement. I gave Angel and his biker gang the name *Bikers for Christ*. I made the fictional Angel more honorable and devoted to his spouse, even before accepting Jesus into his heart. The real Angel lived a violent lifestyle. I don't know if he received Christ in his heart, but a close friend said she witnessed to him. So, I prayed and believed Angel had received salvation. I thought about Angel from time to time and prayed for him. I considered my prayers also to be planted seeds. I believe planted seeds reap a harvest and never return void.

Little Traye represents a nine-year-old child I met in Shreveport, LA, when I assisted my mentor, an inner-city children's ministry leader. Gang members had mistakenly killed this precious child in a drive-by shooting. There was a rumor that his brother had been the intended victim. I never got over it and still think about this baby all the time. It was hard to understand, as we always prayed for these children's safety. Unfortunately, I never met this child's brother, so Marcus is fictional. I also heard it rumored that his grandma had him placed in protective custody.

For years, we went to recruit children for leadership classes. It started as an energized rally. I hated it when this outstanding outreach ended. These young men and women boldly ministered to their classmates, teachers, and school officials through leadership classes. Professional businessmen, women, and attorneys visited the classes, giving their testimonies and encouragement to the children, teaching them there are no limitations to their future. As a result, many straight-A students advanced to college. I am still involved in this ministry.

Marcus is African American. The Gypsy Jokers were a biker gang in San Francisco. I can't remember their nationality, but it seemed Angel was Hispanic. However, my Jokers are fictional and Hispanic. It was true that many gangs were segregated, associating only with their nationality. Except Marcus had favor with Angel and Alfred. He had known them since he was 12 years old and looked up to them. He went ballistic when he found Alfred dead and saw Antonio holding the weapon that killed him. Marcus then grabbed Alfred's gun, fired, and killed Antonio, a rival Italian gang leader. He then called Angel; Marcus was holding the weapon when the police arrived. Some of the officers knew his grandmother, Brenda. She always asked them to place him in protective custody when he encountered danger, and they obliged. They honestly wanted to protect him when they arrested him, though the police didn't see how they could since they had caught him red-handed.

Marcus was sixteen; Angel hired Charles Hanker, who reminded the officers that they couldn't treat Marcus as an adult without the court's permission. Angel told Marcus he didn't have to speak to them without an attorney present. He then took Marcus from the police station since there were no charges at that time.

Marcus had a suppressed traumatic memory. He was recovering with the help of a Christian psychiatrist who changed everything for him. Marcus feared he would lose his freedom for killing Antonio; he didn't realize his actions resulted from his mental illness.

Larry was a minister in Minion and was Summer's first love. Summer was married to Mike when she reencountered Larry. This young woman fought her feelings for him because of her loyalty to Mike. Shortly afterward, she became widowed when A man killed Mike when Mike attacked him because the man had once attempted to assault Summer. He had post-traumatic episodes because he had witnessed his sister Ruby's fatal accident with a harvester. He was helpless to protect Ruby, and he was determined to protect Summer. Mike had to learn the hard way that God is the protector of us all. He knew it through the loss of his life.

Summer's talking about Jesus triggered the first episode. Deep in Mike's subconscious, he had blamed God for Ruby's death. Mike had trashed their hotel room without being aware of what he had done. Trashing the place was all he could do because he knew he couldn't touch God. He wanted to protect Summer; he wouldn't have hurt her. When she left him, he realized how much she had meant to him.

When a coworker made sexual slurs about Summer, it triggered Mike's fight-or-flight reflexes; only his foreman had intervened. However, Mike didn't want to let it go, so he harassed this man continually. Finally, Dr. Cecil Thomas, pastor at Glad Tidings and a clinical psychologist, warned the foreman that firing Mike would be dangerous. The foreman then told Mike he had to get help for his illness or he would be terminated. Mike agreed to treatment, except he wanted to let Summer know about it. Mike went to Minion and seeing Summer stirred his emotions. He pleaded for her to come back and promised to get help for his illness. Summer loved Mike, and they had reconciled. Mike also reconciled with God. He and Lynn had become close, and Pastor Thomas baptized them on the same occasion.

    I took a few classes in psychology at a Junior College when I lived in San Francisco. The illnesses I addressed were from the case histories I read in my college psychology books on repressed memories due to traumatic occurrences. I also researched *Repressed Memory* online. It contains the past, research, causes, and also criticism by skeptics. There are close to a hundred references. But the case histories I read about in Junior college were more interesting cases to me, and I never forgot them. They gave me more understanding of people and why they react as they do. I had previously judged them, but this knowledge gave me compassion for them. It helped me pray for them more efficiently and accurately. I used a couple of these mental illness examples to describe Mike's and Marcus's illnesses.

    I witnessed much crime in the Tenderloin district. Criminals committed crimes in broad daylight for all to see. I had severe paranoia—I felt the perpetrators were after me because I had witnessed knifings and shootings. Except in the Tenderloin, the code of the streets was that you see nothing, and you know nothing. I was not caring, and it placed an apathy in my spirit. I stopped being nervous, shaky, and paranoid. I just stopped feeling, period. We are dead when we stop caring for our fellow man. It never takes long to become hardened in these kinds of circumstances. Jesus is the only one who can break through. The Jesus Movement is direct evidence that many breakthroughs had taken place.

    Sexual predators such as Earl "the Beast" ran rampant in the city. God had sent me protectors, and Angel was one of them. I never approved of his harsh treatment of people, but I loved him and still pray for him, even though I don't know if he's still alive. An Angel of God abated Earl; it impacted him that the man never attempted to molest another woman. When he had his born-again experience, he was grateful. God loves us all, and people don't like to think it includes sexual predators. But as his word states in Romans 3:23, *"For all have sinned and fall short of the glory of God."* We all have the same opportunity. The best example is the famous serial killer Ted Bundy's last interview with Dr. James Dobson. You can find it on the *Pure Intimacy* website in an article titled "Fatal Addiction." In the interview, Ted Bundy claimed he had accepted Christ into his heart. Many people will never accept this, even though God stated in his Word, *All.* Anyone can change and become a new creature. Remember, God won't forgive us if we don't forgive others. And if God doesn't forgive us, we hinder having a place in heaven.

I was older than Summer was when I left to live in San Francisco. However, I was unhappy at home as a teen, and, like Summer, I would have run away had I met a real-life Mike. I am glad I didn't. My family suffered enough heartbreak at my expense. Lindy is fiction, more of the mother I wanted to have than the one I had. My mother, Irene, still favors my sister. My heart changed when I accepted God as my Father, and I received my mother and loved her unconditionally with God's grace. And it was indeed God's grace, as my stubborn heart wanted to remain apathetic toward her and the rest of my family. Then God would remind me of my mother's kindness when I was sick or hurting. Sometimes I feigned illness to seek her kindness.

My father, Kelton, was a U.S. Navy retiree. I never knew him until I was almost grown. For many years, I blamed him for leaving me in a situation with unfair treatment. I felt he could have chosen a career that allowed him to be home more. Then God would remind me of when my father suffered from *Post-Traumatic Stress Disorder* (PSTD) because of the horrors of war and how he adored me when I was little. I have to admit I was the one who stopped valuing.

Kevin, Summer's father, lived at home but worked consistently, both at the office and home. Summer resented him more than she did her mother. She resented Autumn the most because she was allowed to mistreat and disrespect Summer. Either parent never disciplined her. Summer took matters into her own hands by fighting her, and then she had to flee to escape Lindy's wrath. Lindy felt guilty for her unfair treatment of Summer and imagined the worst in her absence. When Summer returned home, Lindy would be overly affectionate. This confused Summer, so she didn't return her affection—she had built a wall to protect herself against hurt.

Autumn was primarily fictional. Marilyn was aggravating and annoying when we were children, but she is the most accomplished person in our family. My sister has a bachelor's degree in sociology and worked for Louisiana and Florida in elderly protection. She was a hero, as she would protect these people at all costs. It would have been easier at times to look the other way, but she never did.

I also have a brother, Bill, but he doesn't represent any specific character in the book. Bill hated the dishonesty that was a part of his job, so God eventually blessed him with a job in a high-quality hotel. He also kept the family navy tradition and was active in the Vietnam war. He's the role model for some of my other honorable characters, such as Bill Blake, the Metro manager. Another character is Andrew Marks, the Christian private investigator, and Dr. Craig Williamson, Marcus's psychiatrist. My brother is a devout Christian man. He and my sister both have successful marriages and have been married for decades.

I also have three fine sons. The character of Lindy represents all praying mothers. I certainly felt my mother's prayers. And believe they protected me and kept me safe. I also recall many nights awakening around 1 a.m., fervently praying for one of my sons. My youngest, John, kept me on my knees the most because he was into substance abuse. John matured and is employed by companies that create utility resources. He has had several promotions. Yet, I still wake early in the mornings to pray for him. My middle son, Dustin, lives with me off and on. He is disabled with some physical and mental problems and lives on disability. Even when he was in the house, I prayed him out of danger. He's pretty intelligent and frequently educates himself online. He's proficient on the computer.

My oldest son, Dennis, is another family navy retiree. He has severe health issues. I never allow worry to take control. Prayer is far more powerful. Once, the military considered medically discharged from the Navy when I prayed he remained in the Navy. Until retirement. God blessed him because Dennis blessed me many times when I needed him. I was once in an automobile accident, which totaled my car, and I could not work. Dennis helped me with most of my expenses. I had some compensation from my insurance agency, but nothing substantial; he also helped me buy a brand-new car. Another time he helped me buy a house. All of my sons have generous hearts and have been there for me. My youngest son was there for me when I was in the hospital. My carpet in lousy shape, and he ripped it up and put down brand-new tile. My middle son has lived with me off and on for years and helped with household expenses.

Ella represents my best friends in school who cared about me. One whom I treasure to this day is Leona. Lynn represents my Christian friends in San Francisco. Even though it was Summer who led Lynn to the Lord, it was my friends who led me—a gift I can never repay. I also have a treasured friend named Lucy from San Francisco. So many people in my life have had a positive influence on me and encouraged my salvation. I can't mention them all, but I pray that they will know their characters when they appear.

Glad Tidings Temple was the real name of a church I attended in San Francisco. Floyd Thomas was a wonderful pastor, but he wasn't a pastor and clinical psychologist as my character is. The church in the book isn't Glad Tidings Temple, only Glad

Tidings. I loved the name. The true church in San Francisco had many outreach ministries, mainly in the Tenderloin. Teen Challenge was the addiction recovery ministry.

You can research San Francisco's various districts online, such as the Tenderloin, Sunset, Twin Peaks, and North Beach, etc. I lived in San Francisco for almost ten years, yet I have been away for decades. So I visit Glad Tidings Temple's website from time to time to see how updated they've become.

Summer made wrong choices in choosing her friends. Parents seldom realize lack of supervision allows children to be out of control. Then children choose the terrible friends, especially those who are unsupervised. Parents allow this to happen without realizing it. When they don't listen to their children's problems, sometimes these children become runaways.

Summer was in danger when a serial killer approached her. But God was with her, and, once again, he protected her supernaturally. Diesel Hamilton had murdered Andrew Marks's daughter. Andrew was a private investigator who had taken the case to find Summer. While on this case, he finally found and apprehended Diesel. Diesel also had an encounter with God when he attempted to slay Summer. God's presence was threatening to him. He feared and believed God would harm him if he touched Summer. He had to question Summer because he had always followed through with a murder, only this time he couldn't. Through Summer, he accepted Jesus into his heart and declared it publicly. His victims' families hated him, but Chaplain Neal and Warden Sam ministered to him because they knew his commitment was sincere. He had no family, so he wanted Summer to be his family as he went to walk on the streets of gold. Summer felt good about this decision, but she still backslid. In Luke 19:40, Jesus says to his disciples, *"I tell you if you remain silent the rocks will cry out."* Summer was no longer a follower, yet she was a rock God used to cry out for Diesel.

I have been married more than once. Unfortunately, I never chose wisely in selecting a mate. Mike and Larry are fiction—

they represent the relationships I have always wanted. God has been my faithful spouse. He has always been there for me. God also sends me loyal friends such as Maverick, who has been a rock. He loves the Lord and has pushed me to keep the faith. We have fasted together frequently and prayed continually. He represents himself as a faithful follower of God.

I learned about soul wounds when I heard testimonies at church from hurting women who had suffered abuse, especially sexual abuse. Some women had abortions and realized the people at the clinic lied to them about the procedure. A close friend of mine had an abortion years ago. She was in love with the baby's father, and, afterward, she was an emotional wreck. She knew she had murdered her child and couldn't live with it. Right before she accepted Jesus into her heart, she had contemplated suicide. She still went through an agonizing process before she would forgive herself. Then she realized she would one day reunite with her child, which gave her peace. She also asked God to help her forgive herself. But many women wouldn't forgive themselves, and their wounds would fester. Self-forgiveness is essential.

God's forgiveness and closure are required to heal a soul wound. I mentioned many kinds of wounds in this book. Summer's unfair treatment at home, Mike's suffering traumatic episodes because he witnessed Ruby's death, Larry losing a lifelong friend to death, and Angel resenting living in the hood. Marcus lost his baby brother and role model and then learned his father sexually abused his mother. Many people do not realize they have a soul wound—a wound only God can heal that requires forgiveness, even self-forgiveness—a wound beyond the heart.

I need to dedicate this book to my mother, Leona Irene Young Crisp. On February 3, 2018, she passed away at the age of 99—three months shy of being 100 years old. She represents Lindy Logan. I also want to dedicate this book to my father, who passed away on January 23, 1997. My siblings and I miss our mother, but we are happy that she finally reunited with our father.

I also want to thank the rest of my family: my siblings and their spouses—Bill and Pou, Sid and Marilyn; my sons Dennis, Dustin, John and his wife Diana and my grandchildren; my niece Kelsey and her husband Chuck; my nephew Prather and his wife Wendy; and my great-nieces and nephews. They are all a vast support system for me.

My brother Bill went home to the Lord on January 7, 2019. He was almost 74 years old. I had planned a spring trip to visit him in Florida. But it was evident he probably wouldn't be around for it. So I couldn't afford to fly out for a visit—I reserved my finances for other issues; however, I did have an emergency reserve, and God convicted me to use it for this purpose. So I visited around Christmas time, and it would be our last Christmas together.

On December 14, I had written a poem in his honor and now in his memory. I included it below. I texted this poem to his wife, and she read it out loud to him and his family, and they were overwhelmed. I thought the poem would be enough; then, God convicted me to make an appearance. I was happy to spend one more time with him and have the time to enjoy all the rest of my family. This reunion was my best Christmas present.

My Brother

You were never one to make a spectacular entry
But you were always there
At times it seemed you would disappear, but your presence was ever there
My mind keeps going back to our childhood when we played in the wild woods
I remember when I was twelve years old and our dog Blackstone
Mama thought he was a nuisance
But you kept this sweet pup in the zone

SOUL WOUND

And Mama's heart softened to keep his presence
You melted her heart and later Daddy's too as you'd hide Blackstone in your bed
One day she accidentally found him there
But you knew how to talk fast and keep your head
You two played ball together, and it seemed Blackstone knew how to punt
But it was Blackstone who chose to leave
His desire in his heart was too strong, and he had to go and hunt
I was sad when you graduated from school
I knew you would soon leave
You went and joined the Navy rule
but you wouldn't let our hearts grieve
Then there was the day when my heart was glad when you found your beautiful bride
Not long after, there were children, and your heart burst with pride
You never knew that I knew that you advocated many times for me
I couldn't believe all along you were on my side, and with this my heart was made free
I only know God declares man's time on the earth to be brief
And if there's time for expression and truth. Then it needs to set us free.
If we let this precious time slip past us, Then the heart has created a wound to heal
I have been proud of you for your service to our country. And also, your service as a husband and father of children with great appeal
And with delightful grands who kept you forever young. The picture I will remember the most is of you holding them in your arms

Mama and Daddy are now gone, so each other is what we have
But it is a greater treasure than all the earth's gold
I have my brothers and my sisters, and God who always takes hold

On October 17, 2020, my middle son, Dustin Daniel Hall, passed away. It was the most devastating challenge in my life. I haven't written a poem for him; however, I had a supernatural encounter with him the morning and exact hour that he passed away. Therefore, I included this as well as his picture and obituary. He died of lung cancer, and it happened so quickly. He was a heavy smoker, and I don't think he believed that cigarettes were deadly, even though his doctors had warned him. He's gone, and his brothers and I are left in the excruciating pain of loving and missing him forever. I only pray that smokers and other substance abusers will think about their loved  ones and quit their deadly habits. The best action would be never to begin them. Think about your loved ones. I know Dustin would never have started; smoking had he known how we'd all be suffering his loss.

He ultimately repented before he died. I prayed for his healing; however, I believe he never wanted to be faced with any more temptation; he wanted to go home to Jesus. I'm grateful for that comfort.

My beautiful son, I will never stop loving you. But, Lord, please let him know what he means to me.

He came to me supernaturally the morning he passed away, wanting my consent. I had kept pressing him to pray for God's healing; however, God called him, and I had to comply. I can't repeat these words without tearing up in heavy sobs. God gave me these words to send him into His presence. "I can't be selfish anymore. I believe Dustin wants to see his visitors coming today. I just don't want to burden him anymore regardless of my pain and loss. I'll never want to see him leave, yet, it's not about me. He doesn't want the things of the earth anymore. Go in peace, Dustin, leave the burdens of the earth." It wasn't long when I received the call that he went home to Jesus.

Dustin Daniel Hall

A memorial service for Dustin Daniel Hall, 47, who passed away October 17, 2020. He was born on October 7, 1973, in San Francisco, California. He attended school at North Desoto High until 1991. His church home was Shreveport Community Church, where he served and was involved in many church functions.

He is survived by his mother, Gloria Knight, two brothers, Dennis Vaughan and John Knight, and wife Diana, many nieces and nephews. Uncle and Aunt, Sid and Marilyn Jones, Aunt, Marion Crisp, and many cousins. He was preceded in death by his grandfather, Kelton W. Crisp, his grandmother, Leona Irene Crisp, and one Uncle, Bill Crisp.

A Memorial service is set for Saturday, October 24, 2020, at 10:00 A.M. at Shreveport Community Church in the Rodney Duron Chapel. In lieu of flowers, please give donations to Cancer Research.

Final Thanks

I had an excellent editor who edited this book. Her name was Martha Ellis, and she was a giving and caring person. Unfortunately, she passed away on March 6 of this year. I knew her for almost two years, I felt close to her. Thanksgiving 2019, she lost her son, Andy. Sharing the same loss connected us; I voiced my grief with her when I lost my son, we both asserted our sorrow, and it was excellent therapy. She's with Andy now, and I envy her, and yet I am happy for her. She was very involved in the writing of this book; I must give her credit. I'll always miss her.

Made in the USA
Columbia, SC
01 August 2021